Ab

Liz Tyner grew up (…)
by stories and story(…)
high school, Liz oft(…)
romance novels ar(…)
manuscript someday(…)
acreage where she enjoys spending her evening gazing
at stars, sitting around a campfire, or at a concert where
it's prudent to wear hearing protection.

Visit Liz at liztyner.com

Regency Reputations

Regency Reputations:

English Rogues and Grecian Goddesses

LIZ TYNER

MILLS & BOON

First Published in Great Britain 2020
By Mills & Boon, an imprint of HarperCollins*Publishers*
1 London Bridge Street, London, SE1 9GF

www.harpercollins.co.uk

HarperCollins*Publishers*
1st Floor, Watermarque Building,
Ringsend Road, Dublin 4, Ireland

REGENCY REPUTATIONS: ENGLISH ROGUES AND
GRECIAN GODDESSES © 2021 Harlequin Books S.A.

Safe in the Earl's Arms © 2014 Elizabeth Tyner
Forbidden to the Duke © 2015 Elizabeth Tyner

ISBN: 978-0-263-30062-8

MIX
Paper from
responsible sources
FSC® C007454

This book is produced from independently certified FSC™ paper
to ensure responsible forest management.

For more information visit: www.harpercollins.co.uk/green

Printed and bound in Spain
by CPI, Barcelona

SAFE IN THE
EARL'S ARMS

To Bill, who encourages my dreams and
who buys me chocolate.

Chapter One

Being wrapped in a shroud of sailing cloth—a shot ball secure at his head and one at his feet—and tossed into the Aegean Sea could only increase Warrington's spirits. He linked his fingertips together, braced his elbows against the railing and ignored the sting of the wind slapping his hair on to his face.

His brother's sparring remarks didn't help.

Warrington turned his head from the words. 'I swear you are not related to me,' he grated out, interrupting the flow of Ben's jests. 'You talk more than any two women I've ever heard.'

Ben chuckled, moving so their shoulders touched briefly. 'And you've made me proud on the voyage. Not of you, of course. Of myself. I'm a fine captain to be able to have an old melancholy miss like you on board and still keep from throwing you over the side.'

'You've sailed us to an island that doesn't even have the comforts of hell.' Warrington used both hands, pushing back the hair from his face, and then he rested clenched fists on the railing of the ship.

'You do not give me the respect due me,' his brother said, shaking his head in exaggerated dismay. 'I saved our lives by steering us here when the ship caught fire. You may have the title, but an earl drowns just as quickly as a mere captain when a ship sinks.'

Warrington didn't speak, hoping to let Ben have the last word and himself some silence.

He'd had to leave England—he'd thought his memories would be easier to bear at sea. He'd been wrong. His wife's face wouldn't appear in his mind, but he could see the letters of her name carved on to the crypt.

He leaned into the rocking of the boat, letting it numb his mind from the endless days of sameness broken only by tribulation aboard the *Ascalon*. He wanted dry boots, freshly blacked, and not covering sodden stockings. Sea-misted trousers dried stiff and looked no better than a stable master's discards.

Across the water, he saw the longboat returning from shore, and hoped the *Ascalon* could cast off with the next tide. With the crew back and the repairs almost finished, surely they would leave soon.

In minutes, the longboat thumped against the side of the ship. Gidley, the first mate, reached his gnarled hands to the top of the ladder. His face came into view. The mate's eyes twinkled and he'd not yet moved on to the ship. 'We have us another one of them problems yer so good at solvin', Capt'n Ben.'

Warrington watched his younger brother take a forceful step forward.

'If anyone has stolen a goat this time, I'll personally throttle them until they are unconscious.' Ben straightened his shoulders and stared at his second-in-command.

'Not goats, Capt'n.' Gidley pulled himself on to the deck, his face showing a barely reined-in pleasure at whatever news he was about to speak.

'What, then?' the captain asked.

'It be a woman.' Gidley spoke slowly and stepped aside

to give the other three men from the longboat a chance to board. They rushed in behind him, feet thumping on to the deck, faces anxious to hear the response.

'A woman?' Ben straightened and strode to Gidley. 'The island is practically afloat with whores.' He spat the words out. 'Why can't the men understand how to handle a simple transaction and be done with it?'

'Well…' Gidley gave a demure smile. 'This one claims she be savin' herself for the capt'n.' He stepped back against the railing, one arm resting on the wood, and with the other hand pulled his gangly chin whiskers. 'I tried to give myself to her in yer stead, but she'd have none of it. *Capt'n*, she said. Kept insistin' she had a treasure for the capt'n.'

Ben smiled, his even teeth too white in the sunlight. 'Is she lovely?'

Gidley shrugged, but his grin flashed back hearty approval. 'She's some kind of mark here.' He touched above his breast. 'The birthmark…' he smiled '…pulled my sight right to her breasts.'

Not a ripple of emotion passed behind Ben's eyes. He turned to Warrington, indicating the shoreline with a quick tilt of his head. 'Go ashore and see what the woman wants.'

Warrington could not believe his brother's words. He examined Ben's face and took a step towards him. 'No.' Warrington shook his head.

Ben's eyes lost all familial ties. 'Captain's orders.' The smug words slashed in the air.

'I'm an earl.' Warrington's voice was tight.

'In case you're unaware, we're not on English soil. Captain ranks higher—*here*.' His brother bit out the commanding words and adopted the cocksure stance he'd perfected by five years old. 'And my crew does obey me. See to the woman, or I will have you left on the island when we haul anchor.'

'Like hell.'

Ben smiled. 'You're going to have to have a go at another woman some time. You might as well get some use out of your little man as to let it wither up and wash overboard.' He raised a hand, summoning three other seamen who'd stilled to listen.

Seven men were ready to toss Warrington on to the longboat should he not go on his own. He stared at his brother's face. He would kill him.

'So go ashore.' Ben crossed his arms. 'Take care of the matter for me—and you might be able to return to England on this vessel.'

'I—' His hands clenched.

'No. No,' Ben interrupted, head dropping but his hand still high. 'Trust me. Once you've been called captain by a woman in that breathless moment—you'll fashion yourself a captain many times over.' He waved his hand in the air. 'Correct?'

Seven male heads quickly gave assent, eyes flashing amusement and watching Warrington.

'Fine,' Warrington snapped out, moving to give his brother a shove from his path, but Ben moved aside—the man was nimble as an eel—and Warrington strode to the port side, stopping to give Ben a bitter glance.

He grabbed the railing and turned, scrambling down the woven ladder. He saw the first mate's boots next on the rope rungs. They would see him to the woman.

When the men reached the bank, the boat's bottom grated into sand underneath. Warrington jumped from the longboat into the water. He stopped for a moment. The immobile land beneath his feet jarred him. He'd been at sea too long.

He sloshed to shore. The others splashed behind him,

then pulled the boat free of the waves, showing no more effort than moving a child's toy.

They started on the path. Water sluiced from Warrington's boots. Gidley slogged beside him. 'She's near the town. Said we'd find her 'fore we reached Castro.'

The blowing wind pushed whiffs of the tainted egg smell that lingered at the base of the island. The shoreline reeked as badly as a demon's breath—a scent Warrington supposed left over from volcanic eruptions centuries earlier.

Warrington nodded sharply, but gave no other acknowledgement. He trudged up the path and soon the sand gave way to a coal-hued surface. Glass-like shards of earth now crunched beneath his feet. The unusual land piqued his interest, but the scent didn't. Warrington wished they had risked another island to recover from the ship's fire, which had nearly cost them their lives. This one stank.

Gidley expounded on what a woman such as the one he'd seen could do for a man's pleasure. He described the mark at her breast in fifteen different ways and each one included more details of skin than he could possibly have seen.

The mate spoke so earnestly and with such conviction, he'd convinced at least one of the other seamen the woman was a descendent of some goddess. Warrington wasn't certain Aphrodite herself would be so free with her charms as Gidley recounted. The sailor loved his mythology—but it was all Gidley's tales, not the ancients.

The road disappeared into a growth of olive trees and brush.

Warrington wondered about the woman—this bold woman who shouldn't disturb an earl who'd been a month without a decent mattress, longer without a decent night's sleep and even longer without a deliciously indecent tumble.

Meeting the woman might be interesting, he decided. He would return and tell his brother what it was like to bed a goddess in the flesh. No matter how the events unfolded, Warrington would manage a supreme tale of unsurpassed passion.

Gidley stopped where a path shot out from the road. 'She lives in one of them red-roofed houses up this trail—a home overlookin' the sea.'

Warrington stopped and turned to the seamen. 'I will continue the rest of the way alone.'

Gidley and six other pairs of feet ceased all movement and their faces weighed Warrington's words.

Gidley spoke softly, his downturned lips showing hurt at the exclusion. 'We want to see yer meet her.'

'I can meet her alone and need no help,' Warrington said.

Gidley stepped nearer Warrington, facing him. Gid's worn cap slid into a jauntier position when he raised his head. He clapped Warrington on the arm. 'I wager a earl knows a bit about pleasurin' himself. I mean…' he paused for effect '…with a woman.'

The others snickered. Warrington raised a brow and gave them the glare that hours spent with a fencing master had made him confident to use, and that hinted *Swords or pistols and choose your seconds.*

Gidley took a step back and turned away with a disgusted grunt. 'We be takin' the longboat back to the boat in an hour or so,' Gidley muttered. 'Sun will be settin' not long after. Ought to give you enough time to meet 'er, fall in love and get yer trousers back on.' Gidley's words faded away as he left along the road.

Warrington pushed through a clump of tree branches over the path and saw the roof of a house. The structure had two storeys and the stairs leading to the upper floor had no railing. He knew from his first day's visit to the island that the house was made as the others he'd seen. The first level—a barn—held the livestock. He supposed the tradition of making homes in this manner started because of the houses built near the sea. If a low-lying area flooded, the animals could be released and water would be less likely to harm the house's upper contents. Besides, the structure took fewer materials than if two were built.

He saw a nanny goat grazing near the corner, a kid at her side. And near the cliffs, a woman sat on one of the boulders overlooking the sea. She turned to him. In the chilled air, her red scarf fluttered around her face and she stood. He didn't move. Let her approach him. She'd summoned.

The covering on her head showed scarlet enough to use as a beacon and another garment draped around her shoulders had only a little less colour. She pulled the covering snug as she walked. The wind didn't warrant bundling so.

When she strode closer, he caught his breath. Even with the breezes constantly tossing the head covering against her, she drew his attention. Brown eyes with lashes thick enough he half expected them to flutter in the breeze, as well. She held her shawl closed with one hand and with the other brushed back the hair that kept blowing across her face. A waste of effort.

'I'm Melina. Are you the *Ascalon* captain?'

Her words shocked him. She spoke King's English and with only enough accent to give her words an exotic flair. And her voice—it purred into him, causing a jolt in his midsection that reminded him of how tempting a woman could be.

Melina appraised the man before her. She'd expected someone silver-haired. Perhaps scarred a bit. This one— she could see how he kept from being mangled. His body showed strength. She doubted he'd be able to scamper across the rigging as she'd seen French seamen do, but he could probably toss another man up to do the job for him.

His clothing fit tight over parts that held muscle, and loosely everywhere else. When the wind blew at him, he stood impervious. His stare trapped the breath in her and caused a pleasing quiver in her stomach.

She'd waited months for an English ship to anchor in the bay because she had to leave the island and discover the truth about the treasure. She had to be right. Her sisters must eat.

'Where did you learn such speech?' He asked his own question, ignoring hers.

'I wish to go to London.' She kept the scarf tight around her.

'I wish for a soft bed at night, but the ship doesn't have one,' he said. 'And it has no room for passengers.'

'I've payment.' She raised her chin. She would not give away this chance. Not willingly. Only certainty of death would back her down.

His shoulders relaxed and he gave her an apologetic smile. 'We've had a fire. Our vessel is near ready for departure and we're finishing the last repairs, but it might not withstand a storm. Another ship will be along shortly. Bargain with them.'

She took a step forward, closer than she would normally stand near someone who'd docked on the island. She looked up at him. 'Before you decide, I must show you something.'

He gave a tilt of his shoulder and raised one eyebrow. 'I told you I'm not interested.' Then she saw his gaze drift to her chest and quickly move back to her face.

She pulled her shawl tight. 'In the stable,' she bit out, taking a step towards the structure.

He reached for her, trapping her arm, but his grip wasn't tight.

She snapped her head in his direction and stood ready

to push him back—first with words, then with force if she needed. He had to see her discovery.

'I don't wish—' His voice softened, but he didn't release her arm. His eyes, not true dark but reflecting the same colours as the almost leafless tree he stood near, showed compassion. 'I can't take you to London with us. Wait for another ship.' His voice lowered. 'Or stay here. The world is not kind for women away from their homes.'

Words fled her mind and she couldn't look away from him. He'd trapped her—not with his hand, but with his gaze. His touch warmed her skin and his gentle grasp had taken her will to move.

'Come with me.' She thrust the words out, recapturing her strength.

He shook his head, still not releasing her arm. The grip held her firm, but she didn't feel imprisoned. She knew a quick tug and she'd be able to slip away.

'I... The ship is no place for a woman—even a...' He tried again. 'I'm sure you could have many times your passage back in your pocket in the time it will take us to reach London—but the men don't need the distraction. They'd be competing for your favours instead of thinking of their duties. You'll not go with us.' He put his free hand in his waistcoat pocket, brought out a coin and held it to her. 'Take it.'

She stared and didn't move.

He kept his hand extended. 'You may keep it. For getting me from the ship for a few moments and for letting me hear a woman's voice. I want nothing more.' His eyes softened. 'I did not bring more funds or I would give them to you.'

She jerked her head in refusal of the coin.

He released her, putting the gold away, and took a step back. She reached out, grasping his sleeve, stopping him.

He turned, his mouth open, and seemed to struggle

for words. 'Miss. Truly. I do not want… And we cannot take you.'

He could keep his words—she needed a man who'd free her from the island.

'Let me show you,' she said.

'As long as you understand you're not stepping foot on that ship. The men…'. He finished his words with a soft tone. 'They would not be able to ignore…'

'I must show you my treasure.' She turned away and strode inside the barn, knowing he would not resist following her.

They walked over dirt packed solid from goats' feet, breathing dust from manure the animals kicked about. She moved towards a small stack of firewood branches. She knelt, reaching into the sticks, and pulled out the cloth-wrapped marble she'd hidden there.

She turned back to him, pulled away the fabric and handed the work to him. Even in the dark interior, the richness of the stone glowed.

He took the carved marble in his hands. The arm was slightly bigger than a human arm would be and the delicateness of the fingers proved the hand to be a woman's. 'It's a part of some statue.'

'Yes.' Even as he touched and examined it, she rested her fingertips against the stone. 'A learned man came here two years ago. He told us the island should have artefacts—worth coin to him—but he found nothing. I uncovered this—and more, after he left.' She watched this one, noting his study of the arm. He looked at the hand the way a woman might look at a baby.

'Take me to London,' she said, 'and you'll be paid my passage once the British Museum discovers what I have—'

'This is well done. When I get to England, I'll get someone who understands art to look at it and he can send payment back if this marble is worth something.'

She jerked the carving from his hands. 'I have to leave now. Not next week. Not the next ship. I must go.' Already her neighbours had warned her. The man who led the island was planning to marry her soon. She would have no choice.

She turned, picking up the cloth she'd used to protect the arm. When she looked up, she caught his eyes on her. Her shawl had opened and her mark showed. He stopped moving. Her clothing fell open a bit more. With her free hand, she brushed the edge of the birthmark, letting her fingers rest a moment. Desire darkened his eyes.

She took a slow breath. Neither smiled. She stopped the words of caution blowing inside herself, pummelling her with the knowledge she could never turn back if she continued her path. 'Is that what you want for my passage?' she asked.

'Yes.'

'Then we've a bargain.'

He shook his head. 'No. The captain will not let a woman sail with us.'

'You're not the *archigos?*' She pulled the arm into her grasp, cradling it. He didn't answer, but she could read the truth in his face. She'd just offered her body to a man who could not, or would not, say yes. Her mind hammered in rage. Controlling her desire to hit him across the face with the stone took all her strength, except for the amount she used to keep herself from shouting.

'I'm the Earl of Warrington,' he said. 'I own part of the ship, but I don't sail her. I'll take you aboard the *Ascalon* and you may speak to the captain.' His head moved sideways, indicating the direction of the vessel.

'Very well.' She could see his thoughts in his eyes. He believed the captain would refuse her. But if the ship's leader had the same mind as most men, once her foot touched the deck, she would make it difficult for him to say no.

'I will sail with the ship.' She challenged him with her stare.

He turned and walked back into the sunlight.

Melina knew that once she stepped on deck, she'd find a way to stay, no matter what she had to do. Their father had given them enough to live on while their mother lived, but now he'd forgotten his daughters. Without funds, she could no longer escape a forced marriage to a man whose touch made her stomach roil. She could not let her sisters starve, or sell their bodies.

The arm, and a description of the goddess, would let the museum see what she had and they would tell her what the beauty was worth. The statue was valuable. Her heart told her so. She could support her family by selling the stone woman.

She ran to the steps of her house and grabbed the small satchel she'd stuffed together after talking with the other sailor. She'd told her sisters her plans. They now watched from the window. Melina waved and then took a step to the path.

The first footstep was easy. But then she couldn't move. A hollowness in her heart told her she was leaving her home for ever. She squeezed her eyes tight and planted one foot forward, then the other.

Chapter Two

Melina rushed to keep up with Warrington's long strides. As she reached the first bend in the path, her satchel strap slipped from her shoulder to her elbow. The weight pulled at her arm, but she kept the stone cradled. The bag bumped against her leg, slowing her pace.

She paused and he immediately stopped and turned to her. He'd been as aware of her footsteps as his own.

Warrington reached a hand out to her, gesturing for the bag, and she met his eyes. Reassured, she hefted the rock in one hand and let the errant strap slip into her grasp. He took the weight from her, tossing the leather sling over his shoulder.

Muffled tones reached her ears. She focused on the sounds. Two men talked as they moved towards the path. Her heart thudded when she recognised the voice of Stephanos, the man who planned to wed her. He was moving in their direction. A few more steps and he would see them. She'd be trapped.

'*Skase,*' she whispered, and then remembered her English. 'Quiet.'

Warrington studied her, but gave a small lift of his chin in agreement.

She brushed past him, nodding for him to follow her.

Snaking through the gnarled trees, she ran towards a knoll that rose just enough that they couldn't be seen from the path.

She reached the hiding place and pulled him beside her, hoping they would not be seen. Listening, she realised the men no longer talked. Stephanos and the other man were silent—unmoving.

Fear crept into her body, clutching at her insides. If Stephanos saw her with Warrington, the Greek would not ask any questions, but would find his own answers. Stephanos and his friends always carried knives and they were skilled with them.

After a few moments of nothing, she heard the word, *gida,* and relaxed. Goat.

The men continued on. She heard their voices fading away and her breathing returned to normal. Warrington put a hand on her shoulder, the warm grasp somehow reassuring. He tugged her around to him and put his face so near hers that the breath of his whisper touched her cheek. He didn't release her, but his grip was soft.

'Have you stolen the stone?' he asked, words quiet, creating a haven around her.

She would have confessed all if she'd done wrong. 'No. The man who owns the land where I found the treasure knows what I have planned. We are in agreement and he has said he'll keep my secret. I trust him.'

Just the gentlest touch of his hand again, moving over the crest of her shoulder and the merest bit down her back, and the waiting look in his eyes, trapped her in an intriguing web and she could not stop her words. 'When they are sure I am safely gone a long distance, my sisters are to say I've been forced away by a man from a ship.'

His eyes widened and he stepped back as if she'd prodded him away with a burning stick.

He opened his mouth to speak, but she closed the distance between them, stopping almost against him. She could not risk him raising his voice.

'You must understand our reasons,' she said quietly. 'No one will know who you are. My sisters will not describe the true person.'

He pulled the satchel from his shoulder and she could tell he meant to leave her there and go on his way.

'No,' she whispered, closing her fingers over his roughened hand, preventing him from giving her the bag. His knuckles were large in her grasp, startling her, and she knew she didn't keep them closed by her strength any more than she caused the tides. Confusion flashed behind his eyes and something whispered in her that she had trapped his hand—that he could no more move his fingers than if their grasps had been reversed and his strength held her.

She could not lose her advantage. 'I am not a thief. I merely wish to get to the British Museum and find out what my treasure is worth. Then I will be able to sell it.'

'But *kidnapped?*' He remained with his face almost at hers. 'That's a bit much.'

She closed her lips and let her breath out through her nose before she answered, 'I have no choice.'

'I do.' He kept his words tight and lines appeared at the sides of his eyes and mouth. 'I am not at ease with purchasing a woman and I certainly wouldn't steal one.'

The words pleased her, yet they were not what she wanted to hear.

She had to convince him. She held his gaze with her own. 'It is necessary. My sisters can't be hurt by my actions. The man who rules the island would be enraged at them if he thought they had helped me leave and did not search him out to keep me. They would suffer. They could be starved, or beaten, or forced into marriage or worse. I cannot escape and leave them behind to face torture.'

She felt his movement and looked down to her hand. She'd tightened her grip on his fingers. He slowly slid his hand from hers.

'You're leaving behind a man.' His words were thoughtful.

She had to make him understand. 'Our land doesn't support my sisters. The rocks only grow more rocks. I care nothing for the man who wishes to marry me, yet his mother often sees that we have food. If I stay, I will have no choice but to wed him. She wishes for it. So does he. He is powerful.'

Stephanos controlled the island and did so easily. But he had other secrets. He often left the island and returned with goods. One of his shirts was mottled with faded brown stains. Blood.

She could barely keep the kindness in her words when Stephanos called on her and she had to speak to him. Perhaps, as the others whispered, she truly had been tainted by her English heritage.

'I have promised myself to no one,' she said.

Warrington shut his eyes.

She put her palm flat on his chest. When his lids fluttered up, she could feel the change in his gaze. She wouldn't beg, or ask again. She didn't think she needed to.

He spoke harshly under his breath—the words directed at himself.

His hand closed at her elbow and he turned away, again taking the lead, only this time, his steps were careful and he watched the wooded areas around them.

She followed, knowing her sisters depended on her and she risked her life to be able to save them. But it wasn't a choice. It was what she had to do. She was the eldest and that meant sacrifice. If she died at sea, or at the hands of a stranger, then she would know she did it for her family. Her mother's last words to her had been *Take care of your sisters.*

Warrington forced himself not to stare at Melina. They stood hidden among the cragged rocks, watching the longboat and waiting for the sailors to return. The hem of her head covering fluttered in the wind and kept calling his attention to her.

He wished he could see her chest again. Her birthmark did have an interesting curve to it. He remembered the child's game of imagining wisps of a cloud as objects and tried to recall the exact shape the mark formed.

He heard the first mate's voice before he saw him emerging from the road. Once the men reached the longboat, he hurried Melina to them.

'You ready to heave to?' Gidley gaped at the woman even as he directed the words at Warrington.

'Yes,' Warrington snapped. 'Hurry.'

Gidley's voice became butler formal. 'Will his lordship be having a guest?'

'Launch the damn longboat.'

Gidley put his forefinger to his lips in a silencing motion and then lowered his hand. He mouthed the word *lady.*

Warrington mouthed back words for Gidley that neither would repeat in front of the woman. The other seamen beamed as if enjoying a particularly good scene at Drury Lane Theatre.

'Yes, yer lordship.' Gidley helped the others push the boat into the waves, then scrambled into the boat, and took the seat in front of her, facing the woman. Warrington made a forceful circular motion with his hand, commanding Gidley to twist around. Gidley's eyelashes gave an innocent blink as he looked at Warrington, then gazed back at the woman, giving a bow of his head as acknowledgement, and turned in his seat. 'Beautiful day for bein' at sea.' He spoke to no one in particular.

Warrington stepped over the side and took the empty plank beside Melina. His shoulder brushed hers. He thought he detected the scent of rosemary about her, but he wasn't sure he even knew what the herb would smell like.

The other men thumped into the boat, voicing polite comments on the calmness of the sea and the beauty of the island as if speaking in front of their grandmothers. Gidley continued his teatime reminisces as the men rowed, recounting with the other seamen the polite sights they'd seen in their travels.

Warrington shut his eyes briefly. He had no idea where these dainty men came from.

'Correct, yer lordship?' Gidley asked.

'Most certainly, my dear,' Warrington answered. He heard a smothered snort from someone else, followed by a coughing attempt to disguise the sound into politeness.

Melina gathered the bundle closer. He hated that she felt discomfort.

Warrington kept his voice calm. 'The next one of you who makes a sound before we board is going to let the rest of the crew watch him swimming around *Ascalon* and the first seaman who can bounce a biscuit off the swimmer's head can give him orders until we're home.'

Silence followed, except for the rhythmic sound of oars slapping the water.

Her shoulders relaxed and he wished he could retrace his steps. Bringing her on to the longboat had been foolish and she was the one being misled. He'd let himself be blinded by a little spot of skin and now she was on a longboat for no reason. They both should have stayed home.

He didn't feel he'd had the option, though. The Foreign Office knew of his ship and had asked him for help. The trip had been a worthwhile diplomatic mission, in that he could tell them the Greeks still planned to rebel against the Ottoman rule. He didn't know if the Turks suspected or not, but he had the information he'd been sent for.

When the boat tapped against the hull of the *Ascalon,* the men tied the longboat. The men closest to the ladder left first. Then Warrington or Melina would go on deck.

Melina stood and didn't move forward, still holding her bundle and her satchel strap draped over her arm.

He touched the small of her back and she turned to him. He reached forward, taking the sculpture. 'I'll get it on deck. If you dropped it into the sea going up the ladder, we'd never get it back.'

She released the bundle and gave her shawl and scarf each a quick knot. She picked her way to the ladder, lifting her skirts to step over the seat in front of them. A simple, everyday movement. His mouth went dry. The image of her legs sealed itself around him. His imagination began to fill in the rest of her body while his mind generously unclothed her. Long limbs, smooth, and welcoming.

He brought himself back to the moment and saw her at the ladder, staring at the ropes.

'Just go up as if you've done it every day, quick, and don't stop.'

She took a few deep breaths, pulled at the waistband of her skirt, trying to keep the fabric away from her feet, and grabbed both sides of the ladder. She snatched the hemp in a stranglehold and moved upwards. Arms reached out to help her on board.

And now he held her parcel. He couldn't risk dropping the rock.

Warrington looked up and called out to the man who

stood at the side. 'Toss me the end of a rope. I need you to haul something up for me.'

In seconds, a rope dropped at his feet and Warrington bound the end around the package. 'Pull it up,' he shouted and the arm went aboard ship. He shook his head at the waste of effort. The rock would be returning to the island soon.

The men were good sailors, but not a one of them was of the clergy and it would take at least that to ignore the woman. He'd send a decent crewman back with her to escort her home safely. No, he'd have to make do with a well-threatened one. All the decent ones were on other ships.

Stepping on deck, he saw the men assembled as if Ben demanded them for a meeting, but he knew the captain did no such thing. The cook sat on an overturned bucket and the cabin boy tangled himself in the rigging like a prisoner in stocks, waiting to hear what was said.

Warrington saw Ben's stare. 'You brought a woman because—' Ben spoke, hands on his hips.

Melina stood, her scarf still knotted tightly and her jaw firm, and stared at Ben. Ben was getting sized up from the tip of his pointy nose to the last thread in his canvas trousers.

Warrington edged just to the side between them so he could see each face. He confronted his younger brother. 'Since I am not the captain and do not have authority as such on this ship, she asked to talk to you.'

Ben didn't speak, but his eyes darted up to the heavens in a disgusted manner.

'Explain your request to the captain.' Warrington spoke to Melina and clasped his hands behind his back. He leaned towards her, challenging them both.

She looked at Ben as if she stared across a battlefield and saw him as a target in front of her, then took a gentle breath—so small to be almost invisible. But the movement signalled a change in her.

Her shoulders dropped no more than a hair. She didn't move her feet forward, but she swayed with the movement of the ship. Warrington was certain she leaned towards Ben as the ship moved and when it rocked back, he did not see her retreat. He locked his jaw and forced himself not to step between them or pull her back.

'I wish *taxidi*—to travel to England.' Her voice became lower—her accent turning into a siren's husky whisper. Her hands reached to grasp the tied ends of her shawl and pull the knot free. 'I have an agreement with this man.' She spared a glance at Warrington.

Warrington commanded himself to remain still. Her voice dripped into him like warm pebbles of desire, bringing back the image of her legs and the spot at her breast. Perhaps he would take her back to her home and work out a true bargain there. The longboat could return him to the ship in the morning. He struggled to attend to the words of the conversation, making his plans for the night.

She reached up and pulled her scarf from her head, sliding the cloth away from her face, and the movements also caused the shawl to drop completely from her shoulders. Warrington watched two seamen collide in their haste to return the garment to her.

Ben's expression glazed over. When Warrington saw that, his eyes followed his brother's gaze.

Warrington stared, his mind not working. The scarf had kept drifting across her face before. He hadn't truly looked beyond the spot on her breast.

Her eyes, he knew they were brown. And her lips red. And her nose, a normal nose. But somehow the arrangement of them and the curve of her chin, and dusts of her hair falling loose from her bun, swirled themselves around her in such a way as to bring them all into a delight for a man's senses.

And that was before even looking lower to a mark that peeked out from the bodice, making one wonder what lay beneath—or making one fill in the imagination of what lay beneath in a stirring way.

'You are in agreement,' Melina said.

'I would prefer not having a woman aboard…' Ben's voice sounded as a kindly father's '…but since we can accommodate you with little effort I'll allow it.' Ben touched a flat palm to his chest. 'I, of course, will be happy to share my quarters with you to make sure you are—'

Warrington knew too much of his brother's life. Snaking an arm around Melina, Warrington pulled her close, sweat forming at his temples. 'She and I have already discussed… the particulars. She will travel with me.'

'Oh?' Ben challenged, lowering his palm from his shirt. 'I—'

'Yes,' Warrington said, feeling her brushing the length of his side. 'We have discussed it. I will handle any expense she might incur. She will share my quarters.' He levelled a glare at his brother. 'I believe you mentioned that it might be best for me to have a woman's company.'

'Should lessen your growls to snarls, I hope.' Ben smiled as he spoke. He looked at Melina. 'If you could do that, miss, the entire ship will be grateful.'

Warrington could feel her hip through her skirts, pressed at his thigh, and smell the spiced scent again, which hinted at mystical pleasures. He felt nothing like growling.

He pushed the thoughts away and loosened his grip. Any tighter and he feared she would be gasping for breath. As it was, he felt on the edge of it and she seemed to have lost her words.

The captain looked at Melina. 'Are you willing to sail this very night?'

She nodded.

Ben turned to Warrington. 'While you lolled around on the island, the repairs ended. The wind is perfect, and the tide right. We can be at sea as the light fades. Show her your cabin, then get to the foredeck and give a hand.'

Warrington leaned his head towards Ben and spoke in a low voice. 'Helping on deck is not what I had in mind.'

Ben smiled. 'See the tears on my face.' He turned and walked away, his boots clattering on the deck louder than before. With every step he shouted a new order to get ready to sail.

Melina whipped the shawl back around her shoulders. She took the parcel from the man who'd lifted it on board.

'Follow me,' Warrington said to her.

His berth was in the foredeck. The captain and the first mate had quarters in the aft deck, close to the wheel.

Warrington led Melina to his cabin, opening the door, which barely swung wide enough for his shoulders. He stepped back, letting her inside. He remained in the doorway and saw her survey the surroundings.

'Take the bunk,' he suggested. 'I'll get some other bedding.'

The hesitancy in her movements made him want to reassure her, but he couldn't. He stood immobile, looking into the cabin. Everything appeared differently to him than when he'd first decided he would sail. Then, he'd seen the surroundings as an efficient use of space. Now he was not impressed to stand in the centre and be able to touch both walls.

The berth took no more room than for a man to lie on, with storage above, and below an open cabinet with a rail-

ing around it to keep supplies from escaping and a brace
midway.

He could not sit upright on the bed and felt he slept in
a casket for a man of slight build. He had a chair cinched
to the wall and his sea chest sat underneath a table. He
had floor space slightly larger than the length and width
of his bed.

'Are you certain you wish to sail with us?' He spoke the
words to her back. 'This will be the room you and I will
share. You can change your mind now and I will see that
you are returned to your home. The ship can wait to leave.'

She didn't turn to him. 'I have no choice.'

As he heard her, his mind knew what her mouth said,
but her voice barely touched him. The curve of her shoulders and the delicateness of her skin—those things reached
him. And he knew without a doubt in any hidden crevasse
of his mind he'd not overcome his weakness. Not even facing his own death had changed him.

He could never curse a woman as much as he cursed
himself for his foolishness.

At least on Melos she had a home and family. She'd be
soon lost among the dockside lightskirts at Wapping docks,
trying to entice men. But it wasn't his concern. He had tried
to keep her from the ship.

Thinking of her on the docks, plying her trade, made
him feel angry again. She only thought she moved into a
place to improve her circumstance. The stews of London
took no prisoners and willingly released no one alive.

He forced the concern from his mind.

The seamen could have their abstinence. He didn't mind
so much when solitude was his own choice. But he did prefer to see noses without close proximity to whiskers. Before,
he'd not noticed how women's presence made the world
feel differently, until he found himself surrounded by men.

He missed Whitegate, his true home, but he'd left it well before he boarded the ship.

He'd left a perfectly sound home behind for the chance to sleep on boards and inhale salt water through his nose. And instead of a crystal decanter, kegs held stale water. The biscuits sometimes had to be broken into pieces and slowly mushed away in his mouth.

He'd not thought past his wish to keep her from Ben, or his own desires, to realise he was putting himself in such closeness with a woman. He'd never shared a room with a woman. Or awakened with anyone. Not even when he was married.

The act seemed intimate. More than a quick tumble would be. Sleeping near her, very near her, could be… His breathing increased. Pleasant.

Or not.

He examined her carefully, thinking of the rumblings from the ship at night. 'Do you snore?'

She stood and looked at him. 'Do you?'

'No.' He supposed he didn't.

Her eyes opened wide, too wide. 'If I sleep loud, will you go somewhere else?'

He smiled. 'It's an old sailor's legend that if a woman snores it's because she hasn't had enough bed play to tire her into a sound slumber.'

Her nose went up. 'It's a Greek woman's legend that if a man *ronchalizo* it's because of the air moving about where his mind should be.'

'We'll have to find something to do together so neither of us sleeps.'

'I do not snore…' She paused and her gaze narrowed when she realised what she said. Her words were strident. 'And it has nothing to do with bed play.'

'It could.' He returned the innocent look she'd given him earlier.

She huffed, not answering. He preferred the anger over the dread he'd seen on her face earlier. Before he sailed, he'd been concerned about the trip—and he knew his brother was a seaworthy captain and the crew was experienced.

Even so, he'd not liked the voyage and he'd hated the first climb up the ratlines.

'I need to give you a bit of advice for sailing,' he said.

She waited, eyes daring him.

'Stay out from under me when I am climbing above. I am not as experienced as the others. If I fell, I could hurt you.' He paused. 'But if you decide to go up the ropes, please wear trousers. Otherwise, the men…would find it distracting.'

He hoped anger might help her forget the newness. Inside, he smiled at the way she ruffled from his words. Talking with her made the water seem smoother. His clothing less rumpled.

Melina saw the spark of humour in his eyes. He jested. She let her shoulders drop and her lips turn down. 'Then I will merely lose my grip and see how the man below feels about breaking my fall.'

His lips thinned, but not in anger. 'I could catch you.'

'But you would not be able to keep your grip. The fall would frighten me so, I am sure my elbows might flail about.'

'Would you like to test that?'

'No.' She made herself shudder. 'I need to put my satchel away.'

He turned to the bunk. 'Shove the bag under there. Wedge it tight or you will be fighting to keep it from sliding about.'

She moved, kneeling to be able to see and reach into the space. She lodged the bag inside and a tendril of her hair fell forward, loose from the bun. She finger-combed it back into place as she rose and then took one step to the door. 'I would like to watch the sails as the ship begins to move.'

He moved in front of her, blocking her way out, his expression cold and dark. 'I have to insist you not go about the deck. For the duration of the voyage, your attentions are mine alone.'

She opened her mouth to protest, then realised what he was saying. He thought her planning to sell herself to the men.

'I—' Her denial stopped before she could finish the sentence. She had sold her body and to him. It would be hard to convince him she didn't use her attentions for funds. Every man on the ship thought her a *porni*.

Melina didn't want their eyes on her. She already knew how sailors looked at the women they thought to purchase. She'd known it not safe to get too close. And now she was locked on a vessel with them. Her stomach roiled.

'How many men are on this ship?' she asked.

'Thirty-three.' His lips formed each sound of the word quite distinctly.

She didn't like where his thoughts were going. 'Women?' she asked, her fingers gripping the back of the chair beside her.

'One.' Nothing in his expression changed.

She controlled her words. 'I think I shall stay inside. I would not want one of the men falling from overhead when I am walking below. Nor would I wish to get tangled in the ropes. I have heard how things move about when ships are underway and sometimes mistakes are made.'

'It would be wise of you to keep out of the way.'

She didn't ask what he would have done if she'd not

agreed to stay inside. From the look in his eyes, he would have been content with locking her in. And she would be able to do nothing about it. She tensed. She had stepped into a world where she was entirely alone.

'Does the door—' She had to ask. 'Does it latch from the inside?'

He shook his head, one very definite movement. 'No one would dare enter without my permission.' His words held in the air.

Relief surged in her, until the next words he said reminded her where she stood.

'And you cannot lock me out.'

'I did not think to do so. I know what I have promised.'

He indicated the island with a turn of his head. 'You can go back. Now. Last chance. No rock is worth going from your home. Leaving the people who can care for you.'

'But it is worth leaving for the people I *do* care about.'

He stared at her, his eyes disagreeing, and left the room, leaving her alone with the reality of her actions slithering into her body.

Chapter Three

—◦◦◦—

Warrington worked the davit, listening to the creak as it lifted the longboat to be secured on deck. He mustn't keep thinking of her. This would be a bad time to get himself injured.

Taking one last look at the shore, he memorised the sight. If the fates were with him, he'd never see Melos again.

And if he had his way, he'd keep alive until they reached England. He had no sailor's wish to be buried at sea. When he died, he wished to be boxed and put into a properly marked location.

He could understand fascination with sailing. The challenge of it. Men stood on rigging as comfortably as they stood on land.

Now the sailors unfurled the foremast sail, working from the middle, out to the side, and it dropped more softly than a lady's skirt.

When the sun set the magic of the sea came out. In the night, the sails stiffened in the wind and the waters whispered a mesmerising sound. To stand on deck, with the blackness reflecting the heavens and the ship racing across the surface, a sailor could feel as if he were flying in an otherworldly vessel.

The moon rose well overhead and Warrington heard the bell, which signalled midnight and the end of the watch.

'Well, old man…' Warrington heard his brother's voice '…I suppose you should go examine the trinket you've stored in your cabin.'

'I'm in no hurry.' Warrington watched Ben. 'I'm not a man given to speed, but more to quality.'

'It's what we all say,' Ben muttered, looking into the darkness at the rigging, and then patted the mast. 'But I prefer to let the women boast about me.' Ben called out, walking away, 'And if you need instruction, return to me and I'll explain how the deed is *properly* done.'

Warrington stopped, turned back, Ben's form outlined in the moonlight. 'Little brother, I see the error now. You've thought all along it is to be done properly, while the women most enjoy an improper tumble.'

Ben turned, waving Warrington on his way. 'Get along, old man. Talk does not get the job done.'

When Warrington opened the door to the cabin, he noticed the lantern light flickering in the room. He looked to the bed. Empty. She sat in the chair backed against the wall, a bucket hooked at her feet by her heels, and looked up at him, her face ghostlike in the light.

'I have lost…' her voice followed the movement of the ship '…most food…' another gentle sway of the boat forward, and her chin dipped over the pot '…I have eaten in the past year.' The ship moved with the rocking motion of the sea and the breezes pushing them forward. She glared at him, but the look seemed more pitiful than angered. 'No one told me…a ship would float so rough…trying to turn my insides…outside.'

'You get used to it.' He hung his cap on a peg. 'About the time we hit land.'

She groaned.

Turning, he reached into the cabinet to move the brandy bottle aside and take out a cloth bag about the size of his hand. 'Comfits. Don't tell the men I have these. Wouldn't want them to think me weak.'

He reached the bag to her, but she waved it away. He didn't move back, but kept his hand firm.

'I had some made with ginger. A servant I have, a former seaman, swears it helps when a man is at sea and his stomach refuses to settle into the ship. Just let it rest on your tongue.'

She frowned, but took the parcel, opened it and pulled out one of the orbs. She put it in her mouth and kept the bag clasped in her hand.

'Since you're not using the berth...' he said, reaching to remove his coat and place it on the remaining peg, and over her shawl.

She closed her eyes and leaned her head back, thumping the wall behind her. 'I can't lie down. My feet keep moving higher than my head.'

'Interesting.'

He usually sat in the chair to remove his boots, but no matter. Perching just on the edge of the berth and letting the bottom of the cabinet above him press against his shoulders, he tugged off his boots. Then he lifted them by the tops and pressed them into the railed opening beneath him so they'd not slide while he slept. He took off his waistcoat and stored it. Slipping his shirt from the trousers, his hand stopped when he looked again at her face. Her lashes rested against her cheeks. Her lips pressed together in a thin line and skin showed the same colour as the sails in moonlight.

For a moment he stared, torn between letting her alone and a need to brush tendrils back from her face.

He shook himself from his fascination and reached to the water pitcher, lodged in place and filled by the cabin boy earlier in the day. Warrington took the flannel lying inside the small raised edge, which kept it from sliding to the floor as the boat moved. He dampened the cloth and stepped beside her, putting it to her forehead. She held the compress in place. Their fingers touched, but she didn't seem aware he was even in the room.

'Try to think of something pleasant.' He spoke to her, and in response her lips tightened. 'Sing to yourself—some peaceful tune,' he instructed. 'It might help.'

'Are the seas always rough?' she asked.

He couldn't tell her this was calm. 'You get used to it.'

She nodded. 'I hope.'

Her parcel lay beside her. He took it and her gaze flicked to him.

'The rock can't slide around. Might break or cause one of us to fall.' He knelt at his bunk, trying to keep from brushing against her, and well aware that she pushed herself to the other side of the small room. He tucked the arm away carefully, knowing she watched every movement. Still kneeling, he looked across at her. 'The light needs out.'

'No,' she whispered. 'In the dark, the room moves faster.'

He frowned. 'You cannot fall asleep with the lantern lit.'

'I am not sleeping.'

Warrington stood and undid the top fastening of his shirt, then snapped the garment over his head, putting it on the remaining peg.

He pulled open the covers and slid between them. He turned his head and she looked forward, her gaze locked on the wall.

'Would you speak of something soothing?' she asked.

He stared at her. 'I'm going to sleep.'

'Say anything. Anything to take my mind off my stomach and the treacherous waters. Talk about your home. Your mother. A dog. Anything. Please.'

'I remember a tale of a young child eaten by wolves on a winter's night. What of it?'

'Nothing with food in it—please,' she mumbled.

He studied her face. The pallor only made her lashes seem longer. He decided he didn't need sleep as badly as he thought.

'Ben, the captain, is my brother. This is his first sailing on a ship he is captain of—but he was born with the taste for sea life in his blood.' He stared into the wood above his head. 'I've another brother, Dane, who is looking after things at home while we're away. And a sister, Adelphinia—named after a batty aunt, who even refuses to answer to the full name. We call my sister Adele, which she much prefers over Phinny.' He stopped. 'Perhaps from our telling her the horses called her when they whinnied.' His voice softened. 'She thinks brothers are a curse.'

He looked at Melina. If the sound of his voice eased her, then the rise and fall of her breasts eased him. The little mark on her might be a scar.

'Keep talking,' she said.

He gave a grunt of complaint, but continued. 'I like Hoby boots, on firm land. I like to be able to look out my window and see oak trees. Solid trees on solid ground. I like my horse, Chesapeake, and I hated leaving him behind. I'm never getting this far from him again. He'll probably wish to bite me or throw me when I get home.'

'You miss...your horse?' She slid the flannel from her cheek.

'Ches—' He shut his eyes. 'I don't know what I was thinking to leave him.'

'There is no person you miss?

'For—' His voice rose, but he stopped himself. He remembered his home. He'd not wanted to speak of family. 'I have a son. And there's his sister. She's younger.'

He thought of Jacob, the morning after Cassandra's funeral. At first light, the boy had darted into War's room and bounded upon the bed with a question or two about death, then a concern about cat's ears.

Silence and darkness around him, he spoke again. 'My wife died a year or more ago. I've not forgiven her. I've not forgiven her for anything.'

She didn't speak.

He didn't want the sombre mood surrounding him so many times to engulf him again.

He turned his head back to her. 'Chesapeake enjoys the same journeys as I do. You can jest and call him any name you wish and he doesn't care. Chesapeake's a good mount. His sire and dam—he inherited the best of both. Father's size. Mother's grace.' The shadows in his world jostled him, taking his mind from the horse. Even though he knew he didn't lie, he left out so much.

She daubed the cloth at her face. 'I already miss my sisters.'

'Women are different.'

'Yes. But you have your brother nearby.'

He grunted his displeasure. 'I intended him to tell you that you could not sail with us.'

'I know.' She patted her cheek with the cloth and stared at him. 'No wonder you don't talk of missing anyone but your children. You've no heart.'

'Chesapeake would disagree.'

'A horse.' She near snorted, and if she only knew—she'd sounded a bit like Chesapeake. He wanted to tell her, but when he saw the paleness of her face he changed his mind.

'A fine chestnut. You'd never get him willingly on a ship.'

'So he's *exypnos*—clever.'

'Very.'

'How did you come to be on the vessel?' she asked, holding the comfits and flannel in one hand.

'My brother convinced me to invest in something he could captain. We both own half.' Warrington let himself settle into a more comfortable place. She needed to snuff the light so he could rest. 'Ben can make having fleas sound like a lark.'

'Should I expect fleas on this journey, as well?'

'Not unless you get too close to the men.'

He saw her lashes sweep up as she checked to see if he jested. Let her guess. 'You'll have to put out the light,' he reminded. 'We've had one fire too many already.'

'In a moment.'

Her head was against the wall. Graciously long neck. A delicious amount of skin creamy beneath it.

'What is that mark at your breast?' he asked.

Without looking, she reached to the colouration, running a fingertip along the skin, tracing the outline.

His gaze locked on her fingers.

'I was born with a smudge and it seems smaller than it used to be. My sisters have the mark, too, but none of ours is in the same place or shape. I think of it as an hourglass—to remind me to be useful because there is only so much time.'

'Reminds me of…' he paused and looked again '…two horses' hooves close together.'

Again, she moved her fingers briefly to the mark and then stood, using both hands to brace herself against the table. She edged herself around the furniture and then doused the light, putting them in darkness.

'How did you pry yourself from Chesapeake to get on a ship?' she said, her fumbling movements leading her to the chair.

'I hoped to see different sights and learn about the Turks, but mostly I've seen water not fit to drink, heard jests not worth repeating and eaten food with no appeal at all. I think this ship has no rats because they starved.'

He heard the slop bucket slide as the ship moved and pushed himself from the bed. 'I'll empty the pot for you—otherwise one of us might put a foot in it before morning.' And he didn't intend to sleep with the smell.

Not having illumination didn't concern him. The walls were so close he could feel his way for what he needed. He slipped out through the door, his feet bare, and walked to the side, tossing the contents downwind. When he returned, he opened the small door to slip the pail back inside the cabinet.

'I would like to keep that nearby,' she murmured, stopping him.

He put it on the floor at her feet, and he saw the shadow of her pulling the bucket close so she could hook it again between her shoes.

'Take the bed,' he instructed, standing above her. He would have to pull together something so he'd have a place to sleep.

'No,' she insisted, moving her head. 'I'm best here.'

'Wake me if you change your mind.' He reached to the bunk, took the pillow and then pushed it her direction. 'At least put this behind your head.'

After she held the pillow, he took his shirt, rolled it and tucked it in the berth.

He slid back into the sleeping space. 'My brother needs to get sailing out of his veins, return home and start a life there.'

'You can't fault him. The boat is his Chesapeake.'

'Well, he'll have to convince me we'll find gold, silver and mountains of apple tarts to get me on board again.'

He could hear her silence. It wasn't only that she was quiet—she was immobile. Not moving. Then she spoke. 'Treasures convince people to risk much.'

Chapter Four

Warrington stepped out of the cabin. He'd not fallen asleep until dawn and the climbing temperatures of midday had awakened him. The sailors cleaned the deck, a daily job. They couldn't risk growth of the green muck that flourished at sea emerging where men might slip.

Ben walked to his brother's side, looking every bit a man without a care—even with clouds bundling above them. Air filling with steam. The sea too calm.

The unconcern in the men around him didn't give Warrington a feeling of ease. He knew the men all too well. They didn't fluster over a storm. They knew they'd either live or die through it and, either way, they'd still be at sea.

The captain leaned close to Warrington and spoke so no one else could hear. 'Did you sleep well?'

Warrington ignored him. The young ferret could sniff for morsels awhile longer.

'I'm thinking the earl is wantin' for Stubby's job.' Gidley walked up. His whiskers quivered when he spoke. 'Men said he emptied the pot three times in the night.'

'Oh.' Ben's brows shot up. 'I may have heard that rumour, too. When we get to London, I'm thinking he might become a lady's maid.' Ben looked to his brother and then jumped aside, dodging the boot swung at his heels.

'For that…' Ben's chin went up '…you're invited to spend the afternoon, *and night,* at the wheel.'

'The woman's in my bed.' Warrington kept his voice light. 'Mine. Slop bucket or no. My cabin. My bed. My woman. She's perfection,' Warrington added. He remembered the night before. Perfection—if you didn't mind the greenish cast to her face. And seeing her fingers rubbing her own heated skin didn't do him any favours. She must have touched that mark a thousand times and each time he'd become aroused.

And now a storm to toss the *Ascalon* about more. He was going to die before they reached port and without getting his own mast climbed. No. No matter what, he'd discover the real treasure before the storm hit.

'You have any more of the medicinal you mentioned when we started out?' Warrington spoke to Gidley.

The older man's chin wobbled. 'Two draughts.'

'See that Melina gets them,' Warrington told the first mate. 'And remove the chair and table from my cabin. Get some bedding for her.'

'Do as he says,' Ben instructed Gidley, his voice light. 'He's not getting any younger and he needs all the help he can get.'

Gidley left to get the medicine and Ben looked at Warrington, saying, 'I'd suggest, brother, that you attempt to manage—if you're able—more than only a single tumble. I speak from experience when I say it *is* possible.'

Warrington's hands tightened.

Ben put his hand at the back of his own neck, shut his eyes and rolled his head, then yawned. 'I've had more than a lifetime of women already in my tender twenty-six— no, twenty-seven years—and probably your share, as well. That's why you're looking so sour at just past thirty. You're fading and I've bedded more women than you could ever hope to count.'

'If we take away the ones you've paid, how big would the number be then?'

'Only ones worth having.' Ben gave another stretch.

'Said by a man who has only the single way of attracting a woman.'

'At least when I pay,' he drawled out the last word, 'I manage to get her bedded.'

'I'm sure they do so quickly so they can see the last of you.'

Ben laughed in response, but Warrington knew his brother had a point. In the night, he'd wanted to touch Melina. And he hadn't. He'd not been able to reach out for a moment.

'Ben...' Warrington looked at the darkening clouds above '...do you ever fear dying at sea?'

Ben shook his head. 'Man has to go some time. Best to be doing what he loves when his toes turn up.'

'Then I will feel no regret for killing you if you don't relieve me from the wheel before the storm hits.'

Ben laughed. 'Give the medicinal time to work. Later, I'll give you time to go "courting". When you get to her, explain you must finish quickly so you may return to your duties.' He tilted his head and stared upwards. 'What's a brother for if not to give the elder an excuse for rushing about?'

'I have not *once,* in my entire life, concerned myself with your bedding habits,' Warrington grumbled, glaring at Ben. 'Not once.'

The captain tilted his head sideways and his tone was mournful. 'Sadly, I know why. You would be distraught at what wonders you have missed in your own experience.' He turned, glancing over the deck, appraising the ship. 'I have some good wine. Come to my cabin and have a swallow while you're resting up for the woman.'

Warrington shook his head and walked towards the aft deck, ducking his head from the ropes jutting out above. He could use some refreshment after the night he'd had, but he didn't relish more of his brother's company.

'The wine is quite good. Worth what I paid.' Ben lowered his head as well when he stepped beside War. 'And I'll not needle you any more.'

Warrington snorted, but followed Ben.

The quiet click of their boots as they moved to the cabin blended with the movement of the boat, and the murmurs of the sailors keeping their voices low so orders could be heard.

Inside the room, Ben reached to pull a bottle from a crate. The cork slid free of the neck with a comforting pop. Ben handed the drink to Warrington, who leaned against the door.

Warrington looked to Ben's berth, which didn't have the storage overhead. The bed wasn't bigger, but the room itself was more than double the size of the others, with two windows instead of one. A miniature was affixed to the front of the cabinet and Warrington knew, if he looked closely, that the painting was of a mermaid—Ben's version of a perfect woman.

The wine's sweetness rested well on Warrington's tongue. He handed the drink back to Ben, who dropped himself in the chair and helped himself to a hearty swallow.

Warrington snatched the bottle before Ben had a chance to put it down. 'Every time the boat touched the smallest ripple, the noises she made woke me. She turned green to her toes, I wager. I'd have had more rest on deck—except the men would have made too much sport of it.'

'You brought her on board.'

'Had to stay awake to make sure the lantern didn't falter. She couldn't stand the dark—made her worse. Every time I convinced her to turn out the light, in a few minutes I was lighting it again. I finally persuaded her to lie down in the berth.'

'So you were able to enjoy her.'

Warrington took a long swallow of the wine, frowned and looked at Ben. 'Think of the width and height of my berth. Two squirrels could hardly mate in it.'

Ben raised his brows and put a hand to his chest. His voice became overly concerned. 'I feel saddened for you and I don't wish you more distress. Send her to my cabin. I'll play nursery maid tonight.'

'Not bloody likely. I did everything but rub her feet to soothe her. I will be enjoying the lady's favours.'

'Maybe you should have rubbed her feet.'

'She wouldn't let me.'

'What can I say, old man, except send her my way.' Ben clasped his hands behind his head. 'I've a special remedy that eases any discomfort a woman might have. One look at it and she forgets all else.'

'You'd best see the ship sails like treacle poured across a plate tonight, or I will be pounding on your door.'

Ben held out his hand, indicating time to return the bottle. He might as well have been looking over the top of spectacles in a schoolroom. 'I think you let her make excuses.'

'I do not,' Warrington repeated, and then smiled. 'Every time I looked at her I could see that little mark, like a drawing of breasts.'

'It looks like a woman's bottom.'

'No.' Warrington spoke with certainty. 'Breasts.'

They were silent for a moment, then Ben held his hand out, palm raised, and didn't lower it.

Warrington gave him the bottle.

Ben took a drink. He put the wine in front of him. 'Just don't forget she'll be plying her trade on the docks when we reach port. Saw an opportunity to get to London and she took it. Doesn't change what she is.'

'I don't care what she is. She's in my bed and she's going to do as she agreed. Then we dock and she goes on her way.'

'Now you're thinking. Not like with—'

'Stubble it, Ben.' He didn't need reminding about his dead wife, the beautiful Cassandra, who always wore chemises that smelled of roses.

He knew he'd been a fool with her, two times over. And both his brothers knew. And the servants. Or at least they all imagined they did. He didn't think anyone but himself realised how truly addled he'd been. At least afterwards he'd been able to let them believe most of his feelings were rage towards her.

But he'd grieved for her and not been able to pretend otherwise enough to fool his brothers. Only the misery of being trapped on a ship at sea, with conditions that might have otherwise driven him mad, had brought back his mind to reality.

He could see Cassandra for what she was, but that also meant he could see himself for what he was.

He'd not been able to stop wanting her. He'd hated himself for his desire.

'Oddest thing came to me when I shaved.' Ben gave a slight shake of his head. 'Think I've seen your berth mate before.'

His thoughts snagged on Ben's words. 'The island?'

'Never been to Melos before. Couldn't be.'

'But how could you forget a woman with a face like hers?'

'Didn't exactly forget her. Just can't remember where I saw her. And I know I saw her.'

'You told me all women look alike to you.'

'In bed.' Ben shrugged. 'But I don't think that's where I saw her.'

Warrington felt the betrayal of his past again and anger with himself for having concern for a woman he didn't trust. 'I suppose I can ask her why she speaks so plain. It would not be unusual if she spoke French, or if she spoke a few words of rough English. But she speaks better than some of the seamen, even with her Greek flavour. I noticed on the island, but once she dropped her shawl, I lost interest in her speech.'

'But she's not said *eros*. Perhaps it's the company she's keeping.'

'So you remembered one word from the tutor you tortured. *Eros*. I am not surprised. But she's been paid—her passage—she'll say it. And you'll leave her be.'

'Of course.' Ben stretched out his arms, before clasping his hands behind his neck and grinning. 'But don't be surprised if she changes affections and decides she can't stay away from me.' He leaned back enough that the front legs of his chair lifted, completely at ease with the ship's motions.

'You touch her, little brother, and there are not enough men on this ship to keep you alive.'

'You talk *here* and the woman is in the cabin regretting she did not get her captain.'

'When we get to London, I'm sinking my half of the ship.'

Ben again leaned towards him. 'Let's just hope you don't sink my half before we get there.'

Warrington kept himself from kicking the legs out from his brother's chair. He truly didn't want him hurt, but unsettled would be nice. Warrington crashed the door shut behind him when he left and hoped his brother's ears rang.

He went to take his turn at the wheel, but knowing, before the night was out, Melina would soothe the memories that plagued him.

Chapter Five

Melina didn't know whether she'd stepped closer to devastation or further away. The boat wobbled so much she thought her knees would buckle as she stood.

The cabin boy fidgeted at the door, holding several biscuits in one hand, and a cup of liquid in the other, which smelled the same as soured goat milk. 'First mate says to drink the broth he had made from his special mix-up and we don't have no choice when he says things. This won't kill you, but it'll give you some ballast in your stern. Keep you from going belly up.'

She took the offering from him.

'Anything else you be needing, I's your man.' He plunked his finger against his chest—or where his chest would be once he grew. She didn't think him aged more than most men's boots. His red hair was streaked with dark strands. The locks fell across his eyes, but didn't conceal the watchfulness behind them. 'Gidley says I'm not to leave your side until you drink the last drop. He says I'm not to let you pour it overboard, either. Gidley says I should watch you with my own vision. Gidley says not to trust you 'cause of you being female.'

'How old are you?' she asked.

His face furrowed. 'I be old enough. I keep working like

I do—I'll have my own ship some day. I want to sail on a man-o'-war. I'll be...' he straightened his shoulders and glowered '...tougher than any privateer, pirate or first mate. Gidley says first mates are toughest of them all.'

'*Malista,*' she answered. 'Yes.' She nodded, about to step back and shut him outside.

He put one scruffy bare foot to block the closing of the door. 'Only toes I have, 'cept on the other side. Would sure hate to lose 'em.'

'If I drink this, you might not wish to see the results.'

He waved a hand, indicating unconcern. 'It's your belly.'

She firmed herself and drank half the cup. 'I'll not take any more and the rest goes into the pot and neither of us will tell Gidley.'

'Won't pickle me none.' He grinned at her, the smudge of dirt on his face wrinkling. 'I'll empty your slop bucket and no one will know.'

She stepped back so he didn't knock her askew when he moved inside. He grabbed the pail, held it for her to pour away the medicine and looked at her.

He whispered, but his words near shouted he spoke so loud. 'Where's the treasure?'

She didn't answer.

He bunched his lips, then moved his jaw from side to side as if the movement helped him think. 'Gidley said you had a treasure for the earl. I figure it has to be in the parcel Warrin'ton hauled up. Jewels?'

She shook her head. 'Some stone. Nothing you'd be interested in.'

'Like rocks?' His eyes lit up. 'Gold ones?'

She shook her head. 'Not gold.'

He frowned. 'I was hoping to see me some gold. No use for rocks on *Ascalon,* 'cept for ballast.' He turned, rushing out, barely letting his dirt-encrusted feet skim the planks.

Melina looked at the boards above her head, remembering the catacombs she and her sisters had explored, but they never stayed long in the darkness. She'd only explored inside to prove her bravery. Now the shadows outside the window increased her fears even as she told herself nothing had changed, but the sea had roughened.

Each lunge of the ship into the unsettled water slapped her stomach with the feeling of being in front of a battering ram. She stood, reaching out to the door, palms against the wood.

The image of Stephanos, the man she had fled, entered her mind.

'I hate you, Stephanos,' she whispered to the empty room while wiping away the moisture at her brow—for a moment, uncaring if the ship dropped under a wave, and kept plunging. Sinking would still the movement and silence the ship. *Ascalon* creaked and groaned, complaining more than any person she'd ever heard. She didn't see how something could stay afloat while protesting so much.

The shadows in the room grew longer. The rocking motion made the walls move as if they reached to squeeze her in an embrace. Her lungs could hardly fill with air. She already felt she was drowning.

Without thinking, she jumped up and pulled open the door. She had to escape—to breathe.

Stepping on to the deck, she could see enough in front of her to realise the vastness of the water. The liquid reached to the end of the world. And she could run no direction to escape.

Melina would kiss Stephanos's feet—each naked toe if he asked—to get back to her home. She pulled the door shut behind her and pressed her back to the wood, her fingers grasping for something to hold herself still. Now she didn't care that she'd planned to leave the island for months and swore she'd do whatever the journey took. The sacrifice was too great.

Taking a breath, Melina took stock of her surroundings. She didn't smile or look directly at any of the men. She did not want more concerns.

Two men sitting on crates immediately dropped their heads and studied the frazzled bits of rope in their hands. They continued twisting the frayed hemp back into shape. Everything on deck, but the boxes the men used, was lashed down.

She let out a breath, putting her hand at her stomach. Walking to the railing, she leaned against the barrier keeping her from the water, facing forward, feeling the comfort of the breeze.

Only a day before, Melina could not have imagined herself drinking a vile concoction, after spending the night inside a bobbing box at sea, with a silent man watching her cast up her accounts and him trying to calm her so he could bed her.

She'd bargained with Warrington and taken a risk, and she didn't regret it, but she wasn't certain her promise wasn't troubling her stomach as much as the ship.

Shutting her eyes didn't help. When she opened them nothing had changed.

Something—a hand—grabbed her elbow and she jumped, darting back from the railing.

'You needin' help, miss?' The reedy voice of Gidley jarred her, and even in the dusk, she could see enough to recognise him leaning towards her in concern.

'I'm well,' she muttered. 'I just needed air. My—' She pulled her elbow from his grasp and touched over her stomach, taking care not to pat it. 'I am not good over water… and…' Things kept moving in front of her when she knew they were really immobile. 'I keep being ill.'

He stepped back, a bundle tucked under one arm. 'If yer need the earl, he's at the helm.' He lowered his voice, whispering, 'He can prob'ly hear us yappin' now. 'Less the wind is howling, yer can hear a sniffle from anywhere on deck. But yer need to take care. This be the bit of quiet before the storm slaps our masts up our…nose.'

She shook her head. Her bun slid back on her head and she hoped the darkness covered her dishevelment.

'Yer want me to show you how well sound can carry, I'll start singin' and in a whisker shake, his lordship will start swearin' at me to shut my mouth.'

'No. I thank you,' she answered.

He tipped his chin to her. 'Well, I'm puttin' this bedding inside yer cabin.' He let his words ring loud. 'Yer get tired of that peer and want to see what a real man can do, just say the word. Might not be the sea makin' you ill. But the comp'ny yer keepin'.'

He gave her a fatherly pat on the arm before scooting her aside to open the cabin door and toss the bundle inside. He left, humming.

'Melina.' She heard the muffled shout of Warrington's voice and turned towards the sound. She crept slowly until she saw his outline at the stern, holding the wheel. The night made him darker, and maybe taller, she wasn't sure. Even the wheel seemed smaller with him holding it.

'You should be in the cabin. You could fall against something, or stumble overboard.' He raised his voice. 'Or have to speak to someone like Gidley, who can't sing and wouldn't know what to do with a woman.'

She heard a chuckle wafting back through the air—and then another.

One more voice—a strong baritone she didn't recognise—called out and she wasn't even sure of the direction.

'When I'm finished with a woman, she's the one singing—my praises. Send her my way if she can't sleep.'

Warrington snapped out, 'You're going to find yourself upside down and hanging from a mast if you don't take care.'

'Best leave his lordship be,' an unrecognisable voice shouted.

Melina guessed the words came from Gidley, but she wasn't sure.

'His mama didn't teach him to share,' the man continued to taunt.

Warrington put his words low, snapped them together and spoke to her. 'Are you pleased with the discussion you have caused?'

'The only grumbler is his lordship,' Melina said.

'You tell 'im, sweet,' a voice rang out.

'Anyone touches her, they go overboard,' Warrington said, his voice not overly loud, but with enough force to take the sound to the tips of the sails.

'Including the captain?' someone asked from the shadows.

'*Especially* the captain.'

Melina crossed her arms and put challenge in her voice. She turned to face him. 'It is a good thing I am fond of his lordship, then, so no one will have to go into the sea.' Her lips turned up and she put her chin closer to his. 'Besides, he's the only man who's ever emptied my pails.'

Whistles sounded, mixed with a few muffled hoots.

He stepped sideways enough to hold the wheel with one hand and snake the other around her waist, pulling her so close she could feel the heat of his breath and hear his rough whisper. 'I should never have brought you.'

She turned, her hair catching in the bristles on his chin.

'I know,' she replied in kind. 'But I'm here and the ship can't turn back.'

His fingers loosened on her waist and as she moved away, he took a step, scooping her closer. Before her feet settled, she found herself tucked between the wheel and a firm male. Both his hands steered *Ascalon.* She had room to breathe and little else.

'You might as well learn to guide the ship.' Warrington leaned to whisper to her ear. 'You're not going anywhere for a while.'

She tried to push away, but he trapped her and she couldn't leave.

'Let's not let the seamen think we're having a lovers' quarrel,' he whispered.

'I don't feel well.' She spoke between gritted teeth.

'Then try to miss the boots.'

Chapter Six

Melina's warmth overpowered Warrington. He gripped the wheel hard, trying to ignore her body—but he could not ignore anything about her. He could only tell his heart to quit beating so loudly she might hear.

Her skirts tangled in his legs and when she moved the slightest, her backside brushed against him, causing his fingers to lock on to the wheel's spindles with such force he expected the wood to shatter. And when she put her foot down on his boot, and then sidestepped to avoid his feet, even more of her pressed against him. He was stoked into heated readiness.

The sea's moisture penetrated her clothing, bringing the scent of a stringent soap to his nose along with the spiced fragrance he'd noticed. But he inhaled again—because mixed with her skin, the soap reminded him of a woman's purity—something he'd never felt before in his arms.

He savoured the moments with her and, for the first time since the newness had worn thin, relished a moment at sea.

'I think you've impressed the men enough with your mastery over me now,' she whispered. 'You may release me.'

He didn't answer immediately. Instead he lowered his head. 'I do not think they are convinced—yet,' and as he said the last word, his lips tasted the skin at her neck. He wasn't disappointed.

A shrill, vulgar whistle interrupted and he pulled back.

'I cannot believe you men are ignoring your duties,' he called out after he'd turned his head so he could raise his voice without hurting her ear, 'simply because Melina cannot stay from my side.'

He heard her intake of breath, but before she could speak, he put his fingers lightly over her arm. 'Don't say more,' he whispered, 'and they'll go back to their work.'

She gave a quick nod and he dropped his fingers.

'Melina.' He made sure no one could hear. 'If I release you...' inwardly he cursed himself '...will you go straight back to the cabin?'

She opened her mouth to speak and then took a breath before answering. 'Yes, but...'

'You may stay if you wish.'

Her voice was hushed. 'The room—the walls—it reminds me of a cave... I hate caves...'

He held her waist and his hand instantly warmed from her skin. 'I understand. I was daft to step foot on this ship. I never plan to let my feet leave dry land again—but I'm pleased I sailed. I saw what I left behind.'

'Your wife is gone, but you have a woman there you care for?'

He shook his head. 'I do not.' He heard the coarseness of his tone and softened his words, speaking low, near her ear. 'I've spent little time with a woman this past year.' A breeze blew over his face and whipped at his clothing.

'My wife, Cass, died nearly a year ago, or beyond,' he said. 'I'm not sure. I refuse to remember the dates. The days. She left behind two children. But I have to get home to my son. I've left him too much. I had him brought to my town house to visit me, but I've not returned to Whitegate since my wife died.' He paused. 'No. I have no woman. I have not had one for a long time.'

'I would have still bargained with you had you been wed. I had to leave.'

'I understand.' His lips were only a shudder from her ear, and he let his face rest against her head. 'But my brother would be holding you now, not I, if I still had a wife at home.' She shivered, but he didn't know if it was from his actions or his words or his nearness.

'Truly?' she asked.

'Yes, I suppose. Perhaps not. But Ben would have known had I been untrue to Cass and that would have bothered me, though he wouldn't have cared. As I am the eldest, I should lead the family.'

'Not all the oldest of the family lead.' Her voice, soft, brushed against him like a caress. 'My mother cared for us on Melos. Father would leave for a long time and then he would return, laughing at how much we'd grown. Sometimes he would stay a short while. Sometimes a year or more. Mother still took care of our home just as she did when alone.'

'My wife left all in the hands of the servants, but they took great care not to anger her.' He'd never spoken such to anyone. Nights with poor sleep and wondering if he might die when the ship caught ablaze, and then having such warmth in his arms melted into him had loosened his tongue. And made his memories not so harsh.

'In her youth,' he continued, 'my wife nearly died and her family feared for her life.' He brushed at the hair fallen from Melina's pins. She had as much of her locks on her shoulders as she had in place. 'Her parents adored Cassandra. Plus, she was a beauty and they treated her as porcelain. Her older sister, Daphne, missed Cass when we married, so I welcomed Daphne to visit. Daph loved her sister so much. In no time, Daphne was family to me and Cassandra was a doll we both adored.'

He stepped back, moving aside. The talk of Cass had stirred unpleasant memories. And he had a woman in his arms who could take his mind from Cassandra. Now was not the moment to think of the past. Any longer with Melina and he would not be able to keep his hands from roaming her body. 'Your hair is falling to your shoulders. Go to the cabin and try to sleep if you can,' he directed her, feeling a distant coolness replacing the warmth of having her close. 'I will follow soon.'

She gave a quick nod and walked away, staying away from the outer rails.

He sniffed the air. He was not a seasoned sailor and he knew a storm was on the way. The seas had roughened. He called out for someone to take his place at the helm.

And while he waited, he told himself to remember that Melina was little more to him than an imagination. When they docked, she would disappear—just like the dream he created of her.

Melina sat on the floor, head back against the wood, eyes closed, propped against a bundle of bedding. He clicked the door shut behind him just as lightning flashed at the window. She jumped, blinked twice and struggled to find words. 'The sea is rough,' she said, voice unsteady.

'We'll take your mind from it.' He leaned towards her, took her hand and pulled her to her feet. Just the touch of her made every bucket worth it. He slipped his arms around her and buried his face against the soft skin of her neck. He smiled when a hint of sweet spice reached his nose. She smelled like something of a holiday. Of gaiety. Mulled wine. Exotic treats.

Her clothing bunched under his hands and he covered

her back with his touch. He needed nothing more than her in his arms. She soothed him—something he'd not expected. Feeling the softness of her earlobe with his face, he savoured her. But she remained still, letting him caress and giving no response.

Warrington stood back from her and took off his coat, putting it on the peg. After wishing the ship's movement hadn't hit her so hard, he remembered the rough days when he'd first set out. No one should feel so unsettled.

Warrington took her chin, lifted it and brushed a kiss across her lips. His body flamed from just the merest touch of her. He whispered against her skin, 'You'll have to imagine all the fine things that should surround someone as lovely as you.'

He understood her reluctance. She didn't know how they'd find the room, probably expecting nothing more than the sort of encounter a rushed man gave a woman who had to be on to her next business. The two of them simply could not fit on the bed. Not only could they not lie side by side, but the cabinets overhead prevented other arrangements. He'd spent some time thinking of the best way to accomplish a blissful encounter. Even as he released her, the ship kept rocking in such a way they could hardly keep from stumbling into each other.

Warrington reached for the bedding bundle, which rolled about, knocking into his legs, and with a few tugs and a quick flick spread the bedding on the floor. The chair and table were gone. She stepped back, flattening herself against the wall.

Pulling the mattress and coverings from his berth, he put it against the ones on the floor, adding softness. He fell to his knees to finish making the pallet. He'd never, ever knelt in front of a woman—but no matter. Running a hand over the bedding, he smoothed edges together.

He stood, examining her in the lantern light.

Brown eyes—lovely, enticing—stared back at him. She didn't look pleased to see the covers on the floor, but he couldn't fault her.

'I assure you, if we were in London, I'd find a bed for us so soft you'd think of clouds.' He wanted her to understand—he took this seriously.

The pallor in her face slowed his movements. She had to know the bed wasn't his choice.

'There's no bigger cabin, except Ben's,' he told her, 'and he is captain, so it's rather hard to shove him out through the door.'

'I'm… This is fine.' She dropped to her knees, pulling the top covers in place and brushing her hand across them. She lowered her chin. 'You know I'm not… The ship is moving more and…' She touched her stomach.

He knelt, reaching out for her shoulder, feeling the roughness of the sleeve. 'Melina—if you've any compassion at all, try to keep from being ill for a bit longer. I can… But with the storm coming and…'

She pulled back. 'This is not the storm?'

He'd said the wrong thing. 'A few raindrops. Ben thinks we'll sail through without a bobble.'

The ship heaved and she moved backwards, sliding with the makeshift bed. He shifted with the momentum, putting his arm around her and arranging so his back was to the wall and he held her at his side. He felt stronger than any wave—but she didn't.

A blast of anger hit him. The fates—he knew them well, they were his bedfellows—they were conspiring again. They thrust another wave against the ship and he held her tight, seeing the press of her lips.

He was not some rutting beast—and she would still be here tomorrow—assuming they didn't die in the storm.

Warrington stood, extinguished the wick and looked to the window. He had no time to get a hammer and nail a covering over the opening so the flashes of lightning wouldn't illuminate and accentuate the discordance outside.

He'd been graced with this woman whose ancestors could have been from Thessaly, where mythology began, and he would not be allowed to touch her. Lightning wove gold threads into her hair, but illuminated the pallor of her skin and reminded him she didn't feel well.

At least on deck he would be forced into thinking of staying alive. He reached to the door, but her voice stopped him.

'Please,' she said, and touched the bed beside her. 'The ship shakes so. I don't want to be alone. I feel better with you near. Here.'

Lightning kept flashing through the glass—giving her a mythical glow, freezing the unmoving image of her into his mind, painting her like a statue, a work of art.

The intensity of her gaze caused him to stare—her eyes clear as a harvest moon, surrounded by lashes dipped in the flashing light. He dropped to his knees, landing beside her, entranced by the flickers of lightning on her skin. He swept his finger over her bottom lip. Now he knew what magic felt like. His skin tingled with anticipation.

More thunder crashed. He heard a crack of lightning. With the sounds, and the sight of her, sensual energy surged in him, heating him until an internal maelstrom engulfed him. The memories he made tonight would some day take on larger-than-life images in his mind. Melina, different from all he'd seen before, and all he'd see again, would remain in his thoughts—like a precious gem hidden away in a safe. A secret only for himself to have.

A wave tilted the ship and she wrenched her body

around, clasping the front of his shirt. She buried her head against him and he held her.

'Have you ever been in seas this rough?' she asked.

Lightning crackled much too close. The very air could not be still, as if it had an awareness of their moments, and told them to hurry, hurry, hurry, and grasp every second of sensation.

He ran his fingertips across her back, and the lightest touch of his hand against her took his breath. The fierce waters faded from his mind.

When he could speak, he said, 'Once is too many times. I didn't tell you before. Suspected you'd worry if you realised how brutal the waves can be when the sun heats the water in the day and the storms take us at night.'

He pulled his coat front aside, sliding into a sitting position, and then tucked the garment around her back, hugging her inside with him. 'This ship was built to handle such weather and the men are the best sailors in the world. Nothing will happen.' Assuming the repairs held and the storm did not get too violent.

'Shut your eyes, and think of... Think of this,' he said.

His mouth closed over hers and the kiss was nothing more than a simple touch, almost the same as he might give a tavern maid who'd plopped down on his lap, before he scooted her away to get to his ale or talk with his companions. But the pulses stirring in him ignited.

When he pulled back, she reached out, running her hand along the side of his jaw, seeing him with her fingertips.

'I have wanted to touch your face since I first saw you,' she said. 'You're so foreign from the men I have known all my life. And the other sailors. I think you even look at me differently.'

He rested his forehead against the side of hers. 'I wanted...since I saw you...so much more.' His lips explored her skin and he cupped her breast, letting the fullness feed the sensations in his fingertips. The fabric didn't prevent the yielding flesh from rolling beneath his caress with her softness and he discovered the hard nipple, and stretched his hand over her, so he could take in as much of the feeling as his mind would allow. No corset. He'd never felt through a woman's clothing to find so much of her underneath.

Just as she had explored his face, he traced her, keeping the fabric of her garments as a barrier between skin and mapping out the feminine twists and turns of her.

The storm would frame them and their bodies would gain sensations from the hint of danger in the air. And she would be the essence of every sensual mythological being ever imagined.

He couldn't read her expression and didn't know if it was a flaw in him, or if she hid herself well. But when she parted her lips and moved towards him, he didn't have to. She slipped her arms around his waist, mumbling his name, muffled words against his chest, and she clung to him. Her breasts pressed against his shirt, causing his clothing to feel tight over his body. She moved with the lunging waves, too, but not in the same way as he. She kept herself upright by pushing herself into him at the same time as she pulled. He braced against the wall, one hand clutching the edge of the bunk, leg jammed against the opposing side. His body was forced still within the movements. And she burrowed and snuggled and wove herself against him, holding on like a handkerchief might be wrapped around a blowing limb. When the ship created even the smallest distance between them, she moved to fill the space, keeping him as her anchor.

Using all his strength in one arm, he kept them steady while he held her with the other hand.

He found her lips with his and at first she paused, but when she moved again her hands wouldn't be still, roaming his body with a hunger in her fingertips, searching him out as if she were afraid she might miss touching some exquisite part and wouldn't be able to bear it.

Somehow she'd settled herself into the movement of the ship and now used it to keep herself thrust against him. He savoured the desires her body created. If she was a goddess to lure men to their doom, he was prepared to die.

'This helps. And the waves are not so strong now,' she whispered, and he could feel the movements of her lips against him as she spoke.

'Just ripples.' But they weren't. Everything had intensified. He reached to pull free the last bits of his shirttails, which remained tucked in his trousers, and her fingers tangled with his, helping him.

The water outside crashed against the hull, but he no longer cared.

She leaned into the side of him that he used to hold them steady, leaving him one hand free to rub the small of her back. But her fingers remained under his shirt, clasping him, leaving heated handprints, which encased his whole body.

'You feel so…pleasant,' she whispered into him, her face moving up so that her lips were at his neck.

And for the first time since he saw her, she was in exactly the right place, saying exactly the right thing.

Letting her sway into him, her rocking against him when the ship moved caused the fire inside him to smoulder so intensely he wondered if he should just let their clothes disintegrate into ash instead of removing them. He had no time to wait for such an event. He didn't fear her not holding up well in the storm—he felt concern for himself not surviving the intensity within him.

His lips lingered against her hair, and skin, taking in all of her he could. This truly was the woman of his imagination—the night cravings that woke him with seconds of pleasure lingering in his mind and hours of hollowness facing him. But this time, he would sleep after the dream, untortured—soothed.

He buried his face into the curve of her neck. She did feel like Aphrodite—and he had the imagination of her vanishing from his arms, fading, mocking him for desiring her so intensely. But he couldn't be imagining this because he'd never tasted a dream and he tasted the nectar of her lips, and this time, he relished the hint of saltiness at his tongue.

His fingers brushed over the strands of her hair loosening from the pins and he slid his palm down, closing his eyes and closing all his senses except the ones at his fingertips.

He knew they had to separate so he could get past the clothing. But one moment apart was a moment for ever lost. He savoured her cheek, her ear and the hollow of her neck. A banquet for his starved senses.

She might as well have already undressed.

She kissed him, he thought. He wasn't totally sure. He pulled back, only enough to look into her face to make certain she was real. Dark eyes stared back at him.

She'd not tugged at his clothes again, or spoken much, but she didn't need to. Her expression now told him all he wanted to know.

For the second time in his life—and he'd never tell her—he felt like a virgin. Yet a different sort of innocent. One who knew all the pleasures he could unleash with his hands, his mouth and his body.

He forced himself away—aware of his own breathing echoing in the cabin—knowing if he did not move back, he couldn't get closer. Melina's hands, hesitant but bold, didn't lose their purchase easily and that knowledge alone washed him with a satisfaction he'd not experienced before.

He pulled off his coat and lifted his shirt over his head.

The luscious heat of her—against his chest—hit him harder than any wave could have tossed him. When he touched her breasts, running a finger over the mark just at the top of her bodice, he could barely breathe. This was his Aphrodite. She would vanish soon, but not until she left him truly sated for the first time in his life.

'You are to be savoured.' He wanted to feel all of her and adjusted her on to her back, moving her so she was tucked between his body and the wall. He released the buttons of his trousers. The sight of her, in this thrown-together bed where another woman would never rest, clutched at him, filling him with a reverence that arrested him. He stopped for another moment, just a moment, to look at her. He wanted to see her face even when he shut his eyes. He needed her locked into his mind so that all other memories of women on the earth were erased—Melina alone remaining in his thoughts.

For this, he would have sailed around the world—twice—to capture her so she could bring him to his knees and let him rise back up, unburdened.

He kicked his trousers free at their feet.

Hooking his arm under her leg, he pulled her knee to his mouth for a chaste kiss on the coarse cloth of her skirt. Now the fabric felt leaden, thick and suffocating for skin soft as hers. Much too rough.

He wasn't quite sure how her clothing worked. This wasn't the same dress of an English woman, which slipped off easily, only to reveal rigging underneath as well structured as the ropes holding the sails.

She sat up and reached behind, tugging her garments. She slipped the blouse over her head and removed her chemise after pulling it from her skirt. His jaw fell. Nothing tied underneath. Not a thing. Lightning flashed again, somehow only illuminating her breasts. Even though the burst lasted less time than a blink, the image of the white softness with pebbled peaks lodged in his mind. His body reacted with the same intensity of the storm.

Then she reached to the side of the skirt and undid a knot, and slid herself out. The thunder increased. The bursts of light showering the room must have meant he'd done something right in his life.

'You are perfection,' he whispered.

Leaning forward, he cradled her and swept her back to rest on the covers. Her eyes widened. She reached up and clutched his shoulders. The wind almost drowned out her whisper. 'I am not a whore.'

'It doesn't matter,' he reassured her. This time, he didn't care who'd been before him. He was with her. 'We are the only two people in the world. We must savour this.' His fingertips traced the mark at her breast and he trailed downwards, over her nipple, and to her stomach and the curve of her hip.

When he bent to kiss her and let his hand rest at her thigh, she slid sideways with the ship's movement and he followed the momentum, but didn't let his full weight go against her. His bent knee rested over her, his foot pressed against the ledge that had once cradled his mattress. He reached up, holding the edge of the bunk to keep them from rolling back.

'Are you hurt?' he asked, his face resting against her hair.

'No. Please don't let me go.'

He had no intention of it. Nor could he have. She rested inside the crook of his arm. Her hand nearest the deck captured his shoulder, the other held his back.

When the ship lunged and she grasped, fingernails clenched at his skin. Instead of feeling pain at her fingertips, he ached for her. His cock nudged her thigh, pressed against her smooth skin.

The weather slammed the ship down and he held firm so they would not slide backwards. He hooked his heel inside the opening at the bunk, lodging his leg over the ledge that framed the base next to the deck planks. His hand was momentarily freed to trace the outline of her hip and, with her head still on his arm, he reached out to grip the base at the other end of the bunk. He was as comfortable as in a cradle. The waves rocked them.

He felt where her waist curved in and then let his fingertips trail downwards into the soft curls and the wetness beneath. She was ready.

But he wanted her more than ready. He wanted her gasps and cries and release. If they died in the storm, he wanted her to be pleasured first, more than she'd ever felt before.

He began a rhythmic caress while his mouth rested against her face, her neck and her hair.

Her teeth grazed his shoulder and her hands pinched into his back. She writhed and he felt his own pleasure bursting inside. He watched, mesmerised with the moment, until he knew she peaked, her gasps plunging desire into him so that his whole body burned an aching need for her.

Forcing himself to wait, he pulled his hand from her and gave her a chance to recover while he brushed his face against her, lips caressing her.

He tugged, sliding her so she could move above him. Both her hands went out, resisting movement.

Releasing her, he pulled back from the kisses. 'Sweet. It might be better if you got on top. The waves. The hard bed.'

She breathed her answer. 'No…' Her disagreement registered in his mind, momentarily giving him pause. But only for less time than it took for lightning to flash.

Brushing his face against hers, he rose over her and gently lowered himself, entering her, and her fingernails plunged into his back, and she gasped.

Something forbidding flashed through his mind. An unease hit him. But the moment couldn't be stopped or interrupted. He held the woman of his dreams, bodies bound together with intensity.

Carefully, he rocked into her, whispering tenderness against her ear.

Her legs, he felt one wrap around him and he forced himself to go slow, to savour. To let the riches of her body wash over him.

Now the ship seemed to smooth, to ease across the waters, and the storm raged inside—inside him. The waves rolled through his body, taking him on their skyward roll, their deepening depths.

'Are you...' He meant to ask her something, but his mind got lost in the feel of her and he could not form another full thought. She was everything at this moment—a world for him.

He tried to move a hand up to brush back her hair from her eyes, but he couldn't. He could not let the ship control his movements. He had to be careful, gentle and not let himself plunder her, but show her the tenderness he felt for her.

'Melina,' he whispered. The sound of her name, even that increased the sensations. He could feel so much more of her. Not just where their bodies touched, but the way she breathed, the richness of her voice, all the things of her that made her who she was.

The room brightened briefly again and he saw her face clearly. The sight of her was too much. He could not last any longer for her, didn't want to last any longer for her, because he wanted those seconds, the endless flashes of time where they were completely together, taking them into another realm of the world.

He released, but it was something different. A connection and blending of their bodies, holding close, melding together in just those heartbeats.

Moisture covered his body, as if he'd felt the rains and they'd cleansed him,

He pulled her against him, falling back with the ship.

When the room became silent—silent even with the storm mocking the tempest that had raged inside the cabin—Warrington's mind hurdled ahead. Instead of a wash of satisfaction overtaking him—dread nudged the warmth into oblivion. His stomach churned.

He looked into the shadows of her face and slowly pushed himself to the side. Lightning still splashed through the window, but the storm no longer concerned him. She made a sound, no more than a sigh, but the illegible sound of settling in for a jaunt through her own thoughts.

The ship lunged and he reached out, not wanting her to be overwhelmed by the movement of the waves, and pulled her firm against his side.

'Had you…before?' he asked, hating the words. Dreading the answer.

She murmured, 'No.'

She could not have understood what he asked. She could not have said what he heard. He spoke to the walls, letting his mind untangle the puzzle around him. '*No one's* a virgin.'

He tried to examine her face in the flashes of light. He saw the truth. 'How could—'

She scooted forward, pulling a bedcover over her. 'I decided—for passage. I knew what I was doing. And tonight, I wanted to know…how you felt…'

'I didn't know, though. I didn't know. You didn't… tell me.'

'Yes.' Her brows bunched. 'I said…something.'

He sat up, looking over his shoulder at her. He felt betrayed. How could he feel betrayed again—this time? 'I thought you were a lightskirt.'

'I told you I wasn't.'

'I thought you meant you weren't a common whore. That you expected more… That you chose who you…' He'd been misled again. He didn't know what to think or do. She was *not* supposed to be an innocent.

'I had to bed you or Stephanos, the man who controls Melos. We have leaders, but he is the one who has coin and the leaders do not cross him.' She sat, pulled her knees up and put her chin on them. 'I would choose anyone over Stephanos.'

He stared at her. Strength left him. He could barely keep himself from sliding with the ship.

'But… You offered— I did not misunderstand you in the barn. I did not. You said…' He heard the volume of his voice rise, embarrassing, and he regained control and pushed to his feet, unconcerned by his nakedness. He noted her quick intake of breath and jerk of her head when the lightning illuminated him. He reached to the washstand, bracing, and poured some water on to the flannel, then lodged the pitcher securely back to its base.

She could avert her eyes, close them or watch. He did not care.

He pressed the cloth to his forehead. 'How could you be an innocent?'

'Stephanos. Years ago, he put it about that if any man touched me, his family would be punished.' She raised her voice. 'I have no care for Stephanos. But unless I gave myself to him, I couldn't marry. I didn't mind not having the choice of another—but Stephanos decided he was tired of waiting. I was not.'

He knelt beside her, followed the length of her shoulder to her hand and placed the flannel in her palm.

Then he stood. The oilcloth coat left behind by the previous seaman didn't fit his shoulders and the arms of it stopped just below his elbows, but he dressed quickly, donning the coat last.

He hadn't been Cassandra's first and had been too green to realise it until she taunted him with it.

Now, when he least wanted one, he'd bedded a virgin.

Chapter Seven

The sky sparked and the rain pounded with an unthreatening insistence. Nothing inside Warrington flowed as serene as the sea.

Lowering his head from the drops hitting his face, he kept close to the ship's upper cabin walls, moving slowly towards the bow. He stood with the wind behind him, facing the bowsprit, and his back pressed into the outside of the cabin. Shadows concealed him. Only men who must stayed out in the weather and they would be too busy staying alive to notice him.

He'd had to be away from Melina and think.

A virgin. She'd been recompensed, but he'd actually paid nothing for taking her innocence. Having her on board the ship had taken no funds from his pocket.

The London docks at Wapping couldn't come quickly enough. He should not have agreed to the journey. He'd never step willingly on a ship again, unless the whole of the world began to fall into the ocean, and then he would consider sailing briefly before drowning at peace with his decision to avoid the vessel.

A movement at his side, not in harmony with the rhythm of the sea, caught his attention and he stepped sideways, avoiding being stumbled into. The slight build could only belong to one person.

'Stubby.' He spoke to the small form of the cabin boy, who'd huddled into the space beside him. 'You are not to be on deck. Go below. Now.'

He heard no sigh, but saw a heave of thin shoulders.

'Gid says this storm's still just a baby. Shouldn't scare anybody but a lady. Supposed to get worse by morning, though.'

'Stubble it. You're to be asleep.'

'Can't sleep. The thunder pitched me from the hammock.'

'Stub. The bed wraps around you. It's hard to fall out of the hammock once you're in it.'

'But once you're out, it be hard for me to crawl back in without help. I'd sleep under it, but I'd be rolling around all night.'

'I'll get you a place to sleep.' He moved to the stern of the ship, borrowing one of the quartermaster's lanterns, and Stubby trudged along behind him.

'You be out here because the woman's in your berth?' Stubby said, his voice still imbued with youth.

'Yes.' Warrington truly didn't want to speak.

'I want to stay here with you.'

'You're going below.'

The lad who could scamper through the rigging faster than a breeze immediately changed his speed to that of a sore-footed turtle, grasping at the sides of the ship's cabins, as if he could hardly stand upright. Warrington locked his jaw and grabbed Stubby's shoulder, turning the lad around the edge of the cabins and towards the opening to the lower decks.

Stubby stopped. 'Gidley says the woman's showin' you

her treasure. You seen her treasure?' His voice bounced with excitement.

'Just a bit of marble stone.' He gave another push, moving Stubby faster. The lad would not take a step without a nudge. Warrington kept a hand on Stubby's shoulder, propelling him forward.

'Can you show me?' Stubby moved to the steps to go below deck.

'No.' Warrington ducked his head and followed Stubby down the rungs, into the bowels of darkness, the lantern giving just enough light to guide their way. They followed the men's snores, which made *Ascalon* sound like a beast with a rumbling stomach.

'Why?'

'Stubby.' He spoke sternly, hoping to quiet him.

'I know. I know,' the cabin boy grumbled in the darkness. 'Stubble it. Stubble it. That's not my real name. But I been called Stubby so much I forget the other one.'

'You'll remember some day.' Warrington hoped he told the truth. 'Or you can pick out something you like.'

Stubby paused, a delaying tactic. 'I'm trying to think of one.'

Warrington reached the crowded hold and, clutching the shoulder of Stubby's shirt, walked by hammocks with sleeping men until he found an empty one. He hung the lantern, the scent of burning oil mixing with rain and musty men.

'But that woman I give the medicines to—is she hidin' gold?' Stubby's voice was a whisper, but the kind that bounced from walls.

War stepped back to the empty hammock and knelt to make a step with his interlaced fingers for Stubby's foot.

'I wager it be gold,' the waif continued, moving close to Warrington.

Stubby's small fists held the edge of the hammock. He secured his foot in Warrington's hand and tumbled into the ropes. 'Gidley says having gold is better'n having teeth 'cause if you have gold, then someone will chew your food for you.'

'Go to sleep,' Warrington said, turning to retrieve the lantern.

'I'd like to have me a big hunk of gold. I'd like to have me a gold ring to wear in my ear and a gold sword to fight pirates, and gold buttons and gold—'

'Do not go back on deck tonight.'

'If Capt'n says all hands ahoy, I will. Capt'n says all hands ahoy, even cook goes.'

'Not in this storm. If Captain Ben and Gidley both think the storm will be angry, then you should stay below. I'll take your place.'

'I be man enough. Been in more storms than you could even think of. I be a sailor.' His head wobbled with pride, then his voice dipped to smugness. 'You be just an earl.'

'One big enough to thump your backside. You will not go on deck.'

Stubby didn't answer, but turned his head. 'I be real sleepy now and you be keepin' me awake.'

'You had better not go on deck before sunrise.'

'I might need to piss.'

'Then you best hold it.'

Warrington turned away, leaving with the cabin boy scooting around in the bedding and swinging the hammock even more than the waves did.

Warrington returned to the spot where Stubby had interrupted him. Stubby's chatter had reminded him of Jacob and caused a longing for his child. But he could not expose Jacob to the risks of the sea and he had not been able to stay on land where the memories were disastrous. Now he wanted to get home and see his son, and throw him up in the air, and pick him up around the waist and carry him like a sack with flailing legs.

And Jacob—how could anyone ignore a blast of life like him? If Jacob were on the ship and saw the men climb the rigging, he would be serenely waiting until a head was turned and he'd be scampering to the top, five years old, thinking himself a man.

Warrington was only days from seeing his son again and this time, he'd not leave him. Jacob needed a father. Well, he decided, perhaps Jacob did well without a father. The child had a nursemaid, servants around who doted on him and an uncle for guidance. Jacob would do well—father or not. But Warrington knew he needed his son's laughter. Now, when Warrington was too far to see his son's face and too far for the sound of delight to carry, he knew where his heart belonged. Warrington wanted to be the one Jacob followed.

Being away had helped him find his compass. He'd put the starkness of the *Ascalon* into his past, along with this woman he'd happened upon, and begin anew with his life.

And if Jacob ever saw the scar across his father's back, and asked about it, the version he heard would be a tale of a cutpurse attempting a crime.

He'd send his past into the depths and not even let Melina linger in his thoughts. But he could still feel the brown-eyed siren. She had skin softer than any touch of silk. Lips that caused his body to boil with desire—not to mention the mark that drew his eyes more than any breasts or arse.

But she wasn't a goddess. She was human. Like everyone else. Their coupling had been a transaction for her passage. She'd been straightforward. And no foolish words of love. *Anyone would be better than Stephanos,* she'd said. No false praise there.

She was, in a way, the perfect woman, drawing his eyes,

setting a price for her affections and taking herself away
when they docked. But he'd not touch her again. Not risk
giving her a child.

If he could only forget she'd been a virgin.

'All hands ahoy.' The voice rang out, carrying through
the cabin walls.

Warrington opened his eyes, coming awake instantly.
A true storm was upon them.

Melina sat with her back against the wall and her feet
stretched against the base of the berth. She'd wedged herself, holding firm when the ship moved. Her hands held the
slop bucket. Lightning illuminated the room and her head
was relaxed back, and her lips were softly parted in sleep.

He'd not undressed earlier, knowing the call would
sound in the night. He left the cabin, giving a quick glance
over his shoulder before pulling the door shut.

The wind popped the sails like a whip. The *Ascalon*
rolled and he braced himself. The storm bucked the vessel
and raindrops pelted like thrown pebbles against his cheeks.

'Get the helm.' Ben appeared from starboard side.
Flashes of light illuminated the rain-soaked strands of hair
spiking from under a cap he wore.

Warrington gave a quick nod and moved past the quar-
terdeck. He had no more time to think when the ship jerked,
tossing him forward.

The bow of the ship plunged downwards, well into the
waves, then bobbed up again, like a drowning person gasping for breath, only to be slapped back against water. He
forced his eyes open in the onslaught of wind and rain at-
tacking them. Water saturated his hair, but none ran in riv-
ulets down his face, instead the wind dispersed the drops
like shattered glass.

When he stood at the wheel, Warrington braced his feet

and locked his body so he could find enough force to control the rudder's movements while the momentum of the ship pulled him forward, then pushed him back.

The main sail was furled. Warrington thought of nothing but keeping the bow of the ship sailing into the waves. He stood, each muscle in his body used to keep tight control and every sense focused on his job.

He couldn't tell how long he'd been fighting the sea, but he had lost the strength to protest the movements and only survived them, when he heard shouts, and saw men scrambling. They were taking risks moving swiftly on deck in a storm and only one reason would cause such a pace. A chill scraped into his stomach and he forced himself to remain on task. Whatever had happened—the sea moved with such quickness and finality that even if he could have dashed to help—the outcome had already been determined.

Pushing aside the knowledge of possible tragedy, he couldn't risk letting his mind wander or make conjectures. If he didn't know, then everything remained the same. He had no choice but to stare forward, ignoring the water blasts in his face and the thunder around him. The ship needed him now more than anyone else.

'Yer had yer two hours.' The shout at his side surprised Warrington. He'd been so focused in his concentration he'd not realised Gidley stood near. 'Yer need to see Capt'n.'

'Why?' Warrington did not release the wheel. Now, instead of bracing himself against the storm, he steadied himself for the first mate's next words.

'He tossed agin' a spar. No blood coming out his ears or mouth, so it looks to be a bump.'

Warrington stepped back as Gidley clamped a meaty hand on to the wheel spoke. 'That boy bounces better 'n any frog I ever seen.'

Warrington left, keeping close to the cabins, grasping

rigging to keep balanced and praying Ben was not deeply injured. Warrington had always spent more time with his middle brother, Dane, than Ben, until this venture. Dane shared a more serious view of life. But Ben—

Both the older ones had watched over him and tormented him. His sister, Adele, would never forgive him if he let anything happen to Ben, just as she'd never forgive Ben if Warrington went overboard. Well, she would forgive Ben. He was the youngest.

When he reached Ben's cabin, he opened the door. A scent of camphor, or some similarly pungent medicinal, hit his nose. The light cast everything into garish shadows. Stubby sat in a chair, feet hardly touching the floor, and looking as if a jib had caught him between the eyes. His thin face had grown in just hours and his nose would likely bear a reminder of the night for the rest of the lad's life. A streak of dried blood caked between his nose and lip. Stubby's wet shirt plastered against him.

'We'll both be a bit colourful in the morning.' Ben's words sounded tugged from his lungs.

Warrington looked to his brother, resting on the berth. His arm lay over his stomach and the fingers of his right hand gripped, but held nothing. He wore no shirt, only dry trousers. His sodden clothing hung from a peg.

'Gid says you thought to dance in a storm.' Warrington moved inside and pulled the door shut against the rain. The water pooling at his feet added wetness to the planks.

'The wind led the waltz and gave me a turn I'll never forget,' Ben said. His cheek looked to have been dragged along one of the stones they used to clean the deck. Pain pinched his face.

'He saved me. That he did.' Stubby's words ran together and he looked at Ben, adoration bursting from the young eyes. 'The capt'n just caught me and snatched me back from that wave like it was nothing. Capt'n didn't say a word. Just scared that water into letting me go.' His voice dropped, memories floating behind his eyes. 'Was a big fight.'

Stubby rose to his feet. The words were too important for him to speak while sitting. 'A big ol' wave.' He raised his hand high over his head, and tiptoed. 'A wave. Jumped 'cross the boat and reached for me, just reached out and— Then I was—' His words became faster. 'I grabbed with my toes to the deck because my hands was full of water. Capt'n pulled my shirt, but couldn't hold me. He seized me and a spar and fought that wave—bigger'n two ships and a house. The monster came back.' He made clawing motions. 'Capt'n, he squeezed on to me.' Stubby made a choking face, with his tongue out. He collapsed back into the chair. 'The wave—it were really angry 'cause it couldn't pull us overboard or drown us while we was standin' and just slapped Capt'n hard into the spar.' Stubby's adoration for Ben shone from his eyes. 'Capt'n is stronger 'n sea devils.'

'You able to get out of your clothes by yourself?' Warrington asked Ben.

Ben nodded at the same time Stubby answered for him. 'Capt'n had to have Gidley pull his shirt and Gidley even had to put dry trousers on him. I'm supposed to be watching him now—Gid says—see if Capt'n goes belly up before the storm finishes, but I don't think he's going belly up. Capt'n still holdin' to all his fingers—even if some of them's more crooked than they're supposed to be. He's not missing any halves like Gidley or quartermaster. Gidley said he bit his own fingers off because they was on his nervous side—and he says I get on his nervous side, but I don't think he's going to bite my fingers off because he says I'm wormy and he don't like worms.'

'Stubby—put your hand over your mouth and hold your lips shut.' Ben's voice rasped in the air. He closed his eyes.

'You do look like you've been mopped around the deck.' Warrington moved closer, studying his brother.

'I've moved across the ship on my backside before and I dare say I'll do it again. Best way to check for splinters I know.'

'You find any?'

Ben's lips twitched, but he took a moment to find the strength for words and open his eyes. 'Gidley gave me a scant spoon of laudanum. He said he's saving the rest in case someone gets hurt.'

Stubby looked at Warrington and the child's voice became a loud whisper. 'Gidley told me about the demons of the deep afore. I know it was them. Capt'n said no. Said a mermaid sent the wave because she wanted to meet him 'cause he's so manly.' He cocked his head. 'You think a mermaid can make waves do that—or you think it was a spirit tryin' to swallow me whole?'

'*Captain* Ben Forrester,' Warrington said. 'You're filling his head with nonsense.' Then he turned to Stubby. 'It was just a wave and no spirit or mermaid.'

Ben's eyes were shut. 'It's not nonsense,' he muttered. 'It may not be truth, but it's not nonsense. It's a *yarn* and we seamen spend much time on yarns.'

'Stubby…' Warrington turned to him. 'Don't believe anything anyone on this ship says but me, unless it is something you see with your own eyes.' He stared at Stubby. 'And even if you see it yourself, on this ship, you will check with me to see it is true.'

'I saw the wave reach for me.' Stubby's chin quivered and the purpling on his face seemed darker. Warrington's throat closed. Stubby was scarcely bigger than Jacob. Warrington put his hand on Stubby's shoulder, resisting the urge to pull him into his grasp as he would have his son.

'It was a big hand.' Stubby pushed free and showed the

actions with his own arm and fingers. 'Reaching out to pull me to the bottom of the sea.'

Warrington watched the boy. 'You'll have to learn not to believe sailors' tales.'

'Why not?' Ben's eyes were shut. 'Mermaids are truly handsome. Sometimes they leave seaweed behind, though, and they don't always smell pleasant.'

Warrington met Stubby's eyes and then shut his own while frowning and shaking his head.

But Stubby spoke to Ben. 'Do they make mermaids in my size?' he asked. 'I hope to see one 'fore long.'

Melina slept sitting, with her back against the wall, and one hand clasped over her fisted other one. She woke when the pressure of a foot sinking into the pallet jostled her.

She didn't move, even when he slid beside her, scenting the air with a salty-tinged masculinity. He tugged at the covers and pulled them around himself.

'Pretend to be asleep,' he muttered. 'Just don't step on me when you get up. I've been awake two nights straight, part of a third—and I must rest. Drowning is starting to sound pleasant.'

She could tell he rolled so his back was to her. She couldn't move. Her stomach was hanging on to her insides and as long as she kept her back straight she could believe she had stayed alive. The waves had lessened in their violence. Even the thunder had moved on.

'Once we get to London, I'll see you have passage back to Melos.' His voice broke the silence.

'I can take care of myself.' She spoke before she intended, jerking her face in his direction. She bit the inside of her lip, reminding herself to be motionless.

She couldn't see his eyes, but she watched him turn in her direction. He examined her, his face a mask.

His words sounded unwilling. 'Your stone won't be enough in England to protect you.'

She spoke again, controlling the intensity of her words. She'd risked everything on this ship and this stranger. But once she reached London, she could find her father there. He could help her raise funds and search for more artefacts. She was certain she'd seen more carvings at the place she'd found the woman. But the woman was the prize. 'We're too far at sea. You can't turn the ship around and return me.'

He touched the bare skin of her arm, soothing her. 'Once we get to England,' he repeated, 'I'll stay a few days in London. I have to meet people to discuss the details of the voyage. And if you wish to return home, I'll make sure my brother finds a way to get you back to the island.'

She gave a quick toss of her head. 'I will find my way. The arm will help me.'

'This Stephanos. Surely you can find someone you prefer better than him?'

She shrugged.

'The men you see at the docks will have one thing on their mind when they approach you—and they won't pay generously. They'll haggle over a pence and be angry with you for any coin they give you. And then they'll take your body and they won't be kind. They'll feel they've paid you so they don't have to be gentle and they'll want every ounce of your skin for their coin.' He paused. 'You can't find a more troublesome lot of humanity. I'm sure they're even worse than this Stephanos you think so highly of.'

'It's not your concern. I won't sell myself because I have the arm. The museum will want the rest of her.' She turned her face from him and bundled herself up, raising her knees and resting her arms around them. She dipped her chin. 'Go to sleep.'

He sat up and clasped her shoulder. She was amazed

at the warmth a single touch could send and pleased deep within herself that he wanted to protect her from selling her body, but angry he would send her back to the island. She could not go back without funds.

His words were soft—sleepy. 'If I'd known you were an innocent, I'd never have let you set foot on the *Ascalon*.'

'If I'd know you were such a tender heart, I'd have thrown myself into your brother's arms.' She considered the words she'd just spoken, and realised the untruth of them. When she looked at Warrington, she could see behind his eyes. The anger she saw wasn't directed at her, but at himself. And sometimes she saw pain, moving quicker than the flashes of light in the night, showing through the struggle she saw within him.

'You've no sense at all if you prefer my brother.' He rested back into the covers.

'I'll find my own way in England.'

He tugged her down beside him and she kept her body stiff. Being held by him teased her of a life she'd never have, unless she made enough from the sale of artefacts to have a dowry not just for her sisters, but also one for herself. A husband of any value could cost a considerable amount.

The warmth of his breath touched her when he spoke, his words little more than a haze of sleepy murmuring. 'I won't waste a worry on you, then. Just be still and quiet for a moment so I can drift off.'

She didn't move, knowing he should fall asleep soon. But even if he slept, she couldn't move from him. His arm around her trapped her with the strength of iron.

'I can't let you be like her.' His voice confirmed tiredness when she heard his slurred words. 'Cassandra. My lovely wife. Not a man on *Ascalon* who wouldn't have given all they owned for her. Even our captain. And I was the lucky one.'

'She's gone.'

'Not to me.' His words barely rose above his breathing. 'The bitch still burns in my heart.'

Chapter Eight

Melina opened the door and stepped into the morning air, pleased to have her shawl keeping out the chill. The *Ascalon* briskly skimmed the water, bow up, proud.

The men showed the effects of the night. They worked, trance-like, eyes focused on the task in front of them, whether it be the ropes in their hands, the buckets or the stones they used to scrub the slippery mould from the deck. She looked to the stern and saw Gidley at the wheel. His eyes had the red-rimmed look of too much wind and too little sleep.

'We near lost 'em both.' Gidley's head trembled in a negative shake and he turned his face to the sea.

'Who?' Melina asked, stopping a few inches from his side.

'Capt'n and Stubby.' He turned back, searching her face. 'Warrin'ton didn't tell yer? Guess a man's thinking of other things when he's close to a woman.' His voice faded. 'Stubby wouldn't ever grow old enough to make a single whisker if not for Capt'n.'

Melina waited, feeling a coldness splash into her. 'Both are well?'

Gidley shrugged. 'Stub's shook or he'd a been dancing 'round my feet this mornin'. Capt'n Ben—' He paused.

'Take more'n a bump to do him in. Prob'ly be walkin' again before we get to shore. One leg's lamed up and he's prob'ly listenin' to a few ribs shouting at him. Though none stick out. Always a good thing when the bones stay skinned over.' Gidley squinted at Melina. 'Yer ever took care of a sick body?'

'My mother.' She hated to say the words. Her mother had died slowly, death taking her by squeezing health away a heartbeat at a time and replacing everything inside her with pain.

'Well…' He took his time saying the word. 'Capt'n is sayin' for you to care for him. I've some laudanum in him and when he wakes he'll not be fine, but I'm needin' to keep my eye on the sails.' Gidley tilted his head, indicating the cabin closest to the helm. 'Go see to him.'

She gripped her skirt, raising it just enough so she could walk quickly, and moved to the captain's quarters. Melina rapped on the door and when no one answered, she peered in. He was asleep.

Melina took stock of her surroundings. The cabin, spacious by comparison to Warrington's, gleamed with polished wood and accentuated the paleness of the captain's face.

He slept because of the tonic and she knew not to give him any more until he complained of pain. She touched his forehead and didn't feel burning. His eyelashes fluttered. Compassion stirred in her. He'd survived the night, but death from an injury could wait days. And she owed him. Without the captain agreeing to let her sail, Stephanos would still be a threat.

She moved back the covers to look at the bruising on his chest, then sat in the only chair and settled herself for whatever care he'd need.

Hours later, when the door opened, she jumped awake and Warrington strode in—his eyes appraising everything.

The light emboldened his ragged features. Whiskers darkened his chin and blended with the shadows under his eyes. His hair—neatly combed—contrasted with the rest of him.

'How is he?' Warrington moved to the bedside, staring at his brother.

'He rests *eirinikos,* well enough, but I believe it is because of the draught he was given. He did wake long enough for a thimbleful of water. But he has the right speech and doesn't appear worse than he was earlier. His side is bruised. Leg is straight, scraped some, and his knee is swollen nearly as big as his head.'

Warrington studied her for a moment longer than necessary, then he turned to his brother. He stepped to the edge of the berth and put a hand lightly on the captain's shoulder.

Ben's eyes flickered, but remained closed. 'The boy still alive?'

Warrington's head jerked up in answer. 'Stubby is doing better than you. You look like a man who danced with the wrong fellow's wife.' Warrington's voice remained gruff.

Ben opened one eye. 'You, on the other hand, look like hell.'

Warrington's smile changed his face, bringing a life to his eyes she'd never believed possible.

'You infant,' Warrington continued, his words light. 'You'll try anything to convince me to sail the next voyage with you—but it won't work.'

Ben kept his eyes closed and talked, barely moving his lips. 'I guess expecting a soft old earl to be able to sail is daft.'

'I'd better get to the helm.' Warrington took his hand from Ben's shoulder, still smiling. 'Since Captain Lackbeard looks to lie about all day.'

'Remember,' Ben said, 'keep the masts to the sky. The hull side to the water.'

'I'll do what I can.'

'So will I.' Ben's brows rose. 'I will rest here and look at Melina all day to ease my suffering.' His head didn't turn, but he glanced sideways. 'Would you give me a drop of brandy, sweetness?'

She rose, which caused her to brush Warrington. He gave a haughty smile to his brother. Then Warrington reached around Melina. His hand was firm at her side and the quick motion surprised her. She stumbled against him.

His lips closed over hers before she expected it. Her heart pounded warm blasts throughout her body. The taste of him was not something she could name, but the flavour of strength and warm male.

He pulled back and kept his hand at her waist while he spoke to his brother. His voice had challenge in it. 'Take care, little brother. Don't test me on this. Or you will get *truly* hurt.'

For days, Melina knew she had less sleep than the seamen while she cared for the captain. She'd not known a person could complain so. He had her searching his cabin for a silver toothpick once, as if his very life depended on it, and then he remembered he'd lost the shining bit on a different voyage.

The captain would send her in search of a sailor he wanted to speak to and she'd find the man at the very spot Captain Ben mentioned, doing exactly what he had expected. Even Warrington did as commanded.

Gidley would sometimes stop to check on Captain Ben, and invariably, the captain would send her on a task. He'd need a biscuit, or for her to take a question to a crew member—she suspected the duties unnecessary ones so he could talk privately with the first mate.

The captain was keeping Warrington from the cabin when she was in it, or else Warrington had no wish to be inside if she was there. She was too tired to sort her thoughts.

They only passed each other briefly, an impossible occurrence—unless planned. From the humour in Ben's face, and the glare in Warrington's, she didn't think it the earl's suggestion.

She'd seen Warrington on the ropes once or twice, with his lean legs scurrying up the rigging. She'd been wrong about him—he could climb the ratlines as well as the others. Perhaps better as he'd kept himself balanced using his legs while he worked.

Almost as soon as Melina reached her cabin and fell upon the pallet, she heard a tap on her door and forced herself upright. A voice through the wood told her the captain requested her.

She stood, pushing at the knot of her hair, pulling at her skirt to straighten it, and left the room. The cabin boy waited. If she'd dallied longer, he would have knocked more insistently. 'I think I have stolen your job,' she told him when she walked through the doorway.

His bruised face burst into a smile. 'I be fine with it. Won't be long till I be an able-bodied seaman. Gid says I have some growin' left, but I'll get that done quick enough and be taller 'n him.'

She found a shirtless Ben sitting in his bed, a map sprawled around him. He looked up at her when she entered.

He hadn't worn a shirt since he'd been injured and his side had darkened more, leaving a yellowish cast around the bruising. She heard the ship's bell. Warrington would be leaving his post. The captain grinned. He rolled up the papers, his hands moving slowly and with excessive care. Finally he tipped the cylinder in her direction. She put it in the cabinet. 'I'll try sitting in the chair for a while. Lend a hand,' he said. He put his palm to the bruise.

'It would be better if Warrington or the men helped you. Your weight is too heavy for me,' she answered.

'They move me about like a potato sack.' He stretched out his naked arm, rubbing the muscle. 'I'm sure you'll do just fine.'

She scooted the chair several inches closer, leaving enough room for him to stand beside the bed before sitting.

She let the captain's weight shift on to her, and helped him to the chair. Just as he was pulling his arm from around her neck, Warrington walked in. She supposed an earl never knocked when entering his brother's quarters—at least one didn't.

The captain slid his arm back to Melina's shoulders and took a bit more time righting himself.

Warrington's hair gleamed with the mist of seawater still on it. His coat hung open, but his shirt looked crisp underneath.

The three of them were nestled in the cabin so tight they could reach out an arm and touch the others.

'I believe I've wrenched my shoulder,' Warrington said. 'I need Melina's care.'

The captain kept his injured leg motionless in front of him. His mouth opened, but he didn't speak. He shook his head at Warrington in an arrogant wobble. She moved to leave and Warrington turned to follow her.

'Stay a moment, War, I need to talk to you,' Ben said.

'I've better things to do than listen to a man who lies about drinking brandy all day.' His eyes were chips of coal. 'Much better things.' He looked at Melina.

'I know. But it won't kill you to spare a few minutes with your brother.'

'Might not be so good for you, however.'

Warrington opened the door, standing aside. Melina moved to step out, but when she passed Warrington, his hand caught her waist and he stopped her movement.

When she looked into his eyes, nothing light looked back at her. But he brushed at a lock of her hair, leaving a trail of warmth she could feel to her toes. 'If my brother is tiring you too much, Melina, you don't have to assist him. Stubby can.'

She saw the intensity in his eyes, and more behind it, and gave the barest of nods. 'I'm well with it.'

He snorted in response, but handed her gently out through the door. 'Rest, sweet.' His voice caressed. 'I don't want you overtired.'

As the door closed, she heard the captain's muttered comment to his brother. 'Arse Hat.' She didn't understand Warrington's reply exactly. She didn't think she'd ever heard the word before.

Inside the captain's quarters Warrington glared impatiently at his brother. 'I'm not letting you keep her from me any longer. I only have scant time left with her.'

'I would never get between a man and his sweetheart.' Ben's eyes half closed. 'I am merely a weak younger brother, not as strong as you, and I need help getting back on my feet.'

'Having a bed that smells of a woman's warmth, and no woman in it, is not doing me any good.'

'You'll survive.' Ben stretched, gingerly, keeping his movements slow. 'But I know where I saw her. I remembered.' Then he let the room fall into silence.

Warrington remained on his feet. 'Tell me or not, I'm leaving.' He wasn't letting Ben trap him into a long discussion. He had better ways to spend his time. One way in particular.

'Somerset House. A painting.' Ben touched his chest. 'The spot. I remember the spot on the girl. The painting captured the mark. Odd to leave a blemish and I noticed it more than her face. At the time I decided the artist added it to make his painting different.'

Warrington waved away the words. 'Any artist would want to capture her.'

'War.' Ben shook his head. 'She has ties to England. Ties we don't know about. She speaks too well. And she has some piece of marble you say she believes she has to get to London.' He waved a hand. 'Probably has a man she's going to. Using the stone as an excuse.'

'If she has a man in England, all the better.' Warrington spoke with authority. He only needed Melina long enough to get the past behind him. To get over his foolishness of letting his lust control his mind. No, that wasn't what he needed to stop. He needed to stop letting his foolish heart control his actions. Lust was much safer than love.

When he returned to Whitegate, he'd have no time for a woman while he took back his duties. He wanted to teach Jacob about the country estate. And Warrington would be travelling back and forth to London after taking his seat in Parliament.

Someone knocked. A double thump, pause and double thump on the door let Warrington know Stubby stood outside. He opened the door without taking his eyes off Ben while Stubby bounded in.

'Melina will be on her own soon after we dock. She thinks the cracked rock is a treasure of some sort and will earn funds,' Warrington said. 'She's wrapped the thing in cloth and it stays under the berth. She put my second pair of trousers around it and has the stone secured tight. Has a bit of rope tying the parcel snug to the edge.'

Ben shook his head. 'You've seen it. Does it look like it could sell?'

Warrington didn't take his hand from the door. 'No. It's cracked badly. I've no idea why she decided it valuable.' He held his arm out, moving his fingers into a grasping position. 'It's an arm shaped like this. One of the fingers is broken off, as well. Just an arm. Should be tossed in a dust bin. Like your collections you've stored around the town house.'

'Then she must have a man in London who wants the stone. A sweetheart she hopes to see again.' He grinned at Stubby. 'But she does keep good company. Believed me when I had her searching for a toothpick.'

The boy, only a hint of bruising left on his face, glared at Ben.

Ben winked at Stubby. 'Every cabin boy has to search for a silver toothpick. Proves their mettle by how long and deep they dig before giving up.'

Warrington looked at Stub's mutinous jaw. 'He *did* save your skin and I *did* tell you not to come on deck.'

The little face didn't soften. 'Well, my looks is ruined for ever. Now I don't know how I'll get me a woman when we get to London.'

'Stubby.' The shocked word shot from both Warrington and Ben at the same time.

'The men say they can't wait to get home and get a woman,' Stubby said. 'They be wantin' her apple dumplin' or a tart. I like confectioneries and if I have to smile pretty at a lady to get me some sweets…' he showed a toothy smile and touched his stomach '…then I be plannin' to have a belly full of smiles.'

War looked at Ben. 'You need to have a talk with him. If you can figure it out yourself.'

'I'll tell Gid to explain—' He stopped. 'No. Cook would be better.' Ben sat, rubbing his knee, and grimaced in pain. 'Not so sure our lovely Melina doesn't have some bad luck with her. A lifetime of sailing and I've never been hurt this bad.' He probed against the trouser leg. 'I suppose I should have expected it. We do have a woman on board. Never know whether they'll be bad or good fortune until afterwards.'

'You've spent too long bobbing about. You're starting

to sound like Gidley.' Warrington kept his fingers on the open door, ready to go to his cabin. Stubby stood listening, nodding as if he'd sailed a score of years and seen everything to see.

Ben's voice lowered, and he fell back on the bed. 'I shouldn't have sent you in my place to meet Melina. I would have just...' he raised a brow at Warrington '...put a smile on her face and we would have sailed smoothly home.'

'You may be right. You see me unhurt. I put a smile on her face.'

Ben interlaced his fingers on his chest and turned his head towards Stubby. 'Go get Gid. Tell him I need him. The earl's imaginations are giving me pains.'

When the door closed behind the lad, Ben's eyes darted to Warrington's face. 'I don't trust her. You won't keep her near once you get to land?'

Warrington didn't immediately speak and he frowned. 'When it is your concern, I'll tell you. But, no. She'll be on her way soon after we dock. I'll remain in London a few extra days because I have to meet with the Foreign Office. Then I'll see Jacob and deal with...Whitegate. I can't leave it all in Dane's hands for ever. He'll be wanting to get back to his confectioneries.'

Ben turned his head to the wall, but his words carried directly to Warrington. 'Don't make the same mistake twice.'

War stepped out of the door. *The same mistake twice.*

When the sea air hit his face, he slowed, thinking. Dane had been wobbly-legged foxed one night after Cass died and damn near cried when he told Warrington how they'd hated Cass. They'd seen the truth before he had. With Melina, he didn't need to be warned. Just like Cass, she made her plans and only said enough to further them. A woman in a household wasn't necessary or needed. He'd had enough of broken crockery, tears and lies to last a lifetime. The whirling dream of love he'd had had turned into a whirling nightmare of the wrong kind of passion.

Instead of going directly to his cabin—or whatever part of it he might share—Warrington paced the deck, trying not to long for Melina's touch. Every time his heart beat, desire pumped through his veins. He shook his head gently, trying to force her from his mind, but he couldn't. And his feet didn't co-operate and wouldn't take him a second turn around the ship, or let him stay out in the air. He had to get back to her.

When he walked into the room, he looked to the floor. Melina lay fully dressed on the pallet. Her hair still remained in a twist and she had the shawl pulled over her for a cover. Her half-parted lips and regular breathing reassured him. She hardly looked old enough to be the woman she was.

He knelt, his fingers barely grazing the skin of her cheek. 'Wake.'

She half opened her eyes. 'My legs are near run off. The captain keeps me at his side while he sleeps, and when he stops dozing, he sends me to sleep. When I begin to dream, he calls for me again. He's unkind.'

Warrington shook his head. 'No. He's not. Gid's keeping Ben's mind in a fog so the pain will not get to him. The medicine has addled him a bit, and the injury, and he's used to a life with men around him.'

'And bad women.'

'He's not called Saint Benjamin, but Captain Benjamin.' Warrington braced himself again against the empty bunk, still devoid of any mattress. 'He's keeping you from me.'

Warrington rocked back with the movement of the ship, and sat, tugging his boots from his feet, taking stockings with the footwear. He slipped his scuffed boots under the bottom railing. He wished for a bed. A real bed. With bed coverings and pillows that didn't smell as if a horse had used them first.

'I know.' Melina shut her eyes as she spoke. 'Neither of you wish me to sleep.'

Warrington knelt, taking her face in his hands, and her eyes quickly opened. 'I hope for you to savour being awake with me.' He saw the tightness of her lips. 'This time will be better. I'll show you what it can truly be like between a man and a woman who—'

He stopped. How would he know what it was like to be with someone who loved him? After Jacob was born, Cass had once taunted him by calling him by someone else's name when he bedded her.

But he hadn't given up on Cassandra—at least not then. She glowed at soirées, entertained society with the charm of royalty. Everyone wanted to be within the beam of Cassandra's smile. When she desired, she would sit and converse with him in such a way he could feel the love in his heart and believe so easily she loved him.

Then one day, during the flash of her smile, he caught the smugness behind in her face and he knew that the sweeter she talked, the deeper her machinations were. And he looked pleasantly back at her and continued laughing with her while his world crashed.

She was Jacob's mother. The woman he truly loved. And she was flawed. No matter that she had no true love in her, she went through the motions on occasion. She did want the appearance of perfection. And without a doubt, she wanted to be a countess and enjoy the luxuries he could provide. He'd purchased a wife, just as he'd acquired the carriage she rode in. Only he'd not realised it at first.

He looked at Melina. 'It's all for pleasure.' He took her hand, but the memory of holding Cass's fingers when he asked her to marry him flashed in his mind and his vision blackened. He couldn't keep thinking of Cass.

He pulled his hand back and undid his shirt and slipped it over his head. Then he gazed at Melina. She looked so different than Cassandra. The darkness fled his thoughts and he cradled Melina in his arms. He could not sense artifice in her. She didn't use her body to turn his desire against him and to her own advantage. She felt pure.

'Melina.' He bent, pulling her so her head tilted back and he could let his lips and face take in the soft skin of her neck and nuzzle the warmth of her. He kissed her pulse. 'You remind me that there's a harbour, dry land and real floors. And I want to see you lying in the middle of my bed, waiting for me.'

'You should not think of such things. I have to be on my way once we reach land,' she said. 'I will see to the stone's sale and return to my sisters.'

He reminded himself to take care. In all of his life he'd never bought a woman's body, until Melina. And she'd not been willing to settle for one of the men from the island. *Captain,* she'd said. *You're not the captain?* Now she knew he was an earl. As always, he was the highest bidder. Only because of the small size of the island had she kept her innocence. If she'd lived in London, she would have realised the real treasure she had was in her face and her body.

'It won't be easy to remove a stone from the island if this man you dislike controls the land,' he said. 'He will be angry at you because you left.'

'Stephanos does not own the land of the stone. Yorgos does. Yorgos said the stone was only rocks to him and that I have sand in my head if I think it is worth coin. He will help me slip it by Stephanos, or convince Stephanos to let it go. I am near the same age as his children and he calls me *kori,* daughter. The museum will have to pay the Turks because they will hear of her leaving and have to be given money. It is better to be done while she is still seen as rocks.'

Currents of relief slid into his body. If she meant to

leave him, she could not be planning to ensnare him. But, he couldn't forget himself. He didn't need a child on some island, not knowing whether the babe was being fed or the funds he sent given for some man's ale.

Yet he could not look at Melina without wanting to push her back on to the bedding, and if he thought of her longer than it took to say her name, his body readied itself to join her.

He frowned, rocking back on his heels and leaning against the wall of the cabin, pulling her close. He could control himself for a few moments if it meant the peace of having her in his arms.

He traced the outline of her jaw and then moved to grasp her shoulder, dismayed by the coarseness of her clothes. A body such as hers should only have silks against the skin. Or his touch.

He rested his chin on her head and took her hair down. Having no place to put the hairpins, he saw his coat hanging on a peg and dropped them in the pocket. He finger-combed her hair around her shoulders, pleased deep within himself at the dark hue. 'Not much time left before we reach London. We must make the most of it.'

'I cannot even imagine the towns.' Her eyes were wistful.

'Where did you learn to speak English so plainly?'

'At Melos. I understand French, too. I speak it some.'

'Who taught you?' He didn't really care. All he cared about was the perfect shape of her breasts and to let his lips trail to the mark. But then he remembered Ben's mention of the painting. 'You could have chosen a French ship to take you to France. What ties do you have to England?' Warrington watched her face.

She gave a shrug. 'I see the French seamen often and they talk badly of the English, but I have also heard pleasant tales of London and the English life. And it is the biggest city I know of and the best museum. They will have a larger purse.'

Because of the French vessels harbouring at Melos, he would have expected her to approach one of those ships, but they would have less freedom to take a passenger.

'Your ties to England?' he asked again, just as he repeated pressing his lips to her neck. He shut his eyes, tasting her skin, letting the sweetness of her flow into his body and melt the tightness of his shoulders, and ease his memories.

She pushed him back. 'I do not ask you of your life'.

'How did you learn the language so well?' he asked, stilling.

'We are a natural harbour with many travellers on the island. I speak to them.'

'Melina—I don't believe you are telling me all.'

Brown eyes met his. 'No. I am not. And I won't.'

A knock interrupted her and a voice commanded. 'Captain needs the woman.'

'She's busy,' Warrington shouted through the door. His hand clasped her wrist and he saw reluctance in her face.

'Go ahead. But if you do, I expect a few nights once we hit land to make up for the ones you don't give me on ship.' He let his hand slide to hold hers and knew he made a mistake. 'Melina… Soft beds. Clean clothing. Food made by someone who knows what it is supposed to taste like. Water—real water—fresh, not stale or salty, to bathe in. Compared to this, we'll be royalty.'

He saw her chest rise in a deep breath. 'Very well,' she murmured, her hand at the door. 'With the ship rocking, and the food, my stomach feels one step from death. Hearing the men shout outside the walls and the captain calling me, I feel surrounded by watching eyes. On land, surely the world will not rock so and will have some quiet about it.' She sighed. 'I would like to be free from all the men shouting and scratching. It feels as if we all smashed inside a large bottle and someone has put the cork on it, and shakes us about.'

'We will get out of this bottle, and we'll have a bed of clouds.' He stood with her. 'And now I will go to the captain's cabin with you. I can trust Ben with my life, but I don't want him too near you.'

She touched the mark at her breast. 'He thinks it looks like a fish.'

Warrington snorted. 'He lies.'

He put a hand to her back and guided her to the other cabin, aware of how much the men watched her. He didn't blame them. If they looked the other direction, all they could see would be an expanse of nothing. And to look at any part of Melina was a treat.

When Melina reached to knock on the captain's door, Warrington leaned in, touched the knob and pushed the door open for her.

Inside the cabin, the air was bitter from some stringent herbal. Ben sat on the bed, head back against the wall, eyes closed, chest still bare. His bruising had faded. He half opened his eyes, then frowned when he saw Warrington. In one hand, he held a poultice pressed to his ribs, and in the other, a brandy bottle Gidley must have collected for him.

'Melina will care for me.' Ben spoke with command. 'I like the touch of a lovely woman—even if she is not a mermaid.'

'You tell Gid to quit giving you so much of the poison,' Warrington said.

'I missed you also, old man.' Ben laughed, then winced and moved his shoulders. 'If I wish to see you, all I have to do is call the goddess.'

'Her *name* is Melina.'

'A beautiful name for a goddess. Did she not rise from the sea inside the shell of a giant oyster?'

Warrington walked closer and looked at his brother's

eyes. 'Melina.' His voice was low. 'Let me know each time Gid gets near him with a medicinal and how much is taken. And the brandy.' He glared at Ben, challenging. 'I am telling Gid to ease up on the laudanum. If the sea couldn't have you, then I'm not letting you slink into some addled state. You're daft enough without help.'

Warrington looked at his brother and opened the small cupboard, pulling out another brandy bottle. Then he reached and jerked the one from his brother's hand. 'I'm finding Gid now and giving him strict instructions on Ben's care. And if the captain annoys you, Melina, let me know and I will twist his good leg to match the other.' Bottles in hand, he marched from the room. He slammed the door so hard she wondered the boat didn't roll to its side.

The captain opened his eyes and had no smile behind them.

'I've told Warrington, Melina.' The captain's vision didn't rest on any one thing in the room. 'I've warned him. If he wishes for happiness, he must throw you back to the sea. An appealing woman is no better than a serpent, wishing to put her fangs in you and suck the life from your body. That is why I like mermaids. They are not true women.'

Captain Ben gave her a smile. 'Warrington is right. Probably should keep the medicinals from me. I'm beginning to see fins on you.' He frowned. 'It is the laudanum making me dream of women. The evil ones.' He shook his head, shuddering.

'One,' he continued, 'looked like Cassandra and she had a grappling hook in War's throat.' He nodded. 'I keep thinking of the beautiful Cassandra, and then—then I wonder what memories my brother has of her. No woman I've seen deserved her fate more. War finally had to keep a *companion* for her. A big beast of a woman, who stayed near, and would let him know if his wife strayed, or acted out of hand. A gaoler, at Cass's side every minute, and she deserved it.

Early on, at War's house, I woke up with Cass in my room, on my bed and her hand stroking my cheek. Not a pleasant moment—waking up with a demon in front of you.'

He looked at Melina. 'It is not that I don't find you pleasant, Melina. I do. But you sold your body so easily. Cassandra held out for a higher price—and she received it. I'm sure she's making deals with the devil now.' He laughed.

Melina kept her voice sweet. 'Did she ever wish to put a pillow over your face?'

'I would imagine.' He spoke the words lightly. 'When I told her War would believe me over her and to never come near me again.' He looked around the room. 'I wish War would not have left with the brandy. It's not as if he's still married and needs it.' He raked his eyes over Melina. 'Cassandra wouldn't like knowing you're in War's bed.' He grinned, and then took a breath. 'Thank you for that. I never expected I'd pity Lucifer, but if he is with Cassandra, he should be wary.' His eyes were unfocused and he nodded, the slow movements of a man unaware of his surroundings. 'She might take over Hades.'

Chapter Nine

When Melina returned to Warrington's cabin, she shut the door behind her in a rush. She had to be thankful Warrington had met her first instead of the easygoing captain—who was not so pleasant when foxed. Cassandra had been called whore in Greek, French, English and some languages Melina didn't know.

She saw the empty berth, and underneath, empty. Her pulse stuttered and she fell to her knees beside the bed. She stared at the space. Her body couldn't move, locked in place. The stone was gone.

Warrington. He could not do this to her. The thudding of her heartbeats brought her movements alive again. Warrington could not hide the rock from her. True, she had not kept her bargain well, but the marble was hers. She must have it.

She knelt lower, looking all the way under the berth. She stood, tore at the bedcovers and then opened each cabinet. Nothing. Turning, she ran from the room and rushed to the helm. Warrington stood by Gidley, who steered the ship.

'My treasure,' she gasped.

She ignored the startled look in Warrington's face and grabbed his arm. 'My treasure. Where have you put it?' Her hair blew across her lips, but she didn't brush it aside.

'Tell me. Now.' The words came out too slow. She wanted to speak faster. She wanted to have the answer now and he only looked at her, his mouth half-opened and silent.

'Tell me,' she insisted, her grip tightening on his arm.

'Melina. What are you speaking of?' He took her hands from his arms, stepping back, and pulling her so they faced each other. 'I've not touched the blasted thing. It's a rock.'

'It's gone.'

'It's under the berth—resting better than either of us.'

'No.' She moved backwards. 'It's not. It's not in the room.'

'I'm sure it is.' He nodded to Gidley. 'I'll be back as soon as we get this sorted.'

She rushed ahead, not waiting to see if he followed. Maybe she *had* imagined the loss. Maybe she had become addled from listening to the captain and perhaps the arm still lay wrapped safely.

But when she ran inside the room, leaving the door open behind her—she hadn't dreamed anything. Her treasure was gone.

Warrington trudged in behind her. She stood silent as he touched the bunk, then repeated her earlier movements, looking through the small space.

After he finished searching, he grasped her shoulder. 'You are sure you didn't move it?'

She grabbed on to his waistcoat with both hands. 'My treasure…'

His mouth pinched. 'It's a rock, Melina. Rock. Not treasure.'

She put both palms flat on his chest. 'It's a treasure. The French museum curator visited Melos two years ago. He told everyone on the island we might have artefacts buried in the ground. Most of the others ignored him. But I remembered the rocks and seeing the white shards mixed with the dirt, left from a structure long before my grandmother's time. Every time I could, I went to dig. And then I found the arm, and more. I knew I had discovered what the Frenchman wanted for his collection. Now someone has taken the arm.'

'Melina. No one on this ship believes the marble is anything but a carved stone. And we've all seen carved stones before. And it's broken. Cracked and chipped both. Any sailor here would prefer a drop of ale to your treasure.'

'Open your eyes.' She clenched her fists and wanted to thump at his chest. She would have if it would have done any good.

He touched her chin. 'Don't get overly worked up. How is a man going to take the arm from the ship? It's too big to hide in his shirt or his trousers—and he knows we can search everything he has before he leaves.'

'You truly believe the marble is worthless?'

He nodded. 'Why would you think it valuable?'

'I know more of art than you'd expect.' She spoke the words softly. 'My father told me of art constantly. He spoke of nothing else. He's not dead—at least I don't think he is.' Pulling back, she watched his eyes. 'He's a painter. Robert Cherroll. Have you heard of him?'

Warrington shook his head. 'I haven't. But Ben has. At least, he mentioned seeing a painting of you. In London. It showed the birthmark.'

She nodded. 'I had to sit, for hours and hours, and couldn't move while he painted. At first, my sister Thessa stood behind him and made faces, but then she grew tired of it and left. I ached from not moving, but I did it. I wanted to see my face on the canvas. My mother wanted to keep it, but he refused. He said some day he'd paint another one, but I knew he wouldn't. He took it, along with all the artwork he completed on the island. Taking them to England, always, to sell. He had to have funds to support us, he said. The work had to be sold, he would tell us, and leave.'

She backed away but held her shoulders firm. 'My father once told me of the British Museum.'

She tilted her head. 'If the stone is seen as a treasure, then both the English and French may want it. Think of it—how much more valuable something is the more it is wanted. I already know the Frenchman will make an offer if he can see part of it. I think the English will, too.'

'I'll get it back for you,' he promised. 'I'll spread the word through Gidley and the rest. Your rock is gone. We're hours from sighting land—but the ship will not dock until the stone is found. You'll have all the men hunting and one person who will be discovered. But, Melina, it's only a broken arm.'

She reached a hand out, steadying herself against the wall. 'But I have the rest of her hidden. I found her under the earth and then I covered her back up. I had lived always with shards of rock around me. The Frenchman made me want to look closer. I found the statue, which has a look of my mother's face, and behind the eyes I see the thoughts she is trying to tell me. She is *polytimos,* priceless. When I return for it… If I could get her before Stephanos realised I didn't intend to stay… And I could take my sisters…' She shook her head. 'But now it's stolen.'

'The men on *Ascalon* are good men. Not perfect, but they are loyal. Most have sailed with my brother for years. *Ascalon* was in those waters to meet with leaders and discuss the possibility of an uprising against the Turks. So, though these men are rough, they've been entrusted to an important voyage. They wouldn't steal a rock that means nothing to them.'

She took the lantern from its hook. 'I'll search everywhere myself. I have to find it. I have no choice.'

Warrington followed her while she hunted, moving to each corner of the ship and looking in any space large enough to conceal even half the stone.

She examined the hold where the food stores were kept. Barrels pressed against her back.

'Melina,' Warrington said, 'you'll set the ship afire again if you aren't more careful with the lantern. You must stop rummaging about.'

'I'll find it. It must be reunited with the statue.'

'Think, Melina. The stone did not walk out alone. You've been throughout the whole ship. Nothing was kept from you. The only place you've not examined is Ben's quarters.'

'I was there when it disappeared, and besides, he can't walk. He couldn't have taken it.' She put her hand to her head, pushing at a dampened tendril. 'But that is where it must be. It must have been stored there when I left to look for the piece.'

Warrington took the lantern she held. 'Not unless Ben was asleep. He would never let someone do that to you, Melina. He might send you about for an imagined stick, but he wouldn't take your property.' He guided her along the narrow opening and towards the stairway, to the light and fresher air. She took in a deep breath when she stepped on deck.

The men worked the sails, tugging ropes to tighten them. No one looked her way. No one paused. But their backs turned just a hair more from her. Their faces tensed. They knew quite well where she stood. The ship had little privacy, yet her stone had disappeared.

Warrington moved her into the cabin, hanging the lantern back in place and snuffing it. 'Forget about the rock and think about how you will proceed without it.'

She stood on the sleeping pallet. Sliding the covers aside with her heels, she put her shoulder to the wall so she'd not stumble with the ship's movements. Something had addled her. Because she wanted him to hold her like a child and tell her everything would be well. And he was speaking the words, but they would have meant so much more if he held her close.

'I have no place to go forward without the stone,' she said. 'Only backwards.' She touched over her heart. 'I feel something for the stone woman. She is still hidden, buried. But I saw her eyes and knew she wanted to be in a place of honour again. And without the arm... I do not know. She was going to save us...'

'I'll discover what happened to your treasure, Melina.' He brushed his knuckles against her cheek, leaving streaks of fire where his fingers trailed, and then he did take her into his arms. 'Someone on this ship knows and I'll get the men together and scare it out of them if I have to.' His steps thumped as he left.

She touched her cheek. He would find it, for her. She knew.

When Gidley stood at the cabin door, summoning her, he looked at the wall over her shoulders. 'Warrin'ton be wantin' to speak with yer.'

Her stomach churned, even though the ship sailed smooth. 'My stone?' she asked, searching his face.

'He's thinkin' he's found out who took it.' He raised a hand to silence her. 'But he be wantin' to tell yer hisself.'

Gidley turned and walked away, head down. Executioners had more joy in their steps. She followed, a feeling of death grating in the hollows of her heart.

On deck, Warrington stood by Stubby, who'd perched himself at the edge of the ship, his hands sliding along the polished railing and his eyes inspecting the dark flecks inside the wood. He appeared entranced in some imaginary task. Warrington stared at the boy.

'Where is it?' she asked, standing an arm's length from Warrington.

He turned his head to the cabin boy. 'Come here.'

Stubby moved, taking two dragging steps to stop in front of Melina. He took a deep breath, but didn't raise his eyes from staring at the deck. 'I heard it were a treasure, so I went to see it. Like pirate's gold and silver. But it were evil. I saw it and I knew. Just like the wave.' He lifted his right hand, making a claw of his fingers, and his mouth moved into a snarl as if he had fangs about to pounce.

'Evil?' Melina asked. 'The arm?'

'Yes.' He lowered his hand and raised his eyes. 'White like a drowned body. The spirit who lost its arm is sendin' storms and waves to pull us to the deep and drown us dead so it can have its hand back. Nearly took me and Capt'n Ben.' His gaze, along with his upturned eyes and quaking chest, reminded her of the way her youngest sister had looked when their mother died. 'You wouldn't want us drowned, or sunk. I know you wouldn't want to see me all guts loose and swolled up in my face…' He puffed his cheeks and held out his arms to show how he would look. 'I had to throw the rock back to the spirits.'

Melina turned and rushed to the cabin. She imagined the arm sinking, landing with a silent thud into the mud. The filth from below sweeping around it, locking it into a silted grave. Gone for ever. A new death. And it didn't matter if the arm was exactly as it had been—a world of water prevented her from ever seeing it again. It existed, but was as lost as if it had been crushed into sand.

The arm could never be reunited with the marble woman who stood larger than a true female, with a covering draped low on her hips. The English museum would not want a statue of an armless goddess, even this majestic one.

She still wanted the statue and she'd return to it, if only to see her mother's face. But her hopes of wresting it from the island were now at the bottom of the sea.

She could have stayed with Stephanos—given him marriage in exchange for the carving. But her mother would not have wanted that. She wouldn't have wanted Melina to have been trapped by the rock.

Now Melina wished she could run her fingers over the statue's countenance again. To feel her mother's presence and the life behind the stone eyes.

The statue appeared so serene. Her hair pulled up into a bun. One shoulder raised slightly more than the other. Breasts free. The covering around her hips sliding low, about to fall. Unconcerned she no longer had arms to hold the draped cloth for modesty.

Melina concentrated on the statue's face, trying to ease her own trembling limbs.

Freedom from Stephanos might have been more costly than she expected. At least the women on Melos who sold their bodies were able to return to normal when the ships left. Her life couldn't return to the way it was. If she returned home now, penniless, her value would be nothing. A failure, and not just for herself. For her mother. And her sisters.

Melina had sold her body—something she swore she'd never do. She'd left her sisters, after promising her dying mother she'd care for them. And the dowry she'd hoped to gain for them was gone because now she'd have no proof of finding anything but dirt. The statue might as well be resting in the muck.

She didn't have enough time to try again, even if she

could lift the entire statue. Her sisters were too beautiful to be ignored.

She struggled to breathe, feeling the same silt and water choke her that now clasped the marble.

Warrington leaned against the door in Ben's cabin and his brother sat in the berth. In hours they'd be docked. From a quick perusal of his brother, Warrington saw clear eyes. Now Ben yelped when he moved. A good sign.

But Warrington was more concerned about Melina than he was of Ben. Melina had not been the same since the arm was lost.

'The quartermaster will bring the physician…' Ben said. 'Besides, I'm on the mend. Gid will see to the rest. Go meet with the Foreign Office. They'll need to know of your negotiations. And don't worry about me. Gidley knows how to take over my duties and he'll watch me as close as he would his own son.'

Ben's words brought Jacob into Warrington's mind. He'd still not be seeing him for a few days. He didn't relish the chore that would meet him when he arrived home. The voyage hadn't vanquished Cassandra from his memory. It had only raised more questions in his mind.

And he would help Melina find her father. But her body could put his obsession of Cassandra to rest. He'd made sure never to be in Ben's cabin again while Melina was there. Ben would have been able to take one look at his older brother's face and know lust crashed into Warrington every time he looked at Melina. But he would control it.

Melina might not care a halfpenny for him, but the darkness of her eyes and her hair called to him. And her body.

He'd watched her when he was on the rigging and his imagination had replaced the feel of the ropes in his hands with the strands of her hair across his fingertips. Immediately he'd thrust the thoughts aside—knowing that to let her invade his mind while he was perched in the air could be fatal.

She'd only walked on deck a few times. If she'd slipped or leaned against the mast, every seaman on deck would have been able to describe exactly where she stood when it happened. And unlike Cassandra, he didn't think Melina would have been able to describe each watching male and where he was standing while he viewed her.

Cassandra had been gently bred a lady and had the heart of a dockside whore. Melina, the dockside whore he'd purchased, hadn't yet learned the things she could buy with her body.

And he wanted to be with her. Over and over and over again—with only his body involved. No wondering who she talked about when she whispered with her maid and planned for her day of social calls—with detours.

'Andrew.' Ben spoke the word quietly.

Instantly, Warrington's thoughts returned to the room. Ben had called War by his Christian name. His brother watched him, lips pressed together, but the smile on his face had a rueful curve.

'You know—' Ben gave a soft shake of his head. 'The woman…'

'Yes, I do.' Warrington nodded. 'And she'll help me forget.'

'I agree. But when you clean out one trunk, don't fill it back up. Leave it neat and tidy.'

Warrington forced himself quiet while he heard the unasked-for advice.

'I don't—' Ben spoke softly.

Irritation jabbed Warrington, but he also understood his brother's concern. 'Ben. I know. I remember. Never. Again.

In fact, I want you to plan a return trip to Melos for Melina. She and I have discussed it. She agrees.'

His brother's eyes widened. 'I can. Not immediately, but soon. The repairs we made earlier were only temporary. I have to get *Ascalon* ready to sail for the East India Company.'

Warrington knew his brother had contracted to carry goods for the company and he would be gone at least two years, perhaps as long as three. 'You've enough time. I already asked Gid how long the repairs would take and that gives you time to get to Melos and back again. Melina can return to her sisters.'

'The way you look at her…' Resignation showed in Ben's face. 'I will find the time to return her. Ships are a good thing, War. You get on one. You sail. A new horizon. A new woman.' Ben smiled and flexed his leg. 'Maybe some day you'll be tough enough to handle a true voyage.'

'Once my boots hit land, they'll not be back to sail. I'm not getting over any water deeper than a bath.'

Ben expelled a breath. 'Don't trip over your petticoats when you leave.'

Warrington pushed himself from the door. 'Wasn't me pretending injury so I could lay abed drinking and sending a woman on false errands.' He opened the door and gave a wave to his brother. 'I'll be at either the town house or Whitegate. See me before you leave, infant.'

'Goodbye, old woman.'

Warrington walked out, knowing his trunk had already been taken to his room and letting the sunshine caress his face. Even the sun felt better when not reflected from below by water and not filtered from above by sea air.

Then he thought of the concern he faced. Rage caused his steps to increase. Cassandra had not merely been happy to tangle his life while she lived. She mangled afterwards, as well. He slapped a palm against the outside cabin door so hard his elbow tingled.

His past ate at him, only it wasn't even his past. And it wasn't even in the past, but at his country estate.

Chapter Ten

Melina crouched on the oak-planked bunk in the cabin. The mattress had been replaced on the bed. The pallet gone. Now Warrington's trunk sat in the room, open. He stood in front of it, staring at the silk waistcoat and buff breeches, complaining that he had not brought someone named Broomer along so he could have cared for the clothing. Warrington had already taken out a gentleman's beaver hat totally unsuitable for the ship or Melos.

Warrington was not of her world. She'd seen silk before and touched it. Her father had worn it. She lived in the world of scratchy wool and rough linen.

'I do not like sailing.' She spoke low, knowing her words wouldn't carry though the wall.

'Makes two of us and I own half of the ship.' He gave her a half smile. 'But my infant brother could talk me into buying a bag of bees.'

She shrugged. 'He reminds me of Stephanos. Stephanos has a schooner and sometimes wears nearly the same clothes as the captain.' She gauged Warrington's face to see if he took offence at her dislike of his brother.

Warrington's chest moved as if he laughed, but she heard no sound. 'Ben doesn't take well to being on his back, alone.

And he's superstitious. Though he'll never say so to you, he thinks you brought bad luck to the ship.'

'The only person I brought misfortune for was me and my statue.

Warrington turned from the trunk, preparing his razor, putting soap on his face and scowling into the small mirror. 'I'm pleased you forgave Stubby.'

'I've not—but he doesn't need to know that. He meant no harm.'

'Ben will stay on board a few more days, until he is walking better. Gid will see he has all he needs brought to him.' Warrington shaved as he talked. 'We three brothers have a town house in London. Ben will have to stay on *Ascalon,* making sure she is readied. Dane is at my country house, working with my man of affairs—taking care of the estates.'

He looked out of the window, as the ship sailed past warehouses for unloaded goods. 'I can't yet return to the country house. Whitegate is my ancestral home. My real home—though I've lived in the town house since Cass died. Now that I'm to be in London again, I have to settle a few things for myself. Things I couldn't face before, but now it's time.'

When he finished, he stored his shaving supplies and prepared to depart.

She kept her eyes to the window while he changed clothing. Each rustle of fabric echoed in her ears. He stood so close, she could see his arm when he donned the shirt. She bit down on her lip, trying to keep her awareness of him from changing her breathing or showing in the colour of her face. She wondered what he would do if she turned and watched. Probably continue exactly as he had been the moment before. But she could not let him see her interest and she could not give in to it. She swallowed, and tried to think of the sights she saw outside the window. But nothing beyond the glass had any appeal for her at this moment.

'You can turn now, Melina.' His roughened voice whispered at her ears, jarring her. She jumped forward, but couldn't move much or she'd have her face against the panes. 'I'm all tucked away.'

'The sights of the town are *neos,* fresh, for me.'

He gave a teasing grunt and she could tell he backed away from her. But she was also aware from his response that he remembered well it wasn't only the view in front of her that was new to her.

The clothing he'd worn while he sailed was tossed on to the floor.

'You are not taking those?' she asked, looking at the heap.

He shook his head. 'Gid'll see use is made of the scraps. I will never wear them again.'

She forced herself not to pick them up. Surely they could be sold for a few pence, but they weren't hers to sell. She would have to find her father and hope she was wrong about him. She'd planned to rail at him for leaving her mother. Now she would have to be kind.

She'd not wanted Warrington to know she had a father in London because she felt ashamed he had deserted them. But she'd told him anyway.

'Remember, Ben chose the town house fripperies and hired servants.' Warrington opened the door. 'It'll not be much different than the ship. But when the ship is repaired, you'll be here and able to go back to Melos, and care for your sisters.'

She took the satchel she'd brought, slipping the strap over her shoulder, and wrapped the shawl tight around her, then followed Warrington to the deck. She watched the port come into view. Already she could see the buildings and the people. The ship floated up the waterway, into England.

On deck, the shouts of orders and replies faded in her mind as she saw the city taking life in front of her. The people on the docks appraised the ship as if it were of no more significance than a mug of ale being put before them.

Waves sloshed, and somewhere in the distance, tar burned—from the odour, enough to coat Melos. The city stank.

Gidley waited, watching everything. His legs were braced for the ship's nudge against the dock. The quartermaster steered and Stubby coiled rope. One adjustment to a sail always meant another loosening or tightening would be needed somewhere else.

Gidley had already placed the huge rolls of rope on the outside of the ship, which kept the sides from knocking constantly against the dock while in port. He stood, brow furrowed and showing no pleasant emotion about the chance to leave *Ascalon*.

Preparing herself to be jolted, Melina was surprised when the ship eased in with little more than a brush.

Melina wished she could slip into this new world as easily as the ship had. She'd have to find her father. She put her hopes in a man who'd left her to starve the past few years. But surely he wouldn't feel the same if she stood in front of him.

Until she found her father, she was at the mercy of a man who cursed his wife's name and when he looked at her after he said the words, he glared.

Warrington had sent Stubby for a hackney as soon as the ship docked and ushered her inside the carriage before she had a chance to look around.

Melina used a fingertip to edge back the carriage window shade so she could peer outside. Warrington insisted she not make a spectacle of herself and keep concealed. Never mind she'd just shared a vessel with over thirty able-bodied seamen—now he told her she would have to go about with a chaperon. An odd world.

She would have hated waiting to begin her search, but the sights in London amazed her. Melina had never imagined such wealth and such vibrancy. She could hardly believe what she saw. No city could be more alive. With so much activity, she wondered if the city ever slowed, even at night.

Melina didn't know how the size of the city compared to Melos, but she imagined the whole of her island wouldn't hold London. And she felt smaller and smaller.

The front of Warrington's town house wasn't grand compared to many others she'd peeked at during the carriage ride, but a sturdy shape, and beyond any dreams she might have imagined while on Melos. Curtains billowed outside, through the open windows, and she saw a young boy, pail in hand, trotting from the back of the house on some errand.

She could imagine telling her sisters about the city and not being able to convince them of the size. No one could create such a picture with words. More horses and carriages than she knew existed in the whole of the world. And people shouting out, and sometimes the drifting smell of baked goods pleasantly covering the more usual odours caused by so many people so tightly packed together.

When the carriage stopped, Warrington helped her to the paving stones.

'If you think of this as Ben's home,' he said, standing at the door, 'it will make more sense. Dane and I have lived in it at one time or another—and we all move in and out of it. But Ben stores his collections here.' He looked to the house. 'Dane and I refer to it as *Seascrape.*'

The house was set among other similar dwellings, close to the street, and three levels of windows, with a front that looked as fresh as if it had been completed the day before.

When the door opened, a man stood there, looking down. This giant of a man well outstripped any person she'd ever seen and he would have been frightening if not for the humour in his face. His upturned lips looked to stay in place at all moments of the day and if he were ever moved to tears, he'd still be smiling.

'Ah, my lord,' he said, giving a proper bow. He wore breeches, one leg of the clothing hanging a hand width too low as it appeared to have lost the securing button just below the knee. His yellow vest had a shine to it and his cravat was of the same colour. His brown woollen coat kept his clothes from overpowering the sun, but not by much.

'Step inside. Step inside.' He moved back. 'We've made the house up pretty for when you and Captain Ben arrived.'

'He'll be staying on *Ascalon* a little longer than expected, Broomer.' Warrington stepped inside the door and gave his hat to the man. 'The ship needs repairs—and so does he. He's limping around, grumbling and groaning because a wave tossed him into a spar.'

Broomer frowned.

War nodded. 'It was close, but he's tough. And he looks to be mending good as ever.'

Melina followed him inside and the big man gave another bow.

Warrington spoke to the man. 'See to having us fed soon, but you're not to do the cooking.'

Broomer laughed. 'Can't blame you. But you can see Mrs Fountain's still working here.' He patted his stomach. 'I tell her she could make a dead rat taste good and she says she'll try it some day to see if I notice.' He laughed again. 'If she wasn't so scared of them little creatures, I'd be worried.'

'Does your sister still live in the area?' Warrington asked.

'She's doing work for that sewing lady you told me about,' Broomer said. 'My sister says everybody thinks that woman sews faster than anybody else. They never suspect two women are doing the fancy work.'

'Can you bring her here to meet Melina and fashion several dresses as quickly as possible, and find fripperies to match?' The corners of his eyes creased. 'Tell her we do not want Melina to draw attention.' He gave Melina a quick smile, and then turned back to Broomer. 'Garments suitable for a governess, I suppose.'

'She'll be happy from ear to ear to be putting together something for your woman.' Broomer gave another small bow to Melina. 'She will be honoured.'

Melina saw Warrington's face the moment Broomer called her Warrington's woman. His jaw had tensed first, then he had looked at her and the light behind his eyes changed. He'd not obviously perused her body, but he'd watched her face in such a way she'd known he was remembering her touch, then the side of his lips lifted in the smallest amount before he turned back to Broomer.

'I will pay your sister double if she can have something here by morning.'

With that the large man left and Warrington took Melina to the upstairs. He paused at the top. 'Sitting room.' He indicated to the right with his head.

He opened the door and she stepped inside. The walls were blue. A painting hung above the fireplace. Mermaids.

'You can surmise who commissioned the art.' His brows rose and he seemed to be saying something other than his words. 'He's a collector—of a sort.'

A fish candle holder sat on top of a bookcase and a ship replica with what appeared to be silver masts graced the mantel. The staff leaning in the corner was the serious end of a harpoon. Two sofas sat angled to catch the warmth of the fireplace. A writing desk with good-sized seating for it sat near the window to catch the light. One overstuffed chair was in another corner with the table beside it holding an ivory-coloured object mounted on a stand.

Warrington followed her eyes. 'Tooth. Some kind of fish. My brother strangled it with his bare hands or something. Claims it wanted to drown a friend of his or swallow them both whole. Took it as a sign the day he caught it and said his luck changed.'

She nodded, even more certain she wasn't fond of Warrington's brother.

He shrugged. 'I suppose having a passion for the sea is no different than any other. Ben didn't choose it. I believe our passions choose us—unfortunately.' His look lost emotion. 'Horses. Gambling. Beautiful women. The trick is not to let them become too strong in your life, I suppose.'

He turned away, speaking. 'I'll show you the bedchamber. We have two sleeping rooms on this floor. One is empty and the other is Dane's, on occasion. Two are on the upper floor—one I use and the other one, which has more of the watery mementos, Ben prefers. I believe he even has part of an old sail stored there. The room smells of stagnant water, in my opinion—though Ben says I imagine it.'

He turned to leave the room, then reversed his movements, facing her. 'Tomorrow, we'll go to the British Museum.'

'What of you seeing your children?'

He looked at her. 'I'll have them brought here or I will go there. Soon. I have not fully decided yet.'

She paused, measuring her words carefully. 'I would

like to go to Somerset House. That is the place I sent letters to my father.'

'It will be no bother.' He gave the words no inflection, no importance, and turned. Taking her to a bedchamber, he paused at the door. 'We've had to move some of Ben's collection here. Dane and I keep moving them around to whichever room is unoccupied.'

When she walked inside, Melina saw what she assumed, and hoped, was the most extensive collection of mermaid paintings in the world. The captain did like his mermaids. Or what passed for them.

These were not virtuous sea creatures if one judged by the looks in their faces and the poses they chose. Each mermaid had long flowing hair, which didn't always fall in a modest covering, but more in an accentuating frame.

She kept her composure. 'I suppose they are beautiful.'

'That is not my first thought when I see them.' He looked at her. 'I'll turn them to the wall if you wish.'

'I am fine with them.'

'I do not have a single mermaid painting in my room. Not one. I have sensible art. Not rabid females.' His mouth was so close to her ear, she could feel his breath. 'I would like to show you.'

His hand slipped to her waist, weakening her knees. Her mind flashed back on the memory of his body over hers. Muscles. Male skin so much different than her own. A new world at her fingertips.

'I would have had the mermaids moved had I known I would be returning with you,' he said.

She fought for her voice. Too much newness surrounded her, and yet, none of it took her thoughts as Warrington's presence did. 'I did not know such paintings existed.' Nor such a man as Warrington.

He shrugged. 'I would say they don't anywhere else. I

think my brother has found every one in the world and had the rest commissioned. One artist always has a painting to show Ben when he docks. Ben can't resist any painting of a naked woman with scales.'

He pulled Melina's hand to his lips. 'I prefer a true woman.' He pressed a kiss to her fingers.

She pulled her hand back, sliding her fingers along his. Without meaning to, she'd slowed her movements, her entire concentration on the feel of his skin against hers. Thumping footsteps sounded up the stairs—the movements were exaggerated on purpose to alert them of Broomer's arrival.

She turned her shoulders from Warrington so he couldn't see her face. The paintings could be more proper. But she feared even if an artist painted seaweed over the creatures, they would still be unsuitable. A small painting propped in the corner would be turned to the wall as soon as she was alone.

He put his arm around her. 'I won't have them near you if you wish. Or there is another chamber you could choose... One in particular would welcome you...'

She firmed her voice. 'I think this room is perfect for me. Perhaps the mermaids will keep wicked spirits away.'

'I would not count heavily on it, Melina. I think they would welcome any wickedness.'

She turned, needing to escape the sensations rocking her body, and he followed her from the room.

Broomer appeared in the hallway. He held his hand up and gave a little twist of his wrist near his head. 'Mrs Fountain's hair stood on end when I said you'd be needing a meal, and pots began flying.' He patted his stomach. 'But from the smell of the beef, she's putting on a fine feed. It's waiting on ye.'

Then he ambled to the stairs and Melina looked at Warrington. 'He is so friendly and not what I expected a servant to be like.'

Warrington met her eyes and she saw agreement. 'Broomer left Newgate and landed on a ship to keep from starving about the time Ben first became an able-bodied seaman. Broomer hated every day of it, but they became close and Ben sent him here when they docked.'

He tilted his head. 'After Cassandra died, I couldn't stand the way the servants watched me at Whitegate. First I'd been ill and then I recovered to discover my father had died of the same illness. We had cholera. Things were not smooth at Whitegate. Then, about a year ago, Cassandra became ill, just as my father and I had. Cass died. I worried that the servants thought I had poisoned her. I came here.'

The light from a window at the end of the hallway illuminated his features, leaving shadows that darkened his eyes. She put her hand on his arm, rubbing along the smooth fabric of his sleeve. 'I was miserable after my mother died,' she said.

Nodding, he held out an arm for her to precede him. 'This house gave me a chance to step from the memories even if I could not forget them. Long ago, my father purchased the town house, saying it would be an investment, and I am thankful he did. I think even then he thought one of his sons would live in it. But we all use it.'

He stopped outside the doorway to the main sitting room. 'I was surprised the first time I walked in and the fish-women portraits graced the sitting-room wall.' He looked heavenwards. 'I could not tolerate them—felt I was in some sort of fish harem. The paintings had to be moved to the room you're now in.'

Warrington continued, 'I'd get a bottle of brandy and

shout for Broomer.' He smiled. 'Ben had sworn his friend could be more enjoyment than any Drury Lane performance. He spoke the truth. Broomer would come to the sitting room and spout tales left and right. Never asked a question of my life.' He turned his head so she couldn't see his expression. 'Not even when I returned home one night with blood flowing down my back because a man I'd never seen before was waiting in the shadows to stab me.'

If he'd not moved slightly back, she might not have noticed the way a muscle flexed in his jaw. 'Why would someone wish to kill you?'

'Jealousy over my wife—though at that point she was dead and it didn't matter. But she was carrying my babe when she died. Perhaps...he felt betrayed.'

The air was silent for a moment. She had to keep him talking. 'Did Broomer go for the magistrate and a physician?'

Warrington shook his head. 'Refused. Said all he'd ever known a magistrate to do was lock up people if somebody else caught them. Said all a physician could do was make people die faster or slower and with more pain. I cursed him, sacked him and thought I might as well die. I gave in and let him tend my back.' He raised a brow. 'Don't ever plan a friendly chess game with him, either. He doesn't like to drag them out. I believe he has three boards set up in his chamber and I suspect if he were to find an opponent he believes is truly worthy of his skills, he'd stop at nothing to cadge them into a game.'

He paused, the silence so soft she could hear the sounds of carriages from the street.

'Make yourself comfortable,' he told her. 'I must arrange for a meeting concerning my voyage.'

Before he turned to leave, he looked at her, his voice

thoughtful, and said, 'I do not know what my brother sees in mermaids. Anyone would prefer a goddess over a sea creature. They're much more enticing.'

Chapter Eleven

Warrington waited until the house became quiet and walked the hallway to Melina's room.

Conflicting thoughts battered him. He'd meant to stay from her and he praised himself because he'd kept out of her bed. But now he stood at her doorway.

He raised his hand to knock, but then he stilled and let his hand fall to his side. Melina couldn't refuse him. After all, he'd paid. And now he provided everything she needed and had ordered clothing for her.

The bed she slept in was soft, the pillows softer. The sheets even better. If she became warm, she could go to the sitting room, pull the bell for Broomer, and he would rise from his bed, ask her what she wanted and act as if he'd been waiting to be summoned, and go merrily back to his chamber after doing her bidding.

Or she could take a candle—not a tallow candle or a burning flame from whatever could be fashioned, but a beeswax candle—and peruse the collection of books in the library all the brothers had contributed to.

For the morning meal, Mrs Fountain would prepare her bread—hot, and dripping with butter—a rasher of bacon and chocolate, or tea, and even porridge, because Ben preferred the simple fare and Mrs Fountain always wished to please. If Melina were to ask for a different meal, Mrs Fountain would do all in her power to comply.

He doubted Melina would even suspect such luxuries were at her fingertips.

But she would know he was her benefactor and remember he was the man she gave her body to in exchange for passage. And now she lay in a room of his house, in comfort except for the hideous artwork, and she could not tell him not to lie with her.

Mrs Fountain or Broomer or the maids could say they had another position and leave. But Melina's father had abandoned her once, was likely to do so again, and the woman had no one or anything else. His fists clenched at the unfairness.

Granted, the first night he'd taken her body in exchange for passage. He'd been rewarded by his own inner guilt. She'd been a virgin forced to sell her body or go to the Stephanos man she spoke of.

And Warrington had once felt forced, as well. Forced to remain in a marriage. Forced by his own beliefs not to take a lover. Forced by the insistence of his own body to return to his wife.

He turned, hoping Dane had added some interesting titles to the books, but his feet would not take him from Melina. He searched within himself, trying to understand his need to see her and wondering why he could not shut off the craving he felt.

A clunk. A thump. He stood outside Melina's door and heard shuffling noises. Things being moved.

He rapped softly.

The door opened a crack and wary eyes peered out.

'Is something disturbing you?' he asked.

'Not if— Yes. They are… Those women all…' She changed her sentence. 'In the dusk, the features of the paintings are dim, but the whiteness around the pupils glows. Eyes stare at me.'

Inwardly, he smiled. He could imagine his brother relishing the eyes on him.

She stood there, peering around the door, the thin shoulder of her white chemise showing well in the bare light and the skin of her neck filled with dark hollows, but they were inviting valleys.

'The mermaids—they seem to get more evil the longer I am near them,' she whispered, perhaps so the women could not hear her.

He agreed, though he felt some loyalty to his brother's choices. And in the light, the women did have a certain appeal to a man's base side. 'I don't think they should be in public view, but in a man's private quarters…' He paused. 'I think my brother prefers mermaids because he knows he'll never find one and he uses them to keep—' He stopped. 'I can understand Ben's views, but yours take preference tonight. If he were here, he would feel the same.'

She laughed softly and the sound of it hit him in his stomach, a punch without pain. But with a certain power involved, taking some of his strength.

'Melina—' The night on the ship kept returning to his memory. He had wronged her. And he'd tried to stay from her to make it right in his mind. But he also kept calling himself a fool. She wasn't staying in England and he felt relieved. He didn't need another entanglement. He had Jacob to think of and Whitegate.

He lived in a man's world. Women brought tension. Goblets being hurled across the room, shattering. Servants upset. He'd truly been amazed at how well a house could run with only servants at the helm. A fractious woman could cause more upheaval with a misplaced smile than a general with a battalion of men.

He looked into Melina's face and gently shook his head. 'I'll move the paintings.'

'Warrington.' Her eyes darted down. 'I know...'

He didn't like talking to her with so much between them and particularly standing in a hallway of his house. Broomer could step up the stairs at any moment, probably stomping to alert them of his presence, but all the same—

He gave a soft push to the door and she stepped back, letting him enter without resistance—except in her face. She'd not braided the length of her hair, only pulled it tightly and put a ribbon around it. He'd never seen a woman leave her locks so free when she slept. He took in the dimly lit room and saw the backs of the art now propped against the walls.

The chemise, too full for Melina, hung on her. The garment sneaked into the recesses of his mind because he knew it was the one thing touching her skin the whole of the night.

'I made sure a dressing gown was placed in the wardrobe for you. He will not mind if you use it. Everything in here is for you to use as you wish,' he said.

She absently touched the tie she'd put in her hair, which caused a shifting in her clothing, pulling the chemise across her breasts. He instantly turned, not wanting more images of her lodging in his mind—causing a pounding ache that stirred from below and crept up to his chest until he could think of nothing else.

Reaching to the paintings she'd turned to the wall, he took one in each hand, carried them to the hallway and placed them facing the wall. Then he went back for more.

Passing her, he held two more paintings. 'This is the one way we haven't displayed them before.' He sat the two beside the others in the hallway and returned to her. 'This arrangement might be the best view of them.'

'You don't have to—'

'Yes, I do. They are not what any woman would choose to have around her and only one male I know cares for them.' A single painting remained in the room. 'Melina, take the wrap and wait for me in the sitting room. Let's give these immoral women's spirits a chance to clear out of the bedchamber.'

In moments she was covered and they walked to the other room. The familiarity of being in a woman's presence in such a mundane way stirred pleasant feelings in him. Caressed him.

Inside the sitting room, Melina curled into a chair and the candles he'd lit burnished her face, giving her features an otherworldly look. He stood at the door, but she didn't turn her face to him, avoiding his eyes.

'Melina, if you have any debt to me—*have* had any debt to me for passage or anything else—I release you from it.'

'It's not so simple. Not for me. I am in debt to you.'

'No, Melina. You are not. Not any longer. It's fully paid. You do not owe me anything. I am obliged to you.'

He saw her gentle disagreement in her eyes. He couldn't take her again. If he did, he'd know she only lay with him out of repayment and duty. He would not go to her chamber. He'd already had his fill of a woman's dutiful coupling.

He took another chair and lifted it, sitting it beside her, not so close the arms connected, but close enough she could reach to put her hand on his arm if she wished, or if they both leaned together, their lips could touch.

Before he sat, he undid the buttons of his waistcoat and pulled off his cravat. He lowered himself into the chair, taking the neckcloth and folding it carefully, then placing it on the floor at the side of him opposite her.

'I should have lit a fire, though it's too hot,' he mused, 'because it would make more sense than sitting here staring at a cold grate.' He paused for a moment. 'Do you play chess?'

'No. I embroider. I embroider, and embroider, and embroider. When I am not mending or making clothing. Every night we sewed, or did some quiet chore if we weren't sleepy when darkness fell.'

'Sounds lively.'

'Sometimes we did argue for entertainment, I suppose.'

He chuckled. 'I have seen that happen in my own life.'

He wanted to take her to his bed. She'd go if he asked. But if he did, he'd suspect— No, he'd know she let him touch her in repayment and he did not want that. He didn't want her saying yes because she owed him. For that, he could leave the house and quickly find another pleased to toss up her skirts for quick, uncaring moments, and most happy see the back of him while she tucked the coin away. But he wanted to be with Melina.

'If you wish it—' Her words rocked into the room and he knew without doubt what she meant. Perhaps she could read his thoughts, but even the coal boy would know what a man contemplated when he saw Melina in bed clothing.

'I realise that.' Sadness tinged his words, but he didn't know if she could hear the emotion and wished he hadn't felt it.

He looked at her. She didn't accidentally open her dressing gown and lean in his direction when he spoke. The woman wasn't a jade.

And he could pull her from the chair and roll them on to the carpet and never feel the floor.

'Perhaps I—' He looked at his hands, fingertips touching, resting on his lap. 'I shouldn't. I think I might like you, Melina. And one probably does take advantage of friends, and all, but I fear if I do, it will seem base. Not like before. Before, we hardly had spoken. We were strangers.'

'Better with a stranger?'

'I suppose.'

'You only plan to speak to me tonight?'

He put his hand on the arm of the chair, palm up, inviting. 'Yes. I've not spoken with a woman much in so long. I'm surprised I miss it. I never saw a woman and said to myself, *Oh, she looks lovely. I might wish to spend hours talking with her.* But perhaps I wanted that more than I knew.'

She didn't move at first, but then put her hand in his. The touch, delicate and warm, pleased him more than a seductive rub. More than a teasing smile, or a planned accidental brush against his body.

'I shouldn't have spoken,' he said softly.

'No. I like your voice.'

'Are you comfortable?' he asked.

'I suppose.'

Warrington watched the fireplace as if he could see flames. 'You will not be amiss if you wish to go back to your room.'

She didn't move. 'It's all so new to me. Everything. This world. I had heard stories. Hours and hours of them, telling us what this land was like. But I still didn't know. All of it. I didn't know.'

'Tell me about your days on Melos.'

She began describing her mother, her sisters and her life.

He didn't have to prod himself to pay attention or stay awake. Her voice, filled with a woman's softness, entranced him more than any sound he'd ever heard. Even when she sat back in the chair and her pauses grew longer, and her eyes slipped shut, he kept watching her, soothed by her presence.

And a whisper inside himself warned never, ever to do this again. Never. He could not let his soul be shredded again by falling in love.

When he heard a clock in the dining room give three chimes, he woke Melina, took her by the hand and led her to her bed.

He kissed her forehead.

After he left the room, he moved to his own chamber.

He'd just kissed a woman's forehead. He didn't understand himself. But he did understand the simmering, pulsing need throughout his body. His temporary sainthood was leaving him. He was barely hanging on to his vow of celibacy.

In his chamber, he poured water into the washbowl and used both hands to dip his face into it. He dried, wishing he could shake his body like a wet dog and quiver away his desire for Melina.

His hands stopped on the flannel, resting. He could think of better ways to ease himself of his want for the dark beauty, and all involved her softness.

He could show her so much, but then, he could end up with another man laying claim to his child. The spectre of Stephanos rose up, and tore at Warrington. He could not let Melina go back to Melos with his child inside her and he could not let a woman close enough to destroy him again.

In the morning, Broomer woke Warrington and barely gave him time to get his eyes open before the servant said, 'My sis brought the first dress and I'm asking her to stay until you take a look 'fore she leaves. I'm thinking you might want her to keep the garment.'

War raised a brow and left his bed.

'It's the colour of mud or boot scrapings,' Broomer continued. 'I asked my sister what she was thinking. She reminded me of you asking for something governess-like… She's in a fierce mood now.' Broomer shrugged. 'They're dressing Melina because my sister did bring some of those underneath trappings and you know how those take an age for a woman to knot up.'

* * *

When War saw the garment on Melina, he understood Broomer's statement. The gown was suitable for a stern governess, but it didn't hide her enough.

He turned to Broomer's sister, a woman close to Warrington's own height. Her eyes had the same friendliness of her brother's, but the dark blue dress she wore, and the long line of her neck, gave her a gently bred appearance—the exact opposite of her sibling.

'A pleasant gown,' Warrington stated. Those were the best words he could say about it.

'We will need a chaperon.' He spoke to the seamstress. 'To protect Melina's reputation.' Broomer's face jerked around. Obviously he'd noticed Melina was living in the house with no chaperonage. Mrs Fountain and Broomer were not talebearers, though. And for the day servants, they would not make note of a woman staying with him, thinking her a mistress of no consequence.

But to be in public with Melina was another thing. She would be noticed and that should have the appearance of propriety.

'I could certainly go about with you. If that's what you wish.' The sister looked taken aback, but agreeable.

He nodded. 'But some of the conversations Melina and I will have with other people—you'll need to make yourself scarce for those moments. I'll nod to you and then you can absent yourself for a bit.'

'Whatever is needed.' Her chin went up, sending out a message of complete agreement and perfect servitude. A woman who considered it a show of her loyalty to help accomplish a task and would consider it no challenge at all to do Warrington's bidding.

Warrington first had to give his report to the Foreign Office and then he took Melina to Somerset House. He

stood in the centre of the room, looking up at the paintings lining the walls. Above eye level, he could see about
three more rows of large paintings, under the windows at
ceiling height. The paintings, all ornately framed, weren't
arranged in a neat line, but more like a pleasing array of
mismatched sizes of tiles covering a wall.

This wasn't the annual display of Somerset House, but
he'd arranged for a meeting with the man who'd forwarded
Melina's letters to her father.

He started at one side of the room and checked each
painting, looking for Cherroll's name. Melina started at
the other. Broomer's sister stood close to Melina and he
realised, based on the women's dress, an onlooker might
think Melina the chaperon.

After a few minutes, Melina called him over, pointing to a painting. The chaperon walked discreetly to other
artwork.

'My father did this one,' she said.

At that moment, a man, with a precise cravat and a pace
just as measured, walked up to them. Warrington turned.
'Mr Bridewater?'

The man nodded. 'Yes. I received your message. Please
follow me.'

After they entered a small room with an ornately carved
desk, Bridewater spoke. 'My lord. I believe you went to
university with my son, Marcus.'

'Yes.' Warrington nodded. 'The fellow could outrun a
horse. Never saw anyone who could move as fast as he.'

Bridewater laughed, pointing them to chairs carved in
the same manner of the desk. 'My boy never sat still. Could
hardly keep a tutor for him. Never thought I'd see the day
he finished his education. Soon as he did, he put his nose
in an accounting book and now to get him running, you
have to kick the legs from his chair.'

Warrington sat and noticed this room boasted a selection of paintings that would be hard to equal. 'I want to find the artist who painted a portrait my brother saw and also one that you have displayed. The man's name is Cherroll.'

Bridewater stared a moment and fiddled with a chain hanging from his waistcoat pocket. 'I suppose it couldn't hurt for me to tell you his true name.' He shrugged, stretching his arms out in front of himself, fingers interlaced. 'He paints under a false name and does not show himself in public as the artist. When he was young his family wanted it kept secret he painted and for some reason he still fancies the old name. Always, I handle any transactions for him. Any enquiries or post in the Cherroll name always come to me and I see that he gets it.'

Bridewater leaned back in the chair. 'He paints all the time. Chases art like some men chase skirts or spirits.' He pushed his chair back a bit. 'Lived on some Greek island off and on for years. That helped his painting—because he's not a terribly creative artist and he lacks something. Painting a different culture helped get his work shown, but didn't increase his skill. He repeats himself—never stretches or grows. Never studies others.'

Warrington stood. 'How old is this man?'

Bridewater squinted. 'About my age, I'd suppose. But don't plan on meeting him, even though he's in London now. If he's painting, he won't accept a visitor.' He shook his head. 'Man thinks he'll be more famous than Rembrandt, so he wants to give the world all the art he can.' At that, Bridewater leaned his head back a bit and grimaced at the ceiling. 'Just wish he would push himself to paint better, not more.' He lowered his chin and looked at Warrington. 'You may know him. Lord Hawkins.'

Warrington paused for a moment. 'One of the Duke of Beaumont's brothers?'

'Youngest, or next, I believe. Never was any chance of him becoming duke. He's the old duke's third wife's second son, or some such. Married well.' Bridewater smiled and chuckled to himself. 'Though his father-in-law rather did know how to remind him who the funds truly belonged to. The father-in-law—not a man you'd cross. He loved his daughter and his coins. Tolerated Hawkins.'

Warrington and Melina stood, and Bridewater gave them directions.

Melina spoke as she stepped to the carriage. 'He's married again. Now I know why he did not return to us.'

Warrington sat in the carriage beside Melina, pleased at the feel of her so close beside him. The soft scent of new fabric of the dress clinging to it. He sat back against the squabs, which caused their bodies to brush again, and knew he'd only moved because he liked the feel of her beside him. He looked at her fingers clasped in her lap, and moved his eyes to her face.

Her brows were puckered, and his chest tightened in response. He knew what she was about to discover.

'We'll call on him tomorrow.' *This man who forgot about his daughters.* As soon as the thought formed, his own blackness slogged into his veins. He tensed. Jacob. The rest of it. Once he arranged the next days of his life, he could put everything behind him. Everything but Jacob, and start fresh. He would close away every unpleasant memory and go forward. His life would begin again.

But now he needed to prepare Melina for what she was to find when she met her father, and he didn't think there was an easy way.

Chapter Twelve

Melina rose from the table, uncomfortable with the amount of food left in front of her. The platter held more boiled carrots and parsnips than had been taken. Parts of three different meats remained—one dark and spiced, small game of some kind and her favourite, one with the lightness of chicken resting in a pool of herbed juices.

Warrington ate, hardly looking at anything other than his food, his movements slow, as if he didn't taste the meal in front of him.

He wore a dark coat and a gold-hued waistcoat under. The cravat at his neck drooped so it hardly stood out from the shirt. But when he moved his arm, the sleeve fell back at his hand. She could see the broadness of his wrist and the shape of the bone resting under the darkened skin. Hair spattered the back of his hand, hardly showing. Even the leanness of his fingers gave him a look of strength.

And if she doubted his power, she had only to let herself gaze at his shoulders or across his chest. He was born with command.

He'd not spoken during the whole meal. She'd not felt ignored because she had her own thoughts to consider. When she stood, he immediately put down his fork and rose. Grim eyes met hers.

'We should go to the sitting room.' Warrington stepped beside her, not touching, but close enough she could see a darkness of his jaw, hinting of stubble.

She paused, studying his face. He smiled—one he might have given a convict headed for the gallows.

She didn't move. 'What is it?'

'I was just thinking of...' He shook his head. 'I don't know. My wife. It's too late to ask her questions now, and even if it weren't, her answers... Why would anyone ask a question of someone who has repeatedly told lies—unless to see if the answer is so preposterous as to be laughable?'

He put a hand to Melina's back and shepherded her towards the sitting room. Two candles were lit to dispel the gloom from the drizzling rain outside. 'A man might ask a question of his wife and in his heart he knows the answer, but he wants to hear something to convince him he's wrong.' His voice was low, laced with ruefulness as if he couldn't believe he spoke. 'I suppose Shakespeare has written a play about it, or he should have. Doesn't matter. I wouldn't have liked it.'

When he entered the sitting room, he stopped, frowning. 'If you ever can't sleep, make use of the books we have. Dane's tomes on gardening are quite useful for nodding off.' Warrington stood in front of the large, chintz-covered chair, but he didn't sit. 'I know you can read English because you wrote letters to send to your father, and I believe I even have several volumes in Greek.'

Melina walked in front of the books. She ran her finger over the titles. 'I can't read Greek. Neither of my sisters can. I would not know how to read English if my father hadn't had trouble painting for a while and found it amusing to teach words. A new game and I was good at it. I even taught my sisters later—and when Bellona realised she could read English, she was enraged. Bellona then took the two books my father had left behind and found a French sailor who would buy them.'

Warrington didn't speak and he looked at his hands.

She wondered why he didn't face her—and why he didn't say what he thought. 'Continue.' She shrugged. 'I know you have more to say.'

'Your father has a large home, very old, very well kept—from his wife's family. When you see it, understand he...'

Melina let out a breath and turned from the books, keeping herself calm by force. 'You are telling me he is both wealthy and married. But since it is his wife's funds, I could understand him not sending much to us, but forgetting about us completely was wrong.'

Warrington stepped closer and took her hand. He led her to the sofa and pulled her beside him. He didn't release her fingers, but held them. 'I am trying to prepare you for the luxurious life he lives and I wanted you to know the money isn't his. And I don't think he is able to control it as husbands do with their wife's funds. The father-in-law was quite shrewd. The man profited greatly from the war with the colonies, and then the one with the little Corsicans—ensuring that England had the weapons they needed. And he only had the one daughter to pass his wealth to.'

'So my father had two families. He surely had enough funds to feed us. We did not need much, by English standards.'

Now he held her hand in both his, the warmth touching her, but not driving away the aloneness. She pulled back, feeling the anger towards her father that he deserved, but Warrington raised his grip to hold her wrists.

His eyes fixed on hers, and his voice softened even more. 'Your father hasn't recently married. He had two families, Melina.'

Melina couldn't speak. Her words burned in her throat.

Warrington continued, 'You have a half-brother near my age. And your father has daughters here. If we are to go to his house tomorrow, I know you will probably see them, his wife or their portraits. You'd find out. It's better to know before.'

She jerked free from Warrington. 'Yes. It's best you told me. I will have the whole night to hate him more.'

He stood silently, watching.

'How many children—here—does my father have?' she asked.

'Four, I believe. Maybe only three.' He paused. 'I believe one may have taken ill and died. I'm not sure.'

She heard her voice and the bitterness she couldn't conceal. 'Do they have the birthmark, as well? The one like we have.' She touched the mud-coloured bodice where the mark hid beneath.

'Not that I am aware of. Well, perhaps the son has a small spot near his ear.' He squinted, thinking. 'I'm not sure.'

On Melos, she'd never considered her father could be married to someone else. Maybe a mistress, but not a marriage. She'd seen the seamen dock. Many of them had sweethearts or family somewhere else, but her father had seemed different. He stayed for long stretches of time and he loved his painting. He hardly had time for anything else.

'He *had* to take his paintings to England to sell.' She held her hand out, palm up. 'I should have known.'

'Not everyone has a wondrous family. Even kings.'

'I will tell him what I really think of him and the daubs of paint he calls *techni*. But you heard the man at Somerset House. They are not true art.'

He pulled her back into his grasp, and although his arm was around her, she felt no comfort. The coldness inside her blended with a hot anger boiling into her chest and arms and forehead, causing spikes of pain behind her eyes.

He didn't speak at first. 'The wife's father supported the family while he lived, but when he died, he left all his funds to a favourite nephew. Not a pound to his only child. The father trusted the nephew to allow the daughter to control the funds. The nephew inherited the wealth and made a great show of letting Hawkins's wife have freedom with her father's funds. I suppose the men made an agreement before the old man died.'

Melina shuddered. 'But *my* father would not care about who has the purse. As long as he has pigment and canvas, he is happy.'

Warrington turned sideways and pulled her chin so she had to look at him. 'Perhaps not. A man expects to control the purse strings since a woman's property becomes the husband's on marriage. When your father found out his wife didn't inherit, it's said he had to be restrained. His father-in-law had given Hawkins a grand slap.'

She stared at the harpoon and thought of the man she knew on the island. 'I would not be surprised if Melos was his revenge. If he stayed with us to punish the woman in England. Just enough to annoy but not enough to enrage.' She shook her head.

'I understand it better than you might think—parts of it, anyway. My wife, Cassandra… I think, even our son, Jacob, the heir she'd had for me, and perhaps even the little girl, were merely tools for her to use.'

'If you are saying you know what it is like when someone doesn't care for their children—still, it doesn't make me feel better. My sisters. My mother. He forgot about us.'

'My wife—forgot about me.' He dropped Melina's hand. His voice hardened. 'No, she didn't forget. She didn't care. She left when I was ill and came home carrying another man's child. And she begged my forgiveness—because it was going to be impossible for me to think the child was mine. I was sick, grieving for my father, angry at her for leaving me when I was about to die. I hated her, and yet I could not stop myself from wanting her. She was silken, soft, alluring—when she wanted something—and she wanted to be back in my home, as I had not heard a word from her in months and I severely curtailed her funds. Besides, how powerful she must have felt, knowing I hated what she had done, knew the child was not mine and yet I still desired her. But I had conditions on her return and I insisted she meet them.'

He stood and his words became soft. 'And I hurt the night she died... That was the worst part of all. How could I feel sadness when I was free from such a person? I should have gone out and celebrated. I *mourned* and was disgusted with myself for it.'

He turned back to her, letting his arm rest on the back of the sofa. His knee touched hers. With his arm still aligned on the back of the furniture, he reached out his other hand. 'Yet sometimes I think I miss her. That is the oddest part and makes me the most angry.'

He ran his forefinger along her arm. 'I tell you about my wife so you will know you are not the only one betrayed. That I have experienced disloyalty, too, and I don't want you alone in this.'

She crossed her arms around herself. 'My father is alive and he has no care of his treatment of us.' She shuddered. 'Not even a letter to see if we lived or died. Perhaps that is part of the reason I had to travel to England. If I'd merely wanted to escape Stephanos, I could possibly have found a French sailor from one of the vessels in the harbour. And I could have used them to send a message to the museum in France.'

'I would hope you are pleased you chose *Ascalon.*'

'*Malista.* Yes.' She looked to the rain-splattered window.

He stared at her, his mouth straight. He took her hand, his grasp overpowering her. He pulled her to stand in front of him and the room was silent. He touched her cheek and held her arms. 'I *am* better than the French sailors.'

Even though she felt no true joy, her lips did curl up. 'I said you were better.'

'Not with conviction.'

'You're an earl.'

His voice was petal soft. 'And, sweet, you're a goddess. You outrank me.'

Chapter Thirteen

Melina's fingers traced the delicate lace at the capped sleeves of the dress the seamstress had brought that morning. This gown was more colourful—only because the brown was darker and the ribbon bows at the sleeves were pink. The dress fit better, too, and the fabric was silk. Her birthmark showed at the edge of her bodice, peeking out, reminding her of her link to her sisters. She had asked the seamstress to make sure the mark showed.

When Warrington first saw her in the garment, he took a step backwards.

The step might have concerned her, except the look in his eyes could have lit a candle, and it caused an answering flame to spark deep within her stomach.

And she felt stronger, just from the way he looked at her. A woman might grow used to such attention. She walked towards him. He smiled. Even the silk against her felt more luxurious when his eyes brushed over her.

Warrington hurried her to the hackney. He'd said a chaperon wasn't necessary, as they'd keep the shades drawn in the carriage and not be in public.

As the vehicle lumbered along, Melina could not help stealing glances at the street. The houses. She could not believe a world of so much opulence and then, sometimes, such sad people trudging along. And young boys dressed in tatters. Running freely. Without parents nearby.

The vehicle stopped in front of a home and she looked out. She had to gasp to get a breath of air.

'Is a king's home as big at this?' she asked, not taking her eyes from the grandeur. This creation was someone's masterpiece. Birds flew from a small fountain and a tree had low branches spreading out gracefully, like welcoming arms. Each blade of grass looked exactly as if an artist painted it.

'Yes,' he answered. 'And as far as I know Hawkins doesn't have a country house, only this one.' He moved out of the conveyance and reached back to lend her his hand.

'I would say it is enough.' She put her foot on the lowered platform from the side of the hackney and slid her gloved fingertips into his outstretched hand. 'I was impressed when I saw your home. Five families could live in the town house. The whole of Melos could live in this one.'

'But Hawkins doesn't truly own it. His wife's family does.'

Melina stopped her footsteps and looked to Warrington, raising a brow. 'So could she toss him from it?'

'I doubt it would be that simple.' He put a hand at her back. 'Besides, it doesn't matter. A woman who wants to make her husband unhappy does better to stay at his side.'

She moved up the steps of the grand house—comparing the mansion to the rooms she'd lived in her whole life.

Melina stopped for a moment, thankful the knowledge of her father's life never reached Melos. At least, she hoped her mother never knew.

While she remained at the door, unable to move forward, Warrington stood beside her, one palm on the small of her back. He reached towards the gleaming knocker. He gave two quick raps.

She sighed, movement exaggerated. 'The poor man. Living in a sad state such as this. Nothing to do all day but the one thing he loves. He didn't travel to Melos for revenge. You don't leave riches to live as he did. He is truly mad for his art.'

He patted the small of her back.

When the butler opened the door, Warrington gave the servant a nod. Warrington's hand slid to Melina's side as he walked into the house. He moved between her and the butler, and she had no choice but to step with him. Melina noted the scent of paint. Even after artwork dried enough to be hung, it could be months before the lingering smell of the pigments left it. And she imagined in this house, the scents never completely left.

The entrance was crisp and even the plants she saw placed near the windows knew to grow straight and tall. Not a one leaned one way or the other, or dared a yellowed leaf.

The butler's face took in awareness of Warrington's commanding stride and his determined entry into the house. The servant's eyes narrowed.

Warrington gave the servant a card.

'Lord Hawkins is not at home,' the butler intoned, 'to anyone.'

'I must see him—about a painting of his.' War's voice—soft, a jagged caress of the words. 'I might wish to purchase it if he has it.'

The butler's eyes never changed emotion, but a muscle in his jaw tensed. He appraised Warrington, and Warrington moved his body forward, letting strength add volume to his words.

'I am *the* Earl of Warrington,' he said. 'Tell Robert I am here.'

The butler opened his mouth, but before he could speak, Warrington leaned in, shortening the distance between their faces to little more than a breath. 'You'd want me angry less than you'd want the artist upset.'

The servant stilled and the line of his jaw stiffened, and his eyelids dropped to half mast. She didn't have to look at Warrington to know how he appeared. She could feel the challenge in him from the tone of his words. The breadth of his shoulders gave emphasis to everything he spoke.

'Of course. Follow me.'

A stairway rose, with the hand-carved banister made to look like twisting ropes feeling cool under her touch. And candles. She'd never seen so many lamps at the ready.

The servant led them to a sitting room and marched away without looking back.

'I fancy hiring him right out from under Hawkins...' Warrington led her to a sofa and pressed a hand on her shoulder, increasing pressure until she sat '...except Broomer would have laughed had someone tried that with him. And he would have done something accidental—such as stepping on the man's foot and crushing his toes.'

He leaned in towards her, touched her chin and turned her face to him. 'You're his daughter. His flesh and blood. You have power, too. While it won't destroy an artist to have it known he has a second family, he can't relish his other children knowing.'

Her eyes moved to the walls and she saw the painting over the fireplace. Without thinking, she stood, her gaze locked on the artwork. Talons shredded her insides and she gasped. The painting above the fireplace. Melos. The houses with barns at the base. The olive trees. And shadows in the background, children playing. The shape of her mother sitting on a bench, watching the girls. She remembered that painting and the day.

Melina turned. Anger replaced the pain.

As she opened her mouth, Warrington spoke. 'Quite a

good likeness.' His words flowed with a silkiness Melina had not heard from him before. 'I am impressed.' He tipped his head in acknowledgement. He captured Melina's fingertips.

The rich timbre of Warrington's voice broke into the fog in her mind. 'Painted your home on Melos quite well. I can hear the sea in the distance.'

'How dare he?' Melina could not take her eyes from the wall. He'd captured her world exactly, and she could see a woman in the shadows—a woman who watched three girls digging caves in the dirt with seashells. 'My *mother*.'

'I suppose some people dare anything.'

She shifted her eyes to the mantel and nodded in that direction. 'The one candlestick. The one candlestick—he could have sold it and had enough money to feed us for a very long time. I know it was difficult to get funds to us and he had to make the trek himself to know that it was done. But he'd managed enough before, even with a war going on.' She leaned in. 'Even with a war. He convinced the seamen he was French when he wished to. A penniless French painter who spoke sparsely because the words twisted in his mouth. A man hoping to make a few coins to feed his family. Neither side must have cared much about an artist.'

She sighed. 'I am thankful I did not know the truth then. I might have been tempted to tell the sailors on the man-o'-war my father was a spy. Except it would have hurt my mother. She believed him a great artist. She loved him.' She said the last words and couldn't stop the derision of her voice when she said the word *love*.

Her father walked into the room. Melina would not have recognised him had they passed on the streets of London.

Gone was the scruffy, unkempt look of the island. Now he had the look of a gentleman artist. The only thing unchanged was his turpentine scent from the brush cleaner.

He had a cloth in his hands and kept scrubbing at daubs of pigment even as he looked at Melina.

'Your paintings must be selling quite well,' she said to her father, realising they were strangers. But maybe they'd always been such.

At first, he stared at her as if he knew he should recognise her, but didn't—then he looked to choke, and then he stared at Warrington and back at Melina.

'You.' Her father's voice filled with accusation. 'What are *you* doing here?'

His eyes—his eyes flashed something darker than when his work was disturbed. They showed the same emotion from the day her sister knocked one of the wet paintings into the dirt and that day had lasted for a fortnight.

He was her father, but not the same man from Melos. His hair, even more streaked with silver than before, surprised her with its perfect grooming. The points of his collar were starched and even the flowing covering he wore over his clothes had been cared for—even though it sported a palette of its own.

She wanted the tension in her body to fade, but she shuddered deep within her heart. The man she'd known on the island was gone for ever. He might have never lived.

Her father looked back over his shoulder and spoke to someone in the hallway who Melina couldn't see. 'Leave us.' He tossed the paint-splattered cloth to the floor. 'Why...' The words came out as if jerked from his soul. 'Why are you in my home?'

She could see the next words forming in his mind to tell her to leave, so she sat. Warrington stood beside her, staring at the other man.

'My muse will be destroyed for days because you have disturbed me.' Her father raised a hand, as if orating for a crowd. 'The stem is not quite right on the dog roses and the honeysuckle is lifeless. But my *bee orchis* is perfect. It truly looks like little bees clinging to the stem and I have captured that.' He turned to her, smugness in his eyes. 'No. I will not let you destroy my work today.'

'I know your work is everything to you, Father. I have no quarrel with that.'

'You shouldn't, Melina.' His grey hair fell across his brow.

'Truly. I never cared painting came first in your life. *Mana* didn't, either. It was the natural order for us. The art came first to you. Always. But she should have been second. I hope you received my letter saying *Mana* died. She did not recover.'

His eyes flashed, perhaps guilt, but then he shuddered, shutting away the emotion. 'I knew she was to die. And it would have hurt me too much to see her suffer.'

Darkness clouded Melina's vision and stole her voice. The image of her mother, eyes hollow, cheekbones with only flesh across them, lying in bed, and the whole world around her falling into nothingness, flared into Melina's memory. 'It would have hurt you?' She controlled her words. 'How do you think it was for her? To be abandoned when she needed you most.'

'She understood. She told me to go.'

'She might have understood. I understood. You would not waste a moment on something or someone if it was not to your advantage. And she may have told you to go, but she wanted you to stay. It would have showed you cared.'

'My art is from my core spirit. It cannot be interrupted.'

'But…' she tilted her head to the side and forced her words calm '…think how much your work would have improved if you had had an added measure of grief to draw on. Now you have lost that chance for ever. Your work can never be what it could have.'

His cheeks reddened and his voice rose. 'That is ludicrous. I have felt grief. I know the emotion well and my paintings show the depth of the human soul.'

'No. They don't. They show the depth of your soul and it doesn't go very deep.'

He jabbed one finger towards her face. 'You are lying. You are not to speak so to me. I am your father.'

'Father?' She filled the word with derision. 'Father? What does that word mean? Tell me.'

'I gave you life. And you must respect me for it.'

'No. I do not. I may have respected you when I was a child, but then I knew no better. I esteemed *Mana*. The only mistake she made in her life was in caring for you.'

'I was the best thing for her. She was a Greek peasant.'

'Worth ten—ten thousand more paintings than you could ever create.'

'You have no true knowledge of art. You are here crying to me because you are weak. Did you not take care of her as you should? Did you not see that she had what she needed? Are you feeling in the wrong because *you* did not do what was necessary at the end?'

Melina's whole body shook. Her face burned and her fingers clenched.

An arm snaked around her waist, holding her. Warrington stood beside her. She caught her breath. 'We did all we could. And you did nothing but throw colours on to canvas a world away. That takes no true talent.'

'My painting is art. It was what she wanted. She knew the truth of art. She saw the value of it. You do not. You see nothing beyond your selfish spirit.'

'Selfish spirit? You left us without enough for food, and yet you live like this?' She waved her hand.

His nose went up and his lids lowered as he looked at her. 'It is not mine to give.'

'My sisters need funds,' she continued. '*Proika*. A dowry. They should not have to rely on scraping the earth and hoping rocks grow food so we can eat.'

'I do not give you funds because it is time you each learned to stand on your own legs, not toddle about like children looking for a teat. You should all have wed before now.'

'We have no dowry.'

'Bah…' He shook his head. 'Do not tell me the men of the island cannot overlook that. I am well aware of how they think. You three could each find a husband if you wished. It is only your haughty airs that keep you from it. When you get hungry enough, you will learn what I mean.'

She appraised him. 'We are better off without you. When you left us, I was angry. I thought we needed you. Now I see. We didn't. We were fortunate you left.'

'Melina.' Her father's voice sounded the familiar angry bark he used when disrupted. His eyes flashed. 'You know nothing of life. On the island—it is a different world than England. My marriage to your mother is not legal here and I have no call to support you, now that you are of age. And you have no right to speak so to me. A man has to have a woman. Especially an artist. We must have our senses fulfilled to continue to create. It's nature. And your mother is dead. My life on the island is gone from me.'

She paused and listened to her own words as she spoke them. Hearing her truth as he heard it. 'When I was a child, I had hoped I would some day visit England with you. I worked so hard on my speech and my letters. I am here now and it's not as I expected. You do not have to worry I think of you as my father. One cannot keep what one never had. So I will not miss you.'

Hawkins stepped forward. He stopped only an arm's length from her and he turned to Warrington. 'It doesn't matter who you are.' His words came out as a snarl. 'I will not have it. I don't know what she told you—and how she convinced you to bring her here. Say what you wish—I cannot stop you. But get her out of my home. You will not sully my house.'

'Melina—' Warrington said.

'Don't talk of this.' The man spat out the words and then stepped back. 'Get out. Now.'

Warrington leaned into Hawkins's face. 'You don't deserve her for a daughter and she deserves better.'

Hawkins stepped backwards, to the door. 'I want her gone.' The plain words bit into the room. Hawkins couldn't seem to stand still. He moved a step sideways, huffed a breath and then paced the other direction. 'Gone. Keep your distance from my family. I don't want my—' He turned to Melina. 'You are most distracting. You always were. I do not know why I ever painted you.'

He'd just given her one of his most severe cuts—she was not worthy to be captured on canvas.

Moving quicker than Melina thought possible, Warrington grasped her father's clothing at the neck and pulled the man forward.

'You will support your daughters.' His words were a command.

'No.' She lurched forward, tugging at Warrington's arm, but it didn't move. 'No,' she shouted again. 'I will find another way.' The statue. 'I want nothing from him. Nothing.'

She wrapped both hands over Warrington's sleeve, holding him.

Warrington stopped, jerking his head to indicate the painting. 'How much for that?'

Her father's eyes moved up and he looked above the fireplace. 'It's not one of my favourites. I can hardly stomach it.'

'Price?' Warrington demanded, voice slamming into the walls.

The muscles moved in her father's face. 'I plan to throw it in a rubbish heap.'

'Nonsense. It has small value. Even life has small value— sometimes. Such as yours—now.'

Hawkins waved his hand. 'You may have it. Burn it. It means nothing to me.'

Warrington released him. Hawkins fled the room. Within moments, a door slammed in a distant part of the house.

'Warrington.' She stepped forward, putting her palms flat to his chest, holding firm enough she felt heartbeats pounding through his silk waistcoat. 'Let us leave. I cannot bear another moment of the scent of fresh paint.'

He moved, taking the artwork under one arm, and put his other hand at her back, walking her through the doorway.

Melina stepped into the hall and a woman stood just beyond the open door, staring. Her hair was pulled into a silver chignon. She wore at least four rings on each hand and each jewel outweighed the finger holding it.

She gave Melina a wavering smile. 'Hope you had a pleasant visit, dear. My husband rarely sees visitors this time of day.'

Melina caught herself before she said *I know.* Warrington touched the small of her back, nudging her forward. She took a step, snagging the hem of her dress under her shoe, making a small stumble. Warrington caught her elbow. 'Careful, sweet.'

'Do you need a cup of tea before you go?' The older woman stood directly in Melina's path, but her eyes showed only kindness.

Warrington gave a bow to the woman. 'My pardon...' his voice caressed the words '...as we must be on our way. We have...duties to return to.'

'I understand.' She smiled at Warrington and moved back. 'I hope your trip home is pleasant.' Then she looked at War, puzzlement in her face. 'I believe I was acquainted with your mother before she passed on. The Countess of Warrington?'

'Yes,' Warrington agreed and shepherded Melina out through the doorway.

Melina walked without another mishap to the stairway, but even though her steps were sure, her mind stumbled.

She'd just met the woman her father had married long before her mother and now Warrington had a painting— the only one she knew of that had her mother and her sisters in it.

She tried to get comfortable in the carriage seat, wishing the air didn't seem so thick and hard to breathe. Her father's rage hadn't really surprised her. If he'd acted any other way, that would have been unexpected.

Warrington handed her the painting, but she didn't look at it.

'Of course it's yours.' The calmness of his voice told her he'd been prepared for the fury. But then, he also knew of the older man.

'I suppose I must take it. I don't know, though.' She tilted the art to him. 'The house you see plain. But we are in the shadows. Fitting.'

'If you don't want it, I'll safeguard it for you.'

She held it in front of her face. 'I know the woman is my mother.' She let the artwork fall against her chest. 'I don't remember another picture he painted of her. He did one of each of my sisters, and one of me, but none of my mother. That should have told us something, I suppose.'

'At least he cared enough to capture your likeness.'

She grimaced. 'He said art with people in it sold better—an observer might feel something for them.'

The carriage jostled along and she tried to get the sound of her father's voice from her mind. 'I would rather have the stone I left buried on Melos than this painting.'

'I saw the arm you brought on board.' He looked at her. 'I think you've convinced yourself of the chunk having worth. It's the offering you wanted to give to your father to please him after he left you and your sisters. To show him you'd found something of the past. A value. Something from another artist.'

She put her hand to the small ledge of the window. The clashes of her feelings threw her into turmoil.

'You didn't see the expression on the face of the statue.' She pushed her mind to form the correct words, but wasn't sure she knew them. 'Simple rock became the same as my own skin. Rock—became flesh. The fingers. They—' She held up one hand, flexing, twisting her wrist, watching the movement. 'The sight of her—you could feel life—as if you could blink and look again, and her eyes had changed. The carving started as lifeless stone and then someone touched it, and it became alive.'

He caressed the strand of Melina's hair that had fallen again from where she'd tucked it. His fingers wove into the locks, making her breath flutter. 'Melina, you've more life in this wisp than anything made by man.'

Warrington turned, bringing his body closer to her, and lightly touched both sides of her face. The scent of shaving soap and crisp wool surrounded her.

'No painting or creation from things of the earth could ever reach out to a man as a woman's whisper against his cheek.' He gave a half smile. 'Truly, she could be someone he never wished to see again, but in the right moments he'd still be more impressed than with any art.'

'You are talking of simple lust. To feel art is different.'

He nodded, and by the slant of his lips she could tell he placed no store in it.

'Stone, Melina.' He straightened in his seat. 'Art compares little to life. When my son, Jacob, forgets himself and runs to me, showing me a stick that is nothing but a twig, but for some reason he thinks it is shaped like a bird, that makes any decoration in a house seem meaningless. And the reason the statue means something to you is because you hoped for her to rescue you.'

Melina remembered the agony she'd felt when her mother knew, even though she was sick, that her father wouldn't stay. 'Some believe capturing the likeness helps the person live on. True art,' she murmured. 'Not the captain's mermaids. Or probably even the paintings of my father. But when you look at a sculpture or a painting and you can see thoughts in the face of the person the artist captured... You know the pull of their heart. The dreams they have. You feel something.'

'Melina, I can feel the thoughts of the fish women.'

She shuddered. 'A different kind of painting—but it does speak to Captain Ben—although the things they say are vulgar.'

He smiled, eyes crinkling. 'True.'

'I care for the statue I found. It's as if she has the same heart I do and she's waiting to be freed from her hiding place.'

'The statue is still as you left it and it is cold and feels nothing.' He talked softly, and in the same tone he must have used with his son. 'Forget the marble. Forget your father.' He studied her, his own face concerned. If not for the painting in her hands, she would have leaned into him. Would have put herself against his chest and felt his compassion.

She shook her head, a lock of hair again falling across her eyes and tickling her. 'Father once said he wept when he saw beautiful art. And he had some small pieces. One a sculpture of a Madonna. One a miniature of a woman and a painting only about half the length of my hand—so small, and the woman looked so alive you could have recognised her had she walked into the room. Our home was plain, and to see those things…'

'I know what you're saying, but it's not the same for me, I suppose. The paintings at Somerset House. A nice way to spend the afternoon, admiring them. But…'

'The piece I left behind on the island. I care for her. Both her arms broken and now one lost for ever. Because I did not safeguard it.'

'It wasn't meant to be, Melina. Leave the woman buried. Let her rest.'

'Her face— My mother died before I found the bits of carving. When I dug down, scraping the dirt from the statue, I saw my mother's likeness look back at me.' She took in a shuddering breath. 'I must have this woman unearthed. She cannot remain buried. She should live.'

'It won't bring back your mother.'

Her eyes locked on his. 'Perhaps my grandmother posed for it. Or her mother. So long ago that she's been forgotten. And that is why the stone must be rescued. The woman cannot be left buried. She is so near the surface. I brushed the dirt free from her with my hands. She's ready to return into the world.'

Melina had tucked the statue back into the broken archway and covered her, hiding her. But she had to go back to Melos to save the woman. The thought of the likeness lying buried another hundred years was too much to bear. Melina couldn't imagine how long the art had been concealed.

And how, at one time, someone must not have cared. She'd heard of a war fought on the island long, long before. She imagined the invading army must have knocked the archway to the ground. Or perhaps time itself. She could not be sure why anyone would leave such a work. But now Melina knew she needed to get the woman freed from her grave.

She had to escape the world her father lived in and return to Melos.

'Ben will take you to her.'

'I thank you. My sisters. I cannot abandon them as my father did. I cannot leave the likeness of my mother buried. And I will not tell them all the truth about our father. I would like to tell them he fell on a paintbrush and met a fitful end.'

'Be honest. They are not children.'

'Perhaps. Perhaps they can understand it better than I. Thessa, my middle sister, has already said we should forget him. Bellona, the youngest, truly hates him. She doesn't remember when he was kind, only the way he was at the last. And she'll not forgive him for leaving our mother when she was ill.'

She wanted the statue—whether it was worth all she imagined, or nothing. She'd found it and she wished to have an expert examine it. To tell her that her eyes were right.

The dowry—she'd thought it her only reason to care for the statue. But, no. The stone woman had something in her eyes telling Melina she must be freed. Melina had to get her from the dirt. The woman had to be rescued in the same way a living, breathing person would. The same way Melina would have saved her mother if she could have.

The carriage stopped.

'Leave the painting on the seat. I'll make sure the hackney waits for us, Melina.'

'Where are we?' she asked.

'The British Museum. I wanted you to have a chance to talk with the man about what you've found.'

Chapter Fourteen

When they left the museum to return to Warrington's home, Melina fought waves of despair. The curator could promise her nothing. He could form no opinion. Of course, he would like to be the first to see the find, but he must inspect it and have the statue examined by others before he could even guess at its worth.

She stepped back into the carriage, Warrington following behind. Pulling the painting into her arms, she rested her chin on the gilt edge of the frame. 'I want to get London behind me. To forget my father's ways and find a way to take care of my sisters. I fear that when I go back, Stephanos will have already noticed them because I have left. I warned them many times not to go near him. He pirates for Greece. He plunders and gives the funds to the island, and to people who are planning to overthrow the Turks. If he is caught, it would be dangerous to be his wife.'

She held her hand out to brace herself on the window facing, and then looked over her shoulder. 'Before Father left, he told me Stephanos would make a good protector for me and I would be able to take care of my sisters. Yet he knew of Stephanos's trips at sea and the risk of being seen as too close to him.'

She half turned to Warrington. 'Father would never have

emptied our mother's slop bucket. Or his own. They would have overflowed.'

'I am thankful for the pails, Melina. I believed I had learned my lesson. I would not let a woman's face or body move me should I not wish it. And on a miserable ship when I had no desire in me until I saw you, I was burning to get you to my bed.' His booted foot kicked the inside of the carriage across from him. 'On the blasted ship—I was back at the mercy of a woman's body again. Smelly slop buckets. Ridicule from the mates. And *you* turned out to be…not what I expected. I cannot trust myself to know a woman's true heart. True person.'

'Don't you feel you know me?'

He moved, taking in a breath in such a way he pulled from her. 'I'm not sure. And it doesn't matter, even if I knew. I cannot exorcise the past I helped create, but I must make sure my son has what he needs for the future. I want to go home to Jacob—need to go home to see my son. But I can't yet.' Warrington's eyes firmed on to something in his memories. 'I have to talk with Cassandra's sister. I want to know who the girl's father is. To see if he knows of the babe, though I would think he does. When Cass returned home, most couldn't have easily guessed she was with child—though I suspected the moment I saw her face. She'd changed. And the date of the birth was not something any of us wanted made note of.'

His hands curled into fists. 'I woke up one morning on *Ascalon.* I wished for the sound of Jacob's voice. Before too many years pass, he'll have a man's words. I'm going to lose my little boy whether I wish it or not and I was on a ship, sailing farther and farther from my own responsibilities.'

He brushed a moth from inside the carriage and it fluttered and found another resting place of darkness. 'I feel nothing for the little girl. I keep lingering here, finding reasons to stay. Because I don't want to return home and face a child who looks like my wife and looks nothing like me. I have to get her from Whitegate.'

'You can't leave a child with no parents.' She turned back to the window and indicated the street. 'I see the children here, and even though we had nothing on Melos, everyone had the same nothing. Some of the little ones here barely have clothing hanging on their thin bodies.'

'She'll have her needs met. But before I make any decision, I have to find the child's father. But I can't leave her with him. He is the one who tried to kill me.'

She turned to Warrington's face, the dim interior of the carriage changing the brown eyes into obsidian.

'But you don't fear him now.'

'No. I'm careful in darkness, and besides...' He laughed and reached to his boot, pulling a short dagger from a scabbard sewn into the leather. When he held it up, his hand covered the hilt, but the blade was twice the length of the handle. 'Cassandra may be at rest, but she's not one to sleep quietly. When the man stabbed me, he approached from behind, a fortnight after Cass's death. I turned and grabbed his wrist, taking us down, and the weapon fell aside.'

He spoke his next words as if they meant nothing. 'I can't forget what he shouted over his shoulder as he ran. "Mind my daughter". The man stopped my movement with his words—words with the sound of the street in them.'

He stared forward. 'I've small scars about my body of no particular note, which I don't even think of, but I don't like the thin line on my back. A mark Cass left—even though it wasn't her hand holding the blade.' He touched the edge against his thumb, feeling for the crispness that let him know the blade remained razor fine. 'You can't toss aside a weapon that wounded you so easily. It's not a talisman to bring me luck. I saved it to remind me I survived. But I haven't yet.' His laughter barely reached her ears. 'Never, ever will I return to the abyss of my life before. Not again.'

His eyes locked on her. 'You must understand, Melina. I learned my weakness. Learned it well and I won't risk returning there—to that. I am meant to be alone.'

He let his legs stretch long and leaned his head back, resting against the leather squabs, eyes shut. 'My brother is watching my home and he knows of the attack. I hired two extra servants who have no other job than to make sure my country home is not breached. Cass used to say I imagined too much. How many times she told me.' He snorted and opened his eyes, staring at Melina. 'I never imagined my wife would find so many diversions to pursue. I never imagined she would have someone else's child when I was ill. I should have believed every suspicion I had and it still would not have touched the wicked truth.'

'Leave her in the past.'

'I can't. She left too much of herself behind.' He reached out, pushing back the painting from Melina's body and viewing the art. 'The shadows. What was real for me was only shadows for her. Moments meaning little. *What fools we mortals be.* That saying I remember. I had my golden princess and I put her above all else in my heart. I have had many nights to reflect on my foolishness.'

Taking Melina's hand from the side of the art, he pulled her knuckles to his lips. His kiss touched her and then he released her hand. 'Even when I look at you, Melina, I keep wondering if you somehow convinced me of your virginity when it wasn't true. I wonder if you secretly plan to go back to the island to see Stephanos.'

'I have been honest with you.'

'It really doesn't matter. I tried to turn lies into truths for so long, I don't know how to care one way or the other. I can never trust another with that child in my house to remind me what has happened. I'm sure whoever Cassandra dallied with—her sister knows. When Cass left my house, she lived with Daphne.'

He turned to Melina and his eyes had a raggedness she'd only seen in her mother's face before she died. Melina's fingers tightened around the picture frame as the carriage pulled to Warrington's house.

'I know I must find him.' His words were precise. 'I *will* find him. And then I will kill him.'

Warrington stepped from the carriage after it stopped, reached in and took the painting, and with his free hand he helped her on to the steps.

She saw no anger in his face—no emotion at all. His grip on her hand was light. When he released her fingers, he took a coin and tossed it to the driver and gave a wave to send the vehicle on its way.

'I've already sent a message to Daphne and Ludgate telling them I've returned and asking if they can spare a few moments before I go to my country house.' He walked ahead, unconcerned. 'It will be good to see them again.'

She thought of the words he'd said. She had no doubt he meant to murder the father of the little girl. And she could not let it happen. Except for stabbing Warrington, the man was no different than her father. Warrington would be leaving the child without either parent. He would have blood on his hands and another scar, which might be even deeper than the first and harder to ignore.

Chapter Fifteen

Warrington marched inside the doorway. Broomer gave them both a deferential nod and he had the expression of a perfectly trained butler. But the hair standing up on his head gave him the look of just having rolled from bed and he smelled of lilacs. When he took Warrington's coat, a lopsided grin broke out on the servant's face.

Melina moved up the stairs and Warrington followed. In the sitting room, he stopped, staring at the harpoon. He moved his eyes to the mantel, the room tinged with evening's shadows. 'Let me see how your painting looks there, Melina.'

She stared at the art in her hands. At first he didn't think she would agree. Then she placed the picture against the mantel long enough to take down the other one and exchange them.

An explosion of conflicting emotions rushed through his veins, taking him by surprise. Such a simple act she'd performed and it caused an ache in him. And ache for a woman's care in his world. For completion of the ephemeral dream he'd once had of having a helpmate. A woman who was another part of himself.

He could not let the feelings take hold in himself again. But when he saw Melina stand back from the fireplace and look at the likeness of her family, he ached inside. It was too late. He wanted the dark-haired beauty. But now he had enough control he could keep himself from folly.

'Warrington.' Melina strode to his side. 'You are not concerned that I am alone in your house and you've invited people who might see me?'

He let out a slow breath. 'No. Daphne knows of my trials. We've shared letters. Before Cass died, Daphne visited Whitegate to help Cassandra's spirits when she was going to have a third child. This one mine. Only the sisters seemed at cross purposes with each other. They argued. Cassandra locked herself in her bedchamber and refused to speak to us. Daphne left and Cassandra died a few days later. Daphne wrote to me of the sadness she felt because their last words had been unpleasant.' He huffed out a breath. 'I think my wife awaited the third birth with the same joy I had of the second.'

'Daphne was caught between loyalties,' Melina said.

'She tried to warn me before I even proposed to Cass. I perceived Daphne jealous then. I believed Cass wanted to marry me, not my title.' He turned to Melina and shrugged. 'Titles are handy things—if you don't expect too much of them.'

He moved close to the wall and touched the harpoon. 'Like this, I suppose. Nice to have at rare times. Completely useless in daily life.' He turned to her. 'And I have a child in my house. A child who means nothing to me but a memory of betrayal. My illness. My father's death. All seem tied in the little one's face when I see her.'

'Even your father's death? You jest?' She stepped within reach of him.

'No. I am tall enough that if I walk into a hovel, I will have to bend my head, but an imp no higher than my knee has conquered me, her innocent face a trumpet blaring the past. She makes me remember—when all I want is a new beginning.' He raised his brows and shook his head at the same time. 'I cannot return to Whitegate because of the child Cass left behind. When my wife was alive, I pretended the little girl didn't exist. But I can't now. And she reminds me of everything bad of my old life. And the suspicion I have that I still don't know everything that happened under my roof.'

'You tell me your wife had a child by another man. What more could there be?' She took his hand.

At first, he ignored her question. Instead, he pulled her fingers to his lips to brush a light kiss against her wrist. He caught the scent of her soap and his mind flashed back to the memory of childhood innocence and the sweetness of his youth. Before his mother died and his father remarried. When his life had held the promise of every difficulty being no higher than his knee. Before he realised the littlest-sized hurdle could be the biggest to overcome.

He shook his head. 'I tell myself I'm wrong—and perhaps I am.' He took her arms and moved her aside so he could leave. 'But I believe I'd not even suspected the evilness in my home until now. I believe Cass had a secret that died with her.'

'What?' Melina stood so close. He would not have had to take a step to pull her against him for comfort. But he couldn't.

He had brought Cassandra into his life. And the part that still confused him was that he didn't think she'd loved him, but she'd not hated him, either. He felt certain she'd not hated him.

He needed to be alone. To think clearly. Without memories haunting him or the lustre of Melina's eyes.

And now his hopes were fixing on Melina. A woman whose face caught the light with intensity. Melina had an allure of another world. He could not let an impossible illusion take over his life again.

He shrugged. 'I suppose I can feel another storm coming and it gives me unease. I've not put her to rest yet. I wanted to bury her memory in the sea. I came home—but then I realised I had brought you, another lovely woman. The child is still here. The scar. Everything is just as I left it, only perhaps bigger.'

He walked to the window, peering through the opening between the draperies.

'No platitudes?' he asked. 'No sympathy?'

'No.'

'I left Whitegate when Cass returned after her adventure and did not go back until shortly after the birth. I decided I didn't want a whole nest of other men's children popping up around me. I made my view clear—and I delivered my rules if she wished to stay. And she became faithful. Not by choice, I'm sure. A carriage wheel would not turn without my approval. Nor could she sneeze without my being made aware of it.'

He could see nothing but bare shapes in the dark. He pulled the curtains wide, but the moonlight was hidden behind clouds. 'I tried to go back to where we were. To start over. I tried every day. Every night.'

He breathed in the blackness around him, putting his palms flat on the panes, feeling the coolness, wondering what would happen if he let his strength go and he pushed.

'It's not her I hate. It's myself. I loved her. And I wanted her to have another child. This one mine.' His heartbeats almost made him unable to hear his words. 'She was a wanton of the first water, and after the girl was born Cassandra had to have another child for me. It was one of the many conditions I made for her to continue to live in my world. She loved the illusion around us and wanted it to continue.'

He turned. He wanted to leave the memories he'd pulled back into his thoughts. He already felt the shortness of breath and the darkness so thick he had to push himself to move through it. He had to leave the room. 'I hope you have pleasant dreams, Melina.'

Melina watched Warrington leave, seemingly unaware of the world around him except for the shapes he needed to avoid to keep moving. If ghosts were real, the spirit of Cassandra would have been walking along with him. She didn't believe in any kind of supernatural beings, except perhaps goddesses, but that didn't mean his wife wasn't still with him, as strongly as ever before.

She just wanted to touch him and comfort him. Putting her arms around him might not truly soothe him, but for that moment, he would know he wasn't alone with his memories.

Curling herself into a chair, Melina imagined the life he'd lived. She would have thought his wealth made everything simple. But it hadn't. Even now, as she tried not to think about the things of her past, she couldn't. And she'd not had Warrington's heartbreak. The betrayal.

Melina looked at the brown garment she wore and knew Warrington had wanted the frock made in such a fashion. Touching the sleeve, she ran her hand over it. A soft garment, but still a hideous sack.

In Melos, even a grandmother would not make such colourless clothes. If Melina wished to be unseen, all she'd have to do was stand close to a wooden wall. The strangling undergarment the dressmaker had forced on her made no difference because it didn't matter how much her stomach was pulled to nothingness and her breasts were pushed up, out and over, the brown concealed everything.

She remained in the room, thinking about betrayal, until

the darkness surrounded her with the same pressure of the suffocating cabin walls from the ship. Moving to the mermaid room, she began pulling her clothes from her body so she could dress for bed and remembered she was tied into the underthings from the back. Squirming and twisting did her no good.

With her dress left lying on the bed, Melina went back to the sitting room. She opened the desk drawer and found a penknife. Reaching behind her, she hacked the knife upwards under the ties. This garment pinched and should be burned.

When she loosened the strings enough, she wiggled free of the underthing and let it fall to the floor. She smoothed out her chemise and put the knife back into the drawer.

Taking the damaged garment, she walked the hallway to Warrington's room and knocked.

A groggy 'Yes?' came through the wood.

Gathering her courage, she pushed open the door, peering in. Moonlight fell through open curtains, mixing light and shadows. The scent of shaving soap, and something that reminded her of trees with new leaves, lingered in the air. One pillow was on the floor, leaning against the bed. Warrington lay in the middle of the mattress, his fist clenched around tangled coverings. When she stepped into the room, he slowly opened his eyes.

'Broomer—you've changed.' He spoke without inflection.

She shut the door and moved to the side of the bed. She stood so close she could see the outline of his bare shoulder.

'This *thing*...' she tossed the corset over a boot stand '...is broken. And I do not want it repaired.'

'What is this *thing* you just tossed over my boots?'

'A noose for a woman's stomach.'

'They are ugly. Those nooses.'

'I can't breathe in it.'

'Then I am pleased you removed it.' His words were soft, reverent. The husky tones flowed into her skin.

'I worried about you.' She forced the words out. 'You are alone, though you have brothers and a son.'

'You needn't concern yourself, Melina. Men are meant to be alone more than women. But I am thankful for your thoughts.' He rolled to the side of the bed near her, took her hand and brought it to his lips, brushing a kiss along the closed fingertips. He pressed his face against her knuckles while raising his gaze.

His lips parted and sleepy eyes watched her. Tousled hair fell across his forehead. In less than a second, she locked the image into her mind.

His eyes awakened fully. He moved again, the covers rustling, and he waited.

She pulled her fingers from his grasp. His breathing changed, almost stopping. She pressed closer to the bed, her legs touching the edge. He moved back, pulling the coverings and leaving an empty space between them. His eyes flicked to the bare spot and then to her. 'It's still warm,' he said.

He propped himself on one elbow—a tower of strength capturing her senses so much she couldn't blink. His fingers—still callused from his time on the ship—clamped over hers, tugging her forward. But the burning need in his eyes drew her into the bed.

She slid into the cocoon he'd woven with the air he breathed and with the beating of his heart. He bent over her and the force of a wave crashed into her. He was muscle, strength and sinew.

'Aphrodite has risen from the night and captured me.' His words, roughened by emotion, rolled over her. He looked at her and pulled her deeper into his embrace. 'Is there a reason you've appeared before me? A reason you've graced me with your presence?' He stopped, his breath brushed her lips and her body pulsed alive.

He kissed her, a warmed brandy taste. Her hands reached out and the strength under her palms overwhelmed her senses. The power in his body caused her breath to hitch—and she wanted Warrington even closer.

He pulled back and she looked up, completely overtaken by his presence. 'I can resist you in the daylight,' he said, 'but in the darkness, I believe you aren't real. You're a spirit to tempt me and I am in your power.'

His eyes held emotions she'd never seen before and not known existed. Any goddess would have met her match with him. He was like no mythical creature she'd ever heard of. Perhaps one had been so wily as to escape detection and did not let himself be found in any tales, and now he was before her, more compelling than any imagined.

Warrington took one finger, touching the tie of her chemise, and with a tug he unfastened the ribbon and flared the opening. He only barely brushed against her, but she responded as if she had been stone before and he woke her.

His hands slid over her breasts, caressing, sliding down, covering her hips and reaching the hem of her chemise. Reverently, he pulled the garment over her head.

Her fingertips traced the wall of his chest and the pebbled nipples. She could sense the whole of him with the barest touch. He stilled, as though the sensations overwhelmed him.

She splayed her palm, feeling the hair flattened beneath. His chest seemed to go on and on and on and on, but it was only that time had stilled, magnifying her movements, letting her experience a treasure in the feelings.

He hugged her to him, tightening her against the ridge pressing upwards between them.

She ran her fingers over his shoulders, traced his neck and stopped at the tendrils of his hair, holding him. Her movements unleashed something behind his eyes, but it wasn't as if he turned from marble to a man—the opposite. Awareness left his face and he became controlled by passions and light and pulses.

'Let's forget the ship. Let this be our first time, Melina.'

He kissed her once again. All she could taste or touch or know was the overpowering awareness of his body. Her heartbeat had changed into pulsations—sensations beyond what she ever could have imagined.

He put his hand to her legs—her inner thigh—and up, into the centre of her pleasure. He touched her, stroked her, and the sensations became stronger, building, until they burst throughout her entire being. Something surrounded her and caught her and filled her with intensity and wrung it from her, bringing every possible pleasure she could feel together at once, leaving her stunned, and alive and unable to move.

Warrington pressed himself up, the covers falling free. He rose—not from the sea, but like the earth moving a volcano upwards until it blocked out sun and all the rest of the world. Her hands reached up to him, but she had no control over them. Nothing remained in her control. Not him, or herself.

He touched her legs, opening them, but she didn't truly feel his hand, the pleasure was too intense to belong only to one part of her, or to be felt in one place. He nuzzled his face against hers, whispering her name, and then he moved above her.

The moment his body united with hers—the warm rush of him—she bolted alive, pulling at his back, and pushed herself forward, wanting his touch to penetrate all of her.

And she knew when he lost himself in her. Sounds, simple heartbeats sounded as a thousand drums and even then the world became completely silent.

He looked down at her. She didn't know if a second, a minute or a night-time passed, when he whispered, 'Aphrodite.'

And then he rolled to the side and pulled her into the haven of his arms, but it was really no haven. Nothing could shelter her from the feelings he unleashed.

No person could have experienced what had just happened to her and not be changed for ever.

Warrington rhythmically touched the strands of Melina's hair, her head resting on his shoulder. Melina slept, but he had no weariness in him.

How many times had he left his chamber to go to search out Cassandra in the night? And not once had she found her way to his bed. After his illness, he'd been tempted to find a mistress, but he hadn't. Each time he'd sought Cass out after the betrayal, he'd hoped their joining would mean something more than his body's desire for relief.

Cassandra had never pulled him closer—even before Jacob was born. Her fingers rested against him, but they didn't move. Melina's deep gasps had startled him, but they'd also inflamed him, and taken his control. And her hands—clutched at him, gripping him as if she could not bear to let him go.

He shut his eyes. He'd not known. He thought passion was from the body and had not realised it could begin in the deepest recesses of the heart.

Placing the lightest kiss on her head, he slipped his arm from under her shoulders and pressed the covers close. His movement caused her to roll towards him, and in the dimness, he could see her lashes touching her cheek, fluttering awake.

Her hand clasped the covers at her chest, and she sat up. He forced himself not to run a hand down the gentle ridges of her backbone, but to turn away.

Leaving the bed, he padded to his wardrobe and found his own dressing gown. He put it on and sat in the over-stuffed chair.

'Are you not sleepy?' she asked.

'No.'

Melina sat on the disarray of covers, hair tumbling around her shoulders. Pulling the counterpane close, she moved forward on the bed until she sat near the end. She wrapped a hand around the foot post and rested her head against the smooth wood.

'Do you not sleep afterwards?' she asked.

'Usually.' He brushed back his hair. 'This is different.'

She shut her eyes, face still against the wood, bedclothes tucked under her arms, and he wondered if he dreamed the moments with her. But it wasn't an illusion. His mind could not have conjured something so perfect.

Melina was more beautiful than anyone he'd ever seen and the woman he desired more than any other. And his demons surfaced, asking him how many times his own heart had lied to him.

Chapter Sixteen

Before the day was out, Warrington intended to know who Cassandra had met after leaving him to die at Whitegate.

He dressed and left the chamber after telling Melina who would be visiting that evening.

He wanted to be alone so he could think with a clear head. But perhaps he'd picked the wrong room for solitude. In the sitting room, he stopped after one step on to the rug, looking down as if he expected to see shattered glass. He raised his gaze to the gouge on the fireplace.

The mantel was the most ornate thing in the house. Big, white, carved marble and one of the acanthus leaves had been broken off.

More than two years before, he'd been discussing changes at Whitegate's stables with Dane and a messenger had arrived to let them know Cassandra had had the successful birth of a baby girl. The chair had been replaced afterwards. One of Ben's mementos had been broken—perhaps some kind of ship made of twigs. He raised his eyes to the tops of the curtains. His mind flashed on pulling them down from the walls but maybe he imagined it.

He didn't want to be told about that night, didn't want to know what others knew of it and didn't want it known he couldn't recall the fury. He was thankful he'd been miles from Whitegate and wished he'd been far from any other seeing and hearing person.

Now, when the raps at the entrance alerted him of guests, he walked to the head of the stairs. Broomer wasn't in the house to answer. He'd been sent on another of the special errands he excelled at. The maid of all work bustled from a doorway below, a cleaning cloth in her hands, and rushed to the vestibule to answer the knock.

Warrington stepped back, knowing the servant had been instructed to show the guests directly to him. He waited for them, thinking of a spider's carefully constructed web, and how fragile it was. Success or failure depended on the whims of nature.

Daphne's yellow day dress swirled around her as elegantly as if she glided into a ballroom when she greeted Warrington, her hands outstretched. 'Did you have a grand adventure?' Daphne asked, mentioning the reason Warrington gave for his travels. Her husband, Ludgate, entered the sitting room, his crutch working in tandem with his leg. He stood slightly behind her, watching the welcome.

Daphne had Cassandra's colouring. Cassandra's features. But on Daphne they'd taken a wrong turn. Her azure eyes, pert nose and full mouth were spaced too close to each other—giving her a full forehead and long jawline, which had made her face seem wide. But now, with the thinness in her cheeks, her features blended together. Age favoured her, except for the way the shadows around her eyes seemed to make them shrink into her face.

Even Ludgate had a paleness Warrington didn't remember, but then it had been years longer since the two men had seen each other.

Warrington grasped Daphne's hands, lifting one to kiss the air above her glove.

'I would find another word to describe our voyage besides *adventure.*' Warrington released her. 'Ben can make hell sound like a paradise. He put the hook in my mouth, slowly pulled me in, and I didn't know what was happening until salt water splashed all over me. The dousing was warm, but all the same, a rude awakening.'

'Oh, it could not be so terrible…' Daphne's voice chided, and she reached briefly to pat his cheek. 'A sea voyage. New sights. New lands. Surely you have some good to say of it.'

Small brackets framed her mouth—ones he'd never noticed before. But he'd not seen Daphne since right before her sister's death. Daphne had returned home after the women's tiff. He'd sent his brother Dane to break the news of the death because he'd not wanted to tell her in a letter. Dane said she'd collapsed and later Warrington had received the missive telling him how troubled she'd been because the last words the two women had spoken had been harsh.

Pushing the memories aside, Warrington chuckled. 'I assure you, it was not a grand adventure. You will not again get me on a sailing ship unless it is at gunpoint.'

Daphne continued into the room, walking past him. 'You jest.' She spoke lightly, but her voice had an edge. 'You want to make it sound difficult so men who travel will appear brave and strong. I dare say you quite enjoyed it.' She pulled at the strings of her reticule, twisting them around her finger, sliding free and then roping them around her hand again.

He heard the forced gaiety. He supposed Daphne still suffered the loss of her sister.

'Of course.' He put warmth into his words. 'I slept every night and dreamed of the novelty of getting stranded at sea in a longboat, with Ben's smelly feet sticking in my face, and I would awake to discover the scent of bilge water in my nostrils. Bilge water. Imagine a swamp so distasteful animals will not even drink from it and that is perfume compared to the sloshing liquid in the hull of a ship.'

Ludgate barked a laugh and nodded to Warrington.

Daphne, back straight, looked deeply into Warrington's face. 'You've darkened in the sun. And you look strong enough to lift a horse.'

His smile warmed, but inside, regret sliced him. Daphne had inherited the heart for both the women, but her presence made his palms sweat.

'I had to experience the whole of sailing, according to Ben,' he said. 'Steering the vessel wasn't so bad. But after working the sails, my arms ached as if I had lifted the masts. The first time I climbed the ratlines, my heart pounded in my ears so loud I could not hear the instructions shouted from below. When I put my feet back on deck, I acted as if I could do it over and over. I didn't worry I'd end up swimming if I fell, but missing the water and damaging the deck. If I did, Ben would insist I scrub my blood from his precious ship.'

She moved to the sofa and turned back to him. 'I'm just thankful Ludgate wasn't along—the three of you would have surely overturned the boat.'

The caring in her eyes comforted him. He'd known Daphne so long and they shared truths that bound them. She'd loved Cassandra, yet she saw her sister's flaws just as he had eventually.

He shrugged. 'Never again. Ben's the mermaid hunter, not me.'

Ludgate's laugh bounced from the walls. His crutch wobbled and he followed his wife to the sofa. He used the wood as a balance, lowering himself to sit. The tool had been a part of his life since a childhood accident where he'd fallen from a roof. Ludgate seemed no more aware of the stick than he was of his own fingers. In fact, he used the aid as another extremity.

'Been thinking of investing in a ship myself—though I don't have a brother to sail for me, of course,' Ludgate said. 'Wanted your opinion.'

'One.' Warrington held up a finger. 'Don't.'

Daphne leaned forward, her voice a whisper. 'So dangerous. I cannot imagine.'

'Truly, I am pleased to keep my feet dry. Don't know how I let myself get talked into it.' Warrington made himself comfortable on the facing sofa. He shook his head. 'We saw no mermaids and everyone looks like a sea monster after anything longer than a fortnight from England. Except, of course, Ben. He kept himself dandified. He is more at peace on *Ascalon* than he will ever be on land.'

Warrington paused. Of course, he was pleased to see Daphne and Ludgate, but this visit had none of the familiarity of before. He felt as if he were talking with two people he had just met at a dinner party and didn't quite know if he liked them or not. Ludgate kept looking around the room and Daphne's jaw appeared clenched. Perhaps she suspected he had a question for her.

'You surely favoured some of it?' Ludgate asked.

Warrington smiled. 'It will take a bigger man than Ben to get me from land again. I've had enough sea air—everything still tastes like salt to me.' He made a face as if he had a mouthful of ocean water.

Ludgate chuckled. 'Can't be that terrible if you two youngsters can tolerate it.' He balanced his crutch across his knees.

'We barely survived. Had a fire when the ship rolled a bit and the bail of a lantern slipped loose from its mooring. The liquid flamed about. I didn't expect when I departed on the journey I'd be bobbing around in a wooden bowl coated in a resin to keep it watertight—resin that just happens to be easy to ignite, especially with a lantern dashed on to it. Nothing matters once the fire starts—but putting it out. If I had any chance of liking the sea, it burned to ash in the blaze. After that, I decided if I had the need to sail again, I'd reside at Newgate for a while. Same luxuries—without the chance of drowning, or burning to death.'

'It cannot be as bad as that.' Ludgate patted a rhythm on his crutch. 'Adventure at sea.'

Warrington shut his eyes. 'Misadventure at sea. Not even a good place for ships to be.'

Daphne shook her head, ear bobs dangling, a teasing gleam in her eyes. 'I think Ludgate should go before the mast if he wishes. Then he would truly know if he enjoys it. Maybe a short trip first, of course.'

'No trip at sea is short unless you go gills up.' Warrington nodded. 'The first day is not terrible. The novelty. But the suffering grows with the days. Your clothing turns to a board from the salt mists drying on the garments. Your face burns from the wind and your hair tangles over your eyes. You listen to the everlasting groans of the ship—the vessel complains, as well.' He put an arm along the back of the sofa, trying to relax. 'Ben didn't even consider it a concern when a wave slammed him into a spar and nearly knocked him over the side.'

Daphne leaned forward, eyes wide and her glove touching her cheek. 'He is well?'

'He will be. I'd rue the day I bought the ship with him, but better for him to be sailing on a vessel he knows than risking a rotted one.' Warrington grimaced and stood, walking to the decanter.

He wanted to get the ugly part of the conversation over. He did want to know who had fathered the child in his house and not just because the man had knifed him. He was curious to find out if one could gut a worm.

Before, he'd not truly blamed the man. Warrington understood, in some deep recess of himself, the man's betrayal. The need for a woman's body could be overpowering. But time had cured that empathy. Now the cur was going to pay.

Warrington filled them in on the details of his journey. By the time the conversation lulled, Ludgate had a jug-bitten look in his eyes and Daphne's face kept pinching when she looked at her husband.

Warrington could feel bile in his mouth, knowing he'd soon be able to say the name of his wife's lover. He no longer cared if the man were a footman, a cit or a king. Death treated all men the same.

He tapped his forefinger a slow heartbeat on to the base of the goblet while Ludgate rambled about some tailor's choice of a button. The man had never been so eternally boring before and he refused to meet Warrington's eyes.

Ludgate knew... Ludgate knew who Cassandra's lover was. Of course he would have to know. She carried on her liaisons under his roof. Warrington's gaze locked on Ludgate's face and anger slammed Warrington's body. Ludgate. Could it have been him? But, no, Warrington had seen the man who attacked him. And one thing he knew, knew positively—he would have recognised his brother-in-law. And the man who ambushed him didn't limp or speak the same as Ludgate.

Warrington sipped his brandy, and just wondered if— if perhaps Ludgate could have had something to do with the stabbing. But he wasn't murderous—he practically swooned if his tea was too hot and couldn't even reprimand his horse or command his servants.

When Warrington rose to lift the decanter to refill Daphne's glass, her eyes darted to her husband. Her words were slow. 'Maybe we should—'

'Nonsense.' Warrington wasn't letting them leave. Let his foxed friend ramble all he wanted. Warrington would garble and warble along with him, right up until the moment Daphne conversed on one particular subject.

Warrington poured the wine for Daphne and more brandy for her husband. 'Please stay longer, Daphne. It's so rare I have guests.'

Ludgate talked on, the liquid in his glass sloshing as he mumbled and sipped. He'd discussed the construction of the frame over the mantel and the way the wood had been carved, and now he compared that to the pictures in his house.

Warrington watched Ludgate's brandy nearly spill. Who else would think of the skill to make a picture frame? Apparently Daphne had heard her husband expound on artistry many times. Her stare was fixed on the wall and she looked to be asleep with her eyes open, entranced in her own recollections.

Warrington didn't for one blink think Ludgate could not know about Cassandra's loose corset ties. Ludgate's valet probably knew about the playthings. The sisters talked. Servants talked. Even the wind carried tales when two people whispered and breezes blew their words into another's ears. Secrets didn't go to the grave. They couldn't lie still.

Warrington asked Daphne about her dog, a little hairy creature smaller than a man's boot. She placed great store in the dog and War kept the conversation going while he eased his way to the pull. When the servant peered in, Warrington pointed to the near-empty wine glasses and the woman left immediately.

When she returned, she brought a decanter, filled, and sat it beside the first. Warrington gave a firm shake of his head and indicated for the maid to put the liquid near his brother-in-law. It didn't take long for Ludgate to put his glass down, prop the crutch at his side and cross his arms. His head bobbed a bit to the side and his half-closed eyes fixed on the tooth decoration. Then Warrington saw the lowered jaw and heard the heavy breathing. Ludgate slept.

Daphne followed Warrington's gaze. 'He's going to be aching tomorrow if his head hurts as I think it will.' She sighed, looking at Warrington. 'But he'll get over it. He always does. I suppose we should leave.'

'Daphne, I have something important we must talk about.' He tapped the edge of his glass. Her eyes narrowed.

'We must go.' She stood, reaching to wake Ludgate.

'No, Daphne.' He stopped her movement with his words. 'This is vital. I need you to tell me about Cassandra.'

The emotions behind her eyes blazed, but he couldn't decipher them.

'I'm sure your memories are as strong as mine,' she said. 'I read her letters again from time to time and I miss her so. Really, I can't talk about her. Makes me too sad.' She stood.

'Who's Willa's father?'

Daphne's jaw dropped and she stumbled, almost falling back to the sofa. 'Warrington—this is not proper conversation.'

'Daphne.' His voice brooked no argument. 'I need to know.'

She grasped her skirt in both hands, shaking her head.

He put his glass on the side table and stood. He reached out, moving forward and securing her elbow. 'Daphne, this is about a child's life.'

She turned back to him, eyes flat. 'We won't talk of this. I lost as much as you. Nothing will ever be the same.'

'That may be. But I need to know who Willa's father is.'

'Why, you, of course.' She pulled from his grasp, but he

grabbed her fingers before she could jab Ludgate awake.
She jerked her hand from Warrington's and pounced on
Ludgate, pulling him up while handing him his crutch.

'Time to leave.' She bit out the words.

Ludgate wobbled and Warrington instinctively reached
out to give him assistance. Warrington felt a stab of guilt
while he helped his friend down the stairs. Warrington
hadn't thought of the trouble Ludgate might have walking
should he drink too much. Loading the sotted man into the
carriage was no easy task. Ludgate mumbled his gratitude
before sliding back into the squabs and closing his eyes.

Daphne avoided Warrington's gaze when she rushed into
the conveyance and shouted to the groom, 'Home. Now.'

Warrington turned back to the house, angry with himself, but more displeased with Daphne. She knew. He could
not blame her for wanting to keep Cassandra's confidence
if she'd been alive, but this was a different matter.

Then he wondered if a spider ever built two webs at the
same time. A good practice.

Chapter Seventeen

Warrington walked to Melina's door and knocked. Melina peered out, a question in her eyes. He took her by the hand and she squeezed his fingers. He led her to the sitting room.

'They've left. Daphne claims not to know. But it doesn't matter if she doesn't tell me from her own mouth. Perhaps I only asked her to see if she would speak of it.' He stopped near the fireplace, and stared at the chip in the mantel.

Melina didn't sit. She put her hand on his forearm.

He gave a long blink and nodded. 'My illness before Cass left—I have not been able to get it out of my mind. Something about the watchfulness in Cassandra's eyes before I became ill. Suddenly she was at my elbow every moment, watching me. Even putting a palm to my forehead.' His lips twisted in mockery of a smile. 'She'd never shown such care for me before. Not long afterwards, my stomach began to revolt, my heartbeat changed and I could hardly think of anything except how ill I was. Cassandra's concern vanished and so did she—with my son. To protect his health, I was later told. I wondered if she'd tainted our food.'

When he'd finally regained his strength and reviewed the household ledgers and accounts, he discovered that Cassandra had struggled through his illness at the *modiste's* and the perfumer's, and even the stationer's—and she never neared ink because it might stain her hands.

'Because she didn't care for you, didn't mean she wanted you dead.' Melina squeezed his arm.

'It certainly didn't mean she wanted me alive, either. My father died of the same sickness I had.'

In the days she was gone, Cassandra became visible to him in a way she'd never been before.

She never let herself be alone. In her quiet moments, the maids would work with Cassandra's hair or fingernails, or somehow change a dress she liked, and he would be aware of the gossipy hum of conversation. Not only did Cass know of every movement in society, she knew if the stable master fancied a household servant and who'd bedded whom.

Cassandra held no past, only the present moment. She'd never had a portrait or miniature of Jacob done and the knowledge plunged regret into him. He'd not asked for a painting, either.

Pulling himself from his memories, he spoke again. 'I found nothing in her chamber to indicate she wished me ill.'

His eyes reflected the past. 'Even now, I cannot believe she would do such a thing. I tell myself I must be imagining it, and after the knife attack, I felt some relief, because she couldn't have planned that. No matter how much I say Cassandra cannot rest in peace and would continue her mischief in her death, I know it's not possible.'

He put his hands on her hips, holding her, and she didn't know for sure if he steadied her or himself.

'I could not go back,' he continued. 'But I could not leave her be, either. If I put her from me, she would have other men's children. If I kept her near, I wanted her in my bed.'

He turned and seized a near-empty glass from the table and raised it as if making a toast to the memory. 'At first I saw her in a halo of sunlight and the world bloomed with

the hint of her rose perfume. Now I hate the stink of roses.'
He turned his back to Melina, took a drink, thumped the
glass back on to the table and continued speaking. 'I don't
believe my recollection of her appearance is tainted—
because as I think of her compassion, I see nothing. Her
heart beat for herself.' He uttered something from deep
within that she couldn't decipher. 'She had very little care
for our son, I suspect. She only kept him with her because
if my father and I died, then Jacob would inherit and, likely,
Dane would oversee things. She thought Dane much more
gentle of heart than I was. He'd never shown her his true
distrust. And I assure you, when he saw her put to rest,
he could not keep the smile from his face. I had him by
the throat before I knew it. We both understood the other,
though.'

Warrington touched a marred spot on the mantel, tracing
where the stone no longer matched the rest of the leaves.
'I've had long enough to mull over it. With me dead, Dane
would not be near enough to scold her sweethearts. She
could be in mourning, cloistered with a bevy of suitable
friends to ease her grief.'

Melina saw him pour more amber liquid into his glass
and the bobble of his throat when he took another sip. She
could feel the brandy's warmth in her own body while she
watched him. No woman of sanity would poison a man who
appealed to the eyes as Warrington did. Even in his stained
shipboard clothing she had been aware of him. He had the
form of a lean Hercules. No, much better. She tilted her
head to the side. 'Don't soak your memories with brandy
and make things worse.'

'I've told you my wife could have poisoned me. You
know she had another man's child and you think I'm making things worse?' His voice lowered. 'If she had shot me

while I slept—would you have told me I must have snored and disturbed her rest?'

'You could think of it every day for the rest of your life. It will not punish her. You will only torture yourself.'

He moved back to the decanter and filled his glass, a challenge in his eyes. 'At this point, if a valet nicks my face shaving, I'm certain he is thinking how lucky I was to lose such a wife and that caused his shaky hand, and I blame Cass for the cut.'

'You admit it?'

He nodded and gave a slight shrug. 'She did enough while she was alive that I can feel justified blaming her for every storm cloud in the sky for the rest of my life. I saw Ludgate and his shaking hands and his movements. He didn't act like himself, nor did he once look me in the eyes. He knows I didn't father the child.'

He drained his glass. 'It just jabs at me she has the last word. I cannot see the little chit without remembering. Yet, the child is innocent. Unaware of her circumstances. Born to my wife in my marriage. My property. To care for. And I can hardly bear to be in the same house with it.'

His lips firmed and his fingers clenched on the glassware in his hand. He walked to the mantel and stared at the picture over the hearth. 'I've grown so distrustful I *did* wonder if Daphne would truly tell me everything. Perhaps she is more like Cass than I imagined. So earlier I sent Broomer to watch outside their home. He has coins and instructions to be quite friendly to any servants who might be leaving or entering the house. True servants—not ones like Broomer. Ones paid to be invisible and often so good at it their masters and mistresses don't realise they are watched. And the employers often don't understand the hint of information given in front of one maid is often shared with another who might have heard something else until a whole story is pieced together.'

A clattering sounded at the entrance and Warrington turned, listening.

'I know the way,' a female voice carried up the stairs. 'I lost a bracelet and I had it when I was…' In moments, Daphne rushed into the hallway.

'I considered what you asked. And I…' Daphne spoke as she crossed the threshold in front of Warrington. Her gaze stopped on Melina, froze, and Daphne took a step back. Her shoulders dropped, and her voice came out dazed. 'Perhaps we should talk privately.'

'Melina is as much aware of the thorns in my past life as I am.' Warrington walked to Melina and introduced her, not by the Hawkins name. 'She needed passage on *Ascalon* and I agreed to help her locate lost family members here in England.' His hand went to the small of her back, and then to her waist, holding her beside him.

Daphne took a deep breath and registered the situation. The edges of her lips dropped before she spoke. 'If you don't care for her knowing, then I suppose I don't, either.'

She paced to the mantel, making the space seem smaller with her flurried movements, her hands clasping and unclasping. Warrington stayed at Melina's side. Daphne faced them both.

'Warrington…' Daphne spoke cautiously, at first, and threaded her fingertips together. Then her words rushed out. 'I know Cassandra wasn't always as demure as a wife should be. When you were ill, she came to my house and I took her in. She was afraid for Jacob's health. But…' she shrugged '…you know how she was…'

'You cannot simply give me the name of the man?' Warrington's voice slashed the air.

Daphne strode to the window, and stared out, her back

to the room. 'After all I'd done for her. I took her in—and I believed every word. I knew her. She spent more time thinking up lies and missteps than most people spend awake. She lied, but never to me—never—I believed. She hated your father. Hated him. I understood. He was a tyrant. But you'd been so good and she came to me when you were sick.' Daphne turned back to the room, her eyes narrowed and lips pinched. 'You were sick. I hadn't expected that. She left you and pranced right into my house like she owned it.' Her voice became shrill. 'I was supposed to just hand her my handkerchiefs and lend her my maid, and wait until her hair was done before I dared leave the house in the morning, taking her here and there in my carriage.' Daphne crossed her arms. 'Always expected me to put her little world back together. And her...'

'So who do you think she could have met?' Warrington's voice slashed out the words.

'Half the town of London for all I know.'

'Thank you for making me feel better, Daphne.'

Her face changed, softened. 'I didn't mean to say that. I truly didn't. She did things and then regretted them.'

'Then she had many regrets.' His lips twisted into a wry line after he spoke. 'I need to know who the man was. Is there a servant you have now who could help me learn who her last lover was?'

'How are you so certain he was her *last*?' The words tumbled from Daphne's lips.

'Fine, then. Is there anyone who could help me make a list of her last lovers? I can hire an expert in mathematicals if you think I might need help with the numbers.'

Daphne shook her head, rapidly. 'No. No,' she said, a blush sweeping her cheeks. 'I didn't mean that, and I'm certain she—' Her voice became brittle. 'I'm certain she couldn't have had but one affection. She slept half the day and we went to the shops until they closed.'

'I'm only interested in learning who the man was. You can't convince me you don't know. You knew her better than anyone and you would have sensed what she was about. And don't concern yourself about hurting my feelings if he is someone I trusted. Right now, I cannot look at a man in London without wondering if he bedded my wife.'

Daphne spoke, compassion in her words. 'You did care for her, though. I watched you dance with her as if the clouds floated at your feet.'

'I don't wish to talk about how I felt for your sister when I first met her. Our feelings were never simple. After she had another man's child in her belly—after it was too late for me to ever look at her the same again—she told me what a mistake she'd made. She said she hadn't even cared for his touch. I believed her. I knew it to be true by the way she smirked about the agonies she caused him by threatening to expose him. She was full cracked, or evil—or both.'

Daphne's face twisted and she didn't speak, just stared ahead.

'Who did my wife share company with when she left me on my deathbed?' Warrington asked again.

She shook her head and clasped her hands in front of her, but her words snarled. 'I don't want to talk about it any more. I believed you loved her. You're no different than my sister.' She speared a glance at Melina.

He left Melina's side, taking a step towards Daphne. His words were stone hard. 'Yes, I am different. I was faithful to Cassandra—against my better judgement. I am a widower now and I am free to do as I wish.'

'An earl doesn't dally with the servants.'

He stood directly in front of Daphne, towering over her. 'Daphne—you could close your eyes to my wife prancing around with another man while I lay ill and you dare find fault with my behaviour. Nor can you disparage Melina. She has the peerage in her family history.'

Daphne scowled disagreement. 'You and Cass were made for each other. I was going to tell you, but now I won't. I couldn't tell you before because I didn't want you to know that I knew. I knew, but by the time I found out, it was too late.' She turned, her skirts flying around her feet as she rushed out.

Warrington went to the door and kicked it shut, swearing. The slam caused Melina to jump.

'So I misjudged Daphne, as well.' He whirled to face Melina. 'She's a traitor to our friendship. She knows who I'm searching for. I cannot believe she would not tell me. Well, perhaps I can. She is Cassandra's blood.'

'She loved her sister long before she cared for you.'

'And Daphne always protected Cass. Everyone in her family protected Cass. And to listen to my *wife*—how I hate that word... To listen to Cass she was misunderstood and never given her due. She didn't even believe she should have to share the stars.'

Sighing, he made a sweeping motion with his hand. 'It doesn't matter that Daphne won't tell me.' He walked to the decanter and arranged the glasses neatly, and didn't re-fill. 'Just wait with me, Melina, and let me have the silence to collect my thoughts. Before the night is out, I expect to have my question answered.

He sat on the sofa, his body in a relaxed pose of his arm along the back, his feet apart and his fingers tapping.

Within an hour, clumping footsteps sounded on the stairs.

'Broomer's not one to tiptoe.' Warrington's face changed, hard and dark. 'He's not much of a butler, but that face of his can smile and words just tumble out of people. Me included. And he can break bones and describe the snap like a musician describes the sound of the pianoforte. A good man indeed.'

Warrington walked to the door and Broomer bounded into the room, stopping by grabbing the facings.

'I don't know if it's the truth…' Broomer's words tumbled out, between his gasps for breath '…but I've been told every servant in that house believes it's one man who was dallying with the fair-haired woman.'

'Speak.' War near bit the word in two.

'Ludgate.'

The small lines at the sides of Warrington's eyes tightened and his face moved forward, as if he needed to hear the word again. 'Ludgate?' he repeated. He reached to his boot and pulled out the knife. 'Ludgate was not the one who dropped this at my feet.'

'Can't explain that.' Broomer's breath slowed to normal. 'But around that time, enough crockery was flying in that house to keep the servants sweeping up for weeks. The man sleeps with his door locked, *if* he stays at the home. They're married, but they keep out of each other's sight most of the time. Was a rare thing for them to go out together like they did tonight. The maids considered it odd.'

Warrington stood perfectly still. 'I won't need you again just now. I'll see you are rewarded for your efforts. However, do not drink overmuch until after we have discussed this again. I suspect you may be needed.'

Broomer smiled, gave a tilt of his head and then the most proper bow. 'Whatever your lordship needs done.' Then his large form turned and he left, each footstep soft.

Warrington strode to the door, but Melina caught his coat sleeve in her hand, moving forward, putting herself in his view.

'Leave it, Melina.' He tried to shake her away.

'I'm going with you. You won't kill him with me present.'

His voice held irony. 'I would not bet a farthing on that. I fed him drink until he was sotted. Then I mistakenly helped him down the stairs so he wouldn't go head first.'

'At least wait until daybreak.'

Melina felt the cessation of movements in his body, so sudden it seemed more of a jerk than stillness.

'Enough. It's a singular betrayal, Melina. And duelling is outlawed. I see no reason to break two laws. One would suffice for this matter.'

'Murder.'

'I prefer to think of it as justice.'

'And should you be hanged, how will Jacob feel? Proud that his father died by a silk rope instead of a hemp one like the common folk?'

'I don't expect to be punished any more than I have already been.' He pressed his lips together and then seemed to pull words from deep inside himself. His eyes flashed a look, a different kind of anguish than she'd ever seen in anyone's face. 'Broomer will happily attest to the fact I never left the house if I need him to. He'll send for a physician and say he sat at my side, praying for the man's quick arrival. Broomer will have two plans, or three, by the time his foot hits the last stair tread. He is extremely loyal and knows his way around, through, under and above the law. He also knows about justice.'

'Justice?' she gasped, tightening her hold on him.

He pulled free and took both her wrists. 'Melina. You should not know of this. It is not your concern.'

'You are my concern. You have already suffered enough because of your wife. You do not need to have more problems.'

'Don't you understand?' His hands tightened on her

wrists. His hair fell forward, brushing at his brows. 'It is not merely my wife who betrayed me. It is the whole lot of them. Cass. Daph. And Ludgate. All.' He dropped her hands. 'Ludgate. Cassandra despised him. I know she did.' He swallowed. 'But now that I think of her, I wonder if any soul lived she didn't hate.'

'Don't let her hurt you now she is dead.'

He put his back to her. 'Daphne and I have had a family affection since soon after Cassandra and I wed—or so I imagined. We were both in her thrall.' He stood in front of the painting he'd retrieved from Melina's father. 'We were both wronged. I had heard nothing, ever, at the clubs of Ludgate stepping outside his marriage. And when he strayed, he certainly did not look far.' He whirled around. 'I will hear no more kind suggestions. Do you understand that I need vengeance for Daphne as well—and against Daphne? How could she not tell me?'

'She couldn't want to speak the words that her husband bedded her sister.'

'I can understand that. But I will take him out of her life.'

'You will regret it.'

'Possibly as soon as Ludgate breathes his last. But at that point I can make no changes. Now I have regrets he is alive. So I am to be plagued with so-called regrets. At least this one will be of my choosing.' His eyes narrowed. 'Daphne. I don't know now whether to hate her or pity her. Cass betrayed her, as well. Nothing can coat the blade of a knife thrust into a person's back like family blood. The added twist of someone you've known your whole life— who you've shared whispers with and dreams with... And they betray you. With no care. Like Cass did with me. And I know it. How we planned for our son before Jacob was born—but the plans were all mine. She listened and agreed—probably planning her next liaison or slippers.

Daphne told me once how she could close her eyes to Cass's selfishness because she'd never seen her any other way and had loved her from childhood. Daphne's eyes aren't closed now.'

His body racked back against wall and his face turned upwards, before lowering again. He grasped Melina's shoulder. 'And she knows. She must have known since before the birth of the babe. She had too much anger to be unaware.'

He let out a long breath. 'Nothing will happen to my old friend tonight, Melina. That is a solemn promise you can believe. I want him sober.'

Chapter Eighteen

Warrington sat in his sitting room and could not keep his boot from tapping the desk leg.

He felt as if he'd spent the night drinking. He should have named his demons. They'd lived so close to him for so long. And they had not grown smaller. He fed them well.

And now they tortured him and Melina had spent an hour talking, trying to convince him of a higher ground, and the merits of forgiveness, while he watched her lips move, knew words flowed from them and tried to devise a way to make his point with Ludgate.

Before Jacob came into the world, War had stayed at Cassandra's elbow. Awed. She grew even more beautiful.

With the second one, he'd had to shut it from his mind and he moved into the town house. Ben had been at sea and knew little of the true events. Dane moved to the bachelor house with Warrington and each night they visited clubs and sometimes attended soirées, where Dane played the bashful rake while Warrington tried to forget he was married, but couldn't.

Melina rose, walked to him and took his face in her hands, her palms cool. She engulfed him in the scent of cleanliness. He didn't know how anyone could smell so innocent and pure. Perhaps it was the new fabric mixed with her soap. And he was surprised she didn't complain of wearing the formless sack. He thought a plain dress would keep her from tempting him so much. A foolish plan that could never have worked.

'You've a son.' Her voice soothed. 'You no longer have to let Cassandra's memory rule your actions. Let her rest or not. But you don't have to punish Ludgate because she couldn't honour your marriage. Think of Jacob. Is this the father you wish for him to have?'

'Melina.' He took her fingers from his face and let them fall from his grasp.

'My father doesn't care for me,' she said, giving a twitch to her shoulder. 'He doesn't have feelings for my sisters. And I can't believe he loves his other children. I've known all my life that we are not as much to him as art. He's told us often. *My gift is my purpose. My gift must be above all else.* You at least care for Jacob. Do not let him grow up with tales of how his father attacked someone because of an unfaithful mother.'

'He'll surely hear the stories of Cassandra.'

She stood in front of him, face earnest, fist clenched at her breast. 'But she'll only be a wisp in his memory. You are his father and he needs you. And he needs more than ever to be able to look up to you and respect you. Do not let him feel he was born of two tainted parents. At least give him one he can know is noble.'

'I don't want him to have two *tainted* parents. I hardly know him, Melina. My son. And I think of him above all else. But I let that whore be his mother. For that alone he should hate me.'

'I dare say he'll get older and find plenty of other reasons. I could probably name ten.'

Warrington's mouth opened. 'Your honesty is not appealing.'

'Stubborn. Forcing Broomer, a servant, to dishonesty. Bedding a woman and bumping her head into the wall, trying to—'

'Bumping your head into the wall?'

'On the ship. You near knocked me out.'

'You should have told me.'

'No…' She waved a hand. 'You were quite intense. And there was the whiskers…'

He stared at her. 'The circumstances were not the best. I told you I am not that bad of a lover.'

Melina wobbled her head. 'If you say so.'

'You do not have enough experience to know. A woman's first time is never quite what it should be.'

She shrugged. 'You say that to yourself.'

He looked at her eyes. 'You witch.'

She blinked.

'You insult me to take my mind from him.'

She touched the back of her head, fingers probing. 'It's still tender—*odyniros.*'

He pulled her into his arms. 'I didn't mean to hurt you. Not in any way. And I did not bump you into the wall.'

She squeaked her disagreement. 'You were consumed in the moment then. Just as you are mired in memories now. Don't kill Ludgate. You don't want to. You want to kill Cassandra. And you can't.'

He pulled her against his chest. She could feel the cloth of his waistcoat and the movements of his coarse breathing.

'You are a witch.' He whispered the words against her hair.

'I don't think you like nice people.'

'Whose side are you on?'

'The children's. And I've never met them. But I know what it is like to have a father you do not respect. And to be without a mother. I'm old enough to understand it, but I don't think they are.'

Strong arms held her and he rocked her briefly, surrounding her in the scent of warm male.

He stopped the rocking movement and leaned back, watching her face. 'Melina—do you have any fond recollections of our time on the ship?'

'Perhaps.' She looked at him and the heat of her memories weakened her limbs.

His eyes changed and he examined her with such intensity—the same way an artist would study a subject to be painted.

He pulled her into his grasp, holding her tight, but before she could gather herself, his lips closed over hers, overwhelming her with a storm of feelings as strong as any winds or waves from the ship. The swirl of his tongue slipping into her mouth tumbled her thoughts so strongly, she could not have remained standing without his support.

The next kiss to her lips was the merest brush. 'Goodnight, Beauty.' He backed away, staring at her, and she didn't know who or what he really saw.

Warrington had stayed from the house in the daylight hours and returned through the servants' entrance so he could find Broomer. Broomer said Melina hadn't stirred, except to ask about the earl, and the servant hadn't been able to tell her what he didn't know. From the spark in Broomer's eyes when given instructions, he still relished a challenge. Warrington gave him one.

Now Warrington sat in the glow of only one candle on the small table by his side. The painting of Melina's family showed murky in the dimness. Tonight, he would have preferred taunting eyes of black-hearted mermaids.

The thumping steps outside the door alerted Warrington. Broomer had his own ways of getting a job done.

War pulled the blade out, the movement releasing the leather scent from the scabbard, and he flicked the steel back and forth through the flame.

Ludgate walked into the room, crutch under his arm. Broomer pulled the door shut behind them and leaned back.

Ludgate paused, his eyes taking in the room. He turned and saw the exit blocked. His fingers tightened on the crutch and his free hand went across his body and clasped the wood as if he needed even more help to stand. 'I knew you would find out.'

Silence and the flickering of the candle filled the air between them.

Ludgate spoke again, his words gruff. 'I know you're aware.'

'Broomer. Leave us and lock the door with the key.'

Without a word, the big man opened the door and left.

Warrington looked to the flame. 'Had I suspected you, I would not have been so slow to find out who bedded my wife. I held her responsible. No one else. But you betrayed me, as well.'

'If you had cared for her, you would have searched sooner.'

He held the blade tip in the flame and his fingers tightened on the handle. He kept his voice conversational. 'I suggest we not get in a match over who cared more for my wife.'

Ludgate spoke, each word measured. 'She was a woman no man could help but desire.'

Rage boiled in Warrington's body, causing a twitch in the knife blade. 'You should not mention your lust for her, either.'

Ludgate stepped back. Someone outside rattled the door-knob. Warrington ignored the sound.

Warrington didn't speak and he could hear Ludgate's breaths from across the room. 'Don't be in a hurry to leave.' He used the blade to snuff out the candle.

'I didn't know she'd return to you. She told us you were dying.' The words sounded through clenched teeth. *'She said you were dying.'*

'Makes it all the better, doesn't it? I'm breathing my last breaths on my deathbed. You're ploughing my wife.'

'Light a candle,' Ludgate commanded.

'I don't like the sight of blood.'

'Warrington. It's over. She's gone.'

'Not entirely gone. Willa, you know. Little girl, about so high.' He held out the hand with the knife in it to indi-cate Willa's height. He was certain Ludgate couldn't see the blade well, but that Ludgate's heart was pounding every shadowed movement into his mind.

He heard Ludgate bump back against the door.

'You didn't find any irony in the fact that she named her Willa Marie,' Ludgate said. 'Marie is Daphne's middle name.' His voice rose. *'My wife's* middle name and my full name is Robert *William* Ludgate.'

'I didn't know.'

'Oh, I assure you, Cassandra knew. Daphne knew.'

Warrington touched the blade tip to the extinguished wick, scenting the room with smoke, and pressed the string down into the melted wax. 'Cassandra would find it humor-ous. Like a final dusting of face powder to get just as she wished. But I want to know why you set a man on me. A man to kill me—when Cass was dead. It makes no sense. You don't want the child—'

Again, the doorknob rattled hard. Warrington kept

his eyes on Ludgate's form. In seeing Ludgate's slumped shadow, he knew the man wouldn't challenge him.

'Open the door,' Melina called through the wood and she pounded against the door.

'Leave us, Melina.' He bit out the words.

'No,' she said, and he heard a push against the door and her words rushed. 'Daphne is here.'

'Bloody hell,' Ludgate's voice rang out. 'I have an elderly aunt, as well. I hope you didn't forget her invite.'

Warrington kept his words soft. 'Trust me, Ludgate. Still not as bad as watching your wife present you with another man's child. I didn't invite Daphne. I don't know how she found out.'

'She watches me like a gaoler when I am in my home. Sends servants and wastrels to follow me about. I can get no peace in my house and rarely visit it.' Ludgate's voice held the brittleness of an eggshell. 'That's why Cass had to return to you. Daphne was suspicious and her mind was wavering.'

'Fancy that.'

The door rattled again, then abruptly stopped.

'She's gone for the key, I suppose.' Warrington stood, the cool knife hot against his fingers. 'I cannot understand why your wife might be upset to have her husband sleeping with her sister. Perhaps Daphne is overly sensitive.'

'I was insane for Cassandra.' Ludgate grumbled out the words, and his crutch top slid to his chest and he held the oak in front of himself, in a protective stance. He whispered, 'My senses left me.'

'But Cass returned to me.'

'I kissed the ground when she left,' Ludgate said, lips snarling. 'I realised—as soon as it was too late—that Cassandra was not quite what I expected. She put me on a string—in my own house. I had to dance at her whims or she threatened to tell Daphne. And Daphne found out anyway. I'm certain Cassandra couldn't rest until Daphne knew.'

'Cassandra had her own sense of enjoyment. I've had enough of games to last my lifetime.'

'You're ten years younger. You've a blade in your hand and I can hardly stand upright without support. I expected you to be more sporting than that.'

'I was…' Warrington paused. 'Your daughter lives in my house.'

'And if you've a wish to be rid of her, I'll see she's cared for. It doesn't matter either way to me. I almost died when I discovered Cassandra was with child. Daphne cannot have children and…Daphne's not what you think, either, Warrington. Daphne wanted me murdered and for you to get the noose for it—because you forgave Cassandra. I know I have no excuse for my behaviour, but even before I strayed, the two women showed a different side to you. *Both* of them did.'

Instead of a rattling sound behind Ludgate, this time the door opened, knocking into Ludgate. He used the crutch to catch himself and remain upright.

Melina rushed in, a key in one hand. Daphne followed, holding a lamp. Daphne's lips were parted, but her jaw was locked in place.

No one spoke and Warrington waited.

Melina tossed the key on to a side table, grabbed the lamp from Daphne and then moved to the sconce on the wall, lifted the globe and lit the candle. He saw her hand quiver when she touched the flame to the wick. Then she moved to the next one and the branch of candles beside Warrington's chair. The room glowed with light.

'Much better.' Melina sat the lamp base down with too

much force. The sound bounced in the room. 'You must see to kill each other.'

'I can manage in darkness.' Warrington met her gaze. She had the same despair in her eyes that he'd felt for years. He couldn't move for the space of several heartbeats. Then he looked to Ludgate. The lamplight accentuated the wan colour of his face. The man looked twice his age.

'We should be leaving.' Ludgate grabbed Daphne's arm. 'I think Warrington and I have discussed enough for one evening.'

'No,' Warrington commanded. 'We haven't.' He switched the knife to his other hand, holding it upright by the tip, in a pitching stance. 'You had some ruffian cut me.'

Ludgate's eyes narrowed. 'I did not. I felt shame for what I did to you. But I had no reason to kill you. And I would not send someone to murder you. A man your size. I would send two, and one with a pistol at least.' Ludgate ran a hand through his hair. 'I wanted no more to do with you. It would not be beneficial to me in any way and I have enough to live with. Your death would not make my life easier. An earl murdered—oh, that would not be noticed, questioned, discussed... You think I want to spend one more moment on the events of the past—no.'

Daphne pulled her arm from Ludgate's grasp while she turned her head to stare at him. 'Warrington. He said he wanted you dead. He blamed you for Cassandra's death.'

Ludgate let out a strangled gasp and turned to Daphne. 'I did no such thing.'

She gave a twist of her head. 'You boasted. You laughed about having your child under his roof.'

'You are mad, Daphne.' He turned back to Warrington and both his hands grasped the crutch. 'I did not. If I would have killed anyone, it would have been that...' his words stopped, eyes locked with Warrington's '...woman.' His voice lowered. 'She didn't care for me. I was a game she played.' He looked at Warrington. 'If it were possible for her to love anyone, she possibly cared for you. She did marry you and she returned to you. She didn't have to. I would have given her funds to go anywhere she wished. I told her.'

Warrington gave a twist of the knife, turning it point down, and jammed it into the tabletop. The sound of the blade vibrating caused Ludgate to jump. Daphne didn't move.

'Daphne—amazing, isn't it—how much you truly favour Cassandra.' Warrington put his hand on the handle. 'Just now. When you spoke, I saw the image of her in your eyes, your face. And when you looked at Ludgate…'

'Cass and I were sisters. We should look alike.'

'And you and I were both wronged.'

Her shoulders tensed and her chin quivered. She breathed through her teeth, then spoke without opening her mouth wider. 'You had plenty of time to get used to Cassandra's ways. You should have made her remain faithful, but when you didn't… You should have gone after Ludgate.' She indicated her husband with a quick nod. 'He betrayed me. With my sister.' Her hands were fisted and she stared at Warrington. 'You should have kept her under control. But you didn't force her back home the moment you recovered from the illness. And I cannot forgive you for that. I told the man who attacked you not to kill you. I told him to limp when he left and not let you see his face, and what words to say. The fool. Both of you. You'd not even searched for the child's father before. I wanted you to get so angry you had to find out. And then discover Ludgate. I was going to tell you myself last night after I left Ludgate in the carriage, when I was positive he wouldn't hear. But then you had *her*…' she jerked her head towards Melina '…with you and I knew you wouldn't leave her side long enough to do justice.'

His ears heard, but he didn't want them to. 'Daphne—I treated you as my own family.'

She gave a careless shrug. 'I treated *you* as my own family.' She gave a lift to her skirts to keep them from hampering her movements. 'I truly did.' Her lips turned up and her eyes glittered when she gave a regal toss of her head. 'Truly.'

'Did Cass poison my father? Me?'

She shrugged, looked around the room and then levelled her eyes at Warrington. 'How could I know for certain?' She pressed a hand to her hair. 'All I can say is that I didn't do it. I would have been assured of the correct amount.' She glanced into the distance. 'It is not that hard to do, I assure you.' She shook her head. 'You can see her plan. Jacob would be the next earl. She didn't like your father at all. Not at all. An illness sweeping the house. Who would think it poison?' Daphne walked out of the room, moving as if she had not a care in the world.

'I know I wronged you, Warrington.' Ludgate stared at the open doorway. 'I wronged Daphne, too.' He stood silent. 'She is not the same since I wounded her. She hides it in front of others, mostly.' He turned to Warrington. 'But you cannot live always in front of others.'

Warrington shook his head. 'It feels that I have.'

'Daphne believes she was betrayed by all around her. Everyone. Me. Her sister. You.'

'I did nothing to her.'

'You took Cassandra back. Daphne received a post from her sister, telling her the joyous news that Daphne would be an aunt—for the third time.' He stumbled over his words. 'I no longer fear for her sanity. It's buried under layers of hate. I fear for my own.'

He touched his cravat and, when he raised his hand, his fingers jerked. 'These things take time.' Leaving the room, he mumbled, 'But there will never be enough time for this to heal.'

Warrington reached for the knife with his right hand, jerked it from the wood and tossed it into the fireplace. Melina touched his back. From behind, she slipped her arms around him. He covered her hand with his.

'My wife's love could be harsh in so many ways. It would have been better had she hated me.'

Melina rested her head against his back. 'Now you can let her go.'

He took Melina's hand, brushed a kiss against it and stepped back. He sat on the sofa and stretched his legs out and his stare focused on the candle. 'I no longer feel anger at the trouble Cassandra caused me. I only feel anger that she caused so many others to suffer. Ludgate has his own troubles. You're right. I'd prefer to strangle Cassandra and it would undo nothing.'

He gave a long blink and looked at her. 'When Cass came home, I raged. She had to agree to my terms and they were not easy ones. Cassandra was no innocent victim. I suppose it didn't matter to me earlier who the father of the girl was because I already knew who the father wasn't. It wasn't me.'

He leaned his head against the back of the chair, his face towards the ceiling. He shut his eyes. 'And I can be thankful that Jacob and the girl will not have to grow up living with their mother's penchant for finding trouble.'

Warrington turned his head to the side and opened his eyes, watching Melina. 'I wish you'd seen none of this, Melina. When Ben finishes his next repairs, I'll see that you get passage home and I'll make sure that whatever is needed for your retrieval of the artefacts to be taken care of.'

Melina kept her irritation hid. He talked too calmly of sending her away. She didn't ask that he throw himself on the knife blade, but he might *look* nicked.

'I will be happy to see my sisters.' She blew out one of the candles.

He stood. 'I believe Broomer needs my company. I'm sure he has a tale to tell me and maybe a song he heard at Drury Lane. He's not fit for polite company sometimes, which makes him all the better for me.'

At the doorway, he looked over his shoulder. 'I'll not trouble you tonight, Melina. I know you aren't of the same cloth as Daph or Cass. I knew who Cass was, but until tonight, I believed Daphne someone else entirely. I thought her a sister.' He shook his head. 'Lies. Everything. Lies.'

Chapter Nineteen

That night, Melina had slept lightly. When she woke in the early hours, the stillness of the house seeped into her skin. She slipped from her bed and crept to see if she could find Warrington.

At the doorway to the sitting room, she stopped and saw candles lit on each side of the room, but only one candle glowed in each branch. Warrington sat where the light from the window would have flowed over his shoulder had it been day. Instead, shadows danced over his face.

His eyes were shut and his head sagged to the side. She supposed he and Broomer had swallowed enough ale to drown themselves. His fingers were clasped together and one leg was sprawled out, the other bent at the knee. He still wore his frock coat.

'Melina.' He spoke without opening his eyes. 'Don't stare so.'

He moved only slightly, upright, but not as relaxed. When he looked at her, he took in her body. She could feel his eyes as she watched his face. The instant his eyes lowered to her breasts, she felt the heat ignite in her. His gaze slid to her waist, and lower, leaving a fiery heat trail that moved inward.

'Again, Aphrodite has risen from the sea.' His voice

unfurled. 'Arisen from the shells and stands before me. A vision. Her hair falling over her shoulders. Her eyes reaching into the soul of everyone she sees.'

'You're foxed.'

He shook his head, but his eyes remained on her, apart from his words. 'Yes and no. If I am drunk, then you must blame yourself. Because it's your appearance that has addled my senses.'

'Is that all?'

'Yes. There is not enough drink to wash my memories from me. I tried it once and it could not be done in three days. I would have had to swallow enough to destroy my whole mind and I didn't want that.'

She didn't speak. He kept her there without a word, only the presence of his being holding her captive.

She turned to leave, reassured he was at his home, safe.

'Stay, Melina. You truly do owe me that much if for no other reason than I helped you escape from this Stephanos you detest. But I cannot stand the notion of a man touching you.' He gave a humourless laugh. 'I do not want anyone you do not desire touching you. Even myself.'

'You need to be alone.' The wind outside picked up, reminding her of the night's gloom. But perhaps the true darkness was in his eyes.

He breathed deeply, moving back in his chair, sitting straight and clasping his fingers in his lap. 'I should have drank myself to sleep tonight and prayed to dream of shipwrecks.'

'There's still time.'

'Sweet Melina.' He laughed. 'You so guard your speech.'

'Perhaps.'

He softened his voice. 'I hope not.' He turned his face back to the dark window. His gaze took her in. 'If you were to think of poison, my dear Melina, or wish my death, I would be indeed fortunate to get a second chance. You determined to set sail on a ship of strangers and did. You would not run if the deed were not accomplished. You would try a different route.'

Melina felt a chill at her toes that crept up, but she hid her shiver. 'I have *never* even seen poison.'

'You have yet to marry.' He brushed his hand across his knee, picking at the doeskin. 'My wife killed my son's grandfather. My wife— How do I tell my brothers that our father is not here because my wife didn't want him around any more?'

'I have met Ben. If Cassandra's ways were so obvious— if it could be suspected that she would do such a thing—you know he would have told you. Did you suspect, before you became ill, she might try to murder your father?'

'Do not ask such a question.' His eyes, dark, locked on hers. 'I know you are trying to make a point, but to even suggest I could have imagined such a thing and allowed it to happen is intolerable. And along with my father's death on my conscience, I have her spawn with Ludgate to keep.'

'He said he would care for her.'

'I may not think much of the child, but I do not trust him to find a home for her.'

'I'll help you.'

'You've never even seen her.'

'It doesn't matter. She's a little girl. An orphan, in a sense. My father left me to starve and has no wish to see me. She shouldn't suffer because of something she had no control over.'

'Happens all the time. Though I'll pay her way.'

Melina spoke softly. 'Then let me take her back to Melos. She should have a family. I will treat her as a daughter.'

Warrington shook his head. 'My problem. My responsibility. I will see to it. Broomer can locate a couple willing to raise her as their own. I will examine his choices. You already have sisters to concern you.'

'You would send a servant for such a duty?'

'I would send the best person for the task. And that is Broomer. He knows what goes on in the world outside the peerage because he doesn't always have work inside the house and finds his way among the streets. When he talks, people think he is a simpleton and they don't notice how much he listens. I didn't at first. I've already told him that the little girl might need someone else to care for her and he knows of a place where she might find a home. When she and Jacob arrive here, she can meet her new family.'

'She does have a name.'

'Yes. She was named for her father. Thank you for reminding me. But I had not forgotten.'

'Perhaps you should forget. Remembering only serves one purpose—to cause you discomfort.'

He shut his eyes. When he opened them, he turned his head from her. 'That is one thing I will change. I will make the people who take her agree to give her a new name. Something they choose. Perhaps it will give them closeness to her.' He pushed himself up. 'This isn't her fault. I want the past behind me, and even if she doesn't know it, so does she. She deserves a chance to begin anew.'

He opened a desk drawer, pulling out a bottle of ink and paper. 'I'm sending Whitegate's butler a note. I never took my father's room after he passed. Cass and I had living quarters of our own, smaller but comfortable. Now I want my things moved to my father's chambers. While Jacob is here, the changes can be made. I'll return with him.'

Melina wanted to touch him, but didn't. She wasn't sure if she wanted to caress his jaw, feeling the skin, or slap him to try to shake him from his feelings.

'You're not accepting and forgetting, you're just pushing the reminder where you cannot see her,' she said. 'You still have the rage.'

'I do have the anger.' He dipped the pen in ink and wrote as he spoke. 'I just found out for certain that my wife killed my father. For nothing. No true reason. The only person she really had reason to kill was me. But I know she didn't like my father. Didn't like his wife and didn't like his controlling so much of our lives.' He dipped the pen again and continued writing.

Melina turned her back, feeling like a goddess. One who had come to earth only to discover that men were mortals and could not accept a peaceful world when they had opportunity.

'It is only what is inside you keeping the pain alive for you.' She did not face him, but her voice was loud enough that he could easily understand her words.

'A person who has never been burned cannot know what it is like to have the experience of fire consuming the skin and the way it lingers. The deeper the burn, the longer it takes to heal and to forget the pain.'

'You plan to live the rest of your life alone?' she asked, feeling each word jar into her heart. And she would live the rest of her life with the memory of him remaining in her mind and she'd wonder if he'd ever put the betrayal behind him. She doubted he could. If she thought he would, she might proceed differently. Because she would never forget the Earl of Warrington. And she didn't even know his given name.

'I think it best.' He didn't look up from his writing.

She stared at the bent head and didn't believe he was unaware of her. But she was being dismissed. Just like the child he thrust from him.

The wind pushed against the house. But it wasted its

time. The house was Warrington's. Immovable. Closed tight. And very dark.

Warrington's head jerked up and his eyes narrowed, but he listened. The noise wasn't only the wind, but someone at the door.

Warrington stood. 'Sounds like someone trying to break inside.' Grabbing a lamp, he hastened to the stairs.

Broomer had a flintlock at his side, but he'd opened the door to Ludgate. The frail man stood at the threshold. He looked to the top of the stairs. 'I must speak with you privately.'

Warrington waved an arm, sending Broomer on his way, and gave a nod to Ludgate. They moved back into the sitting room. Ludgate followed and stood just inside the door. Melina saw scratch marks across his jaw. He clasped something hidden in his hand and he paced in place, the crutch tapping along beside his leg.

Ludgate collapsed on to the sofa and pulled the crutch to him, resting his forehead on the wrapped top of the wood. His eyes were closed. 'I am so sorry, Warrington. So sorry. I had no idea.'

'I am making sure Willa is cared for.' Warrington's voice cut the air. 'You do not have to concern yourself with her ever again. In fact, you will not be allowed to.'

'I am not talking of that.' His head moved when he spoke. The sound of Ludgate's breathing drowned the sound of the wind outside.

'I saw…' He paused, finding words, holding a bottle. 'Daphne was too quiet when we returned home. Daphne is…no different than Cassandra in her own way. When I first heard of your back being hurt, I wondered. But Cass was no longer alive. That left only Daphne. I thought she might try to kill me, but never you. And I had never suspected the illness in your house anything but a fever until tonight. I only suspected Daphne of wanting me dead. Nothing else.'

He raised his eyes. 'Arsenic poisoning can look like cholera. Daphne had a bottle of the poison. I rarely live in the house, but tonight I did not leave. When she stirred in the night, I listened. I pried a bottle of arsenic from her fingers. Meant for me and I knew it. She said…' He paused. 'She'd decided since you weren't going to kill me, she'd have to do so. Especially after I told her I would send her to the country because I believed she knew of Cassandra poisoning your father and did nothing to prevent it or to discourage her.'

Ludgate gulped out the words. 'She killed Cassandra. When Daphne returned home Cassandra died shortly after. And when I confronted Daphne tonight, she told me. She said they called the powder their guarantee of a happy marriage.'

'But why didn't Daphne kill Cass before Willa's birth?'

'She didn't expect… They were together every day and she didn't believe at first that the child was mine. I assured her it could not be possible. She didn't think her sister or I could betray her so. When Cassandra left, the baby came too early. Daphne knew the child couldn't have been yours and it had to have been conceived earlier. She knew the dates. And the girl's name was a slap. But Cassandra wouldn't see her. When Daphne received the letter from her sister telling of the chance of another child, Daph visited without telling Cassandra first. She said she had emptied a bottle of the Fowler's Solution medicinal she found at your house and put the poison in it, then told the lady's maid to be sure that Cassandra was given Fowler's Solution as it would ease her discomfort. I didn't know the truth until now, but I suspected. I've hardly stayed in the same house with Daphne since the little girl was born because she made my life a nightmare. I didn't suspect she wanted you to kill me, and when you didn't, she went for what she called the marriage powder. *Till death do us part,* she said. She claims it is why the vows are written such.'

'Will you tell the magistrate?'

Ludgate shook his head. 'No. I am the only one who heard her words. She can easily lie that she said nothing. That I did it. The footmen and butler have her contained now. She's still raging—at me—for the betrayal. I don't want her hanged. I will see she is confined to Bedlam. It is only my word and hers, and I do not want this to become known. I told the servants she has lost her senses and it is the truth.' Ludgate spoke quietly. 'The little girl should not have the spectre of this following her. The truth is bad enough, and what if it is embellished even more? Do whatever you want with the child and send an accounting to my man of affairs. The funds will be paid. I don't care.'

He left, then stopped and looked back. 'But I would place the little one in a home where she can never find out about her true birth, one with a lot of spiritual guidance. She will need it.'

Chapter Twenty

Warrington had stood at the window an hour, waiting for the carriage, watching the place the town coach would first become visible, before he saw Dane, riding Chesapeake. The carriage was next.

Warrington strode to the front entrance, stepping outside as the vehicle stopped.

'Father,' Jacob squealed, opening the town-coach door. A woman's arm reached for him, but missed, and the child scampered out.

'Careful,' Warrington shouted. Jacob dashed to the doorway and threw himself against his father's legs.

'You're back,' Jacob shouted. 'I knew you were back. I knew that's why Uncle Dane said we must come to London.'

Warrington could see the same family traits of his brothers in Jacob's long-limbed stance. He had the jaw that could jut into the same stubborn pose.

'Yes,' Warrington said. 'Did you behave for Uncle?'

He nodded his head. 'We fished. We rode. We did everything.' He stretched the last word out, making it take longer to speak than all the other words he'd said.

Warrington knelt to one knee in front of his son. 'I brought you black rocks from an island we visited, and some shells I'm sure you've not seen before, and a hat made by a wise old woman who said the boy who wore it would grow tall and strong.'

'I'm tall and strong now.' He flexed his arm and made a muscle. 'Uncle says I can carry a sword soon—then we'll fight.'

'Oh, I look forward to that.' Warrington grabbed his son by the shoulders and gave him a quick pull against him. Jacob somehow always smelled like porridge. He let him go, thankful his brother couldn't see his eyes.

'Can I have a real sword?' his son asked.

'Soon.' He stood and deep inside himself he was pleased Jacob wasn't old enough yet to heft the weapon. Jacob stayed at his father's side.

Whatever else Cassandra had done wrong, she'd done one thing right and given him Jacob. Although he was sure that if she'd known how the future would turn out, she'd never have let Jacob be born. If only for spite.

Dane had dismounted and given the reins to the coachman. Then he helped the nursemaid from the carriage. The servant brought out the little girl. The older woman almost stumbled over her skirts as she moved down the steps, but Dane steadied her.

Dane's boots clicked on the walkway as he strode to greet his elder brother. He and Dane could not be any closer in age or likeness unless they were twins. But Dane made his own light and danced through shadows. He just preferred to keep his nose in a book, or a ledger, or a garden.

No one ever mentioned the slight—very thin—scar running from in front of the ear to the base of his cheek, but Dane would complain of it itching. An occurrence that only happened around females who could offer sympathy.

Dane stopped at his brother's side, reaching out to shove Warrington's shoulder. 'When you were late, I was sure you and Ben had a fight and had fallen overboard. I was going to send out a search for you next year, or the year after. Whenever I started missing you and had run through your funds.'

'I had a wonderful time. Would have stayed longer, but knew you'd have my house tumbling down if I didn't return—and I missed Jacob.' Warrington strode around Dane, leading his son into the house.

Broomer walked out from the servants' quarters, giving a huge bow to Dane. Dane handed his hat to the manservant.

Broomer gave another bow and took the hat, holding it in both hands as he left the hall.

Dane's easy smile of welcome stayed on his face. Then he saw Melina at the top of the stairs, stilled and immediately his gaze darted back to his brother, questioning.

Warrington made sure his face showed nothing. He introduced Melina. 'She'll be taking care of the children when the nursery maid needs help.' Warrington looked at his brother, giving him a brief nod. They moved together up the stairs, Dane at the end of the group.

Warrington saw Melina's smile when she saw the little girl.

'You must be tired from the journey,' Melina said to the nursery maid. 'Let me take the little angel.'

With a stoic face, the maid handed the girl into Melina's waiting arms.

'I'll help you get them settled,' Melina said, leading the older woman into the room Melina had prepared for the children.

Dane watched, unspeaking and unmoving.

Warrington kept his hand on Jacob's shoulder, keeping his son near, and led Dane in the direction of the sitting room.

Once they reached the larger chamber, Warrington

smiled at his brother. 'Hope you do not mind finding some-where else to stay. The children and the nursery maid will need rooms. The governess is in the other room.'

Dane's brows rose. 'Not at all. Not at all. I'm sure I can find someone who cares about me who'll give me a pillow and scraps from their table.'

'Aunt Adelphinia is always asking for you to spend more time with her,' Warrington said.

Dane turned to him, face solemn. 'Exactly what I was thinking. I so love playing whist with her and her friends. It brightens my evenings.' He grinned. 'But truly, War, you would not believe the tales those genteel ladies tell. They delight in shocking me.'

'You're easy to shock.'

Dane shrugged. 'True. And did you have all the adven-tures you dreamed of on the journey? You were gone lon-ger than expected.'

'Only because we found an inviting island...full of lovely ladies...' He let his face reminisce on glorious sights he never saw. 'You need to go with Ben next time.'

Dane's head bobbled and his smile was smug. 'Oh, you'll not catch me that easy.' He paused. 'So the trip—as bad as I said?'

'Worse... Your brother...' Warrington grumbled. 'Put a captain's coat on him and he thinks he's Captain Cook without possibility of demise. I would insist you go with him on the next voyage, but that would surely increase the danger. With the two of you on board, the ship would sink. It was perilous enough this time.'

Dane watched him, waiting.

'Ben banged himself up sliding around the ship in a storm. But he's healing.'

'Papa,' Jacob interrupted, looking at his father. 'I have

a boat. I brought it. Nurse is keeping it for me. I want to show you.'

War brushed Jacob's hair from his eyes. He was looking as ragged as the cabin boy. Warrington nodded and Jacob darted out through the door.

'And the, uh…' Dane tilted his head to the left, in the direction Melina had left. 'The woman—you brought her back because we have no suitable English governesses to teach Willa the ways of our country.' His eyes twinkled. 'Instead, you find a woman—I'm sure you noticed—and install her in your house.'

'We will not be discussing it.' He sat on the sofa and looked at Dane. 'And you will keep ten paces from her at all times—and keep your head down when she enters a room.' He grinned at his brother. 'Perhaps you should just leave now.'

'I will visit Aunt Adelphinia. She says I am her *favourite* nephew.' Dane spoke lightly, but he moved to lean against the unlit fireplace. 'And is the mighty Captain Ben returning home before he sails again?'

'He had to stay on *Ascalon* to make sure the repairs are being completed and to prepare her for the next voyage. As soon as the ship is ready, he'll sail. But he will make time to see you and tell us he's leaving.'

Dane nodded, lips pressed before he spoke. 'I believe I'll have to speak with Ben. You might not want to discuss the woman, but I'll wager he will.'

'Captain Little Brother will tell you Melina did spend some time with me. I took care of her when she was ill as I didn't wish for any of the randy seamen to push themselves on her. And he will find great joy in telling you how he made up senseless errands to keep her busy so I could not enjoy her company to the fullest.'

'Ha. If you had that woman near you, then you had enough time to find some comfort.'

'Doesn't signify. She's here. As far as Jacob will know she is merely another servant. I've certainly dressed her in sacks.'

'Those shapeless rags she is wearing do not hide all of her.' Dane teased with his eyes.

Warrington nodded, picturing Melina's form. If he had found Melina before he met Cassandra, things might have been different, but he hadn't. And he had Jacob. Warrington needed to be a true father and he'd already brought enough turmoil into Jacob's life.

'Have you heard from our stepmother?' Warrington asked.

'Yes. You received a letter from her.' Dane paused, moving the fripperies around on the mantel the way one would move chess pieces. 'I did open it. I sent her the funds. And a firm response. From you. You were a bit angry. Much more so than I would have been. You bluntly told her she must stop the wagers.'

Warrington nodded. 'I'm not as understanding as you are.'

'No. You're not. But I'm her favourite, too.' His chin jutted a bit, in the traditional family pose.

'You didn't like it any better than I did when she sold Mother's jewels.'

'I didn't relish it, but it made little difference. I didn't like her from the moment she called on her dear friend Adelphinia to see how she was faring over the loss of her mother. As if anyone who truly knew Adele would call her that.' He shrugged while he spoke. 'You also should be aware that you sent a man Broomer knows to our dear stepmother's house. The man is quite skilled at wagering and is to teach her not to lose so grandly.' Dane grinned. 'I am Broomer's favourite, too.'

'A favoured dung heap is still a dung heap.'

'As long as it is preferred above the other dung heaps, I am pleased.' Dane scratched at his chin and moved beside Warrington so that their boots almost touched. 'You're very close to the favourite, though.'

'I cannot believe I let you watch Jacob.'

Dane laughed. 'Don't worry. I pretended to be you. Stern and aloof.' He plopped himself down on the sofa. 'Now tell me what the trip was really like.'

Warrington began to talk, but his mind stayed on Dane's words. Stern and aloof. Just the way his own father had been.

Melina woke well into the morning. She'd had trouble falling asleep and hadn't slept soundly.

She'd spent the evening with Willa, instantly finding the child endearing.

In the night, she'd heard Warrington's laughter echoing in the house and the raised voice of his brother, telling some bold tale. Warrington had his own way to keep his shadows at bay.

And she wanted to find the place Cassandra was buried and take a hammer to the marker. This woman she'd never seen. A ghost with far-reaching tentacles. A woman who had everything she could have wanted and could have needed, and found her joy in destroying others around her.

Melina dressed slowly, knowing she would be leaving soon and never see England again.

She'd never see Warrington free himself of Cassandra. She'd never know if he could truly have a reprieve from the past.

A knock sounded at the bedchamber door and she hurried to open it. A draggy-eyed Broomer stood there, his waistcoat buttoned askew. 'Miss. You've a caller. An older woman. A real lady. Not one like that Ludgate's woman.' He shook his head. 'I'd have shot *her.*'

He plodded down the stairs, his words fading. 'I put this one in the sitting room because she had a peaceable face. Tired-like. But if you shout, I'll be there with the pistol.'

Melina found her father's wife examining the harpoon, her face only inches from it. She had her braided hair wrapped into a bun and lace ringed the neck of her peach dress. Her eyes were serene, but she had to have known something of Melina's life or she wouldn't have been standing in the room.

Melina could see no lack of strength in the woman in front of her. In fact, the woman reminded her of the stories she'd heard of the mythical Greek heroines. Even the scent Lady Hawkins wore fitted her, not a flowery delicate one, but more bracing, almost the same as the resin the men used to coat the ship.

'Interesting...' The older woman gave her a warm smile when she turned to Melina. 'I've never, ever been near so much of a sailing collection in a home. The seashells are amazing.' She pointed to the collection at the sides of the fireplace.

'Yes. Warrington's brother selected the objects.' Melina's eyes roved the room. 'Few women would choose a tooth, a weapon or a broken ship's bell.'

'Even the blue curtains hint of the water. This man has a fascination. I am impressed.' She touched the tooth. 'I don't believe I've ever been in a room an ordinary man planned—though I have been to Carlton House. One can't consider that an ordinary man's creation, though.' She looked to Melina, her eyes saying she expected Melina to agree.

Melina smiled and nodded. She'd never heard of Carlton House.

The woman's mouth quirked up. 'Like you, I cannot imagine a woman who would appreciate the decorations, but they are interesting.' She stood solemnly, and interlocked her fingers in front of herself. 'You're my husband's daughter, aren't you?'

Melina raised her chin in agreement, not seeing anger in the woman's face, but a searching perusal. 'How…'

The woman touched above her own breast. 'I saw the mark. My husband's sister had one on her arm. She's passed now. And one of my daughters has a smaller one on her back and one has one on her scalp, which is hidden completely by her hair. I doubt my husband is even aware of his daughters' marks.' She examined Melina. 'You have the same nose and perhaps profile of my daughter, as well. My husband doesn't know—but I saw the painting of you. I always made it a practice to see his showings.' She shook her head. 'He never thinks to ask what I do when he paints. I truly think he doesn't know the world exists at that time for other people.'

'I did not mean for you to discover…' Melina felt she'd betrayed her father. Although she didn't think he deserved kindness on her part, she didn't wish to create problems.

The woman rubbed her right hand against the rings on her left, which she wore over her gloves. 'When I saw you in my house, I near had an apoplexy. It took me a day to think about it before I truly accepted that you were in England. I decided to find you. All I had to do was get in one of those dreadful hackney carriages and say I wanted to go to the Earl of Warrington's home.' Her eyes, wreathed in wrinkles, deepened into smugness. 'And to know about my husband's other life—I was fairly certain years and years ago. More than a decade, I would suppose.'

'You spoke to him about it?'

Her eyes flashed anger. 'I saw no reason to speak my doubts if he would not speak his deceit.' Her ringed fingers fluttered again. 'No. I saw no need to talk to him about this. I could not confront—accuse—and demand confession. He would have professed innocence—and other than hiring a man to follow him on a sea voyage, I had little chance of proving my suspicions. I was content to wait, knowing the truth would surface.' She pointed a gloved finger at Melina. 'It does, my dear. Remember that and it will help you sleep better at night.'

'Why did you suspect?' Melina hadn't expected the woman to be so calm about something that should have caused such intensity.

'Too much secrecy. Too much contentment to be from England for long spells. And when I first viewed his painting of you, I saw it at a sideways glance and assumed he'd painted my daughter with a different hair colour. But why would he paint her years younger than she is? Then I saw the shoreline behind her. The sea. Hmm.' She touched a gloved finger to her cheek. 'He told me, and yet, he didn't know he did.'

'You were content with it?'

She shook her head. 'Absolutely not. But it makes little sense to move from a man who is hardly at home and seems to care little when he is. Why make a change when there wasn't a need. My secret, you see. He left for the island. I waved goodbye with a stoic promise I would try hard to survive while he was gone—and cherished the imagination of storms at sea. If he never returned, I would toddle along as always, wearing a lovely shade of black for a while. When he did return, I toddled along as always, wearing a lighter shade of black, for myself.' Hurt flashed behind her eyes, but was replaced with a wide, innocent blink. 'He does not touch me. I told Lord Hawkins my physician diagnosed a serious female complaint for me—and described ghastly lesions, bloody flux and being treated with leeches. I showed him a handkerchief covered in blood.' She shuddered. 'The poor maid had fallen and broken the mantle of a lamp, gashing her hand. But he didn't know.' She patted her silver hair. 'My children—I love. My husband—he is like a picture on the wall to me. I have him for display on occasion.'

Melina smiled at the thought of her father reduced to a painting. 'I was furious. I never suspected him married to someone else.'

'The question probably did not enter your mind with as much insistence as it entered mine. I had months and months to think of nothing else.'

The older woman took a breath, and her eyes darted to the side. This time, Melina could see the struggle she used to keep her voice light.

'Do you mind telling me the particulars?' Lady Hawkins asked. 'Why you came here? Your mother? Other children?'

'I have two sisters and my mother died. No brothers.' Melina looked to the window. 'I needed to come here to see if I could find a way to fund a dowry for my sisters.' She smiled, her gaze locked to the wall. 'Our lives are not the same as here. I cannot believe what I see. The *plouti,* gold and silver—for *buttons or spoons.* Even the servants have fine clothing.' She thought back to the island and the contrast.

The older woman appeared to shrug off the talk of wealth. 'How much dowry do your sisters need?'

Melina told her.

She tilted her head back. 'That's all?' She smiled. 'My dear, I will quietly see to having the funds for you. I think I could arrange it within a few days.'

Melina shivered. To think, she could be on board a ship for Melos—with a dowry for both sisters.

'What will my father think, spending the funds?'

The woman put her hand to her cheek. 'Oh. It was such a horrible injustice to both my husband and me when my father died and left all his funds in the care of my cousin. And my relative, he is such a strange young man. He will not listen to a word concerning the accounts unless it is from my lips. I could throw every pence into the ocean and he would simply say, "It's what your father wanted".' She smiled at Melina. 'You know, I think it never occurred to my husband who might have suggested such a spurious arrangement to my father before he died. It was at a particularly rough time in my life, when I'd just seen a painting of you, my dear.' She reached out and examined her gloves. 'I do feel I owe you.' Lady Hawkins stood. 'I must get home, although my husband will not even notice I'm gone. He painted well into the night and woke early to catch the light. He found inspiration again—and the rest of the world is lost to him.'

Melina rose, and the woman moved close to her, looking intensely at her.

'I can't help but see my own children in your face.' She shook her head. 'And I never really thought to see you standing before me.' Her features eased. 'I didn't know how I would truly feel if I saw you, but you're a lovely woman.'

She looked at the harpoon again. 'I'm sure the painting session will be nearly over when I return home. But…' she touched her hand to Melina's '…should you encounter a problem, I'd be pleased if you send a message to me. I will help you as my own daughter—quietly, of course. I'm not ready to explain the truth to my children. They have been sheltered, I think, from their father's true nature. I would like as little upset as possible in the flow of my life.' Her eyes had a malevolent glint. 'I do like taking my husband's secrets and keeping them from him.'

'I understand.'

Her face softened again. 'I would be pleased if you consider me a friend.' She hesitated in the doorway. 'In some deep part of my mind, I must have wondered since he returned with the painting of the three girls playing in the waves. That one.' She looked to the wall. 'Their faces were obscured.' She winced. 'Such a painting was not his usual style. And when I saw the portrait of your face…and then the mark…' she touched above her breast '…like my own daughter.' Her eyes wavered. 'You were no longer a stranger to me. You were a part of my family. I only ask that you keep our ties private.'

When her father's wife walked out through the door, Melina knew she had no reason not to return to Melos. She could take funds back to her sisters and buy the statue. But now the island felt lonely to her in a way she'd never noticed before. She would be returning to a gaol, locked alone with her heart—and dreams too secret to mention aloud.

Warrington had distanced himself from her and she knew he wouldn't even let his thoughts linger on her. They were still taken by another woman.

Chapter Twenty-One

M elina sat in the children's room, which for some reason smelled like linseed oil—possibly someone's idea of a good cleaning solution. She felt an intense need to be near the little girl who had no true father and whose mother had died.

Willa chewed her doll's painted shoe. The nursery maid slept, lips parted, in a chair beside the window.

Melina didn't know if she should wake the woman up and tell her it was the children's bedtime, or put the little ones to bed herself and let the nursemaid wake naturally.

Quietly, Jacob walked to his sister and snatched her doll from her arms. Willa lunged at him without a cry and her teeth went for his leg. He jumped aside, his hand at her hair, restraining her. All done in silence.

'Give the doll back to her,' Melina commanded. He did, shoving it between her mouth and his leg.

'She bites hard,' he said. He stepped back, staring at his sister. 'Don't you, Ratface?'

'Jacob. Your sister has a name. Use it.'

Willa took her baby and hit him with it, and he grabbed the doll's arm and held on. Willa tugged the other direction. He pulled at the doll once and then released it. 'You can have her back, Willa, Lady Ratface.'

He smiled at Melina.

'Jacob. It is nearly your bedtime and you must behave if you wish to stay up any longer.' Melina stood.

He shrugged. 'Willa likes it.'

Melina kept her voice stern. 'I do not. Do not do it again. The two of you are not to fight. Brothers must be kind to their sister.'

He nodded. 'I am. She likes hitting me with the doll and I like calling her names.'

Warrington opened the door and walked in, making all the noise of a spirit, but Jacob saw him.

The boy jumped from the floor and whirled to his father. He gave a bow and schooled himself into the manner of an Englishman. Warrington reached out and tousled Jacob's hair, laughing when the child used both hands to straighten it.

'I need to show you the picture I drew. It's of Uncle's ship,' Jacob said, then scrambled to pull a paper from inside a book. He unfolded the drawing and handed it to his father. 'You can have it,' he said. 'I'm drawing another one.'

'Thank you.' Warrington took the picture, pulling it closer to his face. 'We must save it. Tell your nursery maid to start collecting your best drawings. I will have them bound into a book and we can look at it together.'

Jacob smiled. 'I'm going to sail with Uncle—Captain Ben, when I am bigger.'

He gave his son a pat on the shoulder. 'We'll see.'

Willa became aware of the conversation. She kept the doll's foot in her mouth and ran to Melina's knees.

The earl's face didn't flicker as he looked in their direction. Instead, he took Jacob by the hand and left the room. Melina could hardly believe the difference in Warrington. He'd not spoken to her privately after the night Ludgate had appeared. Perhaps she was more like the earl than she realised, seeing not the person, but the appearance, and she'd been misled.

Warrington hadn't burst with smiles on the ship, but now he acted colder, and this man's hands would not touch a slop bucket now. She had no question in her mind concerning that.

Willa ignored Warrington much the same way as he avoided her. But she had to be restrained from toddling to Broomer if he walked into a room where the little girl was, and even though the servant acted put out by it, Melina could tell he exaggerated the irritation to please Willa and he made silly faces at her when he thought no one noticed. He'd even given the nursemaid a little carved toy for Willa.

Now Willa sat, pulling at the dress on her wooden doll, the plaything's stoic expression a complete opposite of the little girl's. Willa had a fan, a full-sized one, and waved it over her doll, hitting the toy's face often as not.

Melina stayed with her until Willa fell asleep on the floor. Lifting Willa, Melina placed her on the bed. The nurse woke at the movement, and mumbled that she'd finish getting the little girl to bed.

Melina went in search of Jacob, but truly she knew she looked for his father.

Warrington sat on the sofa in the sitting room, in his usual relaxed pose of his eyes half-closed, legs relaxed in front of him. His cravat hung loose. Jacob slept beside him, looking as if he'd fallen over, and he used Warrington's lap for a pillow.

'I'll get him to bed,' she whispered.

'Nonsense. Sit with us and watch a fireplace with no flames.'

She hesitated. 'It's late.'

'It's getting later and then it will get early and become a new day.'

The melancholy air of the room touched her, but she stayed.

'I hope you remember your time in England well, even if you might now think it is filled with the worst of the world…' His voice rolled smoothly into the room, curling around her the way the flames would have wrapped around burning coals had the fireplace been alight.

'I will remember you.' She walked behind him, putting fingertips on his shoulder.

He reached up and clasped her hand. 'I hope it has not all been difficult for you, Melina.'

'The world has been so different from what I am used to. I miss my *adelfi,* my sisters, and the plainness of Melos. Each day is the same as the day before. And the sea—I liked the sea. Even the smells are different here. The scents there are from the earth and nature. Here, they are from the people cooking and bringing horses about.'

'I will give you a dowry.'

She shook her head, feeling lightness in her next words. 'There is no need. My father's wife has promised to see that we have what we need.'

The uplift of one brow was all the acknowledgement he gave her.

'I've arranged for Broomer to travel with you back to Melos.' Warrington's voice was a husky murmur. 'He'll get you home, safely. Threaten Stephanos or do what is needed. I've told him every woman on the island is as lovely as you. He asked how soon he can leave. I've instructed him to gather his things.'

Melina looked forward, and saw not what she'd seen before, but the world through Warrington's eyes. And knew she was not in it.

* * *

Warrington lay in his bedchamber, trying to force himself to sleep. The brown sacks he'd dressed her in didn't work. Nothing would. His weakness hadn't left him.

Nor was her presence easing his memories.

Something inside gnawed at him, reminding him of the time he'd thought he would have the dream of a loving family. He'd wanted the world he saw reflected when one looked at the portraits of a man, his wife and children, carefully arranged, and all around them tidy.

Clawing desire burned in him, and not just desire for her body, but for a world where feelings were pure.

Warrington pressed his face into the pillow, trying to smother the thoughts torturing him.

At least Melina seemed to care for the girl. She patted the child's back when she held her and he didn't think she even knew she did.

He'd stayed away from Melina and he could feel her presence in the house every moment he kept inside. And when he walked outside, he could hardly wait to return.

He could attend a few soirées, Drury Lane, and he'd surely be able to find a woman with some appeal. The way he felt, he doubted he could find one who *didn't* have enough to tempt him into her bed. He could go to Almack's and find someone he didn't find attractive, and perhaps then he could believe himself safe to bring her into his home. A woman he might have no true passion for and who could not blind him with her body and beauty and dancing eyes.

But before he left, he wanted to—

But if he did what he wanted to do before he left he'd not need to leave the town house.

He rolled himself out of bed and wrapped on his dressing gown.

Warrington went to the door and knocked, then opened it.

'Melina,' he whispered.

She sat up on the bed and he could tell she wasn't fully awake. Her face looked as puzzled as Jacob's would have.

'Come with me for a moment.' He reached out, taking her hand.

When he pulled her to her feet, she brought the covers with her. He took them from her hand and pushed them loose so they slid to the floor.

He saw her open her eyes wide and shake her head, and she moved back.

'Come with me,' he whispered again. 'I wish to talk to you without children or servants about.'

'It would be as easy as closing a door.'

Her feet didn't move when he took her elbow. He increased his grip.

'You're right,' he grumbled, getting her to the hallway. 'I'm awake now, though, and by coincidence so are you.'

He slipped a hand at her back, to guide her to the sitting room. Touching her was the wrong thing to do. He remembered how she felt when he embraced her, skin against skin. And he didn't need any reminders since he couldn't get the thoughts to recede from his mind for even a half-second. But he didn't know if he could let her go again if he touched her.

She moved to the window. Not sitting. He wondered if she didn't want to sit in his presence, afraid of getting too comfortable.

'I would have thought you would lead me to your bed-chamber.' Her words were tart.

In the shadowy dimness, he could tell her hands were clasped together.

Apparently, growing up in Greece had robbed her of the awe she should feel from having the attention of an earl of some funds. And he was certain his mirror hadn't lied. He was not an ogre. Hell, he was better looking than Dane and Dane had a scar on his face and women practically fainted at his feet. But this was Melina. So different than what he understood. He crossed his arms.

'It is silent in here for someone being awoken because someone else had to urgently speak with them,' she grumbled and he heard the rustling of her movements. 'I'm sure the nursemaid thinks we often meet secretly in the night. She smiles in such a way when she tells me to have pleasant dreams.'

'If she thinks we're together, then I certainly hope she believes it is of great frequency.'

He moved to stand beside her at the window. They were as close as two people could be without touching.

'I shouldn't be in a part of your life. I'm to be gone soon. Now I am watching your— Willa,' she said.

'You can call her my child.' His voice held bitterness. 'She and I are stuck with each other for the moment. I realise she is my child, by possession if not by birth. Ludgate doesn't want her and never will, I am certain of that.'

'And how could he have marched up and demanded her?'

'He could have asked for her the other night. Or he could have told me earlier, by post for his own safety. Or through Cassandra when she was alive. My wife, who'd not even written to see if I lived or died while I was ill—though I understand. It would have been laughable for her to express concern when she so obviously felt none. When she returned, she knew I couldn't possibly think the babe was mine. Particularly as I refused to touch her and did not return to her bed until after the girl was born.'

He patted the back of the sofa. 'When I no longer see Willa around to remind me, I can put all this to rest. Maybe now that I…' He paused. 'I now feel such anger for Daphne, too. More than Ludgate, I suppose. Had she come to me and spoken openly—it would have been different. But she paid a man to taunt me—as if I had not had enough. That must have been something she and Cass learned as children. They were so determined in it.'

He moved to a crystal decanter at a side table and released the stopper. He filled a glass with brandy. He didn't put the stopper back into the neck, but instead absently clicked the crystal against the rim. He finally let the stopper fall into the top and slapped it down with his palm. He swirled the liquid, then took a drink. 'Choices.'

'For Jacob, and for yourself—let it go.'

'I would have done so long ago, if I could. I'm trying. Tomorrow I have a couple arriving who might take Willa.'

She gasped. 'Are you sure they are good people?'

'Broomer would not mislead me. Three years ago, they heard of a street woman who had a child she could not care for and they took the boy in. With no recompense from the mother.'

'Perhaps they wanted…someone to help with the *ergo,* the work.'

'Perhaps. But Broomer said the boy is well fed and clothed, and has turned from a scampering street urchin to a whistling child who is being schooled.' He walked back to the mantel, and stared at it. 'I'll be glad to have the girl gone. The last image of my wife. The last ghost.'

'You aren't getting rid of the last ghost. That one is inside you.'

He nodded. 'I can't take a knife and cut it out of me. Or I would. I would rather have thoughts of you instead of memories of her. But I cannot forget what has gone on before.'

Chapter Twenty-Two

Melina stared out of the nursery window, looking into a day that would have been better served with rain, instead of the fading fog and wet air.

When the couple arrived, Melina noted that Warrington's carriage delivered them. They stepped out. The woman adjusted her bonnet, her skirts, and gave the man a hopeful smile.

Melina heard little clinks behind her, of Willa playing with a doll and the feet tapping together.

Melina could barely look at the little cherub face, feeling like a Judas. She could not be a Judas.

Even Willa seemed to sense a difference and Melina felt a tug at her clothing. Willa stood, looking up, with one arm cradling her own baby tightly.

Melina gathered the girl up and took the doll from Willa's hands, holding the girl snug. She used the baby to give Willa's cheeks loud kisses. The little one immediately laughed—her face showing she'd forgotten about everything else in the world but her doll.

A few minutes later, a maid entered the nursery.

'Miss.' The servant stopped just inside the doorway, giving a smile in Willa's direction before her face turned serious and she looked at Melina. 'His lordship has called for you.'

Melina tensed and walked to Warrington's sitting room, giving one last glance at Willa while she stayed behind with the servant.

Warrington stood in the doorway, leaning into the frame. He wore a dark waistcoat and frock coat and had no lightness about him. Tightness lined his face. Sleep hadn't been kind to him. 'They're here. Broomer will bring them when I ring for him.'

He moved from the doorway and stepped back into the room, letting her cross in front of him.

'I saw them arrive,' she said.

'Do they pass your inspection?'

She gave a nod and halved the distance between them. 'I do not want Willa to feel abandoned.'

'Perhaps she will feel like she has a mother and father who care for her—like a true family wants her. She needs a family. You know that.'

She looked at him, hoping for a sign of his compassion for Willa.

He gave the slightest shake of his head, standing straight. 'I don't feel any warmth for the child. I don't. She will grow into her mother's image. I do not want that face in my sight for the rest of my life. This is the only way I can rid myself of Cassandra.'

Melina turned back to the window and stared at the horizon. Willa did deserve a caring family. Melina reached out and pulled the bell.

When the couple entered, Melina noticed the serviceable dress of the woman, but around the neck, she'd embroidered a row of flowers—the same ones Melina had once stitched on her sister's handkerchief.

The man, Sinclair, a furniture maker by trade, bowed.

He stood thin, too thin, and wore dark clothing. After her introduction, his wife almost vanished behind him.

'This is Melina. She's been assisting in Willa's care,' the earl said and guided Melina to sit on the sofa.

'I hope you found the trip comfortable,' Warrington addressed the Sinclairs, moving behind Melina.

'Yes,' Sinclair answered. 'My wife is not one to leave the house often except for Sunday Services. I've promised her I'll bring her to Drury Lane before too many more months pass.'

The woman looked at her husband when he spoke and seemed scared to meet Warrington's gaze.

'You have a boy?' Melina asked.

'Yes.' The man looked to his wife, guiding her to sit. 'Today, he's with my wife's mother. She lives with us.'

'Do they get on well?' Melina asked.

'Very well,' the man answered, sitting straight. 'When Thomas is not helping with my work, he's asking his granny for a story. I do not know where the woman comes up with the tales she tells.' He smiled, and his shoulders relaxed. 'Sometimes, she tells of clumsy knights and dragons who have blackened teeth from their burning flames. All her dragons have blackened teeth, except the one who cannot muster a puff of smoke. That is the one Thomas must hear stories of over and over.'

'Why do you want Willa?' Melina leaned forward.

'My wife wishes for a daughter.' He shot a glance at her and then turned back to Melina. 'We would not mind to have another boy in the house. It would be nice for Tom to have a brother. But a daughter…' He patted his wife's hand. 'Alice would like to have a little girl to keep her company and so she can show her things a woman needs to know for a home.'

'Willa's timid.'

Sinclair turned to his wife. 'So is Alice.'

Melina stood. 'I suppose you should see Willa and she should have a chance to meet you.'

She hurried from the room and returned, slowly tugging Willa by the hand. Melina smoothed down the tufts of blonde hair too wispy to be braided. No woman could turn her back on a doll so fair. And her little woollen dress, the plainness only contrasted to show the beauty of the child.

When Melina sat, Willa stayed near her and leaned against Melina's legs. She burrowed against Melina and her eyes had a sleepy droop.

'She's quite behaved.' Alice spoke, her eyes locked on Willa.

'Not always.' Melina brushed her hand over Willa's hair again. 'But she truly is a good-natured child.'

Warrington's foot moved, tapping several times back and forth, but he didn't speak.

Melina continued, 'Willa does get irritable when she doesn't get her nap, according to her nursery maid, but she will drag you to her bed so she can be tucked in. And she does like to beg attention from her brother with a bit more force than she should use.'

She brushed down Willa's hair, again feeling the baby skin of her cheek, and looked to Warrington. He appeared more interested in the painting over the fireplace than in the discussion.

'She likes porridge—but not cold.' Melina spoke the words to the woman.

'Tommy is the same,' Alice said. 'I have a place at the back of the stove where I sit the pot. It stays warm there.'

Melina nodded. 'Do you plan on taking in other children?'

Sinclair shook his head. 'We didn't plan on Thomas, but once we heard about him and met him, we decided he should have a home with us. He's a good lad and my wife thinks another child would be dear. Tom's six, but she's already worried about him growing up so fast.'

Melina talked more with the couple, aware of Warrington sitting beside them, occasionally moving his boot, or rubbing away a speck on his clothing or a mote from the nearest surface. He looked to have no more attention for the conversation than he might if the cook explained how a chicken was plucked.

Melina rose, pulling Willa up with her. 'We will be sure to let you know of Warrington's decision. But he is still a bit undecided on letting her leave.'

His eyes darted to her. His jaw was locked. His decision was plain to see in his black stare.

He spoke a few courteous words to the Sinclairs as he walked them to the door and left, still talking to them.

Melina hugged Willa tight, but the cherub pushed away, and Melina lowered her to a standing position.

When Warrington returned, he had Willa's nursery maid with him. The woman picked up her charge and left the room.

'I would like to speak to you a moment, Melina.' Warrington shut the door and then walked to her. He put both hands on her shoulders. 'They are good people. The kind of people who should make up the world.'

'But not right for Willa. I want to take her back to Melos with me. I will be a good mother.'

His fingers tightened. 'They are already parents of a son. They are more right for her than either you or I. They can care for her without knowing what has gone before. They will be good family for her. You will start a family of your own.'

'And Willa can be my first child.'

'No. If you want what is right for the child, you can see

the family she will have. She will be here where she can grow up surrounded by those fripperies women like so well. Not on an island that is used as a harbour for ships full of men who've left their morals behind. Willa can have two parents who will have the same love for her they have for their other child. I will see that she has no financial needs. The man does well in his business and he would do well by her should I not send a coin their way, but I will make sure they have no concerns. I will convey a message to them in the morning asking them to let me know when they are ready for Willa.'

Melina wanted to tell him to go to the devil. Wanted to hit him. But it would do no good. She walked from the room. *Cassandra.* Melina hated a woman she'd never met.

Hours after the Sinclairs left, Melina crept to Willa's bed, watching her sleep. The child should have two parents.

Melina pulled a chair near. She'd worried herself about the little girl, but now she felt calm. More at peace. She'd approached Broomer secretly, asking for all he knew of the couple, and he'd told her what decent people they were. He'd told her of his life and how he'd only had one parent, and how he'd wished for a father. She understood why Warrington relied on him so. The man, with all his loudness and size and capability for violence, still had the heart of a boy who longed for the love of a family. She trusted him, as well.

She knew the hour past midnight when Warrington walked in without knocking.

'Have you been hiding from me to punish me?' he asked.

She shook her head, then realised he might not see the movement in the darkness. 'I just had to think. To understand.' She felt spears of anger, but she tamped them down. The hurt ran deeper.

Fingertips touched her shoulders, rubbing gently, sending calming shivers into her body.

'You've been through a lot, Melina. You've slept in a room where the mermaids were.' His fingertips closed over her shoulder. 'I've actually had a fire lit this time. Come with me and we can watch flames instead of unlit coal.'

She rose from the chair and he followed her out of the room.

'It's not easy for me, either, Melina,' he said, sitting.

She sat at one end of the sofa, he sat on the other—his shirt open at the neck, no waistcoat and his hair ruffled a bit, as if he'd run his fingers through it. He looked to have been in bed, then left it and dressed again. His elbow propped on the back of the sofa and his legs sprawled in front. 'I want to go forward.'

She didn't answer.

'Jacob is my child. And he looks…' He smiled. 'Poor child, I suspect he looks exactly as I did at the same age. And I have seen him plan mischief and seen Ben in his face, as well. I will never let him near the sea.'

He leaned forward, moving so his elbows rested at his thighs and his fingers were loosely clasped in front of him. 'I know there is a chance you might have my child in you. I could not let you go if you had a babe that was mine. I could not leave it for another man.'

'I could lie to you.'

'Will you?' His face turned to hers and the firelight flashed one side bright.

She knew she shouldn't have said those words. He'd had enough lies with his wife, but if she'd not said them, he would have wondered anyway.

'I don't know. With a dowry, I could marry before the baby would be old enough to know otherwise, but I would be like you, I think. I would always be seeing your face in the child.'

'I would hope you would not feel quite the same way as I do concerning that.'

'No.' She moved sideways, so she could put a palm flat on his back, feeling through the clothing to the skin, and through the skin to the beating heart beneath. She'd had to touch him. Had to feel him.

'A little higher and you'll be touching the scar.'

She ran her hand over his back and could feel the thin ridge running a slice across his shoulders.

'It doesn't mar you enough on the outside to matter.' She let her fingers linger. 'It's the betrayal you feel.'

'I suppose.' He lowered his face, letting his head rest against his hands. 'I'm thankful that I will no longer have to worry about the past, yet the knowledge I have doesn't rest easy with me.'

He breathed and the movement calmed her worries.

Melina ran her finger to the side of his face, feeling the cheekbones and trailing down the roughened jaw. 'I wish you could have been sculpted. I would like a likeness of you to have with the one I found. To keep for ever.'

'You have an imagination.'

'I don't need one when I look at you.'

He leaned back, letting his arm lie along the back of the sofa, and his other hand touched her. Swirls of warmth swirled inside her caused by the circling of his fingertips along her shoulder. 'I am the same with you, Melina. I would have liked to have been a pirate, hunting treasure, and when I found you on Melos, I would have taken you and kept you. I would have left any jewels, or rocks, or carvings behind. Because I wouldn't have needed them, if I had you.'

She moved into the hollow of his shoulder, hoping that she could always hold his memory alive enough to feel his touch.

Chapter Twenty-Three

At first light, Warrington sat at his desk, penning the letter to Sinclair. The sooner Willa started her new life, the better she would be. She was young. She'd forget soon.

He wondered if his memories would fade, as well. He only hoped they moved to a part of him that didn't feel rage.

He dashed the words across paper, wishing he'd not been blinded by Cassandra's appearance. She hadn't minded if she'd destroyed him, or his entire family.

He touched his fingertips to his forehead. He'd been so ill. And when he heard she'd taken Jacob, he'd been grateful for his son to be safely away. Never knowing Jacob would have been in the most precarious hands of all. His mother's.

He held his own hands out, looking at them. They were as guilty of his father's death as if he'd brought a viper into the house and it bit his father. He didn't deserve someone such as Melina.

Warrington put his pen in the holder and left the room, feeling a gnawing sense in his stomach. His whole world had changed—thanks to Cassandra. She'd taken his father from him and put a child in his house who didn't belong. He went to the nursery to see his sleeping son.

'Jacob,' he called out when he opened the door. He saw Jacob's face, thankful Cassandra had never considered

Jacob a chore. 'Put on some trousers and a rough shirt. Chesapeake is missing us. I'll send Broomer for him.'

Jacob rolled out of bed, moving with a slippery speed.

The boy stopped, bare legs showing from his nightshirt, and his eyes alight. 'I bet I ride fast now.'

'No. We'll not race.'

'Fast walk?'

'Perhaps.'

Jacob gave a confident nod of his head, fully agreeing with the statement. He turned, running to get his trousers.

Warrington strode to the library and waited, only to have Melina walk in. Her hair in a glossy knot, a rushed glow to her cheeks, and he felt desire—even when she wore the hideous tea-coloured gown.

She carried Willa on her hip, looking overloaded by the weight. Melina didn't look at his eyes. Guilt plunged into him. She blamed him for not keeping the girl. The child still wore her night rail and dropped her head to Melina's shoulder.

'Jacob rushed in wanting me to help find his cap,' Melina said. 'He thinks you are taking him riding. Don't you want to wait until after he eats?'

'He will not shrivel into nothing if he is late eating and he'll make up for it when we return.'

'Me go,' Willa said.

'No, Little Doll.' Melina turned to leave the room. 'We're going to find some ribbons for your hair.'

'Make sure the nursemaid has the child's clothing packed,' Warrington said as she walked away.

Melina's back stiffened. She didn't move. 'I will gather the things Willa needs.' Her voice could have had razors attached.

Willa's arms flailed and she pushed against Melina. Her voice rose. 'Go.'

'Not now,' Melina answered, voice still edged, and then it softened. 'Later, though.'

Melina let Willa slide to the floor and stand, clasping her hand.

'Papa.' Jacob ran in, rushing past Melina and Willa. 'I found my cap and I washed my face. I'm ready.'

'We'll see if cook can find us a biscuit, or something, before we leave.' Warrington turned back, getting the message on his desk for Broomer to take—the one he'd penned saying Willa could go to the Sinclairs. He'd give it to the servant now, before any more time passed. The sooner this was finished, the better for everyone.

Melina looked at the paper, leaning forward, and he knew she saw the name on it. She grasped Willa's hand and hurried her away, as if the child could read and understand the words in his hand.

Jacob chattered along beside him, having no more cares than how fast he could ride a horse.

Things could have been so different, but he was tired of looking at the past. Tired of breathing in the memories every moment. Of wearing the past like a cloak around him.

He'd been so besotted with his wife. Besotted. He didn't know how the word had started. But he'd been sotted for sure. And now he was the same for Melina. Getting her from England would surely cure him. He could feel the burning need inside himself for her, but he could not give in. If he did, he risked her returning to Melos with his child inside her.

And he had to keep moving, moving away from her while she was in England. If he touched her again, he would ache all the more when she left.

She wanted to return to her world. Take the dowry. Care for her sisters. Find her precious rock. And as soon as the little one left the town house, he would go to Whitegate with Jacob. Broomer and Ben could take care of Melina and see that she returned safely to her island.

Now he would keep moving and not think again until miles separated them. He trudged from the house, calling Jacob to hurry.

When they returned from the ride, Jacob slid from Nero's back before Warrington could dismount from Chesapeake. The boy dropped to a crouch when he landed, before sitting on his bottom. Then he tumbled forward to his knees before he pushed himself up, laughing, oblivious to the dirt he'd gathered.

During the outing, Jacob had sung, talked about his preferences in horses and the biggest spider he'd ever killed. He'd boasted about seeing rabbits in the flower garden and how upset Dane had been when the deer visited and ate some of the plants all the way down to stems. Now he begged to feed Nero.

'Let the others care for them. It's their job.'

'What is my job?' Jacob asked, looking up.

'To be my son. To learn from your tutor when you are back at Whitegate.'

Warrington reached out, wrapped an arm around Jacob's waist and picked him up sideways, then shook him. 'I must shake the dirt off you before you get inside.'

Jacob squealed and struggled to get free. 'Let me down.'

Warrington released him. 'Didn't help much.'

Jacob brushed down the front of his shirt. 'Cook says I'm handsome and she calls me "your lordship". She keeps tarts hid just for me because I'm a lordship. And she says I'm getting bigger every day because of her tarts.'

'Perhaps you are, your lordship.' Pride flowered in Warrington's body when he looked at Jacob. He could not have asked for anything more in a son.

War reached out, putting his palm at the back of Jacob's head and giving him a nudge forward to the door.

When they reached the children's room, he took Jacob inside, where Melina and the nursemaid sat with the little girl.

Melina was sewing a dress so small it could only fit Willa's doll while the child played with Jacob's soldiers.

Melina raised her eyes—the eyes he'd miss—and he saw her own sadness pool in them. She put down the dress and rushed from the room.

The nursemaid watched Jacob and frowned. 'Have you been rolling in a hayfield? I think your hair is turning into straw.' She stood, reaching out for him. 'I am scrubbing that dirt from your knees. I expect the horse came back a lot cleaner than you.'

'Papa and I rode a long way,' he told the nursemaid as she turned to get the pitcher. 'Papa even let me get off Nero by myself and I didn't get hurt.'

'But you did manage to get dirty.' The older woman sighed.

'I stumbled when I landed.'

Warrington heard them talking and he left the room.

He moved to the room with the harpoon, planning to write instructions on how he wanted his will changed. Jacob would be cared for because of the entailed properties, but the girl could easily be forgotten about. He didn't want that to happen.

Hearing a rustling noise, he looked up. Willa had followed him, hair tousled, and dressed in a blue that mirrored her eyes. Drool glistened on her chin and she had one of her half-boots in her hand. She should not be toddling about on her own with the stairway so close.

Half rising, he planned to summon a servant, but the

little girl sat, trying to put her boot on. It wouldn't hurt to watch her for a moment.

As he wrote, he heard her chatter again and looked up long enough to see her struggling to climb into the over-stuffed chair. In moments, something rustled at his feet and he knew she'd given up on the chair and was exploring under his desk. A sharp, clamping pain hit his leg.

He jumped back. Standing, he pushed down his stocking and saw perfect indentations of teeth on his leg.

'Willa.' He raised his voice, then reached underneath the desk and snatched her out. 'I've horse hair on me, I'm sure. And last I heard, it tastes the same as dog fur. You shouldn't like it.'

Her bottom lip trembled and a sniffle looked to turn into a crying bout.

'Pardon,' he muttered, pulling her to his chest, and patting her back. 'I didn't mean to frighten you.'

Her eyes were wide and she stared at him as if she watched an ogre. She'd not yet made up her mind about tears. He jiggled her as he paced the floor, the same as he'd done with Jacob. 'You nearly drew blood. You must not like me and I understand.'

Her lip stopped wavering and she nestled against him. 'I don't mind that you don't like me. I wouldn't if I were you.' Bending forward, he leaned to put her back on the floor, but she clung to him, her fist tight on his waistcoat.

'No,' she said.

Willa had had no choice in the matter of her parents. Maybe neither of them should suffer any more for Cassandra's sins.

'Poppet, I wish you a pleasant journey and the best of life.'

'Horse,' she said.

'Not today.'

'Horse.'

'No.'

'Horse.' She looked at him, eyes hopeful.

'Some day, when you are older, I'll see that you have a horse of your very own.' He held her back from himself and put her on to the floor.

The wail shocked him. He didn't think he'd ever heard her cry.

He scooped her up, his arm tucked under her bottom, and her face was near his. He patted her back and took a few steps, hoping to silence the wails. Her tears dwindled quickly.

'Willa, you're going to get something special. A mama and a papa both—all in one day. Very soon. I have already sent the letter.'

She reached for his neck.

'No.' He paused, moving his head aside. She grabbed the cravat at his neck to hold herself firm. She tugged his neckcloth and the softness of fine hair tickled his chin. She smelled like Jacob had when he'd held him—a bit like soap and porridge and life.

She'd be all right. He knew she'd do well. The Sinclairs would be best for her.

'You'll like your new family. They're pleasant people,' he said to her. 'You'll have a new brother, and a new place to live, and a new papa and mama both.'

'Papa?' He heard the wavering voice at the door and turned. Jacob stood there, his eyes unsure. 'We're getting a new papa and mama?'

'No.' He rushed out the word. Shocked his son could think such a thing. 'Just Willa.'

'Here?'

'No. Of course not.'

His son stared, eyes searching Warrington's face, unsure. 'Why?'

'Willa's moving to live with her new family. You'll understand when you get older.'

This time, the eyes he saw staring back at him were his son's and he could see his own likeness in Jacob's face. His own eyes. Accusing.

'You're giving Willa away?' Jacob asked, his lip jutting out.

'We'll talk about it later.'

'If she did something bad, she didn't mean to.'

She burrowed against him and he felt trapped between the two children.

He knelt down, never taking his eyes from his son, and stood the little girl on her own feet. 'She needs a mother.'

'Why does she need a mama?' Jacob asked. 'I don't have one.'

'Boys only need fathers. Girls need mothers.'

'We can put trousers on her and cut her hair, and she can be my brother and we'll keep her.'

He saw Melina move into the doorway.

'Explain to Jacob,' he told her, knowing she'd heard the conversation.

Her eyes didn't accuse. They looked troubled and saddened.

She took a step towards Jacob. She dipped her chin and her words were gentle. 'I had a *mana* when I was growing up. It's something little girls need.'

'Why?'

'We do. Like you need your papa. Think how lost you'd be without him.'

'He went to sea with Uncle Ben and I had the tutor and I was all right. He showed me how seeds grow and everything. The stable master took me for horse rides. Uncle

Dane told me stories about Romans and knights. We even saw a shooting star. I asked Uncle Dane, if Papa didn't come back like Mama didn't, would he keep me and Willa? He said he would.' He sniffed in a large swallow of air and stood as straight as his soldiers. 'Uncle Dane would keep us.' His jaw jutted out. 'I want to live with Uncle Dane or sail with Uncle Ben.' He ran from the room.

Warrington heard each word and they went into his heart. They were true.

He went after Jacob, brushed by Melina, and he could hear Cassandra's laughter.

But he was not keeping the girl. He'd already given her away. He had told them he would send a carriage for them on the next day.

Melina heard the steps in the hallway and knew Warrington was in his room. She sat in the blackness, feeling no need for light. Warrington had left after talking to Jacob and not returned until night.

The dark walls suited her well and one face kept floating through her mind. Warrington. Every servant in the house slept, but she doubted he did. And she needed one last moment with him. She wanted to hear his voice. To feel his scent cover her, and the skin that remained hidden from all the world to be hers to savour.

She stood, wearing her chemise, and crept to his bedchamber, standing. He opened the door after she called out, but kept his eyes on a miniature, examining it. He turned the painting so she could see it.

'My father—he lived for my mother.' His voice barely reached her ears. 'If one of his boys displeased her, he would not hear of it. We could have stolen from the church and he would have not been so angry as he would have been from an irritation to my mother. And rightly so. If she had a fault, it was in loving us to distraction.'

He brought the miniature back into his view and put his arm around her, hand at her waist. Her heart beat faster and she felt like a part of him. She let her cheek rest against his clothing. In those seconds, she changed. When he breathed, she felt the movements inside herself. But also, she could feel his restraint. He was not to be hers.

'And yet,' Warrington continued, 'almost the first woman he saw after the funeral, he began to court, thinking it a secret. Less than a month after my mother's death, he told me he would be married as soon as the proper mourning ended. He was bouncing in his boots. He was so happy and could not keep the news to himself.' Warrington moved the picture to his side. 'I vowed…'

Warrington tossed the miniature to a chair. He expelled a breath. 'Yet I lost my father because I was no different than he.'

She touched the softness of his shirt at his chest, feeling the heart beating beneath.

'I never told my father, not once, how I hated the moment he told me he would remarry. Instead I told Dane and we moved to the town house so we would not have to see the blissful courtship. I didn't move back until I wed. Whitegate is large, yet it wasn't big enough for everyone. I'm tired of living in my memories, Melina. They are getting old and worn, and making me feel the same. Like leather rained on and then baked in the sun.'

'I don't think you can simply close them off.'

'I know I have done the right thing with the girl and I will make it up to Jacob, somehow.'

'Don't think about it. Now it's done.' She pulled him close.

He squeezed her. 'You feel… You feel like…' He paused,

swaying her on her feet. 'I can't think what you feel like exactly, but it warms up old leather nicely. Gives it new life.'

She let herself melt into his body and his scent—fresh gardens and the brush of strength. She wanted to be able to close her eyes and slide into the memories of his arms long after she left. And secretly, she hoped there would be a child. She would let Warrington know—after a while. After her heart did not ache so.

She shut her eyes, imagining her own sisters who'd lost their mother and been willingly deserted by their father. 'I think of my family. The ones gone and the ones left. And I can't leave them, either. My promise to my mother...'

He leaned in, wrapping her in his arms, and when he spoke, his voice was at her ear. 'I've thought of nothing but family all day and you dream of yours. Let us take a walk from them and leave them for a moment. They will still be there for us when we return.'

Melina knew she would like nothing better and to be held by Warrington soothed her completely.

'Let me pleasure you.' He touched a tendril of her hair, brushing it back, but his finger returned to linger on her skin.

She looked up and desire stirred in every part of her just from being in his arms. She yearned for the touch of his lips against hers. She pulled back enough so she could tiptoe up, pressing her mouth to his, and feel the strength of his response.

He took her mouth with the same ferocity of needing one kiss to stay alive. One kiss to have another heartbeat.

She no longer stood on her own feet. Warrington held her, his fingers splayed against her back, keeping her aloft.

He moved, or she did, and that merest movement of their bodies, constrained by clothing, and yet freed to feel every whisper of touch, tumbled her into a world where passions conquered all concerns.

He pulled back and she opened her eyes. She'd never seen the expression on his face before. It was too strong for her to take in and too deep to turn from. He picked her up and deposited her gently on the bed.

Warrington pulled his clothes from his body, shedding them with no care for where they landed, but when he lay beside her, he undid the chemise ties, unwrapping her with the care of touching a wisp he didn't want the breeze to blow away.

She felt rich, pampered, treasured—valuable as marble carved by a hand guided from the heart of the greatest craftsman.

'Melina,' he whispered and said nothing else. No question or words. Just spoke her name.

And the sound of it from his lips filled her the same as an outpouring of love.

When he lay beside her, she ran her hands down his body and up again, trying to memorise every surface. Trying to soak in each fibre of him. Wanting to hold the feelings within herself for ever.

He touched her hip and their eyes were close enough to see in the darkness. He bent his head to her neck and his hair grazed against her, the scent of his skin lingering with the locks. Pressing her to her back, he lay beside her and pulled her against his body. He burrowed his lips into the hollow of her neck, his teeth brushing her skin, and his fingertips marked her heart, and all of her.

When he trailed his fingers down her stomach, reaching into the gentle slope, pressing her soft curls, touching the folds, finding the peak, she couldn't think any more. She gasped, lost in the swirls, the pulses of his touch, and she couldn't regain herself until he completed the feelings for her.

She felt him, holding their bodies close, moving them together, in a rhythm of lovemaking, while his hands caressed her, bringing her to the height of her passion again, crashing them together and taking all the power from her body. She relished all the sensations of him.

This would be their last night together.

Chapter Twenty-Four

Melina sat on the floor, dodging the edges of Willa's fan
as the little one worked to keep Melina's face cool. They'd
just finished breaking their fast and Melina hadn't seen
Warrington since she'd left his bed at dawn.

'Melina.' Warrington's shout from outside the children's
bedchamber penetrated the oak door.

'Oh, Little One…' Melina exaggerated her facial expression '…it appears someone is in very serious trouble.
Warrington sounds very, very angry.'

Willa laughed.

The door burst open and Warrington plunged into the
room, holding a letter. 'The Sinclairs are not taking her.'

Melina looked up. 'They are not?' She pulled Willa into
her arms. 'That is terrible.'

He threw the letter from his hand. The paper fluttered
down. 'They wish for her to stay with her mother.'

She brushed her hand over the baby-fine hair and pressed
a kiss to Willa's head. 'They must be mistaken. If they are
addled, it is best for Willa not to be with them.'

'They received a letter, amazingly with mine. And they
sent it to me along with their change of heart. The missive
is from a woman they believe is Willa's mother asking them
to not take her one and only precious little girl. The only

baby she might ever have. That this woman wants her and needs to keep her. She loves Willa. The letter made them think I was forcing her—you—to give the child away.' He paused. 'Blast it, Melina. No one would be better for her than the Sinclairs. They are a good family. You should not have meddled.' He stood over her. 'And stop hiding behind the child.'

'I am not. We were playing.' Melina let Willa move to the floor.

'You were playing. With the child's life. You are not her mother and you should not have written to the Sinclairs. You have no right to do such.' He took a deep breath. 'She could have had two loving parents.'

'She has two loving parents.' She stood. 'Me. And Broomer…'

'What in blazes…?' His voice hurt her ears and he looked as if he had just spit vinegar. Willa's lips trembled.

'*Skase.* You'll frighten her.' She gave the baby a quick hug.

'I should be scaring you.' He lowered his tone and ran his fingers through his hair, pushing it back from his face. 'What do you mean, Broomer and you?' He leaned his head forward as if he could not hear correctly.

'He and I have discussed it. He would like to be a father and feels he might never get another chance. I already love her. We do not want to part with her and we both agree that two parents would be best. He is going back to Melos with me—and he will stay. He will keep me safe from Stephanos and be a kind father for Willa. And she will have my sisters for aunts.'

'I forbid it.'

'You cannot stop us.'

'You *cannot* take Willa without my permission. She is my legal daughter. And Broomer is my servant.'

Melina looked at the window, then turned her gaze to Warrington. 'I would not say Broomer is your servant. He has left. He has agreed to work for me, at no cost, because you were tossing aside a dear child. Broomer and I want her. If you choose anything otherwise…' her voice rose '…then you are a beast. You are less than a man. You are worse than Stephanos. You are worse than Ludgate.' Her fingers fisted. 'You must do the right thing and give her to us. Broomer and I will live on the dowry money. And you do not have to send us a single pence.'

His brows furrowed. 'Are you planning to wed him?'

'We have no notion of it, but the people on Melos will readily assume he is my husband, and it would be best if Stephanos thinks I am married.'

He took a step back. 'You are completely daft. And so was I. I trusted you and Broomer and you both made plans behind my back.'

'Yes. You are fortunate to have two such caring people in your life. Or, should I say, to have had two such caring people in your life.'

'I cannot believe you would do this. Again, a woman misled me.' He glowered. 'And I will *not* let you take the *Ascalon* back to Melos.'

'I have already had Broomer make arrangements with Captain Ben. On the ship. Your brother said he will have no trouble sailing *Ascalon* to the island, as you have already given the command, and he knows it is what you meant. And you might have trouble finding him to give him any changes, as Gidley is not to let you on board. Gidley has to do as his captain commands. He does not believe in mutiny.'

'I own that ship,' his voice thundered.

'Only half. And Captain Ben thinks if he sails his half, your half will follow without argument. He said it is odd how ships work that way.'

'You did— You led them all—' He held out a palm, shaking it in the air. 'You are as conniving as Cassandra. I want no part of you.'

She stood. 'Willa's things are already on board the ship, as are mine and Broomer's. I was just waiting to tell you. And…' she picked up Willa, holding her tight '…I am keeping those hideous dresses. And your pillows. I quite like them and they will make her a soft bed on the ship.' She stopped at the door and turned back. 'And the milled lilac soap. You should probably alert your housekeeper that you are running quite low on it.' She sniffed at Willa's hair. 'It makes her smell so precious.'

She waited a moment before speaking again, her words firm. 'Jacob needs you. He will need you especially now. The governess and a footman have taken him on a walk to keep him from seeing us leave. I told them it might happen.'

Then she left and gave Willa a tight hug, hefting her close. They would manage. They would make a wonderful family on Melos. And Warrington could live in London with his dead wife the rest of his life.

She walked downstairs to the hackney waiting across the street and did not turn back.

Warrington did not move. He couldn't. Women were traitorous wretches who did whatever they damn well pleased and could steal a child without blinking a lash. She'd stolen his daughter—the child—Willa. She'd taken her. Just walked right out.

Melina was gone. She was leaving the country, and she could get on that ship—that floating acorn—and sail to the end of the world. He would give Ben his blessing to take her. He would even send more pillows.

He opened his mouth. Broomer. She even took Broomer. He—Broomer—another scheming wretch.

He didn't care if the man was bigger than a house, he was going to get throttled. And soon. Warrington rushed from the room.

'Papa…' Jacob's voice, hesitant. He stood directly in his father's path.

Warrington stumbled into Jacob. He reached out, catching the little boy, stopping his own momentum.

He righted them both, still holding his son.

'Are you leaving again?' Jacob asked, speaking no louder than a whisper. 'I heard you shouting when we came back. And Willa's gone… I saw the carriage.'

Warrington stepped back against the wall and his hands loosened. His whole body slackened. He slid to the floor and looked at his child. 'No. I'm not. I'm not leaving you. Ever again. You're my son.' He gathered Jacob into his arms. 'My life.'

He waited, calming himself. 'Now tell me what you'd like to do today and we'll see how much we can manage.'

'You're staying with me?'

'Yes. I'm staying. I can't leave my Jacob.'

Jacob relaxed against him. 'I have a bow and arrow at Whitegate. I could show you how to shoot it.'

'That sounds like a good plan. I think I might have one somewhere, too. Perhaps we can have a competition after you teach me how.'

Jacob's head nodded at Warrington's chest. War let his arms rest loosely around his son and stared forward.

'Can we go, Papa? I like Whitegate better than here.'

'I don't know why I didn't think of it. I'm ready to return home.'

Chapter Twenty-Five

The town coach rolled to a stop, and Jacob bounced from his father's knees, but Warrington kept a tight grip on the boy's coat. There had simply not been enough room in the carriage for Jacob to sit anywhere else.

Keeping Jacob in his grasp, Warrington stepped on to the docks and saw the *Ascalon*. Someone had already noted his carriage, he could tell. Two men were moving forward, standing, blocking the way on to the ship.

He easily recognised Broomer, and the other, Gidley. They stood side by side, arms crossed.

Striding up to them, he stopped, looked up at Broomer, and said. 'You're discharged without references.' He stared at Gid. 'You, as well.'

'Well, yer got a point,' Gidley said. 'We, fortunately, work for other folks. I hear Mr Broomer has a lady he answers to.'

Broomer's eyes dropped when he spoke to Warrington and his lips trembled. 'I'm asking your forgiveness. But I had no choice.'

'No choice?' Warrington's words flew from his throat. 'No choice?'

'You'd have done the same thing. A little girl. That sweet woman needing a baby.'

'No,' Warrington snapped. He could not say another word.

'We're here to see my sister.' Jacob's voice broke the stillness.

Broomer took a deep sniff and looked at the boy. 'My pardon, Little Lordship, but we're to say she's not at home.'

Warrington nodded. He turned to the town coach, put two fingers to his lips and whistled.

Three men tumbled out and one of the coachmen jumped from the front. Each held a club. They scrambled up behind Warrington.

'We were at a tavern.' Jacob's voice rose in excitement. 'Papa gave the men sticks, and silver, and he told them they could change the silver for gold if they helped us walk on the ship. We can walk on the ship, can't we, Broomer? I want to see Uncle Ben's ship.' His voice lowered. 'Papa didn't give me gold, but he said if I did everything he asked, I could have a sea biscuit.' He rubbed his stomach. 'I would like that.'

Broomer looked at the men. 'Jack. Mutton. Wilton. Theodoure.' He nodded to them. They grinned back.

'Your sister…' Warrington stared at Broomer '…told us where we might find your friends when I explained how they were needed.'

'You'll have to kill me to get to the lady and that little angel,' Broomer said. 'You can't take 'em.'

'I will not.' He kept his eyes on Broomer and Gidley. 'You have my word, in front of my son, that I will not take her.'

'Papa. I thought you said we—'

'Quiet, Jacob.' He clamped his hand on his son's shoulder. Warrington continued, 'Unless Melina is completely happy to leave.'

The giant of a man ambled back, freeing space for them to come aboard. 'I suppose.'

Warrington stared at the first mate. 'And since you have time left from your guarding duties, Gidley, show my son how a ship works and keep him alive while doing so.' The earl turned to Broomer. 'And if you could take Willa, and keep her with her brother for a moment, I will refrain from telling the men about that particularly warm night in July when—'

Broomer raised a hand to silence him. 'I'll get Willa.' He turned.

'My cabin?' Warrington asked.

'No,' Gid interrupted innocently before Broomer could speak. 'Her cabin.'

Warrington levelled a look at Gidley. If not for Jacob's ears, this conversation would proceed differently.

Gidley chuckled, his whole body moving, and nodded at Jacob. 'Come along, Little Lordship, let me learn yer the parts of a ship.'

Warrington waited until Broomer and Willa's exodus from the cabin, then he strode inside.

Melina's bottom was propped against the edge of the bunk and her hands clasped the edge. She stared over his head.

He took in the room. 'Devil take it, Melina. Is there a pillow left in my house?' He glimpsed the window. 'And the curtains. How long have you been planning this?'

'Since the letter.'

He saw the basket in the corner. Smoked meat. Vegetables.

He grabbed the side of the door for balance. She planned to go to Melos. 'I suppose Jacob can sleep in Ben's cabin and I can try a hammock,' he said. 'I see there's no room in here for me.'

'You have not been invited.'

He shrugged. 'I'll stay on my half of the ship.' He went to the curtain, pulled it aside and looked out. 'My half should follow Ben's half.' He raised a brow and peered at her. 'Or so I've been told.'

The grunt she gave placed no importance in his words.

'I can see it now,' he said. 'Jacob and Willa on a ship and their tiny little stomachs jolting as we sail to Melos. And the waves. Life-threatening storms. They could perish.' He took a step and planted himself in front of her. 'Or you could stay and marry me, and be the one to guide Willa as she grows into a beauty others will pamper instead of making her do as she should…'

'You do not speak fair.'

'No. If she is to be my daughter, then this time, I will choose a good mother for her. I will not make the same mistake again. Think about it, Melina, because if you say no, I will have to tell my brother Dane that he will be managing the estates and bribe him greatly so I can follow you to make sure you are safe. And two babes will be sailing on a ship, away from nice comfortable beds full of pillows.'

Her eyes flashed dark at him.

He shrugged. 'Think of Jacob and Willa.'

'You will move to Melos?'

'And hope to convince you to marry me. The island will never be home to me. But I can live there and return here to visit.'

'I could not bear to see you leave like I saw my father leave.'

He turned to her. 'Never like your father. I'll expect you

to return with me each time. It won't be asking too much, if I am to spend much of my life there.'

He took one stride, pulled her hand to his lips and kissed her palm. 'I can't let you go. I can't. Since you left my house, I have only had you out of my life for moments, and it has been intolerable agony. I cannot imagine days, weeks or years without you. Let me send Ben for your sisters. They can return here. Your family can share our home.'

She studied his face.

He nodded. 'I have a country estate where I promised to take Jacob. I can add another house if needed. And my lonely, wealthy aunt is batty and cannot find enough people to listen to her stories. Your sisters will be comfortable and we will have enough time to become a true family.'

'What if my parentage is discovered? My father was married to another woman at the time he lived with my mother.'

'Your father's wife knows and I don't wish to cause her any embarrassment. I am quite happy with letting the world know you're a descendent of Aphrodite. Who's to say it isn't true? Certainly not me. I believe it.'

She stood and her eyes softened. 'My mother often claimed she had the spirit of a goddess. So I have heard that nonsense before.'

He took his forefinger and touched her mark, tracing a heart over it. 'Do you think Aphrodite will marry a mere mortal like me?'

She thrust herself into his arms, knocking him back a step, holding him tight.

He held her close, shutting his eyes, and feeling freedom, as if a thousand years of curses had left him.

'I will stay,' she said, 'but I'll give you my answer to the marriage later,' she said. 'I am in no hurry.'

'I'll have to correct that.' He put his cheek against her

hair and inhaled the holiday scent of her, and hoped she never lost the trace of all the best parts of the island that clung to her.

Warrington watched Willa and Jacob arguing over her doll while he waited for Melina to return from her walk in the Whitegate gardens. She searched for the perfect spot for her statue. In a few days, Ben should return with the sculpture and with Melina's sisters, and his wife could hardly wait.

Movement beside him caught his eye. 'You do not want the doll, Jacob,' Warrington commanded. 'Give it back to your sister.'

The moment Jacob handed it back, Warrington saw Willa's arm flex. 'Do not hit your brother.'

She looked at Warrington, smiled and said, 'Watface.'

Jacob snickered.

'Jacob.' He glared at his son. 'If you ever teach her anything like that again, you will be forbidden from riding Nero for a fortnight.'

Jacob's body sagged. 'Paapaa…' He dragged out the word.

Willa looked at Warrington. 'Paapaaa…' she copied Jacob's speech and ran to Warrington. He picked her up. Now when he looked into her eyes, he saw sunshine, and when he looked at Jacob, he saw Ben. That was not so pleasing.

'Warrington.' He heard Melina's voice behind him. She never called him by anything but his title, except when they were alone. Then she often whispered to him in her mother's language. Some day he would tell her that his childhood tutor had schooled him quite well in other languages—and his skill with one in particular had persuaded the Foreign Office to ask his assistance with the Greece mission.

'You must be firm with Willa,' Melina continued speaking to him. 'She knows *ratface* isn't a kind word.'

He felt little arms cling more tightly around his neck and a soft cheek snuggled against him.

'Willa,' he said, 'you cannot ride Jacob's horse for a fortnight.'

'Warrington…' Melina put her hands on her hips.

He forced himself not to smile. He was not besotted. He was in love. Totally, truly. And this time, nothing about it felt the same as before. His past wasn't buried. It had vanished. Just like a myth.

'Willa,' he said to her, 'your *mana* and your papa must insist that you only say nice words.'

'Until you are married,' Melina added. 'Then you may speak as you wish to your husband.'

'As you do.' He used his free hand to clasp her waist and pull her close enough to kiss her nose. 'And as I do to you. My Aphrodite. Not a mythological goddess. But better. I recovered the true treasure from Melos.'

* * * * *

FORBIDDEN TO
THE DUKE

To Juanita Ballew, 'Sis', a real heroine.

Chapter One

The pudgy-eyed gamekeeper pointed a flintlock straight at Bellona's chest. His eyebrows spiked into angry points. 'Drop the longbow.' His gun barrel emphasised his words and even without the weapon his size would have daunted her. He'd not looked so large or his stare so bloodless from a distance.

Noise crashed into her ears—the sound of her heart—and the beats tried to take over every part of her. She forced the blackness away and locked her stare with his. Charred hatred, roughened by the unshaven chin, slammed out from his face.

She nodded and tossed the bow into the twining berry thorns at the side of the path. The canopy of sycamore leaves covered him in green-hued shadows.

He put one hand to his mouth, thrust his fingers to his lips and whistled loud enough to be heard in Greece. The shrill sound jabbed her, alerting her that he wasn't alone. She'd never seen anyone else in the forest but this devil. She would be fighting two men and at least one weapon.

'…shoot at me…' He spoke again and the words snapped her back into understanding.

She cursed herself for not taking more care. She'd not heard him behind her—but she should have smelled his boiled-cabbage stench.

'I be bringing his lordship,' he said. 'Your toes be dangling and the tide be washing your face before they cut you down. You won't be shooting at me no more. You're nothing more'n a common wench and people in lofty places be wantin' you to hang.'

Her fingers stiffened, her mind unable to send them commands. She held her chin high. She'd thought she was in a safe land. She'd thought she'd escaped men who wanted to hurt her. Showing fear would be dangerous. 'You—' She couldn't have taken her eyes from his. 'I'm a guest of the Earl of Warrington and I have misplaced myself.'

The man's nose bunched up as he talked. 'But you ain't on the earl's land now, Miss Lady Nobody. You're no better'n me.' He waved the gun. 'You're a poacher and I've seen you here aplenty times before. I just niver could catch you.'

'The earl will be *thymomenos*, angered.'

He snorted. 'But this is the duke's land. His Grace don't lose no sleep over what an *earl* would think.'

She forced her fingers alert. 'You are the one who should think. You must know I live near.'

'But you ain't no real lady. I already told the duke all about you and how you been scattering my traps and he thinks I'm imaginin'. Your eyes is even uncommon dark like some witch borne you. I told him you're half-spirit. They hanged Mary Bateman. If they don't be hangin' you, you'll end up lyin' with vermin in gaol. Good 'nuff for you.'

He indicated the trail behind himself by swinging the barrel of the gun towards it. 'Don't move a feather.' The gamekeeper swaggered. 'His Grace be right behind me. I told him I set my traps near and this time I be catchin' somethin' big. You've ruined your last snare.'

Footsteps in the leaves signalled the approach of another. Bellona rested her left hand on the top of arrows tucked into the quiver strapped around her waist. 'You can go to the devil.'

The shoulders of another man came into view, and Bellona swallowed. She needed all of her strength. Two men to fight.

The gamekeeper stepped off the path so the other one could see her.

The duke stopped beside the gamekeeper and the scent of the air became clean. The newcomer examined her, not scowling or smiling.

She would not have thought this man a peer had she seen him without introduction, but she would have known him for a gentleman. His neckcloth looped in a simple, soft knot. His boots reached his knees and his dark riding coat had plain buttons. He wore every thread as if it had been woven to his own order. Sunlight dappled over lean cheeks. His eyes were the same colour as her own.

Her stomach clenched, but not with fear. She'd made a mistake. She'd looked into his eyes. For the first time in her life, she was afraid of something inside herself.

She stepped back.

'Your Grace, I caught the murderous culprit what's been stealing the hares from my traps and wishin' curses on us all. She be a common thief, a murderous woman and full of meanness, just like I said.' The gamekeeper's words spewed out, leaving even less air for Bellona to breathe. 'You want I should send the stable boy for the magistrate?'

The duke gave the slightest shake of his head. 'You are mistaken, Wicks. I will see her back to my estate safely and ensure that she is escorted on her way.'

'She be a thief, Your Grace, and a bewitched woman. Why, see how her eyes be puttin' evil my direction now. She be tryin' to burn me into ash right where I stand.'

'Miss—' the newcomer directed his words to Bellona and he leaned forward as he peered at her '—have you been poaching on my land?'

She sensed somehow that he jested with her. 'No. Never,' Bellona said, shaking her head. The knife was in her boot. But she didn't want to attack. She only wanted to flee.

The duke's lips firmed and he took in a small breath on his next words. 'Wicks…'

The gamekeeper's stance tightened and he rushed his words. 'She tossed her bow into the briars. She'd kill a man herself for blood sport. She'd cut out his heart and cook it.'

The duke's lips tightened at one side and his eyes dismissed the other man's words.

'I don't eat hearts,' Bellona inserted, directing a look straight into the vile man. 'Only brains. You are safe.'

'Your Grace,' the gamekeeper sputtered, outrage and fury mixed. 'She's—'

'Quiet.' The duke's words thrust into the air with the seriousness of a sword point held to the throat.

He stepped towards her, moving over the fallen log in the path, his hand out. 'The lady and I have not been introduced, but as this isn't a soirée, I think—'

Instinctively, she pulled an arrow from the quiver and held the tip against the duke's grey silk waistcoat— pressing.

His arm halted, frozen.

'Do not touch me.' Her words copied his in command.

His eyes widened and he straightened. 'I was going to take your arm. My pardon. It's usually received well, I assure you.'

She kept the arrow at his stomach, trying to keep the spirit around him from overtaking her.

The gamekeeper moved so the weapon again pointed at her. 'Just give me the word, Your Grace, I'll save you. She be tryin' to kill a peer. No sense wasting good rope round that boney neck.'

'Put the flintlock away, Wicks. Now.' The duke didn't take his eyes from Bellona. 'This woman and I have not finished introductions yet and, by my calculation, the arrow tip isn't exceedingly sharp.'

'It's sharp enough,' she said.

'Miss…' He blinked. He smiled. But they were just outward movements. 'Most people get to know me a little better before they think of weapons. Perhaps you should consider that. It might make an attempt on my life more enjoyable for you if there were some justification.'

She never saw his movement, but his hand clamped

around her wrist, securing her, not tight, but shackle-strong.

'My property.' He stepped back from the arrow. Then he extricated it from her fingers, the warm touch of his hand capturing her in yet another way before he released her. 'My rules, Huntress.' He studied her face. 'Or if my observation is correct, should I refer to you as goddess?'

As he examined the arrow, she took another step back. She gave the merest head toss of dismissal and readied her hand to the single arrow left in the quiver.

His eyes flickered to the sharpened tip of the projectile he held, but he wasn't truly examining it. He twirled it around, tipped his head to her and held the feathered end to her. 'I have met the lovely Countess of Warrington and although you resemble her, I would remember if I'd met you. That means you're the sister named for the goddess of war. The woman hardly ever seen.'

'You may call me Miss Cherroll.' The rules she'd studied fled from her, except the one about the curtsy and she could not force herself to do it. She took the arrow.

She only wanted to leave, but her limbs hadn't yet recovered their strength. She controlled her voice, putting all the command in it she could muster. 'You're not what I expected.'

'If you've been talking to Warrington, I suppose not.' He tilted his head forward, as if he secluded them from the rest of the world. 'What is he fed for breakfast? I fear it curdles his stomach—daily.'

'Only when mixed <u>with</u> entertainments not to his liking.'

'Well, that explains it. I can be quite entertaining.'

'He claims you can be quite…' She paused. His eyes waited for her to continue, but she didn't think it prudent, either to Warrington or the duke.

The duke continued, taking in the words she didn't say. 'Not many are above him, and, well, I might give him the tiniest reminder of my status, when it is needed.' He shrugged. 'Our fathers were like brothers. He thinks he has become the old earl and I have not attained the grandness of my sire. My father did limp— and that knee was the only thing that kept him from perfection. The injured leg was the price he paid for doing the right thing. He once thrust himself between someone and the hooves of an angry horse.'

'I would not be so certain of the earl's opinion.' She paused, softening her words. 'He says you are quite the perfect duke. A duke from heel to head.' Warrington had stared at the ceiling and grimaced when he spoke.

'A compliment. I'm certain. From Warrington.' He shrugged. 'Too many things distract me from perfection. I just trudge along, doing what I can. Hoping to honour the legacy my father left behind.'

He turned to the other man, sending him along. 'I'll see Miss Cherroll home.' Taking a step towards her, he paused when she moved the pointed tip the slightest bit in his direction. 'Assuming she doesn't do Warrington a boon and impale his favourite neighbour.'

When he stopped moving, she relaxed her hand.

'I will manage well enough on my own.' She turned, pulling the skirt's hem from a bramble, and moved closer to the bow. 'I know the way.' She heard her own words and turned back to the duke and leaned her head to the side. 'I have been lost here before.' She pulled the bow into her hand, freeing it from the thorny brambles clasping it.

'I would imagine so. Wicks claims you are here more than he is. I might call on you,' he said, 'later today to assure myself you arrived safely home.'

She shook her head. 'Please don't. Warrington is always claiming I bring home strange things from my walks.'

'My dear, I'm a duke. He won't be able to say a word. It's a rule of sorts.'

'You truly don't know him well, do you?'

'Well, perhaps he might grumble, but his good breeding would insist he appear welcoming. At least in your presence.'

She held the nock end of the arrow as if she were going to seat it against the bowstring. 'You're right in that my English father named me for the Roman goddess of war. And, it's said I'm completely lacking in the ways of a proper Englishwoman. But I do remember one phrase. "I am not at home."'

'Miss Cherroll. I would think you'd not mind sharing tea with me seeing as you have already shared my property.'

She shook her head. 'I have been called on before. I have not been at home.'

'Ever?'

She firmed her lips and shook her head.

'Why not?'

She didn't answer his question. She could not speak of her memories aloud. Putting them into words brought the feel of the rough fingertips to her neck.

His brows furrowed. Even though she knew a

proper lady didn't scurry along the trail, she did, leaving the duke standing behind her.

Rhys Harling, Duke of Rolleston, sat at his desk, completely unmoving. Wicks stood in front of Rhys, repeating the same words he'd said two days ago and the two days before that. Rhys hoped the air would clear of the man's dank scent when he left.

Wicks waved the arrow like a sceptre. His lips didn't stop moving even when he paused to find new words.

Wicks rambled on, falling more in love with his discourse as he continued. If the gamekeeper were to be believed, the woman created more mischief than any demon.

It had been five days since Wicks had caught the woman. The gamekeeper had approached him twice to discuss the lands and could not keep from mentioning her.

Rhys interrupted, his voice direct. 'She did not try to impale me. Neither her teeth nor her eyes—which are not rimmed by devil's soot—show brighter than any other's in the dusk and she is not as tall as I am. You cannot claim her to be something she is not. I forbid it.'

'You can't be faultin' me for lookin' out for your lands, Your Grace.'

'I don't. But she's the earl's guest. You must cease talking at the tavern about the woman.'

'Who told you?' His chin dropped and he looked at the floor.

'Who didn't tell me?' Rhys fixed a stare at the man. 'Wicks, you should know that words travel from one set of ears to the next and the next and before long every person who has shared a meal with someone else has heard.'

'She does stick in my craw, Your Grace.'

He didn't blame the gamekeeper. Rhys couldn't remove her from his mind either. The quiver cinched her trim waist. A twig had poked from her mussed hair. The magical thing he'd noticed about her was the way her hair could stay in a knot on her head when most of it had escaped.

Rhys had known when the gamekeeper first mentioned the trespasser who it would most likely be. He'd wanted to see her for himself.

Wicks wasn't the first person to discuss her. Even the duchess, who talked only of family members who'd passed on, had varied from her melancholia once and spoke of the earl's sister-by-law Miss Cherroll. The foreign-born woman rarely let herself be seen by anyone outside the earl's household and that caused more talk than if she'd danced three dances with the same partner.

'Forget her,' the duke said. 'She's just an ordinary woman who likes to traipse the trails. I can't fault her for that.'

He couldn't. He'd travelled over those same trails countless times, trying to keep up with his brother, Geoff.

Looking for the woman had been the first time he'd been in the woods since Geoff's death. The gnashing ache grinded inside him again, but the woman's face reminded him of unspoiled times.

But she was…a poacher of sorts. Nothing like her sister—a true countess if tales were to be believed.

He wouldn't put it past Warrington to keep this bow-carrying family member in the shadows, afraid what would happen if the woman met with members of the *ton*.

'You didn't feel she could near strangle a man with one look from her eyes?' Wicks asked. 'I could feel that devil in her just trying to take my vicar's words right from mind. She still be trespassin' ever' day. Taunting me, like. She tears up my traps and she lurks out in the wood, waiting until I check them and then she tries to kill me.'

'I'm sure she's not trying to kill you.'

'This arrow weren't whipping by your head.' He pulled every muscle of his body into an indignant shudder. 'And since I caught her last time, she stays too far back for me to snatch her again.'

'You will not touch her.' Rhys met Wicks's stare. Rhys stood.

Wicks's lips pressed together.

'You will not touch her,' Rhys said again and waited.

'I don't want no part of that evil witch,' Wicks said finally. 'I looked at her and I saw the Jezebel spirit in her. I be sleepin' on the floor and not in my bed so she can't visit me in my night hours and have her way with me.'

Rhys put both palms flat on the desk and leaned forward. 'That is a good plan. However, if you sleep with your nightcap over your ears it will do the same.'

'You're sure?'

'Yes.' Rhys nodded.

Wicks's lips moved almost for a full minute before he spoke and his shoulders were pulled tight and he watched the arrow in his hand. 'Well, I'll be considerin' it. Floor's cold.'

'Do you think perhaps she is a normal kind-hearted woman, Wicks, and merely doesn't want little creatures harmed?'

'I wondered. But that seems odd to me. When I gave her my smile—' He bared perfect teeth except for one missing at the bottom. 'She didn't even note. Just raised her bow right towards me and let this arrow loose.'

Rhys rose, walked around the desk and held out his hand. Wicks slowly placed the arrow across Rhys's palm.

'If you see her again,' Rhys commanded, 'at any time at any place, you are not to give her one moment of anything but respect. You are not to smile at her or approach her, or you will answer to me in a way you will not like.'

'Not right,' Wicks said, his nose going up. 'Being shot at while doin' my work.'

'I will handle this. Do not forget my words. Leave her be.'

'I will,' Wicks said. 'I pity her. Has too many airs to settle into things right for a woman's place.'

Rhys glared.

'But I be keepin' it a secret.' He nodded. 'I ain't givin' her another one of my smiles. She missed her chance. And if she tries to have her way with me, I be turnin' my head and keepin' my nightcap tight.'

He used both hands to clamp his hat on his head as he shuffled out, grumbling.

Rhys studied the arrow and thought of his mother's melancholia. How she hardly left her room, even for meals. How she talked more of people who'd passed than of her own friends, and how she claimed illness rather than go to Sunday Services. His brother's death had taken the life from her as well. The one moment the duchess's thoughts had wavered into the present had been when she asked Rhys if he'd heard of the earl's guest, but by the time he'd answered, his mother's thoughts had wavered back into the shadows of the past.

He brushed his hand over the arrow fletching. Window light bounced over the feathers, almost startling him. Raising his eyes, he saw the sun's rays warming the room. He stood, walking to the sunlight, pausing to feel the heat on his face. He lifted the feathery end of the weapon, twirling it in the brightness.

Winter's chill had left the air, but he'd not noticed the green outside the window until now. The woman had also worn the colours of the forest, he remembered. She'd not looked like a warrior goddess, but a woodland nymph, bringing life into morning.

He snorted, amazed at the folly of his imagination. He'd not had such foolish thoughts in a long time. Nor had he longed for a woman's comfort overmuch in the past year. Now, he imagined the huntress and his body responded, sending reminders of pleasure throughout his being.

Leaning into the window frame, holding the arrow like a talisman, he tried to remember every single aspect of her. What she'd said and how she'd looked. Each word and moment that had transpired between them.

He pulled the soft end of the arrow up, looking at the feathers one last time before tapping the nock against the sill, staring at the reflections of sunlight.

This woman at the earl's estate, who was willing

to fight for rabbits, but could keep the servants whispering about her, might be just the woman who could bring his mother back to life. She'd already reminded Rhys that he was still alive.

Within the hour, Rhys was in the Earl of Warrington's sitting room. The duke clasped an arrow at his side and waited as he expected he might. He moved to the window again, wanting to feel the heat from the sun streaming through the panes. Trees budded back to life. A heathen spirit might do the same for his own home.

The mantel sported a painting of three young girls playing while their mother watched. He wagered the painting was of Greece and one of the girls could have been the one on his property. Except for the single painting, the room seemed little different than Rhys's own library.

Rhys looked out over Warrington's snipped and clipped and trimmed and polished world, almost able to hear the laughter from years before.

Only, the laughter was not his, but directed at him.

Of course, both he and Warrington had matured now. They had left foolish prattle and childish games behind.

Warrington strode in. Rhys could still taste the medicinal the others had found in the apothecary jar and forced into Rhys's mouth when they were children. That had to be his earliest memory.

'Your *Grace*,' Warrington greeted. The earl moved to stand at the mantel. He glanced once at the painting above it before he asked, 'So what is the honour that brings you to Whitegate?'

Rhys held out the arrow. 'I found this on my property and heard that you have a guest who practises archery. I'd like to return it to her.'

Rhys had never seen Warrington's face twitch until that moment. He studied Rhys as if they'd just started a boxing match. 'You are interested in talking with *Bellona*?'

Warrington's eyes flickered. 'I'm sure whatever she did—' Warrington spoke quickly. 'She just doesn't understand our ways.' He paused and then sighed. 'What did she do now?'

'I just wish to meet with her,' Rhys said, 'and request that she refrain from shooting arrows on to my property—particularly near others.'

Warrington grimaced and then turned it into a smile. 'She does… Well…you know…' He held out a palm. 'Some women like jewellery. Flowers. Sharp things. She likes them.'

'Sharp things?'

Warrington shook his head. 'Never a dull moment around her.'

'Truly?'

'Beautiful voice—when she's not talking. Her sister forced her to attend the soirée at Riverton's, hoping Bellona would find something about society that suited her. Pottsworth wanted to be introduced. She'd not danced with anyone. I thought it a good idea even though he is—well, you know Potts. She smiled and answered him in Greek. Thankfully none of the ladies near her had our tutors. Riverton overheard and choked on his snuff. We left before he stopped sputtering. He still asks after her every time he sees me. "How is that retiring Miss Cherroll?"'

'Can't say as I blame her. You introduced *Potts-worth* to her?' Rhys asked drily.

'I'm sure she might wander too far afield from time to time,' Warrington murmured it away, 'but your land has joined mine since before our grandparents' time and we've shared it as one.' Warrington gave an encompassing gesture, then he toyed with what could have been a speck on the mantel. 'We're all like family. We grew up together. I know you and I don't have the very close bond of our fathers, but still, I count you much the same as a brother of my own.'

'Much like Cain and Abel?'

Warrington grinned. He waved the remark away. 'You've never taken a jest well.'

'The bull,' Rhys said, remembering the very incensed animal charging towards him, bellowing. Rhys was on the wrong side of the fence, his hands on the rails, and the older boys pushed at him, keeping him from climbing to safety. He'd felt the heat from the bull's nostrils when they'd finally hefted him through to the other side. Laughing.

He couldn't have been much more than five years old.

Warrington had instigated many of the unpleasant moments of Rhys's childhood. Actually, almost every disastrous circumstance could be traced back to War. Rhys had been lured into a carriage and then trapped when they wedged the door shut from the outside, and then he'd spent hours in the barn loft when they had removed the ladder. When they'd held him down and stained his cheeks with berries, he'd waited almost two years to return fresh manure to everyone involved. It had taken special planning and the assistance of the stable master's son to get manure put into Warrington's boots.

Rhys's mother and father had not been happy. The one time he had not minded disappointing his father.

War's face held camaraderie now—just like when the new puppy had been left in the carriage, supposedly.

'I must speak with your wife's sister,' Rhys said. 'I might have an idea which could help us both.'

'What?' The word darted from Warrington's lips.

'I thought Miss Cherroll might spend some time with the duchess. Perhaps speak of Greece or...' He shrugged. 'Whatever tales she might have learned.'

'I forbid—' Warrington's head snapped sideways. 'No. She is my family and she must stay with us.'

Rhys lips quirked up. 'But, War, we're like brothers. Your family is my family.'

Warrington grunted. 'You didn't believe that flop when I said it. Don't try to push it back in my direction.'

Rhys smiled. 'I suppose it is your decision to make, War. But remember. I am serious and I will not back down.'

'I assure you, Rhys, Miss Cherroll is not the gentle sort that the duchess is used to having tea with.'

Rhys gave a slight twitch of his shoulder in acknowledgement. Warrington had no idea his mother was only having tea with memories of death. She'd lost her will to live. With her gone, he would have no one. No one of his true family left. And he was not ready to lose the last one. 'Call Miss Cherroll. Let me decide.'

With a small cough of disagreement, Warrington

shrugged. 'Speak with her and you'll see what I mean.' He reached for the pull. A child's laughing screech interrupted him. A blonde blur of a chit, hardly big enough to manage the stairs, hurtled into the room and crashed into Warrington's legs, hugging for dear life, and whirling so he stood between her and the door.

Bellona, brandishing a broom, charged in behind the little one and halted instantly at the sight of Warrington.

Rhys took in a breath and instantly understood Wicks's fascination with the woman. Her face, relaxed in laughter, caught his eyes. He couldn't look away—no man would consider it.

'Just sweeping the dust out of the nursery,' she said to Warrington, lowering the broom while she gingerly moved around him. The child used him as a shield.

Warrington's hand shot down on to the little girl's head, hair shining golden in the sunlight, stilling her.

Bellona's attention centred on the waif. 'Willa, we do not run in the house. We swim like fishes.'

The child laughed, pulled away from the silent admonishment of her father's hand on her head, puffed her cheeks out and left the room quickly, making motions of gliding through water.

Warrington cleared his throat before the chase began again. 'We have a guest, Bellona.'

Rhys saw the moment Bellona became aware of his presence. The broom tensed and for half a second he wondered if she would drop it or turn it into a weapon. Warrington was closer, and Rhys was completely willing to let her pummel him.

She lowered the bristles to the floor, but managed a faint curtsy and said, 'I did not know we had a visitor.' Her face became as stiff as the broom handle.

Warrington turned to Rhys.

'Bellona is… She gets on quite well with the children as you can tell.' His eyes glanced over to her. 'But she is not as entranced with tranquillity as her sister is.'

'I do like the English ways,' she said, shrugging. 'I just think my ways are also good.'

'But my children need to be well mannered at all times.' Warrington frowned after he spoke.

'I do adore the *paidi*. They are gold,' she said, voice prim and proper. 'But no little one is well mannered at all times. They have life. It is their treasure. They should spend it well.'

'They should also know the way to be proper and comport themselves in a lofty manner when they meet such a person as we are privileged to have in our presence.' He glanced at Rhys. 'His Grace, Duke of Rolleston. Rescuer of lost puppies, everywhere.' He turned to Bellona to complete the introduction. 'Miss Cherroll, my wife's kind and gentle-spirited youngest sister—' his brows bumped up as he looked back at Rhys '—who has called me a few endearments in her native language that our tutor neglected to teach us, and when her sister translates I fear something is lost in the meaning.'

Her eyes blinked with innocence at Warrington for a moment before she acknowledged the introduction with a slight nod.

'I believe the duke wanted to speak with you.' Warrington walked to her, took the broom and looked at it as if might bite. 'And I should see about Willa.'

The earl took two long strides to the door. 'I won't send a chaperon.' He smiled at Rhys as he left. 'You're on your own.'

Chapter Two

Pleased Warrington had left them alone, Rhys's attention turned to Bellona. She'd moved a step back from him and stood close to an unlit lamp on a side table. Her eyes remained on the arrow in his hand.

Perhaps he'd been mistaken about her. She might be unsettled.

Bellona nodded towards the arrow. 'I believe that is mine.'

Rhys grasped the shaft with both hands and snapped the arrow across his knee, breaking the wood in two pieces. Then he held it in her direction.

The straight line of her lips softened. Her shoulders relaxed and she moved just close enough so that he could place the arrow in her hand. Exotic spices lingered in the air around her and he tried to discern if it was the same perfume from a rare plant he'd once noted in a botanist's collection.

'Thank you.' She took the splintered pieces and increased the distance between them. Examining the broken shaft, she said, 'I feared you would not be so kind as to return it.'

'You could have injured someone. My gamekeeper.'

She raised her eyes to Rhys. 'The arrow did what arrows do. I didn't want to hurt him, but he—' Bellona dismissed the words. 'His voice... You should speak with him about *glossa*—his words.'

'Leave the poor man alone. He has been on my estate his whole life and feels as much kinship to the land as I do.'

'A man cannot own land. It is a gift from the heavens to be shared.'

'For the time being, it is my gift and I control all on it. You upset the gamekeeper.'

She shrugged. 'He upsets rabbits.'

'They are invited. You are not. However...' His next words were about to change that, but he forgot he was speaking when her hand moved.

Flicking up the notched end of the arrow, she brushed the feathery fletching against her face. The arrow stroked her skin. One. Two. Three little brushes. Softness against softness.

His heart pounded blood everywhere around his body except his head.

He remembered where he was, but not what he'd been saying. He looked at her eyes, checking for artifice, wondering if she knew how he reacted to her.

'I do not know if this is a good idea.' He spoke barely above a whisper.

'The traps are a bad idea. Wrong. Thinking you own the earth is not correct.' She moved her hand to her side, the arrow tip pointed in his direction.

Traps? That problem was easily solved.

'At the soirée, what did you say to Pottsworth in Greek that was so shocking?' he asked.

She raised her brows.

'Never mind.' He turned away. Walking to the painting, he looked at it. An idyllic scene with a sea in the background. Waves lapped the sand and breezes brought the scent of moisture to him. 'Are you one of the little girls in the painting?' He raised his finger, almost touching the long-dried oils. She had to be the youngest one—the urchin had grown into the woman behind him.

'Miss Cherroll.' He turned back. 'Are you the little one in the picture?'

'It is just a painting. From my homeland.'

'Tell me about yourself.'

'No. You broke my arrow.'

'I beg your pardon.' He turned to her and locked his clasped hands behind his back. This intractable woman and his mother would not get on well at all. Such a foolish thought.

'You do not mean to beg my pardon,' she said. 'You just speak it because it is what you have always said.'

'I'll buy you a score of arrows to replace this one if you merely promise you will not shoot in the direction of a person. I was making a point.'

She waved a hand his direction. 'Keep your arrows. I have many of them.'

'Well, I must be going. You're not quite as I expected. Thank you for your time. I sincerely regret breaking your arrow.' He stopped. 'No, I don't. However, I will see that more are sent your way. Please be careful with them and do not practise archery on my land.'

She didn't speak.

He strode to the door. This woman could not reside with his mother. He did not know how he could have

imagined such a thing. But he just did not know what
to do. He turned back. He could not go out that door.

'You may visit my land whenever you wish.' He
didn't recognise his own voice. His words sounded
parched to his ears—the same as when he was little
more than a youth and requested his first dance from a
woman whose eyes glittered with sensual knowledge.

'I will not shoot near the gamekeeper any more unless he comes too close to me.' Her tone commanded,
but underneath there might have been a waver in it.
His thoughts raced ahead.

'But be aware he is not a nice man,' she continued.
'He has killed—he has killed them after taking them
from the trap. With his foot.' Her voice dipped. 'It is—
it is bad. He does not care.'

He turned away so he could concentrate and put
his hand on the door frame, sorting his thoughts, listening with his whole body. 'He said you shot at him.'

'Yes. I was watching the traps to see if he'd caught
anything. I was going to free the animals. But he was
early. He knew. He saw me and he walked closer and
I thought of the rabbits. The rabbits. What man could
do that to another living creature? I could not let him
near me. I shot at the ground between us. He stopped.'

'It is his job to watch for poachers.' He slid his hand
from the wood and moved just enough to hold her in
his line of vision.

'Nothing should be trapped like that.'

He asked the other question again. 'What did you
say to Pottsworth?'

'The man at the soirée?'

'Yes.'

'I was in the gardens because I did not want to be

with the people. I heard him speak to another man and say I was ripe for his hands. I only told him what would happen if he touched me, although I did not say it pleasantly. I knew he could understand my language. Warrington had told us that most men at the soirée had been tutored in Greek.'

'I have heard that your parents are no longer with us,' Rhys asked, tactfully changing the subject.

She touched a finger to the tip of the arrow. 'My *mana* is not alive. I miss her still. I miss her more now than when she died, because she has been gone from me longer.'

He stepped closer, into the whiff of her perfume—until he realised it wasn't only the exotic scent around her, but that of fresh bread. His eyes snapped to hers.

The arrow tip followed his movement, but he didn't care about that.

'Have you been in the…cooking area?' he asked.

She waved her palm the barest bit. 'The staff here works hard. They do not need me watching over them.'

He edged forward and she stepped back. 'You have a dusting of white on your face,' he said.

She reached up, brushing, but missed it.

A duke simply did not reach out and touch a woman's face, particularly upon their first proper introduction. But he did. Warm, buttery sensations flowed inside him. His midsection vibrated, but it was with the outward pressure against his waistcoat. If he looked down, he knew he'd see the tip of the arrow pressed there again. But the broken arrow wasn't so long and it connected their bodies too closely. His blood pounded hot and fast. Blast. This was not good. He'd been too long in the country where he had to take such care because his movements were watched so closely. He needed to get to London soon and find a woman.

She smiled. 'I use the arrows as my chaperon.'

'Perhaps a maid would be better instead?' He reached the slightest bit to nudge the arrow away, but stopped before connecting with the wood. If his hand touched hers, that would be more than he wanted to deal with.

He moved back, freeing himself in more ways than one, and examined his fingers while rubbing the white powder between thumb and forefinger. He was fairly certain it was flour or some such. Something one dusted on the top of cakes or used in producing meals.

'You *have* been in a kitchen.'

'I—' Her chin jutted. 'I do not…visit the kitchen. Often.'

He shrugged. 'I do not mind. It just surprises me.' He lowered his voice. 'You shot at my gamekeeper—I don't see why you'd have a problem with going into the servants' area.'

He wasn't in the mood to complain about her at the moment. But he must keep his thoughts straight. She had put a weapon against his waistcoat. She ran through the woods, tormenting a gamekeeper. She'd traipsed in the kitchen with the servants, chased a child with a broom in the sitting room and probably would not be able to respond quietly in the bedchamber as a decent woman should. He clamped his teeth together.

This woman was as untamed as the creatures she freed. She might be a relation of Warrington's, but one always had an errant relative who did not do as they should.

'I—' She stepped back. And now the broken arrow rested against her bodice. 'I cannot let the rabbits be trapped. I cannot.'

'I suppose I understand.' He did understand. More than she thought. She had a weakness for rabbits and right now his weakness was for soft curves and compassionate eyes. He must clear his head. No matter what it took, he must clear his head.

'I would like to reassure you,' he said, 'that the rabbits will soon be holding soirées among the parsnips and their smiling teeth will be green-stained from all the vegetables they harvest. The traps are to be removed. You do not have to check my lands. No more traps.'

'Thank you.' She nodded. 'It is a relief.'

'In return, I would like very much for you to have tea with my mother tomorrow,' he said. He heard the youth still in his voice. That strange sound. Too much sincerity for the simple question. 'Please consider it. My mother is very alone right now,' he quickly added.

She moved, still grasping the arrow pieces, but her hand rested on the spine of the sofa. She studied his face. 'I don't... The English customs...'

She was going to say no and he couldn't let her. He had to explain.

'My mother will not know you are arriving and I will summon her once you are there. Otherwise she may not leave her room.' His chuckle was dry. 'She likely will not leave her chamber, unless I insist. But as you understand what it is like to miss a person you care for, I would appreciate your spending a few moments speaking with the duchess. Perhaps she will feel less alone.'

She didn't speak.

'My brother has passed recently. My father died almost two years ago, soon after my older sister and her new husband perished in a fire while visiting friends. My mother is becoming less herself with each passing day. She misses her family more with each hour.' He controlled his voice, removing all emotion. 'She is trapped—by memories—and only feels anger and self-pity.'

'I will visit your *mana*.' She spoke matter-of-factly. 'And if she does not wish to leave her chamber, I do not mind at all. I will visit her there.'

He turned, nodding, and with a jerk of his chin indicated the arrow in her hand.

'Would you really hurt me?' he asked.

Something flickered behind her eyes. Some memory he could never see.

'I hope I could,' she said. 'I tell myself every day that I will be strong enough.'

'You wish to kill someone?'

She shook her head, tousled hair falling softly, and for a moment she didn't look like the woman she was, but reminded him of a lost waif. 'No. I wish to be strong enough.'

'Have you ever…hurt anyone?'

She shook her head. 'No. I know of no woman who has ever killed a man, except my grandmother, Gigia.'

He waited.

'A man, from a *ploio*. A ship. He was not good. He killed one of the women from our island and hurt another one almost to her death. Gigia gave him drink. Much drink, and he fell asleep. He should not have fallen asleep. Gigia said it was no different than killing a goat, except the man was heavier. My *mana* and uncle were there and they buried him. I do not think the men from the ship cared about losing him. They did not hunt for him long. Gigia gave them wine and we helped them search.'

Rhys took a breath. He'd invited this woman into his home, where his mother would meet her. This woman who seemed no more civilised than the rabbits she wished to protect and yet, he wanted to bury his face against her skin and forget.

'I see.' He frowned, repressing his notice of her as a woman. He certainly did not need to be noting the insignificant things about her.

'From your face, I think you do.' Instantly, her eyes pinched into a tilted scowl, her nose wrinkled. She mocked him. His mouth opened the barest bit. Yes, she'd jested.

'Miss Cherroll,' he spoke, beginning his reprimand, holding himself to the starched demeanour his father had used, one strong enough that even a royal would take notice of it. 'Perhaps my mother could also be of some guidance to you.'

Lashes fluttered. A dash of sadness tinged her words, but the chin did not soften. 'I am beyond repair.'

Bits of words fluttered through his mind, but none found their way to his lips. He took a moment appraising her, then caught himself, tamping down the sparking embers.

This would not be acceptable. He had survived his sister's death. He had survived his father's death. Geoff was gone. The duchess was failing. Rhys's vision tunnelled around him, leaving only images from memory. He would take his own heart from his chest and wring it out with his two hands before he let it close to another person.

He turned his body from her with more command than he would ever unleash on the ribbons from a horse's bridle.

'I did not mean to anger you so...' Her voice barely rose above the drumming in his ears.

'I am merely thinking,' he said.

'You must stop, then. It's not agreeing with you.'

'I think you are the one not agreeing with me.'

'So it has never happened before?'

'Not recently.'

'An oversight?' Wide eyes.

'I can hardly believe you and the countess are sisters.'

'If you think we are brothers, then I do not know what to say.'

'You are—' He gave up. If she could use that same spirit to release his mother's mind from the memories snaring her, it would be worth the risk. He had no other options.

Chapter Three

Bellona took the carriage to the duke's house, frowning each time the vehicle jostled her. Darting through the woods would have been so much easier, but when the gamekeeper's eyes had rested on her the last time, a drop of spittle had escaped his lips when he'd smiled at her. The past had flooded back. She'd thought to put the memories behind her, but they'd returned like a wave, currents underneath tugging at her, trying to pull her to death.

Even now, looking out of the window, she could imagine a face peering at her from behind each tree. The eyes reflecting dark, evil thoughts, or no thoughts at all. Knowledge returned of looking into the pupils and seeing nothing human in a face she'd once seen innocently. Nothing behind those eyes which reasoned or thought, but only the same blankness from the face of an animal intent on devouring its prey.

She'd heard the tales of people being fed to lions. Telling the lion to think about the rightness of not clamping its teeth around her neck would do no good. Reminding the beast that she was merely wishing to live out her life wouldn't change anything. The lion might appear calm, but it would be thinking of only how to get a straighter lunge.

Bellona had known Stephanos before he killed— watched him dance and laugh and work as he'd grown older. Nothing had indicated how one day he would look at her with the harshness of death seeping from him like muck bubbling over the side of a pot left on the fire too long and too hot to pull away with bare hands.

The truth roiled inside her. She'd not escaped to a land where she could let her guard down. Men kept their power within themselves, behind their smiles and their laughter. Like a volcano, the fury could burst forth and take every being in its path.

The day her father had raged at her over a painting she'd accidentally knocked over, she'd known he would have preferred her to be the one broken in the dirt. If he could have traded her to have the painting back on the easel, he would have. He would have rejoiced if she could have been bruised and broken and his painting fresh and new.

Nothing had changed. She'd only lied to herself, hoping she'd be able to forget the past and sleep peacefully again, safe, in this new land.

Even the maid sitting across from her didn't give her the feeling of security she'd hoped. Moving her foot inside her boot, she felt the dagger sheath, reassuring herself.

She braced her feet as the carriage rolled to a stop. A lock of hair tickled Bellona's cheek as she opened the door and stepped out. Pushing the strand aside, she looked at the darkened eyes of the Harling House windows. Sunlight reflected off the glass and a bird flitted by, but the house looked no more alive than a crypt.

The entrance door opened before her foot cleared the top step.

The expanse of space between her and the stairway could have swallowed her former home. She could not blame the duchess for not wanting to leave her chamber. This part of the house, with all its shine and perfection, didn't look as if it allowed anyone to stop for a moment, but to only pass through.

The butler led her to a library which had more personality than she'd seen so far in the house. The pillow on the sofa had been propped perfectly, but one corner had lost its fluff. The scent of coals from the fireplace lingered in the air. The figurines on the mantel had been made at different times by different artists.

One alabaster shape had a translucency she could almost see through. One girl wore clothing Bellona had never seen before. A bird was half in flight. She noted a cracked wing on one angel. The hairline fracture had browned. This hadn't happened recently and been unnoticed. Someone had wanted to keep the memento even with the imperfection.

Then she studied the spines of the books lining the shelves. Some of the titles she could read, but the English letters her oldest sister, Melina, had taught her years ago were hard to remember. She asked the maid and the woman knew less about the words than Bellona did.

The open-window curtains let much light into the room and the view overlooked where her carriage had stopped. A book lay askew on the desk and another one beside it, plus an uncorked ink bottle. The chair was pulled out and sat slightly sideways. Someone had been sitting there recently, able to see her arrive, and had left a few papers scattered about.

She settled herself to wait, the maid beside her on the sofa. The clock ticked, but other than that nothing sounded. Bellona stood again and noticed the walls. Framed canvases. These were not just paintings, but works of art. When she looked at each piece, she could see something else beyond it—either the thoughts of the person depicted, the way the room had felt that day, or the texture of the object painted.

They were nothing like her father's paintings. She'd had no idea that such wonderful art existed.

Bellona was seated when the duke stepped into the doorway. She'd not heard him, but the flicker of movement caught her eye.

He stood immobile for a minute, like the figurines, but everything else about him contrasted with the gentle figures on the mantel.

She tightened her fingers on her reticule. When she met his eyes, her senses responded, reminding her of the times she and her sisters had build a fire outside at night on Melos. Sitting, listening to waves and staring at stars. Those nights made her feel alive and secure— the strength of nature reminding her something was bigger than the island.

Lines at the corners of his eyes took some of the sternness from his face, and even though he looked as immovable as the cliffs, she didn't fear him. Possibly because he seemed focused on his own thoughts more than her presence. When he spoke, his lips turned up, not in a smile, but in acknowledgment of his own words. 'I regret to say that my mother informs me she will not be able to join you. She is unwell today.'

Bellona stood, moving nearer to the duke. 'If she is unwell, then I cannot leave without seeing if I might be able to soothe her spirits as I did for my mother. I must see her. Only for a moment.'

The maid rose, but Bellona put out a halting hand and said, 'Wait here.'

A quick upwards flick of his head caused his hair to fall across his brow. He brushed it back. 'I may have erred in inviting you. Perhaps another day... Mother is fretful.'

'When my mother hurt, my sisters and I would take turns holding her hand or talking to her, even if she could not answer for the pain.'

'She's not ill in quite that way, but I think her pain is severe none the less.' Moving into the hallway, he swept his arm out, palm up, indicating the direction. 'The duchess is rather in a poor temper today. Please do not consider it a reflection of anything but her health.'

'My *mana* was very, very ill many days.' Bellona clasped the strap of her reticule, forcing away her memories. She raised the bag, bringing it to his attention. 'I brought some garden scents for Her Grace. I will give them to her. They heal the spirit.'

'If you could only coax a pleasant word from her, I would be grateful.'

Bellona followed Rhys into the room. He gave a quick bow of his head to his mother and the older

woman's eyes showed puzzlement, then narrowed
when she saw he was not alone. Her frail skin, along
with the black dress and black cap, and her severe hair-
style, gave her an appearance which could have frightened a child. She pulled the spectacles from her face,
slinging them on to the table beside her. She dropped a
book to her lap. The pallor in her cheeks left, replaced
with tinges of red.

'Rolleston, I thought I told you I did not want company.' The words snarled from her lips, lingering in
the air. A reprimand simmering with anger.

Rhys gave his mother a respectful nod and looked
no more disturbed than if her words had been soft.
'Miss Cherroll is concerned that you are unwell and
believes she has a medicinal which can help.'

The duchess's fingers curled. 'I must speak with
you alone.' She didn't take her eyes from her son. She
lifted a hand the merest amount and then her fingers
fluttered to the book. 'You may take whatever frippery
she brings and then she can leave. I am not receiving
visitors. Even the Prince, should he so enquire.'

Bellona stood firm, forgetting compassion. Her
mana had been gentle even when she could not raise
her hand from the bed or her head from the pillow. 'My
own *mana* has passed and I have brought the herbs
that made her feel better before she left us. And when
their scent is in the air, I feel not so far from her. This
will soothe your sleep.'

The duchess's brows tightened. 'I sleep well enough.
It's being awake I have trouble with. Such as now.
Leave.'

Bellona shrugged, looking more closely at the

woman's skin. She had no health in her face. Her eyes were red and puffed. 'Then give it to a servant.'

'I will,' she said. She examined Bellona and sniffed. 'Go away and take my son with you. I am not having callers today. Perhaps some time next year. Wait for my letter.'

'I will leave the herbs with you.' Bellona reached for her reticule, opened it and pulled the other knife out so she could reach the little pillow she'd made and stuffed with the dried plants.

'Good heavens,' the duchess gasped. Rhys tensed, his hand raised and alert.

'It is only a knife,' Bellona said, looking at her, flicking the blade both ways to show how small it was. 'After the pirates attacked our ship, I have always carried one.'

'Pirates?' the duchess asked, eyes widening.

'I am not truly supposed to call them that,' Bellona said. 'I did know them, so they did not feel like true pirates, only evil men, and Stephanos was…' She shook her head. 'I am not supposed to speak of that either.'

'You are the countess's sister?' The duchess's voice rose, becoming a brittle scratch. She sat taller, listening.

Bellona nodded. 'We're sisters. She's more English than I am. Our father was not on the island so much when I was older. I hardly knew him. My second sister, Thessa, wanted to go to London. I did not. I like it, but I had expected to always stay in my homeland. But my *mana* died. Melina—the countess—had left and started a new life with her husband here and with Thessa determined that we should leave Melos I had no choice. The evil *fidi* would have— I could not stay on my island without either being killed or killing someone else because I was not going to wed.'

'*You* are the *countess's* sister?'

Bellona smiled at the duchess's incredulous repetition.

'Does *she* carry a knife?'

Bellona shook her head. 'No. I do not understand Melina, but she has the children and she did not have the same ship journey I had. She did not see the things I saw. I really am not supposed to speak of them.' Bellona bunched the things in her hand together enough so she could pull the pillow out.

Rhys reached out. 'I'll hold that,' he said of the knife.

She slipped the blade back inside and pulled the strings of the closure tight. 'I'm fine.' She gripped the ties.

Walking to the duchess, she held out the bag of herbs. Rhys followed her step for step and her stare directed at him did not budge him.

The duchess took the pillow, keeping her eyes on Bellona. She pulled the packet to her nose. 'Different,' she remarked.

'At night, you are supposed to put them near your head and then your dreams are to be more pleasant. I have one. It doesn't work for me. But my *mana* promised it worked for her.'

'I do not think it will work for me either.' The duchess sighed, letting her hand rest in her lap.

'The dreams. The dreams are the worst part,' Bellona said.

The duchess looked at the cloth in her hand, squeezing it, crushing the centre, causing the herbs to rustle. 'I know.'

'Some nights,' Bellona admitted, 'I dream my mother is alive and for those moments she is. But I dream she is the one being attacked by the men and I cannot save her. Those dreams are the worst. And they only grow and grow. I cannot breathe when I wake.'

The duchess nodded, eyes downcast. 'Do not talk of this to me.'

'No one wishes to hear it,' Bellona said sadly. 'I cannot talk about it with anyone. And not to be able to talk with Mana makes it so bad. I did not think I would live when she died, but my sister Thessa started slapping me when I cried. That helped.'

The duchess stared at Bellona. 'How unkind.'

'Oh, no. No,' Bellona insisted. 'I would get angry and I would chase her and chase her and want to hurt her. I will always love her for that.'

The duchess looked thoughtful. 'Child. Perhaps a pat or hug would have been better?'

Bellona squinted. 'That would have done no good. I would have cried more.'

A chuckle burst from Rhys's lips. A light shone in his brown eyes that she'd never seen before in any man's gaze and she could feel the sunshine from it. Her cheeks warmed.

'You might as well sit,' the duchess said. 'You'll make my neck hurt looking up at you.'

While she stood there, unable for the moment to think of anything but the duke's sable eyes, he slipped the reticule from her hand.

'Find me in the library when you leave so I may

return this to you,' he said. 'I have some work to finish and I will have tea sent your way.'

He strode out through the doorway.

'Do not dare slap me,' the duchess warned.

'If you need it, I will,' Bellona replied.

'Do not try it. I will not chase you,' the duchess
added, studying her rings, before indicating Bellona
sit beside her. 'I would send servants.'

Bellona shook her head. 'You've lost enough family members for many slaps…'

The duchess nodded. 'It was not supposed to be
like that. My husband, I accepted he might die. He
was much older than I. But my babies. My children.
You don't know what it is like.'

'I know something of what it is like.'

'No. You don't.'

'Yes, I do.'

'You can't.'

'Then tell me.'

The duchess tossed the packet aside. 'My daughter
had golden hair. I'd never seen a child so blessed…'
She continued speaking of her past, taking tea when
the maid brought it, and hardly pausing in her memories.

Finally, she looked at Bellona. 'You really must be
on your way now. You've stayed much longer than a
proper first visit lasts. One just doesn't act as you do.'

'I know. I do as I wish.'

'I can tell you have not had a mother about. You
need someone to teach you how to act.'

'No. I do not. This is how I wish to be.'

'That is your first error.' She shut her eyes. 'Now go.'

Bellona rose. 'Thank you for telling me of your daughter.'

The duchess opened her eyes again and waved towards the door. 'I may send a note later requesting you to tea.'

Bellona left, hearing two rapid sniffs behind her. She shut the door, listening for the click. A dark hallway loomed, but she remembered her way to the library.

A few moments later, she found Rhys, sitting at his desk, leaning over papers. Her reticule lay at the side of his work.

'Where's the maid?' Bellona asked, walking into the room.

He twirled his pen between his fingertips as he stood. 'Below stairs speaking with the other servants. I think she is a cousin or sister or some relation to many of the women here.'

Bellona walked to the fabric bag, lifting it and feeling the weapon still inside.

He frowned and shook his head.

She ignored him and moved to the door.

'Wait,' he said. 'I'll send for someone to collect your maid.'

'I will find her. When I step below stairs and look around, servants will appear and the maid will rush to me. If it takes many moments, the housekeeper or butler are at my elbow, asking what I need. It works faster than the bell pull.'

'Perhaps you should leave them to do their jobs.'

'Yes. I should,' she agreed.

He smiled—the one that didn't reach his lips, but

made his eyes change in such a way that they became like dark jewels she couldn't take her own gaze from.

'Would you wait here whilst I see how my mother fares?' he said. The words were a question, but he was halfway from the room before she could answer.

'No. I'll be on my way.'

He took two more steps, stopped, and spun around. 'No?' He stood in the doorway, almost taking up the whole of the space.

'You will ask her what I said. How we got on and make sure she is well,' Bellona said. 'I know the answers to that. She mentioned having tea with me again, but she will change her mind.'

'With me, she cannot speak for crying and it has been a year,' he muttered. 'A year… I think the honeysuckle was in bloom when they were taking my brother from the house the last time.'

'It is not quite a year,' Bellona told him, shaking her head. 'Your mother knows the dates. All of them.'

His eyes snapped to her and he pushed his hair from his temple. 'Of my father's and sister's deaths, too?'

'Yes. And her own parents.'

'You must stay,' he said. 'You cannot keep the knife in case someone accidentally gets hurt. But you must stay. I have tried two companions for my mother and she shouted one from the room and refused to speak with the other.'

'No.'

'Miss Cherroll, I fear you do not understand how trapped my mother is in her thoughts and memories. You must stay and see if you can lift her spirits. Otherwise, I fear she will not live much longer.'

She moved, putting the desk between them. 'I cannot.' She had grown up with the myths of her ancestors and tales of men stronger than storms and compelling forces. But she'd experienced nothing beyond the world of her birth until the duke stood before her. He changed the way her heart beat, the way she breathed and even the way her skin felt.

He tensed his shoulders, drew in a breath and his arms relaxed. She looked into his eyes, but lowered her gaze back to his cravat. She could not stay in this house. Not and be near the duke. He held the danger of the pirates, but in a different way. She'd seen her mother's weakness. Not the one taking her body near death, but the one that had locked her into a man's power. The power you could not escape from because it stole a person from the inside.

He strode to the side of the desk, nearer her. 'I will pay you whatever you ask. You can go to the servants' quarters ten times a day if you wish. You can have your run of the grounds. The entire estate will be open to you.'

She held the bag close to her body. 'I will not stay in your house.'

He held his hands out, palms up. 'It's— There's none better.'

'It's not that.'

He continued. 'You can have whatever rooms you wish if you stay as my mother's companion. Take several chambers if you'd like. You can have two maids at your elbows all day. And two at theirs.'

'Be quiet and listen.'

His chin tilted down. His brows rose. 'Yes, Miss Cherroll?'

'I will not stay here.'

He waited, his gaze locked on to hers.

'My sister needs me for the children,' she said.

'I understand completely,' he said, voice agreeing, and stepped to the door. 'You can take my carriage to visit them as often as you wish.' One stride and he would be out of her vision. 'It is not a problem at all. Send your maid in Warrington's carriage for your things. The housekeeper will be with you shortly to help you select a room.'

He was gone by the time she opened her mouth.

She stared at the fireplace. Warrington's estate was not far. She could return to take tea with the duchess every day if she wished; she didn't need to live in this house. Bellona did not care what this man said even if he was a duke. She did not follow Warrington's orders and he was an earl *and* married to her sister.

Slipping the reticule ties over her wrist, she walked to the servants' stairs.

The maid from Warrington's estate was whispering to another woman, but immediately stopped when she saw Bellona and bustled to her, following as they left.

'My cousin did not believe you'd stay such a long time,' the maid murmured. 'My cousin says the duchess will follow her family to the grave before the year's gone. The woman won't leave her chair except to weep in the garden. She gets in such a state that her humours are all gobber'd up. The duke is the only one can settle her at all and even he can't be around all the time.'

Bellona remembered holding her own mother's hand near the end. How cool her fingers were. So thin, and with no strength in them at all. The duchess's hands had felt the same.

'I will visit her again soon. Perhaps tomorrow. I am not certain. I am hopeful the herbs will help her.' She moved to exit the house.

'My cousin said the duke is right soured himself. Servants step wide of him since he became titled. Said he's wearing that coronet so tight it's mashed out everything not duke.'

'A man should take his duties to his heart.'

Her maid puffed a whistle from her lips. 'If he's got any heart left. My cousin says he don't care for nothing except for his duties.'

'He cares for his *mana*.'

'Simply another duty.'

They walked to the carriage. Bellona could feel eyes on her. She forced herself not to search the windows behind her to see if the duke watched her departure. But she knew he did.

She adjusted her bonnet and held the reticule so tightly she could not feel the cloth, but only the handle beneath. 'Tomorrow, when I return, I wish you to stay at my side.'

'What did you do to the duke?'

Bellona's oldest sister, Melina, stood in the very centre of the room. She tapped her slipper against the rug.

'I was nice to his *mana*,' Bellona said, adjusting the quiver at her waist. 'I am going to practise.'

'The duke is here, demanding to see Warrington.'

'Truly?' Bellona asked.

'But War is in London. So the butler said Rolleston demands to see you.'

'I am not at home.'

'I told the butler to tell him we will speak with him. The duke is our neighbour and War's parents and his parents were very close.' She frowned. 'Bellona. You just cannot tell a duke to go away, particularly this one.'

'Warrington does not like him.'

'They are quite fond of each other, in the way men are.'

'I am quite fond of the duke in much the same way,' Bellona said darkly.

'You can't be. You have to pretend to like him. We are ladies—as I must remind you as often as I remind Willa.'

'He wishes for me to move to his estate.'

Her sister's foot stilled. 'You are—imagining that, surely?'

Bellona shook her head. 'He thinks I can help the duchess. His Grace told me I would be her companion. I will visit her, but that is as much as I can do.'

Melina stepped near Bellona. 'She will see no one. It is said she is dying. How ill do you think she is?'

'I do not know. Bones covered in black clothes, with her face peering out. I would not think she would make it through a hard winter or a heavy wash day.' She forced her next words. 'Almost like Mana at the end.'

Melina's hand fluttered to her cheek. 'You must move in with her. It is the thing Mana would want.'

'I do not even want to visit her every day,' Bellona said, shuddering. 'She doesn't have the gentle ways of Mana.'

'You must. Besides, to live at the duke's house...' Melina put a hand at her waist. 'He might have friends visit. And you might meet them. You could learn a lot.

The duchess is a true duchess. She could help you. You are not as wild as you pretend. Her Grace could teach you so much if you just watch and learn.'

'I already know how to say *I am not at home*.'

'Sister. A woman. Her husband gone. Her daughter and her oldest son gone, too, and you are asked to help her and you will not. Mana would weep.'

'I will help her. I just do not want to live in the duke's house.' Bellona turned to leave the room, but her sister's quiet voice stopped her.

'You do not like living here, either,' Melina said.

She couldn't tell Melina what she felt about the duke. Stone and towering and dark eyes. She remembered standing at the edge of the cliffs and looking at the ground far beneath, and knowing if she swooned she would fall—feeling brave and scared at the same time. The duke made her want to step closer and yet, if she did, the ground might crumble away. He reminded her so much of the stones she'd seen jutting from the sea and the cliffs.

'I wish to be here with the children. And you.' Bellona pleaded with her sister. 'I do not want to leave the little ones.'

'You'll never have your own babies if you do not learn how to mix with society. A footman will not do for you and you know that. The duchess could introduce you to someone suitable.'

'I went to the soirée. The men smelled like flowers.'

'Pretend you are a bee. You can sting them after you're wed. Not before.'

'I will not pretend to be anything other than what I am.'

'You cannot go back to the way we lived. You must

go forward and the duchess could help. She could ease your way into society in a way that I cannot. They hardly accept me.'

Bellona hit her own chest with her fingertip. 'That is where we are different. I do not want to be in society. Bonnets pull my hair. Slippers pinch and corsets squeeze. The flowery world has nothing for me.'

'A husband helps if you want children of your own—and it is best for the child to be born within a true marriage, one with love. You know that as well as I.'

'Even children are not worth a husband. I have a niece and two nephews. They are my babies.'

'You are hiding. From everything. From the past and the future. The duchess needs you. You know how long the nights can be after a death and we had each other. We had the three of us, you, me and Thessa. You are just like our *pateras*, our father.' Melina crossed her arms.

'That is an evil thing to say. I am surprised your tongue does not choke you for forcing those words past it.'

'You are like Father. Of the three of us, you are the most like him,' her sister continued, pacing the room. 'Even Mana said so, just not where you could hear her.'

Bellona raised her voice. 'I am not like him.'

'When we angered him, he would go paint.' Melina swaggered with her shoulders as she walked. 'When he did not want to do something, he would paint.' She stopped and mused. 'Did you ever notice how paint brushes are shaped almost like little arrows?'

'You're wrong to speak so. I practise archery. I do not live for it.'

'Even the way you stick out your chin. Just like him.' She jutted out her jaw in an exaggerated pose.

'You always say that when you have no better words to fight with.'

Melina returned her stance to normal. 'I cannot believe my own sister has no kindness in her heart for a woman with no daughters or sisters.'

Bellona raised her chin. 'I will tell the duke I will stay a short time with his mother. It will be better than listening to you. *You* are the one like Father, insisting on having your way.'

'Only when I am right.' She examined Bellona. 'Please arrange your hair before you see the duke.'

'Of course.' Bellona patted both sides of her head, achieving nothing.

'Much better.' Melina paused. 'I expected you to pull a strand loose.'

'I thought of it.' Bellona sighed. But the duke probably wouldn't appreciate it.

Melina reached to Bellona and pushed her youngest sister's hair up at the sides, moving the pins around. 'There. Now you look as well as me.'

Bellona walked past her. 'Now you see why I do not show my face in society.'

Melina's chuckle followed Bellona from the room out into the hallway.

When Bellona reached the sitting room, the duke's gaze swept over her. The rock stood, unyielding.

Even with a scowl on his face, she still wanted to look at him. The thought irritated her.

'I will return to your house,' she said curtly.

The flicker behind his eyes—the intake of breath. She would have imagined he'd just been hit, except his face softened much the same as Warrington's did when her sister walked into the room. The duke inclined his head in acknowledgment. 'It will mean a lot. To the duchess.'

Chapter Four

Bellona arrived at Harling House the next morning and the housekeeper appeared at her side almost instantly. The woman had a sideways gait, but moved forward so fast Bellona hurried to follow.

After being shown a chamber whose ceiling would need a heavy ladder to reach, she mused, 'I could put an archery target in here and practise without leaving the room.'

'We have no targets which are suitable for use inside.' The woman's face pinched into a glare that would stop any servant.

Bellona gave the woman the same look Warrington had given her countless times. 'I suppose if I asked the duke, he would arrange something.'

'Of course,' the housekeeper said. 'This was his childhood room. Let me know if you need anything.' Then she darted away.

The room had the same scent of the storage rooms in Warrington's house and made her miss the sea air. No flounces and lace adorned it. Instead there were walls the colour of sand and darker curtains that required strength to move. She wondered if every trace of the boy had been removed, or if the room had never had anything of him in it.

The huge chamber didn't feel like home, but she was tired of looking for Melos in everything she saw and not finding it.

She placed her bow in the corner. Her mother would not have believed such a large room existed for one person to sleep in.

Someone knocked at the door. A maid, who looked almost the same as the one from Warrington's house, suggested Bellona go to the library to meet with His Grace. Curiosity and the desire to see more of the house pulled her straight to him.

'Miss Cherroll. Welcome,' the duke greeted her. Quiet words, almost cold, but his quick turn from the window, and one step in her direction, caused a flutter in her stomach.

The last year of his life might have been no easier than the duchess's, she realised. If Bellona had lost either of her sisters to death, the world would have become dark and bleak and suffocating.

He surprised her by the merest corner of his lips turning up at the edge. 'The maid who is unpacking for you will store your arrows and knives in a safe place. She will direct the footman to bring them to you each time you need to practise marksmanship and he will take them when you return to the house and make sure they are properly cared for.'

'You are most thoughtful of my property,' she said, thankful he did not know of the knife in her boot.

'Of course.'

'Then let us discuss payment for my stay.'

'Certainly.'

'I want another two score of arrows. The best that can be made. I also require a dagger perfectly balanced. And I must have a pistol that will fit my hand and someone to show me how to clean, load and shoot it. I have heard there is a Belgian hidden-trigger boot pistol in which the trigger does not fall down until it is cocked. I would like to see one of those. You can have someone bring selections of these things for me to choose from.'

'Ah.' The word wasn't clearly formed from his lips, but was more of a sound. 'No duelling swords? Fencing lessons? Cannons?' he asked, blinking once each time he named a weapon.

'Cannons are heavy, and—' she touched the bridge of her nose '—so are swords. A man with long reach can best me any day. I could not practise enough.'

'Miss Cherroll. Any necessities will be furnished to you and they do not include guns, knives, arrows or swords. You will accept the usual payment from me—enough to buy all the armaments you need and Warrington can help you choose the weapons after you leave. I will refrain from paying you until then because I realise what you might do with the funds. Since you do not like to see game injured, I fear what you might plan to do with any weaponry. You will not have such items in my home.' He stood with feet planted firm. 'I myself do not even keep them at hand.'

'No duelling pistols?' She raised a brow.

He looked aside and absently moved the pen at his

desk on to the blotter. 'Yes, I have them, but they were gifted to my father and they are locked away. There is not even powder for them.'

'Swords?'

'Fencing is something we all had to learn.'

'Where are the swords?'

'I believe they are locked in a case in the portrait gallery. The butler has the keys and he will not be sharing them. With anyone.' His voice rumbled from his chest. 'I think you forget you are here to see my mother, a woman of trifling size who is stronger with her glares than most people are with their body.'

'Do you have daggers? Arrows? Flintlocks?'

His head moved enough so she couldn't see his eyes, then, before she could protect herself, he directed his full attention at her, consuming her with it. 'What do you fear?'

'Not having weapons.'

He shook his head. 'I am sure there is a bow and arrows somewhere. I don't think the bow has a string any more. No daggers.' Still standing alongside the desk, he splayed his fingers and gave the top several hard raps. 'Miss Cherroll, you do not have to concern yourself that someone will attack you in my home. I have footmen and stablemen no one would dare confront. I have had no violence on my estate, ever. That will not change while you are here. I realise you had a harrowing experience on your ship journey here and not a pleasant meeting with my gamekeeper, but you are now in what is the safest place in the world. My home.' For a second, he spoke with his expression. Relief. Thankfulness. 'I must let you know I was pleased to see you arrive.'

She didn't think any man, ever, had looked at her with so much hope on his face.

'You are in more danger from a fall on the stairs than anything else,' he added.

Or a fall from a cliff.

'I am exceedingly angry at the duke for bringing you here,' the duchess said to Bellona.

The duchess wore a fichu tucked into her bodice and the sleeves of her obsidian gown almost swallowed her hands.

The older woman had a maid at her side, holding a stack of four books. 'You must know that I cannot take my anger out on him, so it will land about your ears.' She pulled out one book and waved the servant away.

'I am not happy with him either.' Bellona sat in the matching chair. 'I will probably share that with both of you.'

The duchess frowned. 'Why are you not pleased with him?'

'He took my bow and a small dagger.'

'Your mother should have taught you better.'

'Why? I did not need to be better on Melos and I am fine enough to sit in a duke's home.'

She duchess snorted, just as Bellona's own mother might have. She held out the book. 'You may read to me.'

'I would rather talk.'

'I would rather hear what someone else wrote.' The woman thumped the book and held it out again.

'I am not going to read to you.'

'You have no choice. I have asked you to. I am your elder.'

This was not going to get any better. Perhaps his mother would summon the duke to complain about Bellona. That would tip his tea kettle over.

Bellona saw no reason to explain her struggle to read the English language to the duchess.

'It would indeed be an honour for you to read to me,' the duchess said, changing her methods, 'and might dispose me more kindly towards you.'

'I do not mind if you are not nice to me.'

'Well, I do. My prayer book is the only thing that gives me hope. My eyes hurt from reading it and the letters blur. The maid cannot read and I do not wish to replace her, though I might be forced to because I need someone who can see better than I.'

'You may replace me,' Bellona said. 'I do not read English words.'

'But your sister is a countess. And everyone knows she is from the best society in your home country.' The duchess looked at the book. 'So do not feed me such nonsense that you cannot read. Your family would not educate one sister and leave another unschooled. I have received notes from your sister several times. One she wrote when she visited me and I could not see her, so she must write them herself.'

'I am not my sister.'

The duchess shook her head. 'You do not read?'

'I know the English letters. Melina read our father's letters to Thessa and me many times and I could understand most of the written words. It has been a long time since I have looked at words, though. I do not like them on paper. I prefer a person's lies when I can see their face.'

'I do beg your pardon.' Words spoken from training.

'I cannot begin to imagine what my son was thinking to enlist a companion who could not read to me.'

'I do not dance or do any of the other things society women do, except archery. It is my favourite thing next to my niece and nephews. I sew, but only because one must have clothes. I do not like the nice stitches to make flowers. I like the strong sewing. I am from my *mana's* world.'

'I am from my mother's world as well,' the duchess said. 'Every day we had our hair dressed to perfection, our skin just so. We could not move if it might disturb our clothing. I sometimes hated it, but now I see the value of it. One must give others something to aspire to.' She leaned towards Bellona. 'Take a note of that. Because you are a companion only and from some foreign land, I will tolerate some folly on your part.'

'I am thankful I will not have to tolerate any on your part.'

'Child, I say again that I do not know what the duke was thinking to ask you to stay with me.'

'He was thinking I would be a slap for you.'

The duchess showed no outward reaction. 'Rolleston is making a good duke. He has always been a good son. Although he might have erred this one time.'

'He might have.'

'Do not be so quick to agree with me. Surely you have some accomplishments? What entertainments are you versed in? Recitations? Music? Song?'

Bellona smiled, tilted her head to the side and said, 'Would you like to hear a song the English sailors taught me? I am not sure of its meaning.'

The duchess's neck moved like a snake rising to eye prey, trying to get situated for the closest tender spot. 'Oh, my dear, I think you know full well whatever that song meant and I am not daft enough to fall for that one.'

'I already told you that I have no accomplishments,' Bellona insisted flatly.

'How do you spend your days?'

'Archery. The forest. I spend hours with my niece— I miss the little one. Her joy makes me laugh.'

The duchess opened the book. 'I know what it is like to miss someone.'

'You spend too much time with books,' Bellona said. 'If they make your eyes hurt it is not good for you. Poison in the stomach makes it hurt. The head is the same. Your eyes are telling you that you must not read.'

'Oh. Thank you for informing me.' The duchess digested the words.

Rhys walked into the room, greeting them both, a book under his arm. His eyes had a faraway look, but he settled into a chair and asked them to continue as they'd been because he needed to study the accounts.

But even though he stared at the volume in his hands, Bellona felt his thoughts were on her much the same as a governess might have her back to the children, but be aware of their every move. She felt the need to test her idea and knew she would before the conversation was over.

The duchess leaned towards Bellona. 'How did you learn to speak English?'

'My father was English.' Her father was alive, but he was dead as far as she was concerned. 'He insisted we only speak English when he was home. He made us recite to him. Yet he knew Greek well and if we spoke Greek in anger, we were punished. He is… It is hard to talk of him.' She sniffed and lowered her face. That would discourage any questions of him.

'At least you speak two languages.'

'Some French, too.'

The older woman nodded. She appraised Bellona. 'Did you leave behind family in Greece?'

'None close,' Bellona said. 'I have never wed. Marriage. It makes a woman change. And cry. Men are only good for lifting and carrying, much like the bigger animals that do not think well.'

The duke didn't respond to her deliberate prod.

'Well, yes, some of them can be,' the duchess admitted. 'But marriage is not all bad. Children make you change and cry, too. I do not know what I would have done without my own.' A wisp of a smile landed on the duchess's face. 'My three children were the best things that ever happened to me.' Then her expression changed with the memory and she began to sniff.

Bellona searched her mind for a distraction. 'At least I will not have to marry—like His Grace will have to before he gets much older.'

His mother's sniffle turned into a splutter. Bellona didn't have to turn her head to know where the duke was looking. She pretended to look like her own thoughts were far away.

'Yes. He will marry. Of course,' the duchess said. 'But that is not for you to discuss, Miss Cherroll.'

'I hoped that you would call me Bellona.'

'That is a strange name.'

'I was named for the Roman goddess of war. I remember that every day.'

'Perhaps you should put it from your mind. She

doesn't sound like someone appropriate to be named after.'

Bellona shook her head. 'I'm proud of it. To get to England, I had to flee in the night. Thessa's suitor chased us.' She had slept though the final confrontation, unaware of all about her. Earlier, she'd fallen asleep with the rhythm of the ship and woken when her sister had shaken her awake. Thessa's rapid voice had fallen back into the Greek language while she'd told Bellona how the pirates from their homeland had followed the ship, planning to force the women into marriage.

She thought of what Melina had told her of Almack's—a marriage mart, her sister had said.

'Have you ever been pursued, Your Grace?' She turned to Rhys. He did have her direct in his vision, watching her without censure, but as if she were a very interesting…bee, and he wasn't afraid of getting stung.

'Not by a pirate,' he said. 'Only by a very unhappy bull.'

'I'm sure you could escape.'

'I have managed thus far.' He glanced at the book again, but even with his eyes averted, she could still feel his attention on her.

'My poor Geoff,' the duchess said, 'he was once chased by an angry dog and I thought—' Her lip quivered and she reached for a handkerchief.

Bellona did not want the discussion to return to sadness. A slap with words worked as well as one across the face. 'Reading does appear a good way to waste time. A way for people with no chores to be idle.'

The duchess's sniff turned into a choke.

She had the older woman's full attention and Rhys's

book looked to have turned humorous. For little more than a blink, their eyes met. Sunshine suffused her and didn't go away when he examined the book again.

After his morning ride, Rhys heard the clock as he strode into his home—the same peals he'd heard his whole life. The sounds didn't change, but if they clanked about in his ears, he knew the world felt dark. For the first time in a long time, the peals were musical.

His mother had spoken to him repeatedly about the *heathen*, informing him that the miss was beyond help. Each time she'd recounted the discussion between the two, her voice rose in anger. Not the bare mewl it had been before.

Finally, she'd left her room of her own volition to come and find him to complain with exasperation of having to deal with this motherless child who'd been left too long to her own devices. She'd wondered how he could possibly expect his own mother to correct such a tremendous neglect of education in the woman. 'It would take years, years,' she'd explained as she walked away, shaking her head.

He'd quashed his immediate urge to go to Bellona and pull her into his arms, celebrating with her the rebirth of his mother's life.

Thoughts of Bellona always caused his mind to catch, wait and peruse every action or word concerning her a little longer. The miss did something inside him. Like a flint sparking against steel. Made him realise that his heart still beat, his life still continued and that some day he'd be able to walk into a room and not be aware of all that was missing, but see what was actually there.

He turned, moving towards the archery target that now stood in the garden beneath the library window.

Disappointment edged into him when he did not find her near the targets she'd had placed about. He went inside the house, thinking of her hair and the way she reminded him of pleasures he did not need to be focusing on right now. As he passed the library door, he heard pages rustling.

He stepped into the library. Stopped. Stared.

She was lying on his sofa. Around her face, her hair haloed her like a frazzled mess, more having escaped from her bun than remained. This was the moment he would have walked to her, splayed his fingers, held her cheeks in both hands and kissed her if…

Ifs were not for dukes, he reminded himself.

She rested stockinged feet on the sofa. Her knees were bent and her skirt raised to her calves while she frowned into a book. His mind tumbled in a hundred directions at once, all of them landing on various places of her body. The woman should not be displaying herself in such a way.

Courtesans did not act so…relaxed and improper. Even the women he'd visited in London—ones without modesty—would have remained much more sedate in daylight hours.

But he remembered his manners. Perhaps he'd erred, not she. She had not heard him enter the room. He took a quiet step back because he did not want to mortify her by letting her know he'd seen her sprawled so indelicately.

But then he saw the books. A good dozen of *his*

most precious books scattered about her. One was even on the carpet. How could she? It was one thing to trespass, another to shoot an arrow at a man, but... the books...

Books were to be treated as fine jewels—no—jewels could be tossed about here and there without concern—books were to be treasured, removed from the shelves one at a time, carefully perused and immediately returned to their place of honour. They were made of delicate materials. A nursemaid would not toss a baby here or there and books deserved the same care.

She looked up, swung her stockinged feet to the floor as she sat, dropped the book at her side. Her foot now sat on top of a boot, her skirt hem covering it, as she lowered her hand towards the remaining footwear.

Modesty. Finally. 'You may dress.' He turned his back on her slightly, so he would not see if her skirt flipped up while she put on those worn boots. He would have thought Warrington would have done better by her. He would put in a word to see that she had decent indoor shoes.

He heard a thump and the sound of pages fluttering.

'I cannot read this—this—'

From the corner of his eye, he saw the title of one of his father's favourite volumes disgracefully on the floor. He pressed his lips together and gave himself a moment. 'Why are you in the library since you disregard reading?' he finally asked.

'Your mother has insisted I pick a book, study it,' she muttered, 'and be able to speak about it. She is punishing me.'

He heard the sound of her fidgeting about and then silence. He turned.

She glared at him, but she only had one boot on and she held the other in her lap, her right hand resting on it.

'I do not think I like your mother,' she continued. 'The duchess told the servant who stores my bow I am not to have it. The servants are afraid to disobey her.' She stared at him. 'The duchess said it is good for me to learn to read English. That I should not be *unleashed on society* until I have better ways. I am fine with that, as long as they are my ways. I told her I do not wish to be *unleashed on society*.'

'The books?' With his hand, he indicated the floor.

'They have too many pages and not enough drawings.' She frowned. 'Melina taught me the words when I was a child and when I discovered I was not reading Greek, but English, I hid the books. I have only read a few letters since then and they are never more than three pages long. This—' she stared at him as if he had written the offending length '—this has so many words I do not know how the man did not run out of them.'

She picked up the book, holding it in her left hand and shaking it in his direction. For a moment he forgot to be outraged. Her bodice bounced enticingly.

He pushed his thoughts in a safer direction.

He remembered how she'd helped his mother. He took a breath. He must remind himself that the duchess's health was more important than any book that had been in the family for near a century. Even one with hand-inked illustrations which Miss Cherroll had just waved about without any care.

He switched to a ruse she had used, turning it in

her direction. 'Books are actually only meant for the upper classes. Only peers should have them. They are too much for the common folk to appreciate.'

'I agree. Only peers. Common folk have no time for reading. I sold both our books to a sailor,' she said. 'He knew how to read. It did not make him smarter, though, because he paid a good price for nothing.'

Her eyes sparked with a challenge that bolted inside his stomach.

She perched on the sofa like a preening bird and let the books rest about her like so many twigs.

'I suspect his purchase was not as much—' he eyed the books '—as my father and grandfather and I spent for those.' He walked to the sofa and picked up a tome from the floor. 'So when you are not casting jabs about the books, what do you really think of them?'

'They are too much to read. But very dear to sell. I was so happy when I discovered that.' Lifting one volume, she put it atop another. 'I would not damage such costly items.'

'That almost reassures me.' Rhys kept his face unmoved. 'What books did you sell?'

She held her chin high. 'I do not remember. But I remember the necklace we bought for our *mana*. She had it on when she died. We claimed our father sent it with a ship.'

Rhys imagined the three girls giving the gift to their mother.

'Your mother,' she continued, 'says I have been addled because I lost my own *mana* so young. She said I misled her about the pirates trying to capture our ship. She thought I lied about everything.' Bellona's lips firmed and she shook her head precisely.

'So I sang the sailors' song to her. She believes me now.' She lowered her eyes. 'I should not have done it. I do not like that song. It is *erotikos*.'

Damn. The song had probably singed the pages of his mother's prayer book and he would be hearing about it the rest of his life and on into eternity if he made it that far. He waved a palm about. 'You do not sing improperly—not to a duchess. My *mother*. Miss Cherroll, you are to be a companion, not—'

She sighed, shut her eyes and shook her head. 'I do not think she truly minded. I only wish I did not do it because it gave her a reason to trick me into looking at these infernal books.'

Dark eyes, more like some woodland pet than a woman's, took him in. She didn't say one word, but argument was in that gaze. He'd never seen eyes like those. His midsection jolted again and he looked at the floor to push his attention elsewhere.

In one stride he picked up a book and held it in both hands. 'This is Alexander Pope.'

'Well, that tells me nothing.'

Then he saw her eyes turn to the book at her feet. He gasped, and pulled it from the floor. 'You cannot place *The Life and Adventures of Robinson Crusoe* on the rug. I have read it three times.'

'I didn't like the first page. Warrington has a copy. My sister read the first words and I left the room.'

His head twitched to indicate the book. 'You simply cannot judge it by the—'

She contradicted him with her eyes. 'Why not? The first page of the book is about the rest of the story.'

'This one is about a man who lives on an island and

learns to make do with what he has, and he is very happy because no women are about. Just cannibals.'

She snorted. 'I do not see how that makes fine reading. My sisters and I lived on an island.'

'He was marooned.'

'You mean he could not leave if he wanted. How sad…' She smiled. 'And is England not an island? I cannot return to Melos, which is also an island. Melina and Warrington refuse to let me go back home because of the Greek war for independence and they fear pirates.' She snorted again. 'And then there is the man on Melos who wished to marry me, but…one of us would not have survived the wedding night.'

'You were asked to wed?' He studied her, and, yes, he could see how a man might say anything to get her into his bed. She sat, wiggling that one stocking-clad foot, like an asp, tempting him to partake of forbidden fruit.

'If I had not hated him,' she said. 'I might have thought of it. I did not care for him and he had the mean eyes.'

'Marriage is an honourable state.'

'Your mother would be surprised to hear that from your lips. You should have married long before now. She has feared many times you would do as your father did and near destroy everything dear.'

'My father?' Rhys struggled over the words. 'My mother held my father in the highest esteem.'

Bellona nodded. 'Of course. But it was hard for her to love him at first.' She grimaced. 'When your brother was born and your mother became ill, your father stayed in London while she remained here. When he left, he told her he was a duke first, a man second and a father third. He did not mention being a husband.'

He heard her words. He saw her lips moving.

'Do not joust at me. My father is dead,' he said. 'His memory is sacred. I will not have you disgrace him.'

'Your mother said everyone knew. She felt abandoned. When she became strong again, she went to London and reminded him she was his wife.'

He picked up the volumes and placed them back on the shelf while he controlled his temper. Once the books were shelved he turned to her.

The rumours said Bellona's father had died young and left a wife behind who'd been descended from the Greek upper classes. Perhaps the sister Warrington had married was descended from some Aphrodite-like ancestor, but this one was from the wrong side of the clouds. It did not matter to him if she had been born on a gilded mountain-top. Once he discussed her with his mother and repeated what false tales Bellona had just spread about his father, the woman would be gone. He would have the carriage readied and escort her to it himself. A woman could not disparage the duke's father in his own home and expect to remain.

'Nothing my father ever did was disrespectful to my mother.'

Her eyes widened. Pity directed at him. He frowned.

'I must have misheard,' she said finally.

'I am certain you did.'

She glanced away. 'I am certain I did, too. Perhaps I do not understand English as well as I think.'

When she turned her head, he saw a flash of gold at her ears. His mother's earrings. He swallowed.

He had unleashed the worst sort of woman into his very home.

'Your mother fears leaving her rooms,' she said. 'She knows when she does you will think she can manage on her own and abandon her for London just as your father did.'

'I would not *abandon* my mother.'

She looked down. 'She knows you would not mean to. It is your duty. She understands.'

'You are… I am… That is unacceptable. You are a liar of the worst sort. You will return to Whitegate.'

Perhaps that would be safest for them all. For her—because if she discovered how society would truly perceive her, she might be crushed. For his mother—because she did not need a woman near who would take her jewels while spreading lies. And himself—for a reason he did not wish to consider.

Bellona's jaw clenched. She jumped to her feet, and moved to the bell-pull, her boot under one arm. 'I will send for a carriage. I will not have to read at Warrington's house.'

He could *not* believe it. His bell-pull. In his house!

'Cease,' he commanded, hand out in a halting gesture. No one except he or his mother touched this bell-pull. And he would not let this thief leave with his mother's jewellery.

She stopped, still clutching the boot. 'I'm leaving. Even the walls are sad here. No one laughs. No one plays. It is all reading and embroidery and dressing of hair and clothes.' Her nose went up.

'I will see that you do leave. A carriage will be readied.' He waved an arm. 'Come with me. I want my mother to know what you have said about my father.'

'You first,' she said impudently.

He did not want her to dart away with the earrings. 'I insist. You first. I am a gentleman.'

'Then do as I wish.'

He would not stand and argue with her. 'Do not dare run for the door.'

'You tell me to leave and then tell me not to go.'

He stepped forward, but kept an awareness of her and held out his arm for her to precede him. She rolled her eyes, but flounced from the room.

He gave a quick rap on his mother's door and strode inside. She sat in her chair, but instead of the prayer book… He stepped closer. Fashion plates.

She glanced up at the two of them, but then returned to the books. 'Oh, Rhys. I do not know how this poor child will ever be saved from herself and I have such a short time to mend her because I am going to send her packing any day now. She does not listen. She is worse than you are and I never thought anyone could be worse than you…'

He stared at her.

She clucked her tongue, examining the engravings. 'I send her a maid to fix her hair and she complains. I gave her gold earrings and had to insist she wear them. Gold. What woman thinks gold is unsuitable?' She held up a plate so he could see. 'Child…' She held the drawing so Bellona could see. 'This is the gown I had made for me in blue to match my eyes. I don't want yellow for you, but I cannot decide.'

'I do not need any new clothing.' Bellona's words were clipped. 'I am leaving.'

'Nonsense,' his mother commanded. Then his mother's eyes caught on Bellona's boots. She gasped, eyes wide. 'Un-for-giv-able. Where are the slippers I found for you?'

'I hate them. They pinch. I cannot wear them.'

Rhys watched. He just watched.

His mother's fingers shook so that the papers in her hands made a fluttery sound. 'Your stockings are *dirty*. Were you raised in a stable?'

'Above one.' That goddess nose tilted up. Rhys thought she might not have any of the society airs about her, but her nose and eyes could manage well enough and needed no lessons.

'Now. Go. Put on fresh stockings and get those slippers and return to me. I wish to see you wearing them now.'

'You are just like Gigia.' Bellona frowned. She looked at Rhys. 'She is just like Gigia. I will never drink too much around her.'

'Then you were very lucky if you knew someone like me, but obviously you did not pay her enough heed,' his mother said. Her eyes tightened on Bellona. 'And you are just like my daughter was—may the angels hold her tight in their embrace. I thought never to get her wed to the right man.'

Bellona pursed her lips and blew. 'I do not need anyone to find a husband for me.'

'Bellona. I cannot believe it.' The duchess sat, closing her eyes. 'What did I tell you about being a lady?' She shook the paper towards Rhys. 'And you are in the company of a male.'

'But he is only the duke and has already tossed me out.' She shook her head. 'I must return to Whitegate. You must give me my bow and arrows so I can leave.'

Only the duke? Rhys tried not to be offended. That was a phrase he had never heard in his life.

'I forbid it,' the duchess said firmly. 'You are running amok and you have no mother to train you. You cannot leave until I tell you to. You will never have that bow and arrows if you do not do as I say.' His mother turned to him. 'Rhys. She cannot leave until I tell her.'

'I am not running amok,' Bellona said. 'I am doing as I please.'

'Exactly the same thing.' His mother turned to him. 'Tell her, Rhys. Tell her she cannot leave.'

'I believe she should,' he said stiffly.

'Nonsense. Why, no man of any higher level than a nightsoil collector would give her a glance as she is. And she has good skin and rather a startlingly good singing voice. I am teaching her a hymn.'

Rhys took in a breath. 'Is that what she sings to you, Mother?'

'Why, yes.' Her voice calmed and her shoulders relaxed. 'Along with a few old songs from her country.' She looked at Bellona. 'Run along and change those stockings, and hurry back because I want you to decide on a colour.'

'I will not hurry,' Bellona said, leaving.

He cleared his throat, giving the wench a chance to pull the door shut behind her.

He must inform his mother about the tales. Then he would explain to this miss the repercussions of disrespecting a duke's household—*only a duke*—and send her packing that very day.

Rhys forced himself to soften his words. He did not want his mother upset more than she must be. 'She is a talebearer.'

'Nonsense,' her mother said. 'I am quite sure she is honest. She told me the brocade in the sitting room is quite the wrong colour.'

'I am not talking of fashion. I am talking of the deeper qualities of a person.'

His mother's eyes widened. 'She has some deep qualities. They are just deeply common.'

'She has said—things about Father. Even suggesting he might have not seen you for a time after Geoff's birth when you were ill.'

This time his mother put her hand over her open mouth. Her eyes fluttered.

Rhys knew right where this was heading. Bellona would soon be waiting at the door for the carriage to be pulled around.

The duchess clasped her fingertips as if her hands were cold and then whispered, 'I do not know how I am going to teach her what is proper to speak of and what is to remain behind closed doors. A servant could have overheard. Not that I'm sure they... Well, you know how things get remembered like that.'

Rhys drew in a deep breath, studying the truth on his mother's face. His father? His father had behaved so callously? 'Mother. Did my father...?'

'Well...Rhys, I thought perhaps your father had mentioned it to you before his death, or even Geoff. I know Geoff and your father spoke of it. I heard them. So I assumed you knew as well.' She wilted against the sofa back. 'I have just had so much on my mind. It is hard to think of everything.'

His mouth opened. Bellona had moved into his house and discovered family truths even *he* did not know of. And his mother was discussing these things with her instead of with him.

He took the matching chair.

Then his mother straightened and pulled her handkerchief from inside her sleeve and refolded the fabric, her eyes on the cloth.

'Rhys, you understand…' She looked up. 'Geoff had just been born and it was a difficult birth. He was… I was… He cried so much and the nursemaids didn't know what to do. My baby was small and didn't want to grow at first. I felt I'd failed my husband. Your father and I did not always get on well. I may have… been harsh in some of the things I said. Your father was angry because I could not think of anything but the babe, so he left me. But then, Geoff started getting bigger and I became better and your father returned home, after a nudge.'

She daubed the handkerchief to her eyes. 'That was a difficult time. And to think I would eventually lose them both… So near to each other.'

Rhys didn't speak.

'I had all a woman could hope for.' Her eyes filled with tears.

'My father…' He shook his head.

'Rhys, please do not tell me you are such an innocent. Sometimes, things happen.'

He stood again. 'I am not an innocent, Mother.' He straightened the sleeves of his coat. 'I am just surprised that I never knew of this. That no one told me. It's… You know how Father was. He was the perfect duke. Always.'

'Yes.' She straightened her shoulders. 'He was. And

you know, Rhys—in some respects—nothing is forbidden to a duke.'

'Miss Cherroll—a woman we hardly know tells me of this.' He shook his head in disbelief. 'How could you share this with her and not with me?'

'She lost her own mother and has had so many trials. I understood much of the pain she felt and I told her. The words just escaped my lips.'

Since Bellona had been correct about that, perhaps she had spoken truth on one other thing, too. 'You do not have to worry about my abandoning you, Mother, even when you become hale and hearty once more.'

'I know, Rhys. I understand completely. I know you would never wish to leave me.' She exchanged the fashion plates for the prayer book on the table beside her chair. Running her fingers over the lettering on the cover, she sighed. 'But, Rhys, if you do not… If you do not go to London and find a wife, you will be abandoning your title. Your duty to your family. Your brother's heritage. You have no choice.'

She raised her face. 'I understand you must go. I do not want you to marry a wife only to make her unhappy. Togetherness in marriage, I believe, is formed by people who have the same background and the same interests. You must marry a woman you have something in common with. One who shares your dreams for the dukedom and can be at your side, a helpmate. I wish the same marriage for you that your father and I had, except, of course, for the one year when we could not stand the sight of each other.'

'I know what I have to do.' He did. A wife. House of Lords. A son to pass the title to. It did not have to be written in stone to be engraved in his head. Geoff's heritage.

'It's harder for a duke with all his duties and responsibilities and the stewardship of the estate,' she said. 'And women notice the duke, Rhys, rather than the man, as I am sure you are aware.'

Rhys remembered the last soirée he had attended with Geoff. The women had fluttered around Geoff, and the brothers had jested privately afterward about the peerage being far more handsome than any visage. The next event Rhys attended after Geoff's death, the perfume had choked him, the expanse of pale flesh had burned his eyes and the high laughter had been like spears in his ears.

Without Geoff, it was not humorous any more.

The door opened and Bellona walked in, wearing both boots and carrying the slippers. 'They bite my toes,' she insisted. 'I cannot wear them.'

'I know you must have slippers at Warrington's estate,' the duchess said. 'Send for them or trim off a few toes.'

Bellona put the shoes on the floor beside her. 'I will be considering which toes I can spare.'

'Of course,' the duchess murmured, 'you do want your little niece, Willa, to be proud of her aunt...'

The tousled head darted up and her eyes could have flailed the duchess. 'I do have some slippers my sister gave me. I suppose I could send for them and a gown that matches.'

'I have a tutor planned for you tomorrow in the ballroom. Do not be late. He will not.'

'I will not dance. I have a pain in my foot.'

The duchess spoke to Rhys. 'She can practise archery for hours. A few moments' dancing will not hurt her.'

'I will not,' Bellona said again, calling the duchess's attention back to her.

'It would mean a lot to your sister to know you are settled with a nice vicar or man of affairs. Perhaps a soldier who has returned and needs a wife to care for him? Your sister might even wish for a niece or nephew of her own. Someone her own little ones can call cousin. If you do not dance with a suitor... He will see you as thinking yourself above him and dance with someone more...pleasant.'

She held her fingers up as if dusting crumbs from them.

'I will dance the country dance if you insist.'

'Send a servant to me and I will give the order for your bow to be returned,' the duchess said.

'My foot is hurting more now and the pains are moving up to my head,' Bellona said, turned and left.

Rhys saw the jutting chin as she stepped his way, but as she passed by him, the tiny wink nearly did him in.

The door crashed behind her.

The wench would be the death of him.

'I would not say this in front of her, but if she carries on like this, that heathen child will never even be worthy of a tradesman as a wife. It's just...she did lose her mother, as she is *constantly* reminding me,' the duchess grumbled to Rhys. 'I cringe to think what would have become of your sister had it not been for my firm hand.' The duchess stared ahead. 'This one is more like your father's mother.' She nodded and her lips firmed. 'No one ever took that woman in hand

and I will certainly not let this motherless child be so unruly.'

'You gave her the gold earrings.'

'Yes, and the matching necklace. I never really liked them. I'm trying to make a female out of her, Rhys. No man will ever give her a second glance if she does not present herself as a lady.'

Rhys turned to the door. He did not correct his mother on that point. But she was very, very wrong.

Bellona grabbed her cape, shaking it in her frustration. She had to escape the house for a few minutes and practise her archery. The first dancing lessons with the tutor had gone well, but today he had insisted on a much more difficult dance. Bellona had refused. She was determined the man would not touch her.

The maid returned and slipped into the room. 'Please, miss, the duchess is distressed.'

'She must get over her temper fit.'

'She is crying.'

Bellona stopped. 'Tears of anger?'

'Quiet tears.'

Bellona slipped the cape from her shoulders and tossed it on the bed. 'I'll speak with her.'

'Thank you, miss,' the maid said, backing away.

Bellona knocked on the duchess's door and walked inside. The woman sniffled, but didn't look at Bellona.

'You know I don't wish to dance.' Bellona shut the door.

'I know.' The duchess stared at the embroidered bit of linen in her hands. 'If you wish to be a heathen, then you may be a heathen. I wash my hands of you. My daughter. She loved to dance. Loved the dresses. The laughter. I just thought… I just thought you would, too.'

Bellona sighed. 'If you will help me, I will try.'

The duchess dotted her eyes dry. 'The tutor is waiting.'

'No. You must help me. I cannot do it without you. I *cannot*.'

'You are being ridiculous.'

'I am asking for no more than you are from me.'

'Very well.' The duchess stood. 'I am too old and tired to fight you any more.'

Chapter Five

Muffled pianoforte music wafted down the hallways. Rhys stopped, listening. That wasn't his mother playing. She'd long ago ceased, claiming her fingers hurt if she even looked at the pianoforte, though she wasn't above persuading someone else to play for her.

Rhys trekked to the ballroom and then stared.

His mother sat in a high-backed chair similar to a queen's throne. She held her arm out and hummed above the sound of the music, as she grasped a fan like a sceptre and let it bounce in time with her hums. A man at the pianoforte had the music before him, but his eyes were closed as his fingers moved.

Rhys recognised the other man, the dancing master who had tutored every child from every estate in the area. The man danced, his lips in a grim line as he held Bellona and led her through the steps around the room. His hair was smooth at one side and the other stood out as if someone had tugged him around by the white locks. The wench had a disastrous effect on hair. Rhys's own was beginning to grey since he had met her. Only the duchess's hair stayed locked in place.

But when he looked closer, his mother's eyes were red-rimmed and he wasn't sure Bellona's didn't follow suit.

'Shoulders back,' his mother commanded, between hums, her voice reaching a crescendo. 'Bellona, the hand. Stop pulling your fingers from his. You are causing the tutor to miss his steps to keep you close. Hum-hum-hum. Hum-hum-hum. One-two-three. Feet. Feet. Feet. Remember the— Stop. Stop. Stop!' Her voice rose and her fan-tip jumped up.

Bellona immediately stepped back from the man.

Standing, the duchess moved to Bellona and the dance instructor. 'Bellona, you must simply refrain from pulling away from him. You were doing so well in the country dance, but you cannot manage one step of this dance.' She walked behind the man and straightened his back. He winced.

'Mr Mathers, you must, must, must pay attention as well. You do not have quite the grasp of the dance as I had hoped or Bellona would be able to do better. I will demonstrate for her. Dance with me, Mr Mathers…' She raised her hand and stepped into his grasp.

The dance continued, with his mother and the tutor.

Bellona stood at the side. Her eyes showed dark against wan skin.

The duchess and the tutor danced round the room. Bellona breathed deeply.

'It's not truly difficult,' Rhys said, walking to her side. 'Perhaps I could show you since the instructor is lacking.'

He would hold her only for a moment. That would not cause any problems within him. He could not even remember all the women he had danced with.

Her head jerked around, as if she'd not known he was in the room. She moved back, increasing the distance between them. 'I know. But I hate this dance. I hate it.'

'It's so elegant and the music is beautiful.'

'This dance is… Your mother said some people think it improper. They are wise. To be in a man's grasp like that…' She shuddered.

Rhys talked softly, leaning towards her. 'Has the tutor behaved badly to you?'

'Just in the same terrible way he is with the duchess.'

Rhys's head darted and he watched the couple swirl, his mother's voice slightly louder than the music as she instructed the tutor.

'They're just dancing,' Rhys said. 'If anything, Mother is holding him too close.'

'I cannot.' She shook her head slowly. 'I will tell her that I cannot do this…unsuitable dance.'

He studied Bellona's face and he reconsidered where his eyes had roamed on some of his dance partners. He raised his chin and slowly nodded downward. He moved his view over her shoulder and kept his eyes away from her breasts, but spoke in an undertone. 'I am sure, if you tell my mother, she will see that you have someone to fashion a gown for you with an adequate…bodice.'

She looked at him, studying his deliberately neutral expression. 'I don't understand?'

He furrowed his brows. 'Wasn't that what you were talking about?'

Her lids dropped a bit and her face changed. The eyes narrowed. 'What is wrong with my bodice?'

'Nothing.' It was the truth. He spoke dismissively

and assumed the privileged bearing that usually stopped all questions. Whoever had fashioned her close-fitting garment should have been well paid.

Her gaze widened, and he could see the thoughts working away behind her eyes. She grumbled a word he could not make out.

'I thought,' he emphasised, 'you might prefer a more concealing dress—because you think the dance improper. A thicker fabric might give more of a feeling of distance—propriety—of all those things—important things—necessary for a dance. I am just trying to assist.' He heard the soothing tone of his voice and reminded himself he had meant no offence. He did not need to grovel to her.

One of her feathers unruffled. 'I will consider what you said.' She crossed her arms, and patted one hand just at the top of her capped sleeve. Her arm now draped over her chest. 'I will never, ever dance in this dress now.'

'Just wear a dress that's more—less fashionable.'

Her eyes, if they could, became even more lustrous with disapproval. 'I was not speaking of that, although I will certainly take what you say into account when I choose my clothing.'

'Miss Cherroll… You must accept the norms of societal behaviour if you are to live in England.'

Her face didn't lighten. 'No. He holds my hand and around my waist and I cannot… In a moment he could clasp me tightly. I could not pull away if I wished.'

He looked at his mother and the instructor. 'The tutor did not hold you closer than that?'

'It was still too close.'

Oh, this woman was surely unsuitable for any man's

wife. He felt sorry for her and the man she might wed, assuming she didn't geld him with an arrow first.

'I've held women in that manner and none seemed to mind.'

She shuddered. 'I cannot speak for them. But I cannot tolerate any more lessons.' The intake of her breath spoke of her determination.

She grasped her dress, lifted the hem enough to show those unsightly boots and darted from the room.

His mother must have been watching. She stopped in mid-step and shouted a command to the man at the piano. The music ceased. The two men and his mother were both looking at him.

'What did you say to send her away?' His mother stepped away from the tutor. She waved a hand. 'You would not believe how much effort this day has taken to organise.'

This was not the place to mention the bodice discussion. 'I may have made her...doubt her...ability to learn the dance.'

His mother's fingers splayed and her hands went up. 'Rolleston, I cannot believe...' She caught her words. 'I had to near drag her from her room just to get her here at all.' She pointed a finger at the ceiling. 'Just one moment.'

The tutor dropped his head, and a small moan fell from his lips. 'I so must beg your pardon, but I have another appointment, and I do not think I will be able to continue... With the greatest of regrets and sadness. Not today or tomorrow.'

'See what you've caused...' She looked at Rhys. 'We had made an improvement.'

Before she'd finished the sentence, the tutor was

out through the door. The musician stood and tucked his music under his arm, turning to leave.

The duchess raised her ringed fingers, stopping his departure. 'Stay. We will try again. Do not think to tell me you also have another meeting.' She turned to Rhys, her eyes showing the little lines at the side which could grow into quite huge ones depending on her temper. 'Rolleston, you do not realise how very important this is. Wait here,' she muttered. 'I will get Bellona and we will continue and, Rhys, you will show her that she is quite the dancer.'

Bellona sat in her room. She had taken country dance lessons at Whitegate with her sister and no one had ever minded that she did not participate in other dances. She'd merely taken the lessons to appease Melina and the women always practised together. Sometimes even the children partnered them.

The duchess didn't understand, and when she'd mentioned dancing to Bellona, Bellona expected no more attention to the matter than she'd given with her sister.

When the man touched her, she could not think of feet or music or dance. All she could remember was the feel of hands clasping her neck on the ship—all the more terrifying as it had happened after they had escaped Stephanos and his men, and the captain had promised her her safety. Or the night she and Thessa had escaped Greece—when Stephanos and his men had stolen her from her home.

She had made a promise to Melina not to speak of it. She said the things people whispered about, they overlooked. But if their suspicions were publicly confirmed and indiscretions admitted openly, then the *ton* could no longer ignore them. Nobody wanted to be seen as approving an open scandal as everyone wanted to uphold their place in society.

Bellona thought of a gasping fish lying in the sand, eyes wide, breathing air, but not truly breathing. That was how the dance instructor's hands made her feel. That was how she always felt when a man stood close enough that his hands could seize her neck.

Three quick raps on the door sounded.

Bellona forced herself to her feet, knowing the duchess would be on the other side.

The duchess stood there. 'I do not blame you for this, Bellona. I have explained to Rhys that he must mind his ways. The dancing master—I do not think he has even read Thomas Wilson's book or looked at the drawings. He does not know the correct method of dancing. He's left now and I'm sure—'

'He's left?' Bellona interrupted.

The older woman nodded. 'No loss. His posture was not good. Return and I will see that you learn properly.'

Bellona did not ever wish to attend another soirée—she hated them. Even the country dances caused her insides to ache when many people were together. Everyone moved this way and that and anyone could grasp her from behind. Breathing became impossible.

Almost before her thought was completed, the duchess fastened her hand on Bellona's arm and marched her out through the door. 'You must do this. Mothers need children. You must marry in order to have babies. You must attend soirées and dinner parties to meet the men. Even a vicar will expect a dance with his wife on occasion.'

Bellona walked back into the ballroom. Movement caught her eye. The duke stood at the side, talking quietly with the musician.

His gaze locked on her. He studied her—just a blink, but all the same, he'd already had too many thoughts she couldn't decipher. Too much intensity in his gaze.

The touch of the duchess's hand on Bellona's arm freed her to move again. 'Now, dear, don't be awed that you'll be dancing with a duke.'

Bellona paused, unable to take another step forward. He did not make her fear him as the other men did, but when his eyes raked over her, her strength waned.

Bellona spoke to the duchess. 'You must show me.'

She could feel the duke thinking about her, watching her.

'Nonsense,' the duchess said, waving Bellona's words away. 'Rolleston is a wonderful dancer. He knows what he's doing. With his height you might think his legs would get in the way or his feet would crush you, but he's quite graceful.'

Bellona moved her head sideways in refusal, as he stepped forward, movements slow.

'Miss Cherroll.' His words, rumbling just louder than a murmur, barely reached her ears above the sound of her heart beating. He stopped two arm lengths in front of her. His hands were at his side. 'I would be pleased if you would give me the honour of a dance.'

She could not speak.

'Child.' The duchess, all smiles, reached out to nudge Bellona forward. 'Do not be afraid you will step on his feet. He's quite able to withstand it, I assure you.'

'Mother.' Rhys raised his arm the slightest bit. His voice was quiet. 'I can help her. Why don't you ring for tea? Or some wine, perhaps? I'm parched.'

'That would be lovely.' She turned, signalling the musician to begin, before she moved to summon the tea.

'Listen to the music,' the duke said to Bellona. 'Just listen for a bit. Let it get into your thoughts.'

She nodded, unable to move her eyes from his and trying to slow the roar in her ears. His mother stood near. The duchess. All was safe. Bellona knew it. But her body did not feel safe.

He raised one hand into the dance pose, but the other remained at his side. 'Step forward and put your hand in mine.'

She drew another breath into her lungs and looked into his eyes. They were not harsh or threatening or angry. They had softened at the edges, guiding her, and his head leaned forward the merest amount. Now she couldn't escape. She was trapped. But the snare was the velvety hue of his eyes and the rumble of his voice curling into her with the richness of a covering being wrapped around her on a cold day after the cloth had been warmed by the fire.

She moved towards him and put her fingertips in his palm, waiting for the moment when his hand would tighten over hers. The movement in his hand signalled to her that his fingers had flexed, but he didn't close them against her. He hadn't realised she wasn't scared by him, but was trying to keep from letting her life be changed in a way she'd never believed possible. This weakness she'd fought against because she'd seen her mother deserted by the man she'd loved.

'Now put your hand on my shoulder and I will rest my arm at your back, but I will not hold or clasp you tightly. It will be just the barest bit of my hand resting against you.'

Her throat tightened, and she tried to keep her breathing calm and the world from fading so that the only remaining thing was him.

'You will be safer than you've ever been before. I will let nothing hurt you. Mother is here. She's looking at the music and she is telling the man how she wishes to hear him play the piece.'

He stood, as if he were the one who couldn't move.

Bellona put her hand at his shoulder—wool soft beneath her fingers. The scent of shaving soap touched her nose.

He hadn't moved. 'Are you ready?' he asked.

She nodded.

She felt the flex of his shoulders and the slightest touch of his hand near her back.

'Pretend I'm not even here.' His words barely reached her ears over the tune the pianist just started playing. 'It will be simple as a stroll around the room.'

She nodded and he took the first step of the dance.

Bellona stumbled, managing to find Rhys's feet. He tensed his arms, but he didn't try to right her or gasp at her.

When she moved back into the dance, he looked beyond her and hummed a rich, soothing sound.

She listened to his voice, and thought of the music. She could still move. His eyes weren't on her and his thoughts looked far away. She forced herself not to move closer to him. The distance would save her.

The pianoforte music wafted inside her body and it

was the same as being in the forest, free and alone—the moment of the leaves in the trees brushing the air over her and being safe, held by the forest.

Her arm barely contacted with his coat—a mountain of man moved beneath her touch, but instead of causing cold breaths inside her, the world invited her. She tightened the fingers of her raised hand, feeling his palm, and he responded with the merest pressure, silent reassurance passing between them.

She wanted to see his face, but she didn't dare raise her eyes. She didn't want to ruin anything about this moment.

The music stopped and their feet ceased at the same step. He did not move at all until he spoke to the duchess. 'I think she has the grasp of it.'

Then he ushered her to his mother and left the room.

'You did well enough,' the duchess said. 'I knew you could learn. Rhys is a much better dancer than the tutor, if I do say so myself. You should see the ladies at soirées beam when he asks them to dance. I'm sure it quite goes to his head, but it doesn't show. The dance is not so hard, is it?'

'No.'

She appraised Bellona's face. 'You need not concern yourself about the dance again. All it took was for Rhys to show you. Don't expect your next dancing partner to be like my son, though.'

Bellona nodded, and left the room. She didn't expect any man to ever be like him.

Chapter Six

Rhys stood just inside the open window. He'd had one of the servants move Bellona's target closer to the library window again. He suspected she'd lugged them away before because they'd slowly migrated from under the windows. He'd just wanted the arrows going away from the direction of the fields. *True,* he told himself, and the *thwack* of the arrow both irritated him and pulled him like a siren's song. *Liar,* he admitted.

A carriage rolled up. Warrington's.

The door opened, and Warrington stepped out, then turned to help Bellona's sister from the vehicle. His hand lingered in his wife's until a blonde bundle jumped from the opening and both parents turned to her in caution.

The little one dodged her parents and ran screeching to Bellona. Warrington reprimanded her, but his wife placed a gloved hand on his arm and then Warrington moved from view.

Bellona's bow and arrow slid to the ground and Willa bounded into her aunt's arms. The dark head and the light one bumped together. Bellona moved, hugging the little one in a swirling movement.

'Willa insisted her aunt is out with her bow and arrows slaying dragons. She claims you are doing so to rescue her.' Melina's voice carried through the open window.

'Only six dragons.' Bellona's excited voice was no quieter than her sister's.

'You killed six,' the little one insisted. 'But I killed ten for you.'

'What with?' Bellona asked.

The girl laughed, jumping back from her aunt. 'I stomped on them. They squished.'

'That is ugly, Willa,' her mother said.

'Yes,' Bellona agreed. Her hair had half-fallen from its pins. 'You must save them whole so we can have a feast. Dragon's meat is very tasty and is already cooked from the dragon's breath.'

'Bellona, stop adding to her imagination,' Melina said.

Willa shot an imaginary arrow into her aunt and Bellona was putting more drama into the play than any actress he'd ever seen at Drury Lane.

He wanted to join them. He wanted to hear the laugher around him, especially Bellona's.

'Sir,' a voice behind him interrupted. 'The Earl of Warrington did not bring a card, but suggested I tell you—'

'—To roll yourself out of bed—' Warrington stepped behind the servant '—because you are so tired from staying up late looking at your face in the mirror and wondering why the heavens have been so cruel to you.'

Rhys's quiet response would have earned him a fortnight of prayers from the vicar. The butler's lips quirked and he slipped out through the door.

Warrington walked to the other side of the window and looked out, viewing the same scene Rhys saw.

'Have you gambled away the inheritance yet?' Warrington asked.

'No.' Rhys turned to the earl. 'Do you need me to lend you some funds?'

'Like hell.'

'If you throw the first punch, you should be prepared with another one.'

'So how is the duke?'

Rhys tapped his boot toe at the base of the wall. 'It's been difficult managing the properties around London through my man of affairs instead of seeing for myself. I have had to depend on Simpson completely because the duties are so new to me and the duchess has been so distraught. I believe Simpson quite capable, but I need to take responsibility myself at some point.'

'It gets easier,' Warrington said. 'I was fortunate to have my brother Dane to help me after my father died. If you need anything, just ask. I'll send him.'

'Much better than having you around, I'm sure.'

'True,' Warrington said.

Both men stayed at the widow. All three females chattered and seemed to be having no trouble following every word spoken, mostly in Greek.

'So how are things here?' Warrington said. 'The duchess?'

'Mother is better.'

Warrington nodded, his voice soft. 'Bellona doesn't

like quiet. My wife, fortunately, does. Hard to believe they are sisters sometimes.'

Rhys didn't speak, just watched the gestures down below. Bellona unstrung the bow. The little girl wore the quiver. The women moved with each word they spoke.

'You'd think it's been years since they've seen each other,' Warrington said, moving away from the window.

Rhys still watched the scene. 'At least they get along.'

'They do. For the most part.'

Rhys stepped nearer the bookshelves, and considered his words while he looked at Warrington. 'Is Bellona truly nothing like her sister?' He waited for the response.

Warrington chuckled. 'Night and day. It's odd how they disagree on things, but never seem to argue. My brothers and I argued even when we agreed.'

'How did their father die?'

Warrington walked away from the window, and stood at the unlit fireplace. 'He's actually alive and I would prefer that to remain between us. I've been concerned word would get out concerning the pompous goat. That's what they disagree over. Melina wishes to keep him from all aspects of her life. Bellona has visited his wife secretly several times, though she doesn't like the man either.'

'Where does he live—in Greece?' Rhys knew her mother was dead and he'd thought her father was, too.

'On St James's Street in London. He's actually Lord Hawkins.'

Rhys relived the words in his mind. Yes, he'd heard correctly. Bellona's father was an English peer.

Warrington gave the smallest nod and studied Rhys. 'In his youth, he visited the island, married their mother and forgot to tell her he had a wife here. The second marriage was probably a farce to him, but still, the women didn't know of each other. Two families. Two sets of children. He sailed back and forth a few times. The children's ages are near the same.'

'Lord Hawkins?' Rhys could hardly stand to be in the same room with the man. His voice usually carried to all corners when he talked of the great art of the past and no one else's opinion on any painting came close to Hawkins's self-professed judgement skills.

'It's best that people think Melina's father is dead,' Warrington said. 'Better than the truth and having to acknowledge him. Better for the women. For everyone.'

'I can see how that would be.' Rhys watched the women laughing. He could not connect them in his mind to Hawkins.

'My wife thinks Bellona wants so much to be different from her father that she almost becomes him. Hawkins has that nose up in the air, thinking he is above society's ways. Bellona can be uppity, too, around society. Can you imagine Bellona making morning calls or indulging in polite conversation at a house party? She's more likely to be asking the servants how many eggs a day the chickens are laying.'

'She's been a boon with the duchess, though. They have even looked at fashion plates together.'

'Bellona? That is not her normal way. My wife finally reached an agreement with Bellona so that at least her gowns are acceptable. I'm fortunate Hawkins spent more time with his eldest daughter. He insisted

Melina act like a lady. When Bellona was growing into a young woman and should have been learning the same skills, Hawkins returned to England for several years. Probably hoped they would starve. I doubt he cared much either way as long as he didn't have to think of them. It's a wonder they survived into adulthood. I saw how they lived when I went to the island. I saw how hard it was for Melina to leave her two sisters behind, believing coming here was the only way to save her family.'

'Bellona has helped Mother think of something besides her grief.'

'That really doesn't surprise me.' Warrington stepped back to the window. 'One day, I smelled a stench in the hallway, but I ignored it, thinking a chamber pot had been dropped. Then I heard a strange noise and discovered Bellona had been keeping an orphaned pig in her chamber because she thought no one else could keep it alive. A pig. In the family quarters. Willa cried when I said little Snowdrop had to be removed. It was not leaving *snowdrops* in its wake. I was the only one in the entire household who didn't know of the creature.'

'Still, Bellona has something that…'

Her laughter trickled in through the window. Rhys head turned towards the sound.

'You need to watch yourself Rhys.' Warrington shrewdly studied the duke's face. 'Don't make an error which might cause us to kill each other.'

Rhys didn't answer. London. He would have to go to London immediately. If even Warrington could sense his interest in Bellona…

Rhys couldn't even step away from the window.

* * *

Homesick. Heartsick. Bellona touched her stomach, before resting her hand on the fabric of the chair in the library. Seasick on land. She missed Melos, but she could not return. She missed her sisters, but they both had wed—Melina to the earl and Thessa to Warrington's brother, Captain Ben.

In the past, Willa and her brothers had always taken Bellona's mind from the feelings of sadness. Today, seeing her niece again had only heightened her loss. Her *mana* and sisters had laughed together so many times. Mana was gone for ever.

Now, instead of having her peaceful mother, she was sitting every day with a woman who could have tackled Zeus and made him leave the heavens. Bellona could not go back into the duchess's chambers right now. She had told the maid so—twice—when the duchess summoned her.

Bellona had chosen to sit in the library because it had the largest windows, but now the evening shadows lengthened in the room, darkening everything. The duchess was suffering a fit of irritation. The older woman always became more cross as the sun set. She could sit it out alone this time.

Rhys walked into the library. He held a half-full glass of amber liquid. He sat it on a table, but his eyes met hers. 'My mother has asked me to collect you.'

Her chest constricted. She didn't know why she did not have the strength to make her body unaware of him whenever he walked into the room.

She was in the duke's chair. The arms of the chair seemed to grow bigger and the back taller. She rose. She had to free herself from the confines. 'Your chair.'

His head moved only an inch to each side as he shook it, but his eyes didn't move at all. They remained locked on her. 'Miss Cherroll. Please be comfortable. I am just as at ease wherever I sit.'

She raised her chin in acknowledgement of his words. 'I have been here too long. When I saw my family today, I realised how much I miss them. I...' She moved back, planning to tell him she would have to leave.

'My mother just stormed into the dining room where I was eating,' he said. 'She insists you are being contrary.'

'I would not say I am the contrary one,' she said.

He turned to her, eyes shining, lips upturned. 'I would say you are, but with a definite purpose. You annoy her to keep her mind from dwelling on other things.'

'I suppose I must go see how she is faring.' But her feet didn't move.

'Please,' he said. 'Sit for a moment with me. I think you owe me,' he said. 'I soothed my mother and kept her from searching you out. She checked your room, by the way.'

She sat, but kept her back straight. 'I think you are contrary, too.'

'Very.' He sat on the sofa, legs stretched in front of him, one booted foot rocking back and forth on its heel. 'But you do not need to go to my mother right now. She is currently looking for my valet. I have told her when I go to London next, I am going to purchase a waistcoat and cannot decide on the right colour to go with yellow stripes. She is hoping to convince my valet of the proper garments I should buy so I do not look like I have lost my wits.'

'She tires me. All the sadness. It just reminds me of my own. I sit with her and have to remember that I am alive today. All of yesterday is gone. I must be alive for today or I will have nothing.'

'I just study the ledgers or read when I am lost in sad memories.'

'Or ride your horse, or check on the stablemen or write letters to your man of affairs.'

He stared at her. 'How do you know all that?'

'I wake many times in the night and it is too silent. My sisters were always with me when I was young. My mother near. Now I wake up and the room is so large and I am alone in it, so I move about the house. I was— I see you writing at night. I have been in the hallway many times and noticed the light from the open library door. I hear the shuffle of your papers and your sighs.'

'I do not sigh.'

She took in a deep breath, looked at him, parted her lips and imitated the sound of a weary sigh.

He shook his head in disagreement.

'And you grumble. I do not even have to be near the door to hear you complaining to the paper.'

'Next time, just walk into the room.'

She settled back into the chair and let her fingers rest on the arms. 'You must have many sad memories if you spend so much time working not to think of them.'

'A few. Mainly of my brother. We pretended to be jousting knights. We had fencing duels. We took our lessons together. He never was as robust as I, but I never expected him to die, even when he got very sick. I wasn't even here at the time. Now I ask myself, how could I have not known?'

'I hate sadness. Sometimes the duchess's melancholy almost swallows me.'

'She was not this way before. Not always gentle, but never was she like this. She's not the same person.' He raised a brow. 'I understand quite well. If you need someone to make you angry to take your mind from your sadness, search me out. I will do my best.' He gave a definitive nod of his head.

'That is kind of you.' She smiled. 'But I don't wish to be angry.'

'How does a person slap you with their words?'

'By criticising my clothes or my hair. Telling me how I should act. Disparaging my boots.' She kicked out her hem of her dress. 'I like my boots even if no one else does.'

Her chest flooded with warmth. His eyes. He appraised her with something she recognised as laughter, but it was also mixed with the same look Warrington often gave her sister. In this moment, she could look at the duke directly and feel cosseted by his eyes.

'I cannot understand why your boots aren't revered. It's quite interesting how one even appears bigger than the other.' His voice flowed smoothly. 'And the toe appears to have a chunk out of it.'

'I disarmed a trap with it.'

'Perhaps you should have used a stick.' He studied her and, even as he commented on her footwear, he complimented her with his eyes and voice.

'I did the next time.'

'I will be happy to have those beautiful boots replaced for you with an even more lovely pair.'

'No. But thank you, Your Grace.'

'I assure you, I can have someone fashion such

suitable, extraordinary footwear that your toes will sing.'

'You cannot have more *suitable* boots made for me because these are perfect. And I hope you do find a yellow-silk waistcoat with something fashionable painted on it. Perhaps blue slippers.' She lowered her chin. 'You would like to discuss my hair next?'

'Hair like that…' His eyes wandered away. 'A man does not want to discuss it.'

She tightened her jaw.

But when he looked back at her, his eyes had changed. He'd lost the look that made her feel she knew him. 'I'm sure Byron could find something to say about your hair much better than I could.'

She wanted to bring back the feeling of companionship between them. 'Try,' she challenged.

He frowned. 'No. I am no poet.'

'You are every moment the duke?'

He gazed at her hair and his voice dropped to a whisper before his gaze took control of her. 'I do not have to touch it to feel it against my skin. A caress. Unequalled by any other woman's fingertips.'

The explosions in her body took her breath. 'I forgive you for what you said about my boots.'

'I am fond of your half-boots.' The seriousness left his face. 'They are quite serviceable, you do not have to have a valet to care for them and they do cover your feet well.'

She looked at her feet. 'That is the first nice thing anyone has ever said about them and I do think it might be the worst as well.'

He shook his head. 'It might be. But you find them comfortable and you wear them and you do not care if they are not quite the thing. You like them and so they are on your feet. That is all that matters.'

She half-nodded. They also held her knife. 'They are indeed serviceable.' But most importantly, they made her feel safe.

Only even with the knife hidden in her boot, she'd still not recovered her ability to sleep well after the attacks she experienced on the ship from Greece to England—first from Stephanos and his men and then later from the crewman who had tried to strangle her.

She'd been asleep when the pirate, Stephanos, had attacked the ship and she'd only woken when Thessa had burst into the room after everything had ended and Captain Ben had secured their safety. Realising she could have awakened to find her sister gone for ever had terrified her.

Stephanos had always watched every move Thessa made when he saw her and when she and Bellona had fled Melos by swimming to the ship of Captain Ben— whose brother, Warrington, had taken Melina from the island—Stephanos and his men had followed them. The group had included the man who had wanted to marry Bellona… He had the demon's eyes. Eyes that darkened to a soulless pit. All the demons in her dreams had devouring eyes. And they always, always had the same scent of rotted eggs, while jagged-edged black earth crunched under her feet when she ran from a man with eyes growing darker and darker as he came closer and closer.

Captain Ben and his men had fought off the invaders and defeated Stephanos. The pirates had had no choice but to retreat and allow the Englishmen to leave with Thessa and Bellona on board.

'I must keep my boots nearby me at all times.' She studied Rhys's face.

'I feel the same about mine.'

She looked at his feet. 'Your valet is quite good.'

'I surround myself with the best.'

She gave the merest nod of acknowledgment and let the thoughts rummage around in her head. She chose something safer to mention.

'Your mother still says I must leave and when I agree with her, she becomes even more angry. She doesn't want me to go, but she doesn't want me to stay.'

Nothing about him moved, except the rocking of his boot, until he spoke. 'Before you came here, countless times, every day, my mother said she prayed to die.'

He stood, towering up, but she did not feel frightened. 'I would like you to stay. You have no notion how much better she is today than the day before you came. She has not summoned anyone but me since Geoff died. She has not looked at fashion plates since my sister died. You have roused her spirit.'

His eyes stayed on hers. 'You've been a boon to me in so many ways.'

Looking up, she could only nod.

'If she becomes too much for you to bear, seek me out. Any time of the day or night.'

He left. The glass remained along with the lingering scent of shaving soap and leather from the chair. She'd not noticed it before. It had the same earthiness of the duke and it surrounded her on three sides—an embrace.

Chapter Seven

Bellona shut the duchess's door with the lightest of clicks and stood in the hallway. Then she made a gesture she'd seen the sailors use.

The older woman deserved respect, but certainly did not earn it. She'd called Bellona an ungrateful bumble-knot. A foreign muddle-mind. A featherhead.

The woman had been unwilling to accept that Bellona did not want to learn to read English, had managed just fine so far without such a habit, and the letters did not all stick in her head.

Bellona had explained she couldn't read that much in Melos as she hadn't had books and with so much work to do there hadn't really been time. Then she'd been told she was not in Melos now and discovered that the duchess and Bellona's own father had a similar way of expressing their ire. They waged a war on her ears.

Bellona had promised to search out a book and study it—because that was the only way to finally quiet the woman and escape.

The library was empty. Bellona pulled out the first

book she saw, opened it, shuddered and, with a thunk, slid it back on to the shelf. That one was not even in English. She did not know the language at all.

Poetry might be ideal, she mused. That was why people liked poems. A poem did not require as much reading.

If she memorised a verse of a poem that she could recite in a mournful voice and become too carried away to finish… She could honestly claim it to be her favourite verse and favourite book and perhaps that would satisfy the duchess.

Bellona searched until she found a volume of poetry with a long introductory section at the beginning. She skipped that.

Bellona sat in the library with the book, staring at the few bits of words she recognised and the pleasant white space, knowing she would have to study the dribs of ink in more detail.

Pages. Pages and pages. Whoever invented paper must have hated everyone. Whoever decided to put words into sentences should have had to sit in a room with nothing else but paper and ink and a pen and write for the rest of his life.

But this family placed importance on books and if books meant something to them then Bellona would try to read. Especially if it might make the long stretches of night move more quickly.

She tried to sound out the first word. *E. X. P. O. S. T.* The next letter, *U,* she did not recall at all. *L. A. T. I. O. N.* She did not remember enough to read even the first word. She groaned at the fifth line. Books. That word she could read. This poem had books in it, which made no sense at all.

The duke strode into the room. He still wore the clothes of the day, but had discarded his coat. His sleeves would have been out of place on Melos, too much cloth and very white. The waistcoat, obsidian, and the night, took the lightness from his face, creating a cold look which reminded her of the marble pieces she'd seen on her island. They were all crushed and broken, though, and he didn't appear possible to shatter.

His face showed the beard trying to poke through for morning. He raked his fingers through his hair.

'I thought you did not like books.'

She could not make out the first word of the title. She held it up so he could see. 'I don't. This *biblio…*'

He walked closer, bringing all the pleasant scents of the outside with him. He'd been riding. Leather and wool blended into the air.

'Lyrical Ballads,' he read aloud.

She gave a sideways turn of her head. 'I have read enough of it.'

His eyebrows rose in question.

Nodding, she admitted, 'One word was enough. I even like embroidery better than reading. At least when you finish sewing you have something to show for it. When you finish a book, you still have the same pages you started with and tired eyes.'

'You've not read the right story.'

'I've not read any book.' She stood. 'I do not have to eat a tree to know if I would like how it tastes.'

'Sit for a moment,' he said, indicating the sofa. He walked to the shelves behind the sofa.

'Do not try to make me read.'

He tugged a book out and held it so she could see

the title. 'This is a tale you cannot help but enjoy. I'll give you a primer on it.'

'Does your *mana* like the story?'

His jaw dropped. 'Of course Mother likes the book. Everyone does.'

'She expects me to read to her. She said when she holds out the book far enough to read the letters, her arms collapse.'

'She has spectacles. She refuses to wear them when anyone is near.'

'Spectacles? Then I will not worry about reading. If she wishes to read badly enough, she will do it herself.'

He rested the book against the top of the sofa back. 'Perhaps you could just read some *Robinson Crusoe* to her. If you do not like it, then you can truly say you do not like books.'

'If I do not like him, then you will believe me?'

'Yes.'

She settled into the edge of the sofa, her back straight. A crease appeared between his brows, but then his attention returned to the book in his hand.

Letting him worry about the words would be so much easier than doing it herself.

He moved to the chair across from her, whisking the lamp along with him and setting it at the side. He took up much more of the area than she'd believed possible. 'Listen.'

He read aloud for a few moments and his voice became like a soft thunder off in the distance when rain was needed. Something pleasant and hopeful. Her thoughts were pulled along with his words.

'Wait,' she interrupted.

He looked up from the words, his brows knit again, and that caused her own face to tighten.

'You are reading about a man who is being told to be happy he is not of higher birth—that to be born in a situation of middling life, not poor, not wealthy, is the best. Is that how you feel?'

'Of course not.' He turned back to the book, reading again. 'The writer was correct for Crusoe, but not for everyone.'

'Wait,' she interrupted a second time. 'The older man is crying. You cannot like that.'

'Perhaps you should not really listen,' he said, not raising his eyes. 'But only sit there and pretend—to please me.' He took a breath, frowned and said, softly, 'Imagine I am enjoying reading the book and would like to have your company while I do so.'

He continued reading aloud.

Her company, she mused. What an odd thing to say. She intended to tell him she did not want to listen, but when she opened her mouth to speak, his voice increased and his words filled the air. She leaned back in her chair and his tone returned to normal.

She crossed her arms in annoyance, but the story wasn't so terrible. After a few moments she relaxed. If reading made him happy, she could pretend to listen.

The duke read of the man's age. He was only a few years younger than Bellona's age of twenty-two and he was planning to go on a sea voyage. Bellona shut her eyes and leaned back with a sigh the duke could not have missed. She'd been on a ship. If one liked bland sea biscuits and ale—in a gaol surrounded by water—then sailing was the best place of all to be.

Now, the tale told of the young man's *mana* trying to dissuade him from travelling. She nodded in agreement. If her own mother had lived, Bellona would never have stepped on the ship and left her.

Bellona shut her eyes and listened, letting her arms relax. His voice could make even the tale of sailing sound pleasant.

He paused a moment, but she didn't look at him and he continued reading.

She listened to every word and time vanished.

When his voice stopped, her eyes opened.

'See, reading isn't bad.' He handed her the book still warm from his hands. 'Finish the story and then tell me you don't like it.'

She challenged him with her eyes, and smiled. 'I really cannot read English.' She'd been so determined to forget every word of English her sister had taught her. Forced it from her mind, but now she wished she'd kept the knowledge. Not that she wanted to open a book any more than she wanted her skin scraped with thorns, but perhaps her mind might change.

'No matter.' He tossed the words aside. 'As a gift to you for spending your time with my mother, I will have a tutor installed here.'

'The dancing master didn't work out.' A tutor. She shuddered. Brambles in human form.

The duke's lids flickered just a bit. 'I am sure I can find someone you get on well with.'

'I am not educated. Warrington saw no reason for me to be taught if I did not wish it.'

'I do not care if that is how Warrington feels. It is a gift. From me to you.' He spoke as if the words were straight from some ecclesiastical scribe.

'I will consider it,' she said finally. It would not take her long.

'Yes. I am sure you will. In the meantime, I will have someone go to London tomorrow to collect a tutor for you.'

Bellona shook her head, eyes never leaving the duke.

'Miss Cherroll, if you are to move among society with your sister's family it would be an asset for you to be able to read. You may wish to look at the caption under an engraving to see what the ladies are laughing about in a shop. Or, like my mother, read your prayer book.'

She nodded. 'You are right. When that happens, I will learn.'

Three blinks of his eyes.

She smiled. 'Your Grace.'

'Miss Cherroll.' His shoulders relaxed and he leaned back into the chair. 'You did enjoy Mr Crusoe. I promise you would not need a tutor for very long before you would be reading for yourself.' He held out *Robinson Crusoe* to Bellona. She hesitated.

Rolleston leaned forward enough to put it in her hand.

She stared at the lettering and handed it back to him. 'I know most letters. I know some words.'

He turned the book around. 'Then why do you resist so much?'

'You have never met the first mate of the ship that brought me to England,' she said. 'I liked him. He does not read. He said he carries his knowledge here—' she pointed to her head. 'He does not have time to keep turning pages.'

'Some of us cannot carry all the required knowledge and would prefer to have more than is allowed in such a small space.'

'And you see what happened to your sailor,' she muttered. 'Crusoe.'

Rhys acknowledged her words with the merest smile. 'What would it take to convince you that you need this?'

'I don't believe you truly care if I read or not,' she challenged.

'Of course I do. You've helped my mother. I wish to return the gift.'

'Then—if it is so easy, teach me yourself.'

He coughed. 'I do not have time. I have duties. Tenants. Ledgers.'

'Then it is not important.'

She stood and moved to the door.

'I will do it.' His voice rumbled. Strong. Irritated.

She turned. His eyes did not match his face. For a passing second, the boy he'd been peeked out from his expression. Then he became the duke again.

'I must be daft.' He stood and *Robinson Crusoe* slammed back into the bookcase before Rhys stared her way again.

'You do not have to do it,' she said quickly. 'I don't wish to. You punish both of us for doing no wrong.'

'An unwilling teacher and an unwilling student should make a tiresome combination, so we will start tomorrow to finish all the sooner.'

She could change her mind. She could insist on a tutor. But the image of the boy behind his eyes flashed in her memory and tumbled about her body. He'd mentioned she was a boon in so many ways and she'd wondered about those words. He could be just as alone, in his own way, as the duchess. He'd even wanted to begin teaching her the very next day.

'The day after,' she asked, checking his response.

'Oh, no. Miss Cherroll. Tomorrow. I accepted your challenge. I dare say you will be reading quite quickly with me as a tutor.' He took the volume of poetry and walked to her, placing it in her hands. 'Look over this one, too. Mother can recite a bit of it from memory. She might like speaking it while you follow along with the words. It might help her as well.'

'You wish for your mother not to be alone because it will be good for her…'

'Yes.'

'You wish for me to read because it will be good for me…'

'Yes.'

'Have you thought about what you should do because it will be good for yourself?'

'Most certainly.' He stepped back. 'To be a son my father would be proud of. To continue his legacy.'

She shook her head. 'You have only considered what your father's needs would be. Not your own.'

'My needs were formed the moment Geoff died. I cannot let him or my father down. That is what I am doing. And I thank you for reminding me that I should be about my duties. The most important thing I can do is have a son, because if I don't marry and produce a child, everything my father and grandfather did will pass out of their direct family line.'

She pressed the books together. 'Does that not feel as if you are being commanded to do something?'

'No. It is simply another duty. If a tenant's roof

blows away, I must replace it. Now I must put another heir at the table.'

'I am fortunate that I do not have to consider such a thing. I was almost forced into marriage once. I did not like it.'

'A lot of women would wish to be a duchess.'

'I am sure they will also find you tolerable as well.'

Chapter Eight

The poems were mountains and crevasses of words. She could not make sense of them. She'd forgotten almost all of what Melina had taught her. She tried for hours to remember and not enough had returned to her memory.

The only good thing about this situation was that it gave her something to do in the long hours before dawn. She could not have read into the night on Melos, though. They only had the one good lamp.

After studying, she'd fallen asleep and dreamed of being chased. Again she'd awoken breathing fast, her throat hurting and her heart pounding. She'd sat in bed, clasping her knife. When the shadows in the room were replaced by sunlight, she felt herself nodding off.

The next thing she knew, someone knocked.

'Miss,' she heard a woman's voice call through the door.

'Enter.'

A maid, mob cap snug, walked inside. 'His Grace wishes that you might meet with him in the library.'

Bellona pushed herself up. The knife handle showed

from underneath a fold in the counterpane. She swept
the covers back over the blade. She closed her eyes and
wiped her eyelashes with her fingertips, and yawned.

She could not learn the words when she was this
tired. The duke would think her the same bumble-
head his mother did.

'I believe I will sleep longer.'

'His Grace,' the maid said softly, as if the words
should stand alone in the room, 'wishes you to see
you in the library.'

'Please tell him I would be pleased to...' She looked
back at the bed. 'But I cannot meet him now.'

The maid didn't move.

'Could you bring chocolate—several hours from
now?' Bellona asked.

'If you are certain,' the maid said finally.

Bellona crawled back into bed and covered a yawn
before speaking. She didn't know how she would inform the duke she could not read—ever—but she was
too tired to tell him now. She could not even remember the letters of her own name, and could barely hold
her eyes open. 'I am certain. I cannot see him now. I
must sleep.'

The maid nodded. 'I will tell His Grace your head
pains you.'

Rhys sat in the overstuffed chair in the library, a
stack of unread newspapers on the table beside him.
He'd changed from his riding clothes after he'd seen
the maid, eyes averted, rush by the door with a tray.
His mother had eaten. He had eaten. The tray could
only be for one person who was not in his mother's
room, nor in any of the common areas of the house.

He would not go to her chamber and find her. She would have to leave it some time. The woman did not sit about in her room with books or sewing or staring out of the window as his mother did. She flitted around the house and the gardens—a bird moving from one berry to the next with a flight of fancy behind her eyes.

He'd worked the ledgers and made notes for Simpson and now Rhys started with the oldest newspaper, more aware of the sounds of the house than the print before him. He tended to let them gather before he read them. Perusing them in the carriage on his trips to and from London didn't work out well. His eyes could not adjust to the jostling. He'd tried. Now he used the travelling time to review things in his head. On occasion he'd had his man of affairs ride with him so they could plan. The trip certainly went faster, but he didn't like to take Simpson from his home because he knew the man preferred staying near his wife.

The clock chimed one note.

He turned the page. The library had been both his mother and father's favourite place. To be allowed to sit there with his parents and older siblings had been a treat when he was a child. Whoever sat in the library could tell most of the movements about the residents on this side of the house.

He did not think he could have missed seeing Miss Cherroll if she had left her bedchamber. He snapped the paper straight. Five times servants had whisked by the door, certainly having been summoned by his mother or Bellona. The staff was well trained to stay invisible otherwise.

Even the paper didn't look to have been ironed properly. He'd smudged a word with his hand, and the smear vastly irritated him.

Something creaked. A door softly shut. No footsteps sounded, but he could almost feel her movements. He lowered the print enough so he could look over it.

'Miss Cherroll,' he said before she even appeared at the opening.

A rap sounded at the wall. He would wager that was a bow bumping wood.

She stepped to the threshold.

When she met his eyes, the bow was held in both hands, flat to her chest. The quiver cinched the dull fabric of her dress.

'Oh, Miss Cherroll,' he continued, 'I see you have arrived to practise your reading.'

He stood, folding the paper. Shadows rested under her eyes and her hair was more mussed than usual. Compassion touched him. Perhaps the maid had told the truth. Perhaps Bellona had really been feeling ill.

'Do you need a medicinal prepared?' he asked.

Puzzlement. He saw it. Puzzlement in her eyes and then the memory washing over her. The wench had forgotten she was supposed to be unwell.

'I am fine. Now,' she added. Her shoulders dropped and her chin weakened.

He looked at her the same way he'd reprimanded the gamekeeper. 'Wonderful. Then we will read.'

'I must practise my archery.'

'I am rushed for time. I think it would be best if we worked together first.'

'I should have a tutor,' she said. 'I cannot take you from your duties.'

He placed the paper on the desk as she spoke. Now he put a hand on his heart. 'I cannot think of any duty more important than your education, Miss Cherroll.'

'I have changed my mind.'

'I have not.'

'I cannot learn.' She shook her head. 'I have no mind for it.'

'Nonsense. You and I will have hours and hours of nothing but lessons until you learn.'

'You will be wasting your time.' The chin went up. 'I cannot even remember all the letters.'

'Then we will start there.'

She shook her head. 'I have already tried. I have tried and I have tried.'

'Last night?'

She nodded.

If the paleness of her face told the truth, then perhaps she had worried over it. He wanted to reassure her. But he could think of only one way to do that. 'You will be reading in no time.'

'I know you have more important things to do,' she said. 'I will have the tutor.'

'I suspect you will not make progress with a tutor,' he said. 'I think you will somehow manage to convince the man to quit his post. I have seen no dancing tutor of late.'

'You do not trust me?' Her brows rose.

'Should I?' he responded in kind.

The brows lowered. 'You do not know what you ask for.'

His eyes didn't leave hers, but he managed to take

in her whole body. Warmth flooded him, and he felt he could conquer the world, but perhaps not stand upright any longer. 'I know what I am up against. I will fight the challenge.'

She glanced at the book he opened and the ink swirled into the dreaded confusing shapes. The duke stood, watching her. His hair curled the slightest bit at the end, brushing his ears. Some rested at the collar of his shirt, and some hid behind the cloth.

The currents in her stomach increased. How could she learn with the duke near her?

'I would prefer to stand,' she said. 'If you sit at the desk, I will watch.'

'You only want to be able to leave quickly if you can think of an excuse. You are scared of the words.'

No. His words flamed a challenge inside of her. She had survived far worse than this. 'We must start with the letters first.'

After putting the book away, he moved to one of the overstuffed chairs, grasping the back to move it near the desk.

'I will stand.' She shook her head.

He dropped the back of the chair. 'Very well.' He moved to the desk, shuffled the ledgers aside and pulled out a paper and dipped the pen in ink.

As he wrote the alphabet, she spoke the letters she knew. When she didn't remember, he marked it and went to another one. Then he asked her to pick out her name and she did.

'You knew all but four of the letters,' he said, glancing at her. No smile. No frown. 'Memorising them should be easy. You also know your name. I'd say you're more than halfway there already.'

Then he sketched short, quick strokes on the page.

She leaned towards him, watching the movements he made and noting the scent of his hair, bringing back memories of the mornings by the sea, causing a stab of homesickness and a curling reassurance of home.

'And this is a pig,' he said of the drawing, jarring her mind back into the room.

He wrote the letters under it and spoke them aloud. She'd not remembered the G.

'We will name him Snowdrop.' He glanced up at her and she saw sparkling brown eyes and strong lips, half-upturned, and with a private laugh hidden behind them. Then he returned to his mission. He wrote the letters and called them out as he put them down. 'This is the W.' He tapped it with the pen, leaving a drop of ink. 'And Snowdrop wasn't quiet. So we'll have the Q and U.'

'How did you know of Snowdrop?'

'Warrington told me.'

'The earl was wrong. Snowdrop wasn't unpleasant. I kept her in a soapbox with oilcloth under her because the sow didn't like her. The stable boy could not have kept her alive, but I did.'

He digested her words. 'You must not only learn to read—you must let the servants do their jobs. Do you wish to live among the staff or with the people who employ them? If you do not keep your station, your children will not have the same opportunities they could have. The legacy you create for them will follow for centuries. You do not want your children considered less than they could be. If you ignore society's ways, they will ignore you.'

She stepped back. 'I do not think they will ignore me. I think they will banish me. How terrible. No more dancing. No more maid putting her hands around my hair and pulling it tightly, trying to put a stinking mixture on it to make it stay in place. I do not want to anger people, but I do not like their discomforting ways.'

She lifted the hem of her skirt slightly as she retreated so he could see. 'These are my boots. I wear them comfortably in the house. And you spoke to me about them because they are not slippers. The more beautiful my clothes, then the more people will note my boots and talk of them. So I wear the plain dresses.'

'I noted your gown in spite of its plainness,' he said, almost under his breath, as he drew another line on the page.

'Without looking,' she asked, 'what colour is it?'

'Lighter than your eyes. Softer than your hair.'

Seconds passed. She spoke again. 'Brown. So my boots do not appear so different.'

'If you are saying you chose that gown so you would not be noticed so much...' He barely looked over his shoulder at her, but his lips caught her attention. 'You failed miserably. I hope you do better at reading or you won't learn a word.'

'My dress is the colour of leather.' She moved forward again, standing more at his back.

'Leather. Yes. Exactly the colour I meant. Just couldn't think of the word.' He turned sideways in the chair. 'But you did succeed. I did not think of your boots.'

She touched his shoulder, pressing him to turn back to the paper, not wanting him to see the heat she felt in her cheeks.

He didn't continue writing. 'I cannot help jesting with you, Bellona. You need some escape from the sadness at Harling House. So do I.'

She made a light fist and rested the knuckles of her hand against his collar, just brushing at the end of his hair. 'You don't seem sad…'

His shoulders moved under her hand when he breathed out. 'I know. But perhaps I am. And perhaps I am not enough. You are right in what you said. My life is all planned for me now. I no longer have to think what I should do—I only have to think how I should go about doing it. Generations of people have decided it for me and how could they all be wrong?'

'Perhaps.'

'No. I have lived in this world my whole life. I have seen what has happened to those who do not see the failures of others and who do not learn. A person's mistakes are his legacy, too. His children can be lifted by their father's past or have to fight it.'

'I know that well.' She looked at him and let her breath flutter past her lips. 'If the wishes of others are so important to you, then you will have to marry soon. It is what you are supposed to do.'

His gaze looked through her. 'I, too, know that well.'

She tilted her chin. 'All you must do is seek out a woman who is fond of society. You have all that a woman might wish for and can put it at her feet.'

He frowned, but the words weren't from his title but from him. 'It is true, a woman may wish to wed me for the world I can give her, but how is that different from you?'

'My dowry is not so large it will choke a man.' She twitched her shoulders. 'But he may cough,' she admitted.

'I was not talking of funds. You could wed well without a dowry if you would just accept our ways. It is not much for a man to ask.'

'No. It is not much. It is everything. For my sister, she flutters about like a butterfly when people are about. For me, the eyes on me make my stomach feel seasick. The clatter at the soirée made my head hurt. Sitting with others with tea in my cup, pretending to like it, pretending to care about the brim of a bonnet, knowing I cannot even think of the right word to say something pleasant. I feel the same as a speck in the bottom of the teacup.'

Her hand fell from his back and she stepped closer so his gaze met hers. This time her chin tilted down and her eyes levelled at him. 'Would you give up all that you care for to sit and pretend to like the taste of a foreign tea that tastes like weeds on your tongue, while you discuss the brim of a bonnet, and only wear boots that do not fit? For the rest of your life?'

'Most women like bonnets and tea and those things.'

'Then they can enjoy them. I do not wish to take theirs. I am quite sincere in that.'

'Why do you not try?'

'I have. I have sat in my sister's house and I have seen her life. For the two years since I arrived in England.' She held up her fingers. 'I have travelled to London and made morning calls and walked in her steps. We returned home again. She flutters about there and her face shows that she has been in a garden of nothing but flowers. She says I can be a bee, too, and I understand, but her garden is wrong for me. And you—' Her voice slowed. 'You have not truly taken on your new duties. You have stayed in the country rather than go to town to find a wife. Do you not feel trapped?'

'Do not put words in my mouth.' He moved. His shoulders turned. He still sat, but his body faced her. 'There is nothing I want more than to accept my duties. Nothing.'

'You have not wed—'

'I merely have not had the time.'

'You are well over thirty. You've had more than ten years to look for a wife.' She waved an arm. 'Not enough time?'

'Apparently not.' His lips turned down. 'And I am not *well over thirty*. I am thirty-one. At *first*, I was the second son and Geoff was the shining star in the heavens. Every woman I thought fascinating only met me in order to speak with my brother. I could see where their attention went. I remember that well. I decided marriage was not for me—until I met one woman at a soirée and I thought she was the one.'

'Did she reject you?' Her voice wisped away at the last words.

'Not really. I have not asked her yet because... Geoff has not been dead a year. A respectful period of time should be waited. He is—was my brother. And truth be known, I pursued her before he died. Geoff just did not know it. He never missed a soirée where she attended that he did not ask her to dance. He told me he would win her some day—but that she thought him too rakish and said she could not imagine him forsaking his mistresses for a wife.'

Winter's chill settled in her bones, even though the temperature was warm. 'You and Geoff pursued the same woman and he did not know?'

'I have not had a woman in my bed since Louisa said a man must give up his mistress for her.' He picked up the paper with the alphabet and handed it to her. 'Geoff had told me what she'd said to him. I mentioned to Louisa, later, that I had made certain conclusions and that I wished Geoff understood my unwillingness to traipse about with him—to disreputable places. She certainly had to know what I meant.' He made a loose fist and tapped it on the table. 'I pursued her with more determination than Geoff. I selected every word before I said it to her. Now that he is gone, I don't know what I think any more. Except I do not like what I did to my brother. When he died, I received the message at her father's house.'

She looked at the page of letters and wanted to crumple it up, but she didn't. 'I believe I have met Louisa. She is one of my sister's closest friends. We went to the shops. She chose slippers with pink rosettes. When she laughs, no one near can frown.'

'That would be Louisa.' Rhys turned away, suddenly fascinated by the unlit lamp. 'When my brother left the room, I often talked with her. I made her laugh. I did whatever it took to get those smiles. I thought her worth the risk.'

'The risk of hurting your brother?'

She thought his silence meant he would not answer. He didn't need to. He'd not wanted to pursue the same woman as Geoff.

'The risk of—more than that. By then my sister had died. To lose her had been so unfair. I imagined the fire taking her. The pain of it. We'd all loved her so much. I still cannot dwell on it. I did not want to repeat such a thing, and if I married Louisa, how could I keep her safe? But I eventually pushed those fears aside. And then my brother died. And now that I am the duke...' He tailed off.

'You should always be a person before you are a title,' she said, then turned to leave. She'd reached the door when he responded.

'That is not how it works.'

The quiet emphasis of the words rang in her ears and when she looked back, he still gazed at the lamp.

She wondered if he imagined Geoff's face or Louisa's smile.

Chapter Nine

After his morning ride, Rhys walked to the library. A rustle in the room alerted him that someone stood inside.

Entering, he felt a surge of disappointment that Bellona wasn't there. Guilt replaced the displeasure, but then he truly felt pleased. His mother fussed with a curtain. She'd not shown any care of the house in a very long time and to have her standing with the sunshine about her brightened his own heart.

'You would think the maids would have learned by now how to arrange the folds.' She moved them this way and that, frowning.

'Now I am crushed.' He moved beside her. 'I thought you were here to see me and it is only the windows you wish to inspect.'

'Well, I might inspect you a bit, too. Now that I see you in the light, it appears your valet does not know how to keep a man's hair properly trimmed. Or you have been leading him a merry dance again.'

'Guilty.'

She reached up and patted his cheek. 'Rhys. I am

not here to merely note how you have let yourself go because it is possibly a good thing.'

He chuckled. 'How's that, Mother?'

'When you are truly well groomed, it would be so hard for a young woman to keep from losing her heart to you.'

'You must be sure to tell the young women this. I don't think they are able to realise it on their own.'

'Nonsense.' She frowned and fussed with the curtains again. 'I think we have one under our very roof who is becoming rather taken with you.'

'I am certain she might be a bit fond of me, Mother, but I believe she is also fond of the stable master as he has secured archery targets for her. She's also had Cook prepare a poultice for one of the footmen.'

'Your valet talks too much of the other servants.'

'Just as a lady's maid talks too much to the mistress of the house. You should not believe idle talk when someone suggests Miss Cherroll is taken with me.'

'This is not idle talk. It's from her own mouth.'

'Miss Cherroll?' He studied his mother's face, uncertain he heard correctly.

'Yes.' She nodded her head. 'She does not exactly say it in words, but a mother knows. A mother definitely notices when a woman's eyes change if the son's name is mentioned. If she speaks differently when he is discussed. It's obvious.'

'I've seen none of it.'

'I am not surprised. Only concerned. But please do not encourage this woman, Rhys. Such heathenish ways. But she does make the days bearable and she has a heart of gold underneath all that rubbish she spouts. I don't want more unhappiness for her. She's had enough. No parents. Not settled like her sister. I see a poor future for her and I don't wish more unpleasantness on her, especially not under my roof.'

'You have nothing to worry about.'

Her eyes batted his words back at him. 'If you say so. She's not right for society. You should hear the tales of her life. She is of a different world. If it were not for the earl, she'd be making her way at the docks.'

The image of Bellona walking among the toughs and cutpurses jabbed at him.

He pulled open a desk drawer, searching, for what he did not know, but he would know if he saw it. 'I am aware of the role I have to fulfil. I know how uncomfortable a woman as spirited as Bellona would be living this life.'

'How uncomfortable *she* would feel? The whole of the *ton* will be watching whom you choose as a wife, Rhys. They would not be pleased that you have turned your back on their daughters and sisters. They will think you married beneath yourself. And you will have. Remember your father's last request. He counselled all his children on the importance of marriage. He asked for his name to be carried on. He wanted the family to continue. *Wed a suitable duchess*, he said. He said that many times. It was one of the last things he asked for.'

'Those were not his final words to me. They were to Geoff.' His breaths were quick. Taking out a pen, he put it by the first one. He stared at them and then put one back inside the desk.

She walked to the window. 'I worry. I can't help it. I know how easily you could be taken from me. Everything has changed so much. Not quite a year ago,

Geoff was here. A year before that, your father was here. He started failing soon after he told me of your sister's death.' She looked into the rain. 'It was like he died on purpose, so he wouldn't have to…'

'Mother. He was seventy-eight. I don't think he had a lot of choice in the matter.'

'Did you notice the honeysuckle blooming when Geoff died? I'd been in the garden with him the day before and we'd talked about how he loved the scent of them. So do I. His passing was so cruel—taking him in the spring when so much life began around him.'

She pushed back the curtains and didn't speak for a moment. 'He loved honeysuckle. When he was a boy, he'd pick the little flowers and bring them to me and I'd sniff them and exclaim to make him happy, but I truly was the most pleased. The two of you grew up so fast, Rhys. I remember how he felt as a babe in my arms. So many of the things I'd forgotten about while he was here, but after he died I remembered them all so plainly. The best children a mother could have. And the three of you so close. You and Geoff always watched out for each other and your sister. No rivalry at all. I couldn't have been more proud of my children.'

'Geoff was my only brother.' The words sounded normal enough—at least to her.

She turned. 'I wish for the family every hour. Every day I hear myself thinking about how I wish they would return. It's not asking much. To have my family. They were given to me once, but whisked away. Even the grandchildren they would have given me were taken from me. A home of this size should be filled with family. Instead we have servants and more servants and no one for them to take care of.'

Walking towards him, she smiled. 'I don't want you to think you're amiss. You're doing a fine job of managing things since they left, Rhys. I appreciate everything you've done to take over where your father and Geoff left off. I know how much you cared for them, too. How much you loved your sister. They would all be so proud of you. I am proud of you. I want you to know that.'

'Thank you.'

A maid crossed by the doorway with a tray, certainly taking it to Bellona's room. His mother's attention wavered and she waited until the woman could not possibly hear the conversation. 'Bellona must leave or you must go to London.'

He let out a loud breath of disagreement.

'Rhys. I am your mother. It is not only her acting differently. You are too aware of her. You understand quite well what I am really saying. A man's nature is such as it is. You could ruin her. She does not deserve that. You would hurt her. It is not the best situation for either one of you and you know it. She has told me how she is more comfortable with the servants at the earl's house than the guests. She has been there two years.' She paused. 'Think of her.'

His mother glanced at the statues. 'They're just bits of pottery. I don't know why we thought them anything else. Meant to hold memories of the past. They do. Soot left after the fire is gone.' She made a motion of sweeping them away before fixing her eyes on him. 'I don't know why I kept them.'

She stopped at his side, and reached to the loop of his cravat, straightening it. 'Think of *her*,' the duchess said again.

She left, skirts fluttering at her ankles. The maid moved by the doorway again, tray empty. Rhys called, stopping her.

'Inform the stable master to be ready to journey to London at a moment's notice.'

Rhys finished his meal, surrounded by empty chairs. The lamps lit the room as brightly as they always had. He sat at the same place he'd always sat.

He lifted his wine glass, sipped and put it down. Echoes of his sister's laughter, Geoff's jests and his father's half-hearted grumbles bounced in Rhys's memory. His mother, one brow raised in feigned dismay, or lips pressed to hide her smile, had presided over them all.

An infinite world at the time.

If he had known what was to happen, how could he have enjoyed the moments, knowing they were to end? But if he had known the future, the time with his family would have meant so much more.

Nothing could change one second of the time before or since. No oath was strong enough. He'd tried them all.

He stood, took the glass and finished it, sitting it back in the place it had always been and left the room.

No oath was strong enough.

Walking along the hallway, he stepped into the library and picked up one of the statuettes, turning it in his hand before putting it back on the mantel. His grandmother had owned one. His mother had added to the collection and his sister had given one to his mother. The women had thought them precious and he'd seen no value in them at all. None. Except now they'd somehow begun to matter a great deal to him.

Once he'd had to grab his mother's wrists to keep her from smashing them to the floor. They were supposed to have been passed to a daughter's daughter.

'What are you thinking of?' The question jarred him from his thoughts. He turned. Bellona stood in the doorway, staring at him. Yesterday, the message she'd sent to him had begged off reading practice because she said the duchess insisted on helping her. He knew why his mother kept Bellona at her side. He also knew just how long it had been since he'd been alone with Bellona. Two days. That he had kept count disturbed him. That his senses came alive when he saw her concerned him even more. His mother was right.

He watched her study his face. 'I was thinking of the statues on the mantel. How long they've been there. Most of them, my whole life.'

She walked into the room with the assurance of someone who'd never seen a cloudy day, but her eyes belied her steps.

'Your mother. I am concerned about her.'

'She is more demanding?'

Bellona shook her head. 'No. She's more pleasant, but still…'

'The woman you have met is not the woman she was before. She wasn't gentle, but she wasn't the same as she's been. The grief took over. Her worries surrounded her.'

'I run from mine.' She only touched her skirt long enough to hitch it up on one side, before letting it flutter into place. 'Sturdy boots, remember.'

'You can't always escape the things that trouble you.'

'If you say so.' She stepped to the books, grimaced and began to study the spines. 'I am thankful I ran from Melos. I am also making certain I do not have to stay in London if I don't wish it. If I cannot be in my own country, then I have no place to bind me to it. That is why I have decided to learn to read. Your mother said it might be needed some day to write to my sisters.'

'A good reason.'

She tugged at a book, looked at it and put it back.

'Where would you go?' he asked. He hadn't thought beyond the moment.

'I have a friend who thinks of me as a daughter, I believe. And she knows a woman who married well, but is lonely. They have written to each other and the woman says I might visit and, if we get on well, I can stay with her.'

'But you are already a companion to my mother. You must agree you take her mind from her grief.'

'I do. But she tells me she is so much better already and she is.'

She studied the books. 'Your mother said you had another book by the man who wrote *Crusoe*. I thought I might like it better. What was that man's name?'

'Defoe,' he said, not letting her divert his attention.

'I do not know how *Crusoe* ends,' she said. 'But he could not return to the same world. When a year passes. Two. So much changes if you do not see the people often. You cannot return to the same world as before. And neither can I. So I will move somewhere else. Somewhere smaller. While I have the chance to make a new life. I want children. But there are many motherless children. Many. I might gather some about me.'

'You could have your own. Marry.'

'Marriage.' She shook her head. 'Look at the grief

that marriage has caused your mother. A husband and two children lost.' She paused. 'My mother did not truly have a husband. He was gone most of the time.' She took another book as she spoke. 'The woman who thinks of me as a daughter, her husband did not do right by her either. Marriage—' She shrugged. 'The pigs and goats and chickens do not marry. And yet women do. They think they can change—' she looked at him '—nature. Yet the males of the species do not seem that particular.'

'I will be loyal to my wife. A vow is a vow.'

'You say that.'

'I know that,' he said. 'I have— I made no vow yet to Louisa. But for her I gave up other women…to prove to myself I could do it…' He had not thought it possible to go so long without a woman. 'I assure you it has not been easy, but I make no idle promise. I can be a true husband.'

'I am proud for you.' She looked at the book she'd taken out and her mouth formed letters, before she stopped, watching him. 'But I do not know if I can make such a vow.'

'You jest.'

She shook her head and held the volume towards him, letting it rest in the air between them. 'Sows. Ewes. Hens. They do not seem particular about their mates. Women, too, change their affections. Widows remarry. Women on Melos… I saw their hearts change. My mother's did not after she married my father, but I could see that did her no good either.'

'I pity the man who you might marry.' His fingers clasped over the leather, but she didn't release it and he didn't pull it away.

'That is why I should not wed. I wish to be happy. I like to smile.'

'I think you would like giving a man grief, too.' He looked at the book they held. Defoe. *Roxana.*

'*Ochi.*' A definite no. 'I do not want a man close enough to give him any sorrow. It would rebound double on me.'

'Your choice.' He slipped the book into his control and put it back on the shelf.

This woman was no society miss. The *ton* would certainly not accept someone so different, so free of restraints. He spoke his thoughts aloud, puzzled. 'Your sister cannot encourage your folly. She surely wants you to follow her example. I may not always agree with Warrington, but I believe he treats her well. Theirs is a good union.'

'Warrington is kind to her. Her heart is filled with him and the children. They are of such a similar mind.' Her eyes flicked up. 'Similar to yours. I have considered this life in England for two years, and after being at Harling House I know I may be wrong for others, but I am right for me.'

'You met me and decided marriage and society was not for you?'

'I would not say that.' He lips curved into a smile. 'I have been away from my sister and the children. I have missed them, but it is them I miss. Not just any baby or child. I see your mother and I see the damage even good love can cause in a person.'

'Your father. You are letting his actions rule yours. All your thoughts of marriage are coloured by the way he left you all.'

'No.' Her chin tilted and her lips thinned. She

ducked her head, but not before he could read her face. Her next words didn't match her expression. 'I hardly knew him. I remember my mother crying more than I remember him. My uncle did what he could do to help when I was very young. But he died—killed for no reason. We had so little. I do remember that when my father came home, the food was better. Everything. But inside the house was not always better. Our life was a calm sea when he was gone even though my mother struggled so hard. But when he returned there was a storm inside our home. I only wanted the goods he brought. I did not care for him at all.'

Then she made a gesture with her hand. He didn't know what it meant, but he was certain it was not a suitable action for a lady. He'd noticed it before. Her wrist would turn quickly and her lips firmed and words formed in her mind, but her fingers executed the phrase he didn't know.

'You should not say such,' he said, testing his theory.

'A society woman would not,' she agreed. 'Another reason to remain as I am.'

'I surrender,' he said, moving to the desk. He caught her gaze and smiled. 'I have a surprise for you.'

He did not want to argue with her, but he did want to hear her voice. He had lost his mind somewhere among the pins in her hair, but as long as no one else knew and he recovered soon, all would be fine. He hoped.

He opened the desk drawer and pulled out a book, holding it aloft. *Cobwebs to Catch Flies.* He brushed a hand across the leather cover. 'I don't know where it was or which servant found it, but they have all been rewarded.' He smiled. 'Geoff, my sister and I all read this.' For a moment he was held by memories, all good. 'Sit near me.' He waved the book towards the cushions. '*This* one will have you reading.' He opened it, moving to the section with the three-letter words.

Bellona settled on to the sofa and he put the book in her hands and sat beside her. Spices flowed into the air. The memories and scent of Christmas around her made the present feel as good as the best of the past did. He could hardly wait for her to begin.

She took the tome and her lips moved the barest bit, saying the words silently while she studied the page.

Her mouth. He watched it, willing her to repeat the action. She didn't, but she still held the book.

A weakness plunged into him. He relived a memory that kept him strong.

He'd written some bit of fluff to the girl who'd given him his first kiss. The moment had been…a surprise.

He'd not really thought much about what a kiss could feel like. And he hadn't meant to be alone with the girl. They'd happened upon each other by chance. She'd rounded a corner and he'd caught her just as she stepped into him and then she'd trounced his boot and he'd been worried about his boot being scuffed. She'd purposefully rested her foot on his other boot and he'd meant to remove her, but her waist had felt more important than any new boot had ever felt in his life and he'd not been able to budge the little wisp of her. He didn't remember the conversation or how long they'd stayed there, but she'd reached up and kissed him.

His world had changed.

Later, he'd written to her about how her lips tasted—but the letter had been stolen from his chamber before he could give it to her and it had somehow ended up in his father's hands—thank you, Geoff— and his father had called Rhys into the library, told him to shut the door and they had had another talk. The letter had been returned to Rhys and his father said it was Rhys's choice whether he gave the letter to the chit or not, but to remember that words written could never be changed. He should consider how a wife might feel some day to read something which might concern her. Or how their servants might snicker to learn of such a thing about their master.

Rhys's father gave him the letter. Rhys threw it in the fire. He'd disappointed his father.

Just as his father would be disappointed now if he'd walked into the room. Rhys shoved the thought aside.

'Why don't you read aloud?' Rhys suggested, and she did.

Initially, she stumbled over the words, but she could understand them, slowly at first and then more easily.

She closed the book, but held the place with one finger. 'I did not know books were like this. Cats and rats and dogs.' She looked at him. 'I would wager there will be a pig in it, too.'

'I do not want to give away the ending.' He leaned closer, pretending to look at the pages. 'Keep reading. It is good for you.'

'I do not like to hear something is good for me. That usually means I won't like it.' But she wiggled a bit, reminding him of a hen settling into her nest.

Again she read the words aloud.

He watched, half his vision on the book and half on her. The only other noise in the room besides her voice was the occasional sound of the page turning. He listened and then forgot everything else as her fingertips touched the paper.

His thoughts were much safer when he imagined only her hair. Now he watched her hands, heard her voice and could not stop his fascination from growing.

She reminded him of childhood and innocent times, and then she'd turn the page and he'd be ever so thankful to have left all that behind him and be alone with her. She made his chest feel broad and his skin vibrate just because her voice moved towards him through the air.

Her head dropped a bit to the side and her words wearied.

He wanted these moments. They were harmless. Nothing to be concerned about. Nothing he would remember later and feel guilty for, even when he was married to his duchess. No one would know that his mind wandered to places where it shouldn't. This was just a simple moment between two people who happened to be in the same room.

'I am tired of reading,' she said, closing the book.

He took it from her hands and put it on the other side of himself, causing him to move so close their sides brushed. Without her voice, it felt as if the whole world had ceased to have sound.

Rhys spoke softly, not wanting to disturb even a dust mote in the air. 'Tell me why you cannot tolerate dancing. Not the dance itself, but the holding.'

'It has always been this way.' The words were slow and barely reached his ears. She'd closed her eyes for a moment and she opened them when she answered. 'Or at least for a long time.'

'When did it start?'

'I'm not sure. But I know the dreams started on the ship to England. The first night I slept afterward.'

Her eyes flicked to his face. He didn't move, waiting.

'I told you that when I was on Melos…' The purr of sleepiness left her voice, but her lids dropped again. 'Men woke my sister Thessa and me during the night. They forced us from our rooms and one was going to wed my sister Thessa whether she wished it or not, and the other was going to—wed me, and I…could not have survived marriage to him. Or he could not have survived marriage to me. Snake. *Fidi.*'

'And…' he said, barely speaking.

'And Thessa and I swam to the English ship in the harbour. It left. We sailed here.'

He didn't want her to open her eyes, afraid if she did she'd pull back, taking him from this shared moment. He gave a soft sound of acknowledgement, looking at the shape of her face, and the skin, so delicate he feared even brushing his fingertip against it might be too rough.

He slid further from her on the sofa so he could put his hand along the back. His fingertips could have easily held her shoulder or dipped a bit lower and touched the bare skin where her sleeve ended. In his mind, he could feel her. Perhaps he truly did because the warmth of her body flowed outward. He was so close it had to be wafting to him.

'The island men pursued us, but the captain and his crew fought them off. I thought we were safe, but later on our voyage a man decided I was bad fortune.' She touched her throat, slender fingers resting against her skin. 'He tried to toss me overboard to drown in the seas. I couldn't breathe I was so frightened. Thessa pulled him from me.'

Spears of rage hit his midsection. Those words changed everything. They slammed into him as if his own body had been thrust hard against a wooden fortress. His temple pounded. He pulled back, not wanting her to sense the violence inside him.

How dare someone touch her so? He would have killed him without hesitation. He forced his voice to be calm, but it took a moment. 'I am pleased you were unhurt.'

Her lips turned up, not so much in a smile, but in some sort of inner amusement. 'I have a sword. I thought it would protect me, but I almost cut off my own nose.' Her eyes opened and she looked at him. In that second, he felt the same intimacy he might when looking across bedcovers at a woman, only it wasn't the same. This was more intense, deeper—something he hadn't known existed. It was as if she'd just taken over his whole body. As if her spirit was twice his size and had wrapped itself around him, cradling him. He never wanted to lose this feeling.

She leaned towards him, touching, perhaps not touching but brushing, just at the top of her nose, and he almost felt the sensation of her fingertips. The trail of her hand lingering against his skin in the same way she swept her hand above her own nose. 'Can you see the scar?' she asked, voice husky. She slid more towards him. He could not move.

A tiny white line rested just at the bridge. 'How did you do that? Was it that man?'

'It wasn't him. This was when I was living in England. I was taking the weapon from the shelf where I had put it to keep it from my niece. It fell.' She shut her eyes again, only for a moment. 'I didn't know how I was going to tell my sister, since she'd already complained about the sword. But luckily, her babe chose that moment to be born and no one noticed my hand—' she rested her palm over her nose and peered out at him from around it '—covering my face. By the time my nephew was safely tucked into the family, the scratch hardly showed.'

She took her hand from her face. 'He was so tiny. I did not see why her *stomachi* needed to grow so big to have such a little babe.'

He studied her face.

'Your nose is rather a pleasant nose.' The words slipped from his mouth, sounding like a caress. If he raised his forearm just the slightest bit and moved just the merest bit forward, he could be holding her.

'I didn't expect to like the babe.' She grimaced. 'He'd caused my sister such discomfort already and he wasn't a girl. Warrington already had a son and daughter, and I hoped the little girl would have a sister. I wanted another small Willa in the house.'

She pulled herself straight on the couch. 'I told Melina just a few days ago…about the mark. She thought it humorous that I could manage to sail from Greece to here, sleep when the pirates boarded the ship trying to take our other sister before being defeated in their efforts and have no marks to show for it. Then I wounded myself with the weapon I kept for protection.'

She looked at him. 'Let me try reading again. I like it much better when the words are small and the story is about children.'

He moved, securing the tome without looking at it. Holding it in her direction. Her hands skimmed over his as she took the volume, slowly, from him.

She turned the pages to the spot where she'd left off. 'The words are getting harder, though.'

His arm rested at her shoulders. 'Just hold your finger to the word and I'll help you.'

She began to read, and at the first stumble she moved into the cradle of his arm and pointed for him to read the word aloud.

She stayed where she was, and when she paused again he let go of the breath he'd been holding and helped her.

The book wavered because she pointed to another word. He took hold of the other side of the cover and held it.

As the words became longer and longer, he never realised when he became the speaker and she became the listener. His words lingered, so she could follow easily, and he read to her about the happy family of eight children and the merry-go-round.

He read more slowly as he neared the conclusion, and when the story finished they closed the book together, then he pulled back and she straightened.

'I did not want the story to end,' she said. 'I quite liked it.'

'I did as well.'

'A good tale,' she said. 'Better than *Crusoe*.'

He nodded, holding it with one hand. 'Though I enjoyed it as a child, I had not realised before how much interest it has.'

'Sometimes things more scholarly are not always the most enjoyable.'

'They are good for one, though.'

The flicker of her eyes when she heard the words acknowledged his jest.

'So true.' She stood and leaned towards him again, taking the book. 'Do you mind if I keep this in my room for a time?'

He looked up at pale skin, a long neck, a wilful chin and lips that he wanted to touch in all the ways that he could.

'As long as you'd like. It's yours.'

'Only for a short while and then I'll put it back,' she said and left the room.

He wondered if he would be able to move again.

Chapter Ten

Bellona fought, inside the dream, pulling hands from her throat, her grasping fists closing over emptiness. She struggled for air—ale-scented breath suffocating her. His darkened pupils expanded so that she could see nothing else. She scrambled back as her own vision clouded into black, reaching for her weapon, the world of the ship fading, changing to the bedchamber. The image of the crewman fell away into the recesses of the room.

Her eyes opened. She sat against the headboard of the bed, her heart pounding, fingers gripping the knife she'd had under her pillow. Her throat ached, the press of thumbs indenting her throat still choking her.

She swallowed slowly, trying to get air, but keeping her movements still so she could be aware of the room. Shadows brushed her skin with the lightness of spider's legs. Beyond the walls, something creaked.

Slipping one foot from the bed, she braced for her ankle to be clutched. She had to escape from the room, yet the hallway would be dark and someone could be waiting.

She dashed to the door, her back against the wood, the knife held close to her body. Listening. Watching. Waiting.

Wind blew against the window. She forced herself calm. Over and over the dream found her in the night.

Questions would throb in her head until morning. What if the pirates hadn't been defeated by Captain Ben and his crew? What if they had continued to pursue the ship intent on making another attempt to capture Bellona and Thessa? Or what if the gamekeeper had got angry at her because she had been accepted into the house as a guest and he broke in to attack her?

She touched the door latch with her left hand, gripping the cold metal. Listening. She had no reason to fear. None at all. But blood still raced in her veins.

She leaned back, feeling a vibration as she painlessly thumped her head once against the wood. She could not traverse the room and reach the bell pull. Her feet wouldn't let her.

The room didn't feel safe. She couldn't stay long enough to summon a maid. The pirates would not go away. She could not make them leave her dreams and in her dreams she had nothing to fight with.

Soundlessly, she opened the door and put one foot into the hallway. Nothing. Still darkness. No movement.

She couldn't shut the door behind her. Even though the room could trap her, she couldn't close even one possible way of escape.

Sliding her body out, she moved down the hallway. If she called from the library for a servant, the butler would arrive. He stood tall and she could ask him to check her room for a mouse. She'd heard something.

She'd heard a squeak or a creak. A noise had stirred her from the terror.

Or perhaps she'd only dreamed it. The figure of the man squeezing her neck had vanished as she woke, disappearing, as the nightmare always did, taking the stench of death with him. Leaving her room as quiet and still as a crypt covered in dust.

Standing, she waited, making sure she heard nothing again. She forced her imagination away. Those endless fears that plagued her had merely returned, but she didn't want to be alone.

She clutched the knife close to her body, and ignored the chills seeping through her thin shift.

'What—' A gruff voice—behind her—right behind her. Her mind froze, but her body did not. She swirled around, bringing the knife up. His hand rose, clamping on her own, holding her clutched fist with the strength of a vise. In the same instant her hand was caught, he moved forward, pushing her, her right shoulder crashing into the wall. He trapped her with his size.

Neither moved.

'Bellona,' the duke gasped out. 'What the hell are you doing?'

She could not speak. She could not.

'Bellona.' He called her name again.

It was Rhys. Her brain knew it. But her body wouldn't move. Her pounding heart took all the power from her voice. Pushing against him made no more difference than hurling herself at the strongest rock on Melos. Fear overpowered her, and her mind could not free itself from the terror.

'It's me. It's Rhys,' he said. 'Bellona.'

Shudders racked her body.

He still held her knife hand, but his other arm pulled her into an embrace. 'You're safe.' His voice rumbled softly, a caress in words. 'It's me. I won't hurt you. I'd never hurt you.'

The bulwark of his strength didn't frighten her, but terror still controlled her even though her mind translated the scene into the reality of the moment. She rested her head against his shoulder. The only movement she could make.

He pulled her even closer. He murmured to her and he lightened his clasp, cradling her now. Her body shook and he didn't speak again, just held her.

Minutes passed. The knife handle was pulled from her hand. She had no strength to hold it. She didn't have the ability to stand without his help. His other arm went around her.

Her face stayed buried against him, the silken threads of his waistcoat against her cheek. His male scent soothing her. He didn't clench her tightly, but she burrowed into him, regaining her composure as the shaking stopped and her heartbeats slowed.

'I thought…' she whispered.

'You thought to hurt me?'

'No. I did not know. I could not think,' she said. 'I did not know it was you.'

'Who else would it be?'

She whispered again, 'I did not know…'

He kept her folded into his arms, crushing her against the fabric of his clothing, surrounding her with the fortress of his strength.

His chin rested against her forehead. 'I didn't mean to frighten you.'

'I didn't recognise your voice at first.' She shut her

eyes, taking solace from his hands clasping her back, holding her.

'Sweet, much as I'd like to hold you, I have something I must attend to.'

'I don't want to be alone.'

'I understand.' He squeezed her. 'We can talk about it later.'

She gripped him. 'I could have hurt you.'

'I know.' He mumbled the words, his lips against her hair. 'You could have.'

He pushed himself away from her. 'But you must get to bed now.'

She reached out, unable to let him go, and confusion hit her mind. She felt the sleeve of his arm, but he jerked back.

Something was wrong.

'I…' She clenched her right hand, letting her own fingers brush her palm. Wetness.

'I— Did I—?'

'Yes, I believe you did.'

'You're cut?'

'It does feel that way. I appear to have grasped the blade before I was able to get to your hand.'

She gasped. He stepped further away.

'Rhys—we must get a light. You're bleeding.'

'I'll attend to it. You go back to your room.'

'I'll summon help.' She turned to run, but he captured her arm with his right hand, grip warm and tight.

'Shh… I. Will. Attend to it.'

'But, Rhys… Are you hurting? We must—' *He must not be hurt. He could not be hurt.* Her breaths gasped from her.

'Bellona. The servants. I do not want talk, but really I should look at it. There is a light in my chamber.'

'Yes,' she agreed. She slipped from his grip and caught the fabric of his sleeve, pulling him in the direction of his room. 'Quick.'

Inside the room, the stain on his white sleeve looked like nothing more than a shadow until he stopped by the lamp.

Blood dripped from the hilt of the knife.

Red. She gasped. Death. She could hear the screams of the women of her homeland. She could have done to Rhys what the man who'd killed her uncle did.

Her knees weakened, but she did not fall. He put the knife on the bedside table and opened his hand. The skin parted where his palm had slid down the blade.

'You cannot die.' She appraised his body, looking for damage. 'You cannot.'

'I am not planning to.' He pushed the skin together and held it. 'Bring me a flannel. I need to stop the bleeding.'

She rushed to get the cloth and took the fingers of his hurt hand in hers, and he moved his free hand aside while she pressed the cloth against the wound.

'You must remove the blood from yourself as well,' he said. 'You look as if you have been in a fight. Are you cut?'

She noted the red splotches on her arm for the first time. Her own fingers showed red. She examined her arms and hands. 'No.'

'I'm thankful.' He shut his eyes briefly and shook his head. 'I'm thankful I am the one that felt the blade and not both of us. That would be hard to explain.'

'It should be stitched,' she said, bending over his hand. 'I will do it. I know I can.'

He took a step away. 'Damned if I let you near me with a needle. I've seen your embroidery.'

'I will be slow.'

'Bellona.' His eyes widened. 'We have a physician. I have been bled before and I survived. It is merely releasing some of the humours. I do not like it, however. Your method is a bit painful.'

'I will take care of you.' She moved to the washstand and splashed water from the ewer into the basin. She swept her hands through to remove the red. The water turned a bloody tinge, but no cuts showed on her own skin. She turned back. His eyes were on her and his gaze didn't move as she watched him.

She took a cloth, her hands dripping water, and rushed to his side. 'I'll care for it. Sit. Sit on the bed.'

Keeping his hand clasped over the cut, he held his elbows wide, still standing. 'Would you undo my cravat and the buttons on my waistcoat? I'd prefer not to get more bloodstains on the fabric…'

She wiped her hands dry, tossed the cloth to the bed and stepped closer. With a quick tug, she slipped the knot free. Then a swift snap.

The force of her pull on his neckcloth jerked him sideways.

'Damnation, woman. Do not break my neck.'

'Pardon. I did not realise it was wrapped around so many times.'

'You almost snapped my head from my body. You do wish to kill me,' he muttered, then leaned forward again. 'So unwrap it or merely slip it free by pulling *gently* at the sides and front.'

She finished her task, surprised at how comfortable she was this close to him. To be alone with him was quite different from anyone else.

She folded the cravat and put it on the bed.

Reaching up, she slipped the delicate buttons of his waistcoat free, moving back so he could raise his hands as she finished.

At the last one, she stopped, looking up into the dark eyes as she undid the final clasp.

'Are you…' she asked, 'in pain?'

The lightest nod.

When she turned, her eyes locked on his hand. She sucked in air through her nostrils.

'You look a bit rattled,' he said. 'Do not have the vapours.'

'Your Grace. Please. Sit.'

He looked at her. 'Bellona, I believe you can call me Rhys now.'

She paused. 'I am sorry I hurt you.'

'I know. I believe you.' He held his hands clasped a bit more and stepped away. 'What I don't understand is the knife. I thought your weapons were taken.'

'Not the one I carry in my boot.'

'Ah, yes.' He nodded. 'How remiss of me. The blasted boots. Your reticule knife was removed, but it was strictly an oversight on my part not to have someone collect the knife from your boots. That's their charm, isn't it? That's why you wear them?'

She answered with her eyes.

He stared at her bare feet and his eyes trailed up her body clad only in her thin nightdress, leaving warm currents in their wake, causing a *frisson* in her stomach. 'I would say that you do not have another knife hidden about you right now. Is that a safe assumption?'

'No—yes, I do not have a knife.' The words. They scared her. She'd just told a man she was unprotected. The walls in the upper rooms were solid… The duchess would not hear a scuffle. No one could answer her if she called out for help. In the servants' quarters, there was a chance someone might respond, but not here.

He watched her, but without the darkness she feared. 'You should go so I can summon assistance.' She lost all thoughts he could ever harm her. He was injured and he cared that she not be discovered in his room.

The red on his hand reminded her.

She had done that.

'I will summon my valet,' he said.

As he moved forward, she threw her body between him and the pull. 'I cannot go to my room.' He stepped to brush her aside, but she flattened her palms on his chest. His eyes widened. He felt rather like a wall. A wall of muscle and skin and male. 'Your Grace.' She thought it best to address him such at the moment. 'I will worry.'

He leaned close. He'd been drinking brandy some time in the evening. His eyes shone with an emotion that jumped into her and caused a heating sensation that somehow managed to touch her entire body.

'Sweet. It's his job. I will tell him that if I die he must alert the entire household. So, if you do not hear, then you will know I am well.'

'I am not leaving. He may care for you if you wish, but I am to stay and see that it is done right.'

'You cannot be found in my chamber in the middle of the night, particularly with blood on both of us. The man is discreet. He will not speak of it, but I fear he would have an apoplexy keeping silent on that. I would then have to replace him and I simply do not have the time.'

She lowered her eyes to her palms still resting on his chest and then slid her hands away, before looking up again. 'I will care for you.'

'You will?' He smiled. 'Just as you cared for me a few moments ago?'

Surely he would live if he could jest. She nodded and took the cloth from the counterpane, holding it towards his clasped hands. 'Yes, Rhys.' She daubed at the smears on him, taking the red from his knuckles.

When she indicated that she wanted to reach the cut, he did not open his grasp, but extended his fingertips to clutch the cloth.

'Let me,' she said, refusing to release it.

'You've already attacked me once in the night. Don't struggle with me now. I might stumble backwards and knock myself in the head.'

'If you stumble now, you will land on the bed. Sit on the bed so I can see the wound better.'

He sat on the edge. She was no closer than before until she perched beside him, her shoulder aligned with his. She wiped the cut clean.

'What happened to bring you out into the hall with a weapon?' he asked.

She pressed on the wound. 'I awoke from a nightmare and thought you were…someone evil.'

'And you only cut my hand?'

She pressed harder.

He flinched. 'Go more lightly with the cloth. You're making it worse. Leave and I will send for my valet. I just do not wish for him to know how this happened, but I suspect he will notice the cut and the shirt will have to be burned.'

'How dear are the lamps?' she asked.

'I have no idea. They're lamps.'

She sighed. 'Break the glass of one and tell him you stumbled.'

'I can do that. But when you turned to get the cloth, I noticed a bloodstain on your back. How will that be explained away?'

'The maid will not notice after I finish with the garment.' She peered at the cut. 'Move your fingers.'

He did.

She rested her forehead against his shoulder momentarily, then straightened again. 'That is fortunate. Now do not move them again.'

She held the flannel tight against his hand. He reached to pull it away, but she clasped it. Determined, he took the cloth and put it against his palm, closing the fingers of his right hand over it.

'You don't have to tend this. I'll break the lamp, call the valet and now you can go back to your room and get some rest.' Then he pushed her aside so that he could stand, reached with his left hand, picked an unlit lamp from the side of the bed and crashed the globe against the table. The glass shattered and he sat the base back on to the table.

She met his eyes. 'I'm still not leaving, Rhys.' She rose and moved, planning to search out another flannel. But before she left, she gazed over him to reassure herself he was not about to die.

He returned to the bed, stretched out lengthwise, his head at his pillow and his ankles crossed. 'Sweet, you may return to calling me Your Grace at any time.'

She spoke over her shoulder. 'You must recover. You would need a big spot to be buried in and the man who cares for the gardens would grumble if I asked him to dispose of you.'

'Bellona, you do not just dash a duke into a hole in the ground. You must have a bit of a ceremony first.'

'Yes, Rhys. I suppose it would take some time just to dig a hole for your boots.'

She could feel his eyes on her as he digested her words.

'Even if you address me as Your Grace, I suspect you've always seen me as no more privileged than one of the sailors on the ship that brought you to England.'

'That's not true.' She shook her head. 'I've always seen you as a duke.' She continued searching for a useful cloth, only stopping to look at him. 'But the men at sea are quite skilled in things that matter. You are skilled in books and learning, and I suppose that has a place besides writing letters.'

She found another flannel inside the washstand.

'Thank you.' He exchanged the reddened bandage he had for the new one, pressing it once more against the wound. He shut his eyes. 'Would you bring me a brandy glass and the bottle?'

She went for the drink, splashed some in the glass and then returned. He pushed himself upright with an elbow, his injured hand still gripping the cloth. He downed the liquid and held out the empty glass. She refilled it with the same amount. He looked at it, frowned and drank more slowly before handing the glass to her once again. The fresh blood smears on the flannel pressed to his injury caused her stomach to clench.

Putting the glass and bottle on the table, she returned to the dressing chamber and found another flannel for his cut. When she returned with it, he took it from her and placed it over the other one.

His eyes moved over her, reminding her of the way water in a stream followed the movement of the current.

'If you wish to get the dressing gown from my wardrobe, you may wear it,' he said. 'I would not want you to catch a chill.'

She moved to the dressing chamber. She didn't feel cold at all and she didn't think he'd been overly concerned about that. When she opened the wardrobe, she reached out, running her fingers over the silk and linen in front of her. Nothing looked as if it had ever been touched, but everything had rested against Rhys's body. She took the banyan, wrapping it around herself, amazed at how well shaving soap smelled. The garment drooped from her shoulders and dragged on the floor, but felt like a royal robe.

'This is so…' She snuggled into it. Then paused when she met his eyes. They'd narrowed, but she couldn't see behind them.

Padding back, she sat in a chair, looking across at him.

'You can't sit there all night and stare at me.' He pressed against the flannel. 'That will surely enough do me in.'

'If you die because I'm looking at you, I will take note of it, since I have never even been able to pain my sisters by giving them my harshest look.' An army couldn't have taken her from the room. 'I need to stay to make sure if you fall asleep, you don't get blood on the covers.'

'You sound like my mother. You have been spending too much time with her.'

'I think she will agree with you and so do I.'

He adjusted the pillow with his left hand. 'I suppose I should not have been traipsing about in the dark, but I have done it often in the past year. If I walk enough, then I sleep without my own dreams and I prefer that. The nights are so long after I have finished with my ledgers.'

'The dark frightens me. I always had my sisters close by when I was young. I had never been alone in the night until I sailed here. Sometimes I feel smaller than Willa. And now it has caused your injury. I didn't want to hurt you. I would rather my hand be cut.'

'I believe you. I didn't mean to grab the blade. I didn't know you had a knife in your hand until I reached the hilt. Then it was a little late to reconsider.'

'You could have been hurt much worse.'

'So could you.' His voice rose in exasperation. 'Granted, you did me an injury, but do you realise what could have happened?'

'It's better to have a knife than nothing. Even the smallest man is stronger than I am.' Rubbing her fingertips together, she examined them for red. 'It is important I protect myself.'

'Why? Why do you feel it is so important?'

She looked at his hand and let her gaze linger over the rest of him. Tall. Shoulders the same width of Stephanos's. But he tried to see her and not just the reflection of his power from the fear in her eyes.

She shook her head. 'It is…how I must be,' she said. 'How I have always been. At least for a long time.' She crossed her arms over herself.

'The ship?'

'That was the second time I knew I could die at a man's hands.'

The memories she kept in her thoughts always, of the island, and that day of violence, flashed in her mind. 'One day when I was young, I heard shrieks. But I thought it was happy noise. I wasn't close enough and I wanted to see what was happening. I ran to the people and saw them crying, but I could not go on.' There had been more than tears. There had been wailing— begging the heavens to reverse time and bring her uncle back to life.

'I could not see my uncle breathing his last,' Bellona explained. 'I could not believe that it was real. This time the truth felt like a dream. I could see and hear but I could not…feel. You cannot undo something like that. You wish for the moments to go back just the smallest time, but they will not. You long to know it didn't happen, but it did.'

She remembered stopping, and sitting, wrapping her arms around her knees. She could hear the words, and see the people, but they blocked her view of her uncle. More screams. Louder this time.

'So much noise,' she continued. 'Then Stephanos was walking away. Swaggering, away from everyone. Towards me. On the trail, he stopped and watched me. He was not even a true man yet, but he was tall even then. As big as the men. His eyes were evil. *"Your uncle is dead,"* he said. *"I killed the man who stabbed him."* He laughed. Blood was on his face and where his knife was tucked in his sash. *"I could kill everyone on this island and no one could stop me. Even you, little one. I could cut your throat."'*

She'd watched him and felt no fear. But she had known he was thinking of death as a prize—someone else's life a bounty. A proof of power.

'He laughed. He threw back his head and raised his fists into the air. Like a rooster crowing to greet the morning. He was not sad my uncle died. He was happy for my uncle's death because he could kill the murderer in front of everyone. He didn't care about justice. He cared that other people feared him.'

'Not all men are evil.'

'Stephanos was. And only one evil man can cause so much pain. And he liked it. Years ago, Melina was to marry him. She had no choice. He had decided to wed. He was going to marry one of us and he didn't care which one. Melos was too small to escape him. Melina sailed away to bring us funds to help, but when she didn't return, he noticed Thessa and would not stop watching her. She agreed to marry him to stop him looking in my direction. But then the ship came and we escaped. I still have dreams about it. About all of it.'

'Anyone could have nightmares after seeing such things.'

'I see too much in my dreams.' She wrapped her arms around herself. 'Again. I see a man's face with nothing in his spirit but death. The happiness of having power over others.'

'You cannot be feeling true danger from me. You cannot.' He pushed himself up. 'I could not hurt you. I could not.'

She shook her head. 'I don't believe you could. But

there is something in your thoughts you are not saying.' Something she couldn't decipher. 'When you meet my eyes, I see... I am unsettled. If you are in the room, I know where you stand. I cannot think of anyone else when you are near.'

He shook his head from side to side. 'That is just a... Something that happens between a man and a woman. It means little.'

'I cannot think it means nothing.'

'Not everything a person feels or thinks is to be spoken of. That is why thoughts reside in the head. Some things are to be kept silent. No one tells another person all the things inside.'

'My sisters and I, we did.'

'Perhaps women do. Men do not.'

'So they do not think of important things that need to be told?' She moved so she could see the light flickering on his face.

He closed his eyes. 'A man doesn't need to prattle on.'

'It is not prattle,' she said. 'I don't know what it is, though.' She shrugged. 'But perhaps it is not good. Your mother talks so much of death and hurting. And now you are injured. If you do not get well, your mother will never forgive me.'

'I doubt she will forgive you anyway if she finds out the truth,' he teased.

'My sisters and I had a saying, "There is the truth, and there is the truth we tell our mother."'

He smiled. 'My brother and I said it a little differently. "If you tell Mother, I will kill you."'

'I suppose they both mean almost the same.' She leaned closer, seeing his lashes against his cheek. The way the soft fringe and the strong jaw, lean nose and stubbled chin all formed the man.

'I am aware the duchess is on the mend,' he said. 'But I don't want to risk her learning of this.'

She rose and got another flannel and took it to the side of the bed, looking down at him.

He opened his eyes, peering into hers. 'Stop staring at me so.' He reached for the fabric. 'You might as well lie beside me. You're already ruined if anyone sees you here. It will probably look more innocent if we're on top of the covers, looking irritated, anyway. You might as well relax.'

She didn't want to go back to her room. To the dreams. She might have even talked to a pirate to keep from being alone. To be alone with Rhys, though, she would have fought sea savages.

She walked around the bed and sat on the other side, resting against the headboard, snuggling into the dressing gown. 'I wanted to make sure you are not hiding pain.'

'I'm not hiding it at all. It aches. But less than other hurts I've had.' He paused. 'Where were you going when you were in the hallway?'

'The servants' quarters.'

'Were you searching for someone?'

'No. I sometimes sleep there. In my big room, sleeping is difficult. A few nights ago, I could not get the door to latch properly and I could not rest. My bedchamber seemed so large and open that someone could have walked in on me in my sleep and I felt that I had nowhere to hide. So I took the book to a smaller room I had found. I felt safer there.'

'You felt safer away…away from the rest of us?'

She nodded. 'The room is more like my home on Melos. A place so small no one could hide and a single lamp could light to the very edges of the room. In Melos, I would have thought it so grand to have the plainest chamber in your house. It is far better than what I once had.'

'Bellona, do you not respect the servants' world?'

'I do.' She smiled. 'Even your servants would think me far beneath them if they had stepped on Melos and met me right before I left my home. On Melos, the animals lived under my home and the stairs led to the two rooms above, where we lived.'

'You'll never have to live like that again.'

'I miss it,' she said. 'I long for it every day.'

'How could you want to return to that?'

'I miss my sisters and my *mana* being together. The waves. The blue. The smell of the sea. The sand under my feet. But now I must be happy in England. I just do not know how to do that and it has been two years.'

'It takes a bit to recover when you lose what you hold dear.'

'I wish I could share with Mana and I wish she could see the riches here. The only thing I know is— if she had to choose and could, she would have chosen to be poor in order for us to have much. She would be so happy looking down from the heavens, although I don't know if it is possible.'

'Perhaps she does see this.'

'She would not be happy I hurt you.'

He chuckled. 'Of course not. A woman is not like that, especially a mother.'

'Gigia. You did not know her. She would think it

humorous or perhaps be angry that I let you so close to me in the hallway.'

'I can understand a grandmother not wanting her granddaughter to be close to a man in the dark.'

'Oh,' she said and chuckled. 'Gigia was not at all like you think. Not at all. She was not at all like the English and their proper ways. If she were here now she would be angry with me that I had not—'

Silence again. She knew he thought of the same thing she did. Gigia would have been angry that Bellona was not pushing her body against Rhys. But what he didn't know was that she would have been most angry to know Bellona had not been whispering a price in his ear.

Chapter Eleven

His hand hurt like blazes where he'd cut himself on her blade—which was the only thing allowing him to keep a decent thought in his head.

No, he didn't have a decent thought. But keeping his hand pressed against the makeshift bandage while reminding himself that he might still die of a fever kept him from pulling her against him.

She slept completely wrapped in his dressing gown, only her head poking from the top of it, concealed more chastely than any woman he'd ever seen.

She wiggled around, towards him, and the dip in the bed helped him roll ever so slightly towards her.

Miss Roman Warrior Goddess could have killed him with her very sharp knife, but he'd immediately wanted to reassure her when she'd discovered she'd accidentally sliced him.

Flames nicked at him everywhere, but he wasn't feverish.

His body still had the cravings of a youth, but his mind had advanced somewhat. He had rules. He had managed for quite some time to keep out of a woman's bed. He turned over. But now one was in his bed and she was sleeping peacefully.

He should have married before now.

He just wished… He just wished he had wed the previous year. He should have. Then his wife would have been settled by now. Most likely, a child would have been on the way and Rhys could have threaded his fingers through his wife's mussed hair and rested his cheek against her skin.

His boots were on so he couldn't get under the covers. He'd have to call his valet to be undressed. If he did that, she would have to leave. He wouldn't be able to sleep. He'd be lying there, bleeding and thinking of her.

She turned in her sleep. Her arm went around his midsection, jolting him, and he rested his clasped hands at the side, his arm just against her hand, keeping it snug to his body.

It would be for ever until morning, but the time would pass too soon.

Bellona awoke with a dim light flickering in the room and the sound of rain pounding against the house. Rhys sat in the overstuffed chair, which had been turned towards the bed. His left arm propped his head and she couldn't tell for sure if his eyes were open.

She pushed herself into a sitting position.

'It's morning,' Rhys said. 'Or it will be soon. You should leave before someone discovers you.'

'Your hand?'

He held it closer to the light. A blood-caked slice went from the bottom knuckle of his forefinger to the heel of his hand. He waved his fingers.

She put a foot on the floor, and looked at the night table. 'Will you return my knife?'

'Do you truly believe you need it here?'

'No.'

He reached to the drawer, pulled out the knife and handed it to her, the blade facing himself.

'I'll put it away,' she said. She held the cold handle and looked at the weapon. The crumpled flannel, coloured with darkened red, lay on the nightstand.

The knife no longer made her feel safe or secure. Now it felt poisonous. The men who had frightened her in the past had hurt her from a world away.

Next, he picked up one of the shards of glass from the floor and put it on the table. 'You should take the real weapon from this room. My valet will believe the culprit was the broken glass. But I don't want him to see a knife in my room where there has been none before because he would surmise something. What exactly, I don't know, but I don't want to take the risk.'

He lowered his voice. 'Bellona, if you have fears in the night, I will check to make certain no one is there.'

'When Thessa and I were taken on the island, it was from our beds in the dead of night. I fear what happens when I sleep. But this time waking was the most dangerous course. I am sorry.'

She rose, reached for the tip of his fingers and examined his hand, putting the image of the injury into her mind as strongly as she could. This she would remember when she thought of the blood and felt fear, because this could result. She must control herself. She couldn't live in terror any longer. 'The hallway is long. If I have trouble sleeping, I'll sleep in the room below stairs. I feel safer there. If I shout, someone will hear.

I don't want to see anyone's blood again and know I caused it. I can't.'

'You should not be below stairs. You are a guest. We have family rooms all about.' He waved his arm, then he dropped it to his side, grimacing. 'Just no family to fill them any more.'

She turned away. Only one person had the task of filling the rooms and she did not want to think about that.

'I will be leaving to go back to Whitegate soon,' she said. 'There I'll sleep in the nursery near the children if I need to. When I watch them, the world doesn't seem quite the same dark place. It seems like there's sunshine in the night.'

'I know how much better you've made the duchess while you've been here,' he said. 'I suppose there is a reason the mourning time is a year. Perhaps that's just how long it takes for everyone and I shouldn't have been so concerned. But after Geoff passed, she crumpled, seeming to fall into the past, and even I could not rouse her.'

Bellona knew the duchess had been moving about Harling House more. She even talked of other things besides her grief. Bellona could leave without concern, and if she stayed it would be foolish. Being at Harling House when Rhys returned with a wife would not be wise.

'I am enjoying speaking with you.' He spoke softly. 'But if you don't leave soon, someone might see you. I'll walk you to your room. I don't want my dressing gown left about for the maid to see so I'll return with it.'

'We did nothing wrong.' She pulled the clothing

tight around her, tying the belt. 'Except I did cut your hand.'

He moved to the door, waiting to open it. She stopped beside him. His hair had been finger combed and his shirt, rumpled, hung loose from his trousers. She reached, smoothing the sleeve, pressing a hand against it, but the wrinkles were fixed firm. 'You look like you have been in a war.' She didn't release his arm.

'It will certainly not be perceived as innocent if it is known you spent the night here. The talk would rumble about for the rest of our lives. You in my room. My hand slashed. Tales could get quite grand about that. Even I would have trouble believing it all innocent and I am here to see that it is. It might be assumed I attacked you. Or that you meant to hurt me and I had to restrain you. I don't know what would be said, but it would not be good. You'd be ruined. Quite ruined.'

She wouldn't admit the thoughts running through her mind, but she didn't care if she were ruined. She didn't. But for his sake she didn't want any tales put out about her hurting him and people speculating on what had really happened. She didn't even want to remember the night because of the pain she'd caused him and the fear that he might become feverish.

'I am so sorry,' she said.

He cupped her cheek in his hand. 'I see it in your eyes. You don't have to tell me.'

Everything shifted and it was as if his spirit stepped behind her, beside her and all around her.

'I'm leaving Harling House soon,' he said. 'And this will be the only chance I have to tell you goodbye.'

'You would vanish without taking your leave of me?'

'Yes. I would and I should.' He leaned forward. He brushed a light kiss on her cheek. 'I won't forget you.'

'You can't. I've put a mark on you.'

He moved, pressing another kiss on her cheek, lingering this time. His lips touched her as he spoke. 'You certainly have. Deeper than you know.'

He did not say he cared for her, though, and the knowledge washed over her in the same way a winter wind entered the cracks in the wall and enveloped everything inside. She had to make the feeling of unease disappear. She had to warm herself and only by stepping closer to him could she find any comfort at all.

She examined his eyes and he did not move, just looked back at her. Brown. Chocolate. Aged wood. Perhaps not as dark as the men on Melos. But a gaze softened by his lashes. He stood patiently, not speaking, and he didn't smile, but the small lines at the corners of his eyes relaxed.

Then he did smile. 'You shouldn't examine a man so closely. It does things to him... It is the same as if your fingers had swept over me.'

She reached out, putting her palm over his heart. The fabric didn't prevent her from feeling the strength of the man beneath, of the skin covering taut muscle.

He reached up, taking the barest grasp of her fingertips. He shut his eyes and pulled her hand up so that her knuckles brushed against the roughness of his cheeks.

No clock ticked. No sound from beyond the walls reached them.

He snaked the other arm around her waist, using the strength of his forearm to hold her against him, sending shivers into her that she could feel every place her body had ever touched anything and all those senses changed into something burning inside her.

His kiss was her first true kiss. His tongue, warm and hungry, took her, tasting her, melting her into his body and swirling her from her feet and giving her the feeling of when she swam just underwater and sunlight heated her back, only stronger.

He turned her, the door at her back, holding her up and himself, not ending the first kiss, but changing it to a treasure trove of smaller ones, moving to her jaw, her ear and burrowing down her neck, his left hand pulling open the top of the dressing gown, heated fingers pushing the barrier away to make a path for his lips over her skin.

He pulled back, released her, and her knees almost gave way, but as her body seemed to dip, his arm kept her upright.

His eyes stayed on hers, but when he opened his mouth, it took a second for him to speak.

'I am not myself.' His voice roughened, the words barely reached Bellona's ears. 'I do not know what is the matter with me.' He gave her a tight bow of his head. 'Forgive me.'

Bellona muttered. 'You have marked me, too.'

She stepped to the door, stopping only long enough to throw the dressing gown back into the room as she left.

Chapter Twelve

The palm of his hand tingled and burned. The cut had opened twice in the morning, but each time he'd cared for it and the bleeding had stopped.

His morning meal had not gone well. The rasher of bacon left a tallow coating in his mouth and he'd had to wash it away with a drink of chocolate—even that had not been quite right. He'd almost sent to have the cook try again, but he just was not hungry. Eating with his left hand made everything taste off.

The day's lashing rain splattered against the window and Rhys only had the ledger books in front of him so he could look busy if someone walked in. The sums were not terrible, but rather the way he'd hoped them to be. Everything soured before his eyes because of his thoughts concerning Bellona. The woman had injured him and he had fallen at her feet. If his mother had known how simple it could be, she would have been arming all the ladies of the *ton* with knives in their reticules.

This morning, he did not expect to see Bellona moving about the house. She wouldn't be going out to practise archery because of the weather and she'd not slept much.

The decision to leave for London had been taken out of his hands. The roads from his home would be difficult for a carriage and the trip wasn't a good idea. He would get stuck. But he was already mired.

How many times must he go wrong in order to recognise the right path?

His proximity to Bellona had merely misled him. Misdirected him. Natural enough.

He'd relived a certain kiss a thousand times and cursed himself a thousand-and-one times. What if he'd only kissed her because he'd been so long without a woman's touch? Or worse, what if he had kissed her because she was like a meandering stream, winding and winding and seeming to be just a trickle until it pooled into something so wondrous the eyes could not believe it?

He could not do this to her.

His father would have counselled him. He would have shaken his head and closeted himself in a room with his son. They would have discussed the events. Or rather his father would have guided Rhys.

His father's main responses would have been, *'I see. That sounds interesting. I hadn't thought of it that way. What of the other people involved? Your future children? What kind of mother will best raise your son to be a duke? Help your daughters to make the best marriages? This is not a decision for you. It is a decision for your future heirs. And what of Bellona? What is right for her?'*

He forced the thoughts away, determined to make the best decision for everyone.

His sister, his father and Geoff's deaths had pounded his heart into dust. He could not resurrect it and expect to have the strength to carry on with his father's legacy. To let the lands and the estate go to a cousin, while the remains of all those he'd loved would reside here for eternity, was something he could not risk.

He had no choice but to marry a suitable woman, and he had no true heart left to give her. Perhaps that was why Louisa was the perfect wife. He'd not seen any real affection for him in her eyes.

If Louisa died in childbed, and left a child behind, he would be able to care for it and continue on.

He had courted her quietly while his brother was alive, knowing that his brother wanted Louisa—and why not, she was the perfect duchess. Geoff was no fool. Louisa's head wasn't easily swayed. Her thoughts were not altered by a duke pulling her one direction or his brother tugging her another, determined, on this one thing, to win.

When Geoff had died, the letters Louisa sent Rhys had been written in almost the same tone he would have expected from his man of affairs and he had responded similarly. Letter after letter exchanged—with little more personal nature than those he might have sent to Simpson. He'd saved every letter. Every one, and read them over and over, and each one convinced him even more of her suitability. The guilt he felt at courting the woman Geoff had planned to wed only flared occasionally. Now he wanted her for another reason. After he observed the mourning period, he had told himself, he would ask her to marry him.

Rhys had once believed his heart was in the right place. Perhaps. He no longer needed to think about that or question himself. He needed to go forward. Perhaps putting his body in the right place would cause his heart to produce the right response. Louisa knew what was expected of her in the role of duchess. Knew the ways of society. She was pleasant. Kind. Thoughtful. Perfect.

He didn't love her. To love someone else—to release his heart to them, was impossible. He could not give what he no longer had.

'Rhys.' His mother stood in the doorway, whispering loudly. Rhys jolted as if caught in an illicit embrace.

He collected his ducal mien and with his left hand scratched a jagged figure on the page before him. His mother had not entered the library in a long time. 'Yes, Mother?'

'The maid said…' The duchess rushed to his side. 'She mentioned a cut on your hand. The footman saw it when you were eating.'

'It's nothing to concern yourself over.'

'Let me see it.'

He held out his hand, keeping the palm almost closed so the slice wouldn't open again.

She gasped, her thin fingers reaching out to hold the sides of his hand. 'How…?'

'It was just an accident.'

She clasped her hands to her heart. 'I cannot. I cannot lose you, too.'

'I am planning to stay alive for quite some time, Mother. Please do not try to get rid of me so quickly.'

'This is not a jesting matter. You—' She turned and reached to summon a servant. 'I am sending for the physician now.' Her voice rose to almost a scream. Her body shook.

'My babies. They cannot all die. I cannot be left by all my babies, Rhys. Can you not see that?'

'I am almost recovered now, Mother. It is not my time to die.'

'We must have the Prince's physician. We must.'

He took his time with each word, hoping to calm her. 'If my hand becomes infected, we'll send for the man, but the roads are too bad for him to travel.'

'It will be too late by then. Look at it,' she said, again clasping her hands to her heart. She collapsed on to the sofa, her voice rising. 'I cannot live through this again. I cannot.'

Bellona ran into the room. 'Is he bleeding?'

'Bellona. He is injured. Badly. His face is feverish. His hand must be infected.' She clasped her head. 'My baby.'

'He is dying?' Concern flashed in her face.

'No more than I was this—last—yesterday.' He did not wish his mother to know the truth. 'I have a cut on my hand, Bellona.' He spoke precisely. 'A simple cut. That is all.'

'I did not mean for this to happen. I cannot live with myself if you die,' Bellona said.

'He is my only...' The duchess stared at Bellona in bewilderment. 'He is all I have left.'

'Ladies.' Rhys's voice calmed them. 'I am only slightly injured. Not dead. Please do not hurry my demise along by wearying me to death.'

His mother rose, pushing herself up. 'A mother should not outlive all her children and have no grandchildren to carry on. It is not just.' She looked at Rhys, but her question was directed to the winds. 'What have I done to deserve this?' She put her arms out. 'What have my children done?'

'Nothing, Mother.' He moved to her and held out his hand. 'See. A little cut. I'm fine.'

'You promise me you will not die. You must promise.'

'You have my word.'

She snatched his wrist. 'I will keep you to it.' Tears pooled. 'And you will give me grandchildren? Soon, Rhys. Promise you will give me grandchildren soon. I want to hold them before I die. You must go to London as soon as the roads are safe.'

'Yes, I will.'

Chapter Thirteen

Bellona put her hands over her ears even though no one spoke in the room and she was alone. How many times in how many ways had the duchess said how much she missed her family and how Rhys must wed someone from his own world? And how many times had his mother expressed her fear that he might now die if the cut in his hand became putrid?

Rhys had spent the morning calming his mother while Bellona listened, watching his hand to make sure it no longer bled. After he'd left the room, his mother had talked of nothing else but her younger son for hours. Then the discourse had travelled through each deceased family member and five handkerchiefs.

Bellona waited until the duchess tired herself into a nap. *Robinson Crusoe* was in the room at the servants' quarters. Perhaps she had found a man whom she could spend the rest of her days with, this Mr Crusoe, not that she particularly cared for him, but at least he did not have a mother nearby.

Rhys was in the library. She knew it. She could almost follow his movements inside the house without ever seeing him. He varied little from his usual paths and when he did she could tell by the activity that changed in the household. A different servant would be at the stair or she'd hear his horse outside, or a scent of some baked treat brought upstairs would waft her way.

He had told his mother the roads would be better the next day and he would leave for London. Bellona could not let him go without seeing him again.

She walked into the library.

Rhys sat at his desk. He didn't have the usual ledgers in front of him, but a chessboard with several pieces resting to the side and most on the board. His right arm lay on the desk and he moved a white pawn with his left hand.

He turned to her. Sensations of their kiss returned to her body, but this time, his eyes created the warmth swirling inside her.

She could stay at the door, safe, far enough away from him, or she could step inside. She moved forward, unable to do otherwise. 'The duchess was quite fractious today—your injury on the anniversary of Geoff's death.'

He nodded. 'I thought to leave so she might not learn of my hand, but decided it was not for the best, because of the date.' He moved a black knight.

'You have no opponent?' she asked.

'Not for this game.' He grinned at her. 'If you are unarmed, you may join me.'

'I have no knife,' she said, then answered the question in his eyes. 'Or weapon of any kind. Nothing that can jab or hurt you except my hairpins.'

'I suppose one must take progress where it is found.' He nodded to the board. 'Do you wish to play?'

She shook her head. Another thing she could not do. 'How is your injury?' she asked Rhys, stopping near his hand.

She waited, moving closer. He turned his palm towards her. The gash was closed, the skin around it slightly puffy, but reassuringly healthy.

'The valet has told me he has seen a man recover after having his leg cut off,' he said, 'and that his own father died from a toothache. He said when it's my time to go, something will find me. But he said it's not my time to go. He knows this because he peered at the whites of my eyes and pinched the top of my foot. The best check of all, he said, was to slap a cold cloth across my face. I almost let him, but when I declined, he said I passed his test.'

'I have hidden my knife, even from myself. It is with my bow and arrows.'

'Do you continue with the nightmares?'

'I have had dark ones, but I'm fighting back with the knife in my dreams now. It's much better, and when I wake I tell myself I can shout for help. I remind myself I can scream out.'

'Is my mother treating you well?'

'Well enough. She asked me to read to her again. A letter she'd saved from your sister this time. I could read most of it, and when I did not know a word she was able to tell me without looking. She said I have progressed much with my reading.'

'She is correct.' Gently spoken words.

'As a mother must be,' she said. 'When I have my own children she assures me I will understand.'

'I think you understand perfectly well now.'

She stepped to the mantel and noticed a vase, not

as tall as her hand, had been added. Primroses were tucked into it, their perfume so delicate she'd not noticed until she stood near the flowers. She brushed one yellow petal, feather-soft. 'Yes. I do.'

'You didn't want to leave your island. But you did. It was for the best.'

'Best for me?' She let laughter into her words.

'Yes. It has not turned out so bad, surely?'

'No. I cannot mind. I know how things must be.'

'I cherish those thoughts. I would not want you unhappy.'

'I'm not. Though I don't know that I wish to live on Warrington's estate any longer or live in London. I do not think I should stay here now. I want to have true contentment.'

'Do you truly know what you need for that?'

'Yes.' She met his eyes. 'I have known since I was a child.'

She went to the bookshelves and knew just where to find the *Cobwebs* book, seeing that she had placed it back there. She pulled the book out and looked at the title again. 'I thought about how Mana would have rejoiced to see her daughters so well placed. She would have bargained with the heavens that she would suffer so her daughters would not have to. And perhaps she made a bargain in another way to give us more. So when I feel sadness, because she could not share this life with me, I tell myself it is not so bad. She would have been joyous to know how bountiful my life is. And I will not let her struggles be for nothing. I will not.'

She traced a finger over the cover of the book where his hand had rested. 'I even know what would cause me the greatest of unhappiness. The union my mother had.'

* * *

Rhys had to gaze at her. He had no choice. He turned. That crown of hair she wore would topple around her shoulders some day and the man who could see it every day would fall to his knees and give thanks.

'What did your father tell you about love?' she asked. 'Your mother has mentioned it to me.'

'He said if the head could lead, the heart would follow. He said many men have lost their families, their lives and their world by trusting the most untrue organs of the body. He said the heart lies. A man's body lies. But he must separate himself from that and look from a distance. I thought them wise words, but he could not have known he did not need to say them to me.'

'The *Robinson Crusoe*. It was your father's book first?' Her lips quirked up and her expression nearly felled him. This moment was the most precious one of his life. He felt the strength of the world inside him as some mystical force flowed from her eyes, igniting a flame within him.

'I'm certain,' he said.

'Mr Crusoe. A man who wanted adventure and then spent most of his life alone. I don't think I will finish it after all.'

He looked at her long enough to see the smile in her lips and the sadness in her eyes. 'I want you to take the copy of *Crusoe* when you go. You may sell it if you wish. I will never read it again. It would always make me think of you alone on the island of Melos.'

'I would not sell this book. Perhaps I should read it at night when I cannot sleep. I could see how truthful the book is.'

At his side, she took his cut hand, examining it closely. 'I think you will live.'

'I think we both will,' he said.

He reached out with his other hand and let his forefinger touch her skin. She accepted the movement as one might let raindrops linger on the face. His caress slid over the contours of her cheekbone, feeling the silk. One fingertip was not enough. He stretched his hand so he could sweep more of her into his senses.

'I never thought dark colours could be so bright,' he murmured. 'Your eyes. They shimmer.'

His fingers moved to the valley at the side of her temple, where her cheekbone rose. 'They linger in my sight. They take my soul and hang on to it.' He ran his touch over her nose. 'You were created for a warrior god.'

She shook her head, but not enough to move from his fingers, but to brush against them. 'I am blemished. More so than my sisters.'

He chuckled. 'Marred? That could not be possible.'

Her nod moved her closer. 'I have a longing mark.'

'That cannot be bad.'

'My sisters' marks are brown, almost the shape of hearts, but mine is red, more like a scrape that never goes away. With my sisters we believed my mother wished for love for them, but for me, we could not think what she wished for.'

He moved, the smallest bit closer to her. 'Did you ever ask her?'

'Yes.' She stumbled over the word. 'She said she had wished for love for my sisters, but by the time I was born she said she had realised her error. She told me the two red blemishes on my skin are where a heart was torn in half. She said she wished that I would never fall in love. She said it hurts too much. She thought like your father. Perhaps you and I are in agreement on the foolishness of possessing a heart.'

He'd touched her lip when she spoke. She could no longer move. This was not the same immobility of fear, but of an embrace of security. He was fire you could walk into and never be burned, just feel the tingle and caress of the flames.

Now the fingertips from both his hands rested on her skin and his breath whispered against her. 'Your mother was wise for you.'

'She was. I know. Because I already saw my father leave my mother and I want no man near who will not stay with me all his life. Who will not place me above everything and everyone else.'

His hands slid from her face and he closed his fingers. 'I hope to remember the touch of your face. You're the magic I will hold within me for the rest of my life. In a secret part of me that keeps me whole and gives me breath. But I cannot give you what you need most.'

She touched above her breast. 'And I must have a man who puts me above…his father. His mother. Even his children. Who loves me with all the intensity of the sun's heat and his love reaches to the stars.'

'You ask—'

'For what I wish for. Why should I ask for less? I am happy to be alone before I will be with a man who does not cherish me as I wish.'

'A man can say the words easily enough. Words, Bellona. But how will you know if he speaks the truth? And what if he's not sure about his own future? What if he does not even know if he can feel for a woman what you wish him to?'

'If he does not know—then he does not feel enough.'

He swallowed. He moved and his elbow touched an inkpot, knocking it askew. He caught it, but not before splashes destroyed the paper.

Turning, she moved to his desk. Ink had pooled on his work. She put the stopper back on to the empty bottle.

He shrugged and touched a blot on his sleeve and frowned, still staring.

She put her fingertip in the obsidian pool. She paused, studying the letters scratched on the piece of paper. Taking her time and reading. The list of things he planned to do in London. The places he would go and the people he would meet. She dotted her finger over the letters, obscuring them. Then she put another spot at the side of the first one, letting her finger drag over, smearing the lines into darkness.

She looked at his eyes.

Her index finger touched the back of his hand and she left a faint mark.

'Have a pleasant journey.' She walked out through the door.

Chapter Fourteen

A storm brewed, but not in the clouds. The sun warmed the morning, turning the day into a spring confection of promise. Bellona didn't want to go back inside the mansion. Rhys's carriage had just left the estate.

The air moved aside for her arrows, creating the perfect pathway for each tip, taking them so close they clustered together, fighting for room. One *thunk* after another. She stepped back to give herself more of a challenge. It didn't work.

'Miss Bellona.' The shout screeched into Bellona's ears.

She turned. The maid ran from the house, skirt clamped in both hands raising it enough to allow swift movement. 'She's fallen. She's fallen.' The maid stopped. 'The duchess. Down the staircase. She won't open her eyes.'

Fear leapt into Bellona's chest. 'Send a rider after Rhys's carriage.' She dropped the bow. 'Let Rhys know the rider will need to continue on for the physician.' She rushed into the house and found the duchess lying at the base of the entry staircase.

The cook's bulk bent over the older woman, with only the duchess's feet visible. The servant talked softly to the still form. The butler stood at the ready.

The duchess's eyes fluttered. Then she blinked, looked around and studied her surroundings. A puff of air escaped her lips. A sigh.

'Are you hurt?' Bellona knelt beside her, relieved she was breathing. The lifeless form had plunged the memory of Bellona's own mother into her heart like a knife.

The duchess pushed herself up, looking at them all, but not speaking.

'Are you hurt?' Bellona repeated.

The duchess held out a hand to Bellona. 'I had thought to see what heaven might look like. You are not it.'

Bellona smiled and put her arm around the older woman, her ribs feeling as though they were hardly covered by skin. The woman winced, but managed to stand. She reached up and touched her cheekbone. A bruise would be evident soon, but for now there was only a scrape. Then she clasped her wrist and wiggled her fingers. 'I'm fine. Fine.' She pulled out of Bellona's grasp and grabbed the banister. 'I'm going to lie down.'

She took each step up the stairs with great care.

Bellona followed behind her and the cook did as well.

'Just leave me,' the duchess said crossly. 'I fell. Simple enough. I didn't watch my feet. I stumbled. Others cannot stay alive and I cannot die. I cannot *die*.'

The sharp turn of Cook's head alerted Bellona that

the servant was checking her reaction to the duchess's words.

Bellona schooled her face to show no emotion, but she didn't think it worked.

'I'll fix a purgative for Her Grace,' the cook offered.

'No. I'll keep my bile and whatever else I have inside me right there. I just had a fainting spell. I'm fine just as I am.'

The cook looked again at Bellona, and this time she grimaced.

They'd hardly settled the duchess into a chair, with a maid sitting beside her, when Rhys burst into the sitting-room door.

'How is she?' he asked anxiously.

'We don't think she's more injured than a few bruises.'

'What caused her to fall?'

'I am not sure. She said the world turned black around her.'

'She has never fainted before…'

'I fell, Rhys,' the duchess snapped, eyes closed. 'I fell. Do not worry about me. The house could burn around my ears and I would still be standing. Festering boils could appear all over my body and I would still see the sunrise every day.'

'Mother.' One strong reprimand.

She opened her eyes. 'I didn't mean for you to have to return. I am just sitting around every day, waiting for the end.'

He turned. 'You may slap her, Bellona. We will see if she can chase you.'

'Don't be ridiculous.' She shook her head. 'I just fell down the stairs.'

'An accident? Or on purpose?' Rhys said grimly.

'Neither. I was crying over Geoff. The tears were in my eyes and I had to go to the garden. I had to pick some honeysuckle. I'd almost forgotten to pick the honeysuckle for him.' She waved her arms about, her white sleeve billowing. 'I might not have done it on purpose, but I certainly wouldn't have minded waking up somewhere else. When I opened my eyes, I realised the truth. I am in a different kind of purgatory. My back hurts and my face aches. My wrist burns.' She sniffed. 'I would like some port.'

'How will I know you won't stumble again once you take a sip?' Rhys asked.

'Because I cannot die. A thousand times I have asked to be with my husband and children and I cannot. One year ago yesterday Geoff was taken from me. They are all waiting in heaven and cannot be happy without me and yet I cannot join them.'

'I would have thought you might wish to stay here on earth with me,' Rhys said quietly. He strode from the room. Bellona followed.

Outside the door, Bellona caught his sleeve.

'She is just distressed. She means none of it.'

He stopped, face stone. 'I understand that.' He pulled his arm from her grasp and strode to the stairs.

'Rhys,' she called at his heels.

He turned to her on the stairway. 'You don't understand.' His face rested near hers. 'It is not my title. It is not my estate. It was never meant to be. Never.' His words flowed faster. 'I do not know why Geoff did not marry and have children. I was not supposed to have it all. I don't know whether to feel guilty for taking it or angry that it's now mine and I cannot escape it.'

'That has nothing to do with this moment.'

'It is everything to do with it.' His eyes darkened. 'If he were here none of this would be happening. Things would be as they should be. They would be—controlled. The world was taken and torn like little scraps of paper and tossed into the air. All scattered and in bits that cannot be mended.'

'Do you wish to tumble down the stairs as well? Would that make it all better? Leaving a cousin to inherit. Would it be his destiny either?'

He raised his hand, the mark showing. 'I do not care at this moment. I must get to London, find a wife, bed her and produce a child. Hopefully before nightfall.'

'Oh…' She dragged out the word. 'More's the pity.'

He lowered his chin.

'From where I was born,' she said, 'even the people who cannot read have no trouble with that.'

'You witch. It is not quite the same for me.'

'I imagine you will find some way to have pleasure doing it. I have heard it can be done.'

'An unmarried woman is not supposed to know about these things.'

'And what turnip were you born under?'

'Not the same one as you, apparently.'

'Now go to London and do as you must.' She put a foot beside his and moved down the stairway, turning back to him. 'Safe journey.'

'Bellona.' He rushed after her and caught her arm. His voice softened. 'I cannot leave you like this.'

'Yes, you can.'

'I don't want to be alone now, and there is no one in the world I would rather be with than you. And perhaps you are right. Perhaps you are the one able to see this clearly without the heart being involved.'

She didn't answer, but her hand grazed her skirt, above the red blemish hidden from view.

Chapter Fifteen

She continued down the stairway and heard his footsteps behind her. She rushed ahead, moving to the servants' quarters where she could shut out the world above the stairs. No one was about and she moved to the small room she'd taken over.

Only the door didn't shut when she pressed it. Rhys's hand caught it and pushed it open again.

'So this is the room where you feel safe,' he said, stepping inside and shutting the door behind him.

'Yes. It is more my world than any other room in the house. You can see it for what it is.' Even as he looked around, she knew he could only see the room. He couldn't see the truth of her past. This room was a palace compared to where she'd grown up on Melos.

Nothing marred by salt from sea air. Nothing marred by life. This room had belonged to a scullery maid and it was the closest she'd found in the house to what she'd had.

His eyes furrowed. 'I did not know such a place even existed in my home.'

The small bed had a washstand beside it. Resting

on the washstand was a small mirror propped against the wall, a tallow candle and Robinson Crusoe's tale.

'This is how most of the servants' rooms are.'

The bed covering wasn't torn. The walls were solid. She raised her eyes to the ceiling and saw no stains. At the washstand, she pushed against it. No wobble. 'I am sure Mr Crusoe would have been pleased to have such a place on his island. I would have.'

Rhys sat on the bed, elbows on his knees, fingers steepled and his chin resting on them. He raised his eyebrows. 'I have been angry these last few years. Enraged that my sister died, my father and then my brother. Now I anger at even my mother, who suffers deeply.'

Brown eyes, more rich than any silk or sable, peered at Bellona. He smiled. 'But it doesn't matter. Nothing changes. I tried shaking my fist in the air. Pounding the wall. It changed not a thing. Didn't make me feel any better, only more angry because it was senseless.'

'I did not mourn my mother after she died. But I did not need to. While she was ill, I cried and thought my life could not go on. But she talked so much with us towards the end. We talked of everything and she prepared us. I missed her, but the hardest part was her suffering. The last week of her life. That was cruel. She hurt so.'

In front of him, she rested her hand on his shoulder and then let the back of her hand move upwards, along his cravat, to the skin above it, letting sensations engulf her as she talked. 'Your mother will get over this. It is just the valley before she climbs back up the hill of life again.'

'I thought if I went to London I might be able to

put the loss behind me. But when I return, there will be even more. You will be gone.' His eyes flicked to her and one side of his lips turned up.

She brushed his hair from his temple. 'There is the duchess you must find.'

'Do not remind me.'

'Why not? You will do it. You have put your mind to it. Don't tell me you do not think of the woman. How you will approach her. What you will say. How you hope to feel something for her in the way you used to feel before Geoff passed away.'

'When I close my eyes at night, it's not her I think of. When I open them in the morning, she is nowhere in my head.'

'Truly?'

He turned to her. 'Look at my face. What do you think?' He touched the earring at her ear. 'I notice you always wear these.'

She nodded. 'Yes. I think it makes your mother feel better.'

His hands clasped her waist. Warm bands. Strength that made her feel delicate.

'I want to make certain you are provided for,' he said.

'It is not needed.' She held her chin up.

She shook her head and turned her gaze from his. 'When you wed, I will never again see or speak with you. It is for the best. I will not forget the past. The good or the bad. Yet I will not fall into the same trap of the heart that my mother fell into. When it is done, finished, it is over and done with.'

She didn't raise her eyes, but kept the expanse of his chest in her view. The cravat rested close to his heart, but she didn't know what emotions lay inside the man. No words of love reached her ears and only the warnings of her mother sounded in her mind. She would heed them.

Rhys's hand slid up, sparking eruptions she had only heard about in myths. He cupped her cheeks in his hands. One kiss. Then another. So light. Lighter than the one before. Soft. The barest moment of contact and then he pulled back.

She kept her eyes closed, her chin upturned, and savoured the softness of the lace on his sleeve against her face.

Opening her eyes, she said, 'You dressed so fine to go to London.' She grasped his wrist, trapping the thin cloth so that she kept it between them. His jutting wrist bone rested under her fingertips. Then she stepped back and let her hand fall slowly, and land on the buttons of his waistcoat.

'Bellona…' He said her name, but it wasn't really a word. More of a caress. He paused. 'I cannot. Not now. Not ever.'

'Cannot?'

The words sounded pulled from him. 'I cannot touch you because I cannot…*touch* you. You deserve the promise along with the touch.'

Her gaze stopped at his face. She could see him more clearly than she had ever seen another person. Her eyes even caught the tenseness at the corner of his lips and the slight sheen of moisture at his brow.

His eyes darkened, but with an emotion that didn't frighten her in the least. But he still did not move one bit—even one hair closer.

Then she waved fingertips over the silken waistcoat. The fabric working as a barrier between the life of him and her hand. He took in a breath yet still didn't move towards her. Nor away.

He made her think of the statue of an armless woman she and her sisters had found on Melos. If the artist had carved a male, Rhys could have been the perfect model. His face. The stance. Unmoving.

She trailed her hand up, turning the palm so that the back of her knuckles moved past his cravat and caught the slightest bit of roughness on his cheek. He was strong enough to have moved away at any time, but she knew he couldn't. His eyes closed. The back of her fingers stroked his chin. His lashes rested just above her touch.

With the lightness of a feather, his fingers clasped over her wrist. Eyes still shut, he pulled her hand away. 'You must go to Warrington's estate.'

Slowly, his eyes opened. Her heart crashed alive in her body, flooding her with such pounding she could hardly take in air.

She had an arrow, of sorts, and she carefully aimed it. 'When I do, your mother has said there is a kind vicar…that you provide a living for…who might be looking for a wife. I should meet him.'

His lips barely moved as he spoke. 'I will see that he calls on you.'

'You do not have to. I will.'

She pulled back from his grasp but she couldn't walk to the door.

His body remained still, but his gaze didn't. The thoughts she couldn't touch were there, showing in his eyes.

It wasn't fear of dying without him that overtook

her when she looked into the brown, but the truth of living without his touch. And she took the strength he used to stand still and captured it in her body to stand there immobile.

His hand reached to her face, but she flicked her head back out of reach.

'You must not forget, I'm not an English society miss,' she said, 'which your mother tells me is important to you. I have tried for two years to want to be one and I see I am not, and will never be. I will be always free. I may not be a lady by birth, but I *am* worthy to walk the same earth as you.'

'You are.'

'I saw my mother cry when my father left us and I swore I would never beg for a man's attentions. I would have them freely or not at all. Whether he is a vicar or a soldier or a carriage maker, I will find a man who falls to his knees and thanks the heavens for me. And when he speaks words to me, they will be true. How I feel for him is not so important—as how he thinks of me. I am not a goddess. I do not wish him to think I am such. But he will have me in his heart as if I am.'

'I would like to see you with your hair down…' His voice was a whisper with a rumble that could only come from a man's throat and hardly touched the air, but swirled around her at all sides, as if an artist with a thousand brushes had taken her as his canvas and danced his brushes lightly over her body.

She pulled one pin from her hair.

He took it and held it between them, letting it linger in their vision, and she couldn't take her eyes from the fingers that held it so lightly.

'Your hair always looks as if your next movement will tumble the locks around your shoulders. I catch myself holding my breath, waiting. The wisps dance with your body, but the rest of it stays, looking soft and…like you. But even with the pin removed—' instead of returning the clasp to its place he palmed it '—it doesn't fall.'

His hand fell away, as if he'd forgotten what it held. His gaze moved over her tresses before returning to her face. 'A meadow. Did you know, it is always as if meadows or forests surround you? When I was a child, I would lie in the grass and look up at the puffs of clouds, and then close my eyes. Sunshine warmed my face. The grass softened the ground beneath me.

'The world had the same scent of an oak leaf held to my nose. At that moment, if a bird flew over me, it was as if its wings brushed my face and I was alive and everything was quiet in a way it had never been before. I could feel the poetry of the world and now that same verse surrounds you. I can feel the warmth of your hair against this pin.'

She reached out, putting her palm on his chest, cloth caressing her fingers. 'You have been reading—too much of that man who writes about women walking softly at night. Byron.'

'I would never say you walk softly in the night. *"She walks in beauty like the night…"'* His eyes flicked back to her face. 'Those words I do recall and they do apply. I'm sure there's more after that, but when I look at you, I cannot even remember who I am.'

She stood so close she could even see the way his pupils seemed to fade into a softer colour at the edge.

But she could not see herself reflected. She shook her head. 'I do not think Byron knows the true meaning of love either. Words. Perhaps that is why I have had so much trouble thinking of reading. It is bad enough when false words are spoken. To put them down on paper is even worse.'

'I admit, words do not do you justice.'

She stood immobile, and one edge of his mouth moved up. He took a step and reached up, and both his hands went to loosen her hair and she felt strands against her skin. Finally, her hair fell around her shoulders as he stepped away, but he wasn't truly moving from her. He was using his eyes to remain close, looking at her lustrous hair.

Taking her hand, holding it open, he dropped the pins into it. Then he closed his fingers over hers and pulled them up, dropping a kiss over her knuckles.

She put the pins on the table and stood with her back to him. The mirror reflected from his shoulders to his waist.

She took a breath, watching him worry the edge of his sleeve in his opposite hand. Then he straightened his fingers, flexed one hand, relaxed it and ran his forefinger along his opposing thumb, softly brushing back and forth.

She couldn't take her eyes from the mirror.

'If I were to choose one minute in my life,' he said, 'to live over and over again, it would be this one.'

'You say all the right words—almost...'

'I know. I say the easy ones. How hard can it be to tell a woman she is beautiful?' His fingers slowed, curling into a soft, unmoving clutch.

'But you are honest to us both.'

'A man must be more than his wishes, his dreams. He must set his path and follow it. He cannot let himself be swayed by what…he desires.'

'Words of your father.'

His reflection tensed, but his words held no emotion. 'True words. Words I believe.'

'I know. And I do not know if I hate you or love you.'

'Perhaps it would be best if you hated me.'

'I have seen how love withers when a man marries a woman who cannot follow him in his life,' she said. 'I know I am not your idea of a duchess and living that life is not what I see for myself. This simple room is how I wish to live. I am like my mother, except I know not to walk her path.'

'What are you trying to say?'

'Do not think if you lie with me, there will be a wedding to follow. I would not be compromised. I do not have to bow my spirit to anyone. The dowry I have has made that true for me. I do not have to listen to your society's rules and I am not staying in London either. I will find a small place and have a simple life. I will plant my own flowers and cook my own meals. I will work side by side with my husband to make a home that is ours alone.'

She stopped watching his reflection in the washstand mirror and turned, examining his eyes. Her lips turned up, but it didn't feel like a smile. 'I suppose I will feel differently when you leave tomorrow to find your duchess. But today I love you.'

Her lips were soft under his. She tasted of nature. Perhaps it was the spiced scent which always seemed to cling to her, or perhaps it was because she was so different from the women of his past and future. But he didn't care about the reason. Just for a few moments he wanted to experience her.

She clutched at him, pulling him to her. He ended the kiss too soon, leaving their faces pressed cheek to cheek, feeling their breaths mingle. Then he sat on the bed and took her by the bottom, skirts and all, pushing them up just enough so he could sit her astride him. He kissed her again and ran his fingers up her back, through the thin material of her gown, until he touched one of her shoulders. The feel of her under his hand captivated him.

He buried his face in the cleft of her bodice, awash in the heavenly sinful friction of cloth covering soft, delicate skin.

Keeping his lips against her skin for all but the briefest moment, he slipped the shoulders down on her gown, revealing a corset contrasting against the flesh that blossomed over the top of the stiff fabric. Her breasts, like her hair, barely stayed in their constraints, as if waiting for the smallest movement to free them.

Hooks unclasped under his fingertips. The corset ties hardly needed a tug, and when she stirred against him, the corset fell open and the chemise had already slid down her shoulders.

As he removed her clothes she slipped from one form to the next, becoming a woman from another land, a world he'd never seen, and a magical being, female, feminine and with the ability to hold him captive with her spirit.

His hands grazed over her back, taking strength

from her body, filling him with a sense of power. She arched against him.

He had not known it could be like this. To be inside this realm of another person, gaining strength from them.

She increased the distance between them just enough to capture this moment in her vision. To see him. His eyes were shut. Defenceless. Innocent. Never had she seen such a captivated look on a man's face. His nose, aquiline, and lips, soft. She moved, brushing her forefinger over them, and he kissed her and kept one arm at her waist while he pulled back the counterpane and watched as she slid into the bed.

He swept the coat from his shoulders, removed his waistcoat and pulled the cravat away in a silken whoosh. He whipped his shirt up and over his head— stopping her breathing for a minute. He tossed the garment aside. For half a second he stood motionless.

He sat beside her and the narrow bed, not made for two people, sagged with his presence. She placed her hand in the very small of his back, savouring the feel of his muscles beneath her fingertips while he tugged at his boots and then his stockings. The buff doeskin slid from his legs and he lay almost over her, propping himself on his elbows to keep his full weight from her, skin heating skin.

He kissed her and she could taste him, and her heart beat stronger, igniting the volcanic smoulder inside her. Her blood transformed into a lava heat, seeming to flow from her body through his body and returning to her.

His legs melded with hers, and his whole body surrounded her. The shaving spice on his skin mixed with the barest hint of wood smoke and she didn't know what kept her from actually igniting.

He twisted to his side, pulling her almost from the bed and into his complete grasp. The pillow slid to one side of the floor and the coverings to the other. The bed had no room for anything but them. His every movement against her increased the deepness of her breathing, and sent her higher into a cloud of pleasure. Molten.

Fingers explored her, claiming each curve of her body, and the feeling of his hand rolled over her so that even the places he did not reach responded as if he had caressed them.

He touched her softness, her wetness, and she erupted into spasms, lost to everything.

Rhys sat with his shoulders against the bed frame, looking at Bellona. Her hair wreathed around her—more appealing than any he'd ever seen graced with a tiara. He tapped her chin when she closed her eyes and let his knuckles rest at her arm when she looked up at him—sated, he hoped.

Twining his fingers through her hair, he lifted it and let the locks slide free. The second time, he brought them to his face, the delicate ends caressing his cheek. Savouring every strand.

And then something clattered outside the door, hitting the wood.

He knifed his body around, jerking the counterpane from the floor to toss the covering over her, and when he did his elbow hit the washstand, jarring it, skittering the mirror over, and the glass clattered to the floor. The fabric slid in place, partly, just as the door opened.

But it wasn't the aged housekeeper's head, the one with discreet quiet acceptance in her demeanour, who peeked around the door, but one of the underservants holding a wooden pail. Peering in with a question in her eyes.

Her expression changing, her eyes opened wide and her mouth fell into what appeared to be a near scream, but came out as a strangled gasp.

No, of course it could not be the housekeeper, a woman known for her silence.

He closed his lips and watched as the thoughts behind the girl's eyes embedded the scene before her into her mind for ever.

'Leave,' Rhys commanded.

The girl nodded, gave a gasped 'yes' with the uptake of her head and then she snapped shut the door.

He swore, words he'd never said in front of any female before, and the moment they fell from his lips, he knew as Bellona's head turned to him. He saw a different look in her eyes and he much preferred the servant's shocked gaze to the black one befitting a coiled snake about to strike.

He blinked to gather his thoughts because his next words were so very important, but before he could speak them, she pulled ever so slightly from his side.

Her eyes. He'd never seen a darker stare.

Chapter Sixteen

Her hands clenched. Trapped. But she would not be snared. She had lain with him, knowing he would go to London and she had not once asked him to stay. She had wished him well. She had been in his bed and then he swore when they were discovered.

He was not the one who would be destroyed by their actions becoming common knowledge and he well knew it. She was. But he swore. Because now he must do the right thing and offer for her hand. She'd seen how a man could be a treacherous husband and father when he did not wish to be wed. Her father had followed the dictates of his body and had then been angered because he blamed her mother for his lust.

'So, Your Grace, this is a first for you as well.' Soft words.

'In a sense.' Controlled, he said, 'I will instruct her that she is not to speak of this.'

'You may instruct her,' Bellona said calmly, 'but you know how the talk will travel. By the time we have dressed it will already be flying around the estate.'

'We will marry.'

'I would not wed you if you were the last duke on earth.' She reached for the pins at the bedside and in one quick twist she'd secured her hair and pinned it almost in place. She pulled the covers around her and moved from the bed. 'I can do better.'

'The Prince is taken.'

'I am not talking of rank, as you very well know. You trapped me like a hare.'

'No. I do not have to do something like that to get a wife and you know it. I can wed any one of a score of women. A fortnight of courtship and a proposal and I would be married.'

The words buzzed in her head so loud she could hardly think to form her own thoughts. They were true, but for him to speak them, unforgivable.

'Yes. But I am here. You desire me. Your head tells you I am the wrong woman, but your body does not care. And now you think I have no choice. That I must marry you because my reputation will be soiled for ever. You also have no choice—you can say that later, too.'

'No.'

'You heard the maid and you knocked the mirror askew.'

'That was an accident.'

'Accident.' She followed with an expressive gesture. 'That is what I think of your accident.'

He jumped to his feet. 'You cannot for one moment believe I did this to trap you.'

'Oh—' she shrugged '—why should I not? You had a brief moment to think and you didn't. You acted.' She cocked her head to the side.

'You are wrong.'

'I refuse. Refuse. Refuse. To let my children think their father was forced into marriage with me.' She could not control her voice. Let the world hear. 'That he purchased me in his own way. Oh, I have seen that. How many *drachmas* am I worth? Five hundred. Oh, but you have much more money. A thousand, then. And will you shout at me in front of my children to tell me how you paid too much for me? No, you will not.'

His voice softened. 'I would not.'

'No, you will not.'

She stood, securing the coverings, a Grecian goddess draped in white, as in times of old, proud as any statue. She brushed a tangle of hair from her lips.

'I will walk naked down St James's Street before I turn my back on my heritage and before I am trapped into a marriage I don't want.' She swirled the cloth and controlled her words. 'But thank you for asking.'

He inclined his head to her and reached for his own clothing, thankful she did not have a spear and that her bow and arrows had not been returned to her. That was the only thing from this situation which he could be happy with.

'I—'

Her words cut across his before he could finish. 'I will say, *Stubble it, Your Grace*. Or perhaps, *Rolleston, hold your tongue*, seeing that I can only call you Rhys when we are alone because we have no ties at all.'

'Except the ties of marriage,' he added.

'And this is written where?'

If he did not tread very carefully, he knew that not only the servants, but the tongues of the *ton* would get more than a splash or two of *on dits*. This would make the notorious tales of Lady Lamb fall by the wayside.

He slipped on the trousers that had been dropped beside the bed. He picked up the shirt he'd tossed to the floor and donned it. She stood draped in rough-woven bedclothes, and the small amount of light found her, sparkling on the earrings, cloaking her regally.

'In society's eyes,' he said, 'you'll be able to wed no vicar now. You will be a woman known to have been…been in my bed…in the servants' quarters…'

'What about you, Your Grace? If you ask another to wed you too soon, what will you think of her if she says yes? She will be marrying only your title. Your funds. Your estate.'

He continued with his shirt and trousers. 'Warrington will insist on our marriage. Your sister, the countess, will expect it. I will acquire a special licence before first light tomorrow morning.' He held his boot and sat on the bed. He stared at the leather. 'With Warrington and I both in accord, we can have this completed by nightfall. It is not unheard of for a man and woman to share a bed on their wedding day.'

'This is not my wedding day.'

He raised his eyes…waiting.

She smiled. At least her lips did. Her eyes, not at all.

'Yes. It is.' He paused, seeing steel in her face. 'You cannot…' He paused. 'You cannot *refuse*. Warrington has control of your dowry.'

'Yes. Warrington has control of my dowry. I cannot get it at the moment, but I am sure he will give it to me eventually. That was a mistake my father's wife regrets. She has promised she will correct it very soon.'

He knew where this was going. 'And your father's wife…'

Her shoulders flicked up and then down. 'We have

talked. Her relative has the wealth so that my father cannot touch it. It was done that way before her father died because he did not want his money in the hands of her husband, my father. My father's wife can do exactly as she pleases because her cousin moves the funds as she instructs. And when I told her in the past of my wish to be free…' Her chin tilted. She might not have a spear in her hands but she could use her words as one. She tossed the words out and they landed as a challenge. 'My father's wife understands. She understands my need to make sure I am safe at night and that no man can get near me if I choose not to let him. She has a spinster aunt in Scotland. My father's wife owns the house and she would like me to live there with her aunt. That is who I spoke of before.'

'Bellona. You must be my wife.' He looked at his boots again. The floor. The crumpled neckcloth. The waistcoat lying beside it, but even they did not make sense to him now. Could she not understand? Did she not know how many ambitious mothers would put their daughters before him—a virginal sacrifice the daughters would willingly become? His wife would be getting the same life of wealth he shared. The same deference from the whole of society. It was the way of the world. He had no more choice in it than they did.

'I will cherish that request—those words—just as I cherished the words in the books I sold to the sailor.'

'It isn't a request as you well know.'

'And I am not refusing you.' She swept the cover around her as she turned, her cape of bedclothes swirling, and he realised she was about to walk out of the room into the servants' area clad as a heathen goddess. He did not think she would walk quickly up the stairs.

Oh, no. She would possibly meander. Every servant in the area was going to get to see her dressed like this.

'I am merely taking a lifetime to decide. You may wait patiently for my answer.' She opened the door wide and he was suddenly thankful he was mostly dressed.

She pointed to the floor. 'I will be sending someone for the dress.' She indicated the clothing he had removed from her body. 'Please do not let it be misplaced as I will be directing a servant to this room.' Her eyes. No woman had ever looked at him in such a way.

'You cannot go about like that,' he commanded.

The door closed on his words.

The mirror lay at his feet. Unbroken. He picked it up. Hair mussed. No cravat. He looked more heathen than she did.

He slung the mirror on to the bed behind him, put on his boots, kicked the pillow into the wall and looked around the room. Let the servants talk.

For the first time in his life, he was thankful his father was no longer alive.

Chapter Seventeen

Bellona bypassed the servants' stairs, fearing her covering might get caught in her feet on the narrow climb. In the main stairway, she bundled the covers closer and moved towards the family rooms. She reached the top in time to see the duchess open a door and stand with her hand at her neck, and a bruise on her forehead.

'I heard such shouting...' the duchess said.

The woman was not picking good times to leave her room.

Her eyes closed, opened, and then closed again briefly as she spoke the first words. 'My dear, you appear dishevelled.'

Bellona nodded. 'Yes.'

'As if you have been...' The duchess swallowed, examining her.

Bellona met the older woman's eyes. 'I was thinking of taking a bath.'

'It is always sensible to disrobe on such an occasion.'

'I should also like a carriage readied...' Bellona paused. 'I will be returning to Whitegate.'

'I agree.' The duchess nodded. 'But might I speak with you first?'

The duchess stepped back inside the door, keeping her hand on the wood. Bellona followed and sat, pulling the covering with her, kicking it with her feet to clear it from the pathway.

After shutting the door, the duchess stood across from Bellona. 'And should I...should I assume you have been walking about my house like this? And perhaps even been seen?'

'Yes. I heard the butler sputter just now so perhaps he saw me.'

'Were you bathing alone?'

'No.'

'Is there to be a marriage?'

'No.'

'My dear. Even being able to read, dance and embroider adequately will not rescue you from such actions if there is not to be a wedding.' The older woman's head tilted low, but her eyes remained straight ahead. 'You have no choice. You rather agreed to that when you decided to bathe.'

'No.'

'We must consider all options.'

'I am only considering the ones which do not include your son.'

She swayed and grasped the wall. 'It is worse than I feared. Rhys. Rhys saw you dressed such?'

'I assume he saw me quite well.'

'In the servants' quarters? The duke was with you in the servants' quarters?' She panted. 'Well, you certainly made a fine kettle of fish. To trap him into marriage is one thing. *But in the servants' quarters?*' She made a fist. Her eyes narrowed in a way that said she could have easily tipped a boiling cauldron on to Bellona's head. 'I should never have let you step foot in this house. You planned this all along.'

'Not all along. I waited until after I had met him.'

'So you *bathed* with a duke and then walked around in view of the whole household?'

'Yes.'

'Well, that explains nothing.'

'A maid did not knock…when I was unclothed. The bath was not a private matter any longer.'

'Did you pay her to open the door? In all my years a maid has never interrupted my bath. Possibly because a decent woman knows to bathe at night.'

'So do all decent men.'

The duchess raised her hand and reached for the bell. 'Do not move. I will send for your clothes to be packed. You will not believe how fast the servants can have the carriage readied when I am on a tear. You can dress or not for the carriage ride. It hardly matters.' The duchess's hand stopped. She struggled for words. 'And there could be a little…' She blinked. 'Have you and Rhys been *bathing* together…regularly?'

'I would not speak of such things with his *mana*.'

'Nonsense. I *am* his *mother*. It is not as if I did not instruct his father how to handle that little indiscretion Rhys had with one of the servants.' Her eyes narrowed and, this time, she used one finger to jab her own chest. 'And I was *wed* to *his* father and that shackle had to be kept clamped on *his* leg.'

'The duke and I have agreed not to marry.'

Rhys walked swiftly through the doorway, the door knocking back against the wood. His cravat was looped in the most unsettling knot Bellona had ever seen. His hair had somewhat returned to its place and his waistcoat was buttoned. He had her clothing draped over his arm.

'Mother, Bellona and I are betrothed. We must go immediately for the special licence.' He looked at Bellona's covering, took in a full breath and held out the dress. 'And she forgot what she was to wear—in her excitement over the marriage.'

'Rhys,' his mother said, voice high. 'We have more rooms on the upper floors than can be counted. You could have been in one of those where you wouldn't be seen. I cannot believe this of you. I cannot believe it of *her.*'

'However, it is done. Bellona and I are to be married. I have sent the maid to instruct the carriage to be prepared. Mother, please start writing notes to all your friends telling them how I could not wait a moment longer to make her my wife.'

'*Never.* I don't need grandchildren after all. In fact, I've decided I don't like babies at all. They're never well mannered. Cast up their accounts. Spit on silk. Then they grow up and—it—gets worse.'

Bellona took the chance to turn to the door, but Rhys was between her and the exit.

He spoke softly. 'We must wed.'

'I have never heard of so many proposals in one day.' She spoke more words, in Greek, and from the tightening of his eyes, he had certainly learned those from his tutor.

'Bellona. Consider…what we have done.' His words were soft and his eyes gentle, but she had heard the harsh tone from him when the maid had opened the

door. The one that came from his heart. That one she
agreed with.

'I am not thinking of the past,' he said. 'I am thinking of the future.'

'Mine is in Scotland,' Bellona announced.

'Sometimes travelling is very good for you,' his
mother grumbled. 'It is a pity it just did not start soon
enough.' She held her hands up. 'And none of this
would have happened if not for my fall.'

'I must go.' Bellona struggled to reach out her
hand while keeping her breasts covered. 'I need…the
dress…'

He moved forward and she extended her hand, taking care not to hold it out too far. He placed the garment near her and she fumbled to hold everything
together. He frowned, waiting while she managed.

'I would have liked to have wed you, Your Grace,'
she said. 'But—you will spend your days looking at
me as if I am less than you. As if I trapped you.' She
shook her head. 'I knew every moment we were together you did not plan to marry me. Only because of
the maid outside the door did you finally consider it.'

'Rhys. Did you not learn anything from that past
indiscretion with the servant?' his mother asked. 'Did
your father not explain the word *mistress* means to
pay and go away? One does not soil one's own home.'

He frowned at her. 'It is not like that, Mother.'

'You took advantage of Bellona.' The duchess swept
forward as if she'd suddenly gained strength from all
the disappointed mothers of the world, the silver knot
of her hair shaking as she walked to him. 'You took
advantage of…a woman practically alone in the world
and her supposedly under my guidance and care. I can

forgive her more easily than I can you.' She stared. 'You were not raised to behave like this.' With each word her voice strengthened. 'You know better. I cannot believe you did this.'

She stopped in front of him. Her hand swung out, palm open, and she slapped his cheek. 'Get out of my house.'

He didn't flinch and his expression did not change. 'As you wish, Mother.' He turned and left.

The loudest thing in the room was Bellona's thoughts. The duchess had her head averted and stood away from her.

'It wasn't like you think,' Bellona said to the duchess finally. 'He didn't take advantage of me. I needed... I wanted...'

'Do not say it. The two of you created this wrangle and I cannot slap you because you are not my child.' The duchess sighed. 'The only thing I want to hear from you is that you will leave immediately.'

'If the servant hadn't heard Rhys drop something in the room and walked in to discover what made the noise, no one would know. Nothing would have changed.'

The duchess turned to Bellona and the lines at her eyes and mouth had deepened. 'And if the black plague hadn't happened—well, then we would have missed all that death and dying.' She put a hand to her chest. 'I would not usually compare this to the destruction of so many lives, but right now, it feels about the same to me. Get dressed. I have had enough of being a mother for one day. For one lifetime. I am going to have some wine and lie down. And *if* I wish to speak with you when I wake up, I will take a carriage to visit you at

Whitegate.' She made a flitting movement with her hand, as if sweeping Bellona out through the door. 'I would not stand by the door and wait if I were you.'

Rhys sat at his desk, examining the black-ink mark Bellona had made on the page he'd kept. One smear, with another beside it. A heart, or rather two halves of one. Not joined. He tried to find the right oath for how he felt. There simply wasn't one strong enough and even stringing all the ones he knew together hadn't worked. Whoever invented swearing did not make words strong enough.

His father had once said that being a duke was no different from anyone else except one had to always appear perfect. Wise words. Not quite accurate, however.

His father did not mention days when one did not know exactly how one could be so imperfect and not decipher any of it. He could not jump over a broom and then try to leap back to undo the action because then two errors had been made.

'Your Grace.' A footman stood at the doorway. 'The carriage is readied as you requested and Miss Cherroll—' His gaze dropped. 'She is also asking to be taken to Whitegate.'

Rhys felt no surprise. If he did not miss his guess from the flustered servants who had been darting to and fro, his mother was trying to manage the tales to reflect her family in the best light. Bellona would not fare well.

But he would change that. 'We will travel together,' he said. 'Let her know the vehicle is ready.'

The footman darted away.

Rhys stood and walked to the front of the house. He stepped outside and into the carriage. In a few moments, the door was opened. Bellona was half-inside the carriage when she saw him. She halted, but then continued and sat beside him, or rather as close to the other side of the carriage as she could get. She pulled her reticule into her lap and crossed her arms over it.

'Lovely dress,' he commented.

'Thank you for returning it.'

'I see your reticule does not have a blade poking from it.' The carriage jolted forward.

She ignored him.

'Are you going to London?' she asked.

'Eventually.'

'I'm going north.' She looked out of the window.

'Not in this carriage.'

'I do not need your carriage. I must tell my sister goodbye and arrange the trip.'

He grunted. Warrington might have other ideas. And he wagered her sister would as well.

'Are you…wearing a weapon anywhere about your person?' He watched her face carefully.

'Will I need one?' she asked. She didn't turn from the window.

'I might wish to borrow it from you. I don't think Warrington is going to be pleased when he hears of the recent…events.'

'I expect him to be more upset when he discovers his carriage missing and on the way to Scotland.'

'Bellona. Do not be surprised if he is aware something has happened before you even arrive. My mother had many servants scurrying to make sure she got in her side of the story first.'

'No.' Her head snapped around. 'Surely the news… would not travel that fast.'

'I think it moved as fast as it could be written on paper and carried through the woods by the fastest runner at Harling House. Accept that we are to be married.'

'I accept that *you* are to be married. That is no surprise to anyone. You have no choice, Your Grace.' She smiled and touched her earring. 'I do.'

He studied her. 'Well, it is best I find out your disagreeability before we wed. I would hate to be surprised.' He studied his palm before glancing at her. 'Again.'

He was not sure he wanted any wife at the moment. A woman could appear as sweet as the finest confectionery, but then one error at the wrong moment and she stubbornly refused to do the sensible thing and correct it.

'You know that no one can force me to marry you.'

'Fine. That might be safest,' he said. 'Don't marry me. But Warrington will not be pleased. Your sister will not be pleased. Your niece and nephews will miss you.'

'I can write enough words now to send them letters. It is how I will practise.' She tapped her hand to her head. 'Thank you for helping me read. It will be very useful now.'

The face which had been so soft in his hands earlier had changed. Her eyes no longer had the sparkle he'd seen in them before.

He tried to think how he would advise someone else to sort out this problem, after he'd told them they were an arse for getting in such a bramble.

Fine. He knew he'd been foolish, but he couldn't condemn himself for that.

He glanced at his puckered palm, wondering if his senses had bled out with his humours. The memory of her would go with him to his grave. And *if* he ever needed to be reminded he could simply hold out his hand.

'I don't regret what we did, Bellona. I only regret the knowledge of it being something for people to whisper about. If you wed me, and continue in the ways of a duchess, then society will accept you well enough. Your sister, the countess, is quite adept at moving in society. You can be as well.'

'No. If you think because we are sisters, that we are similar, you are wrong. To be a sister means only the faces are near the same. Our thoughts are our own.'

'What is wrong with you that you do not relish the chance to put yourself in the highest tiers of society for ever? To wed me?'

'As I said, I can do better.' She spoke. Quiet words. His second slap of the day.

The carriage rolled up to Whitegate and she jumped out before the door was properly opened for her.

She ran towards the steps. He would not chase after her. At a sedate pace, he followed. The groom watched from the corner of his eye. The servants would discuss this tonight. At least she had looked lovely draped in bed clothing. He hoped that had been noted.

The butler opened the door for her and waited for Rhys.

Bellona was not in sight by the time Rhys crossed the threshold. 'Summon the earl,' he said to the servant.

'I do not think it is necessary, Your Grace.' The butler spoke in the distant way of a well-trained servant, showing no awareness in his face of any upheaval in the household. 'He dispatched a message summoning you at half-past and he did not speak quietly.'

Rhys brushed by the man, not waiting to be announced, and moved up the stairs as easily as if the home were his own. He slowed at the sitting-room door.

Bellona sat on the sofa, not speaking. Spine firm— lips the same.

Warrington stood, arms clasped behind his back, staring at a painting of the three children playing. One chair was overturned.

'Rhys.' Just the one softly spoken word. Warrington didn't move.

'War.' He paused. 'Would you like to travel with us to procure the special licence?'

The pop of Warrington's jaw preceded his answer. 'I don't think you need do so, Rhys.'

'Why?'

'No one will expect you to.'

Bellona's chin tilted a bit, defiant, but her knuckles were white as she gripped the reticule.

Rhys stepped inside and shut the door.

Warrington exhaled sharply. 'She tells me she led you to the room. When you suggested marriage, she refused.'

'I will leave England,' she said.

'You cannot run away from this, Bellona,' Rhys challenged.

'My sisters and I ran from Melos.' She shrugged. 'It has not turned out too badly for them.'

'It doesn't have to turn out badly for you either.' Rhys gestured with his right hand for emphasis.

Warrington's eyes locked on his palm. The earl gave a sharp intake of breath. 'Arrow?'

Rhys immediately dropped his hand, turning the wound away from the earl's gaze. He shook his head in answer and kept his eyes on Bellona. 'Do not make this worse for yourself.'

'I won't,' she said. 'I'm leaving.' She paused for a second. 'It will be best for you, too. You will not have to concern yourself that you could do better.'

'I have never said such a thing. You are the one who keeps saying that. Not me.'

'You don't have to.'

Warrington huffed. 'It is as if I have my children standing in front of me. You both need to listen.' He righted the chair, thumping the legs on the rug. 'I have known for a few days, but I hoped it would disappear. It hasn't. Lord Hawkins has been drinking. The man appears to be losing his mind—perhaps he is succumbing to some sort of illness. Unfortunately, it is also loosening his tongue. He claims Bellona has been trying to get money from him. Claiming she will say she is his daughter to discredit him unless he pays her.'

She jumped to her feet. 'He *is* my father. The funds have been organised by his wife and she gives them freely.'

'I know that,' Warrington said. 'But he is splattering every handful of mud he can in your direction.'

Chapter Eighteen

Warrington snorted. 'Don't look so...gutted, Rolleston.' Warrington's eyes narrowed. 'Neither my wife nor Bellona can help their birth. None of us can, *Your Grace.*'

Your Grace. He heard the sneer in Warrington's voice, but it reminded him of who he was. And he realised who Bellona was. He'd never cared about the *on dits* that Hawkins had a mistress he visited when he left England. When he found out Hawkins was Bellona's father he'd not really cared. But the truth had been secret for so long and now Hawkins was spouting it everywhere.

Warrington closed his mouth and paused before speaking to Bellona. 'Perhaps you should consider the special licence. Even Rhys can't change a marriage after the deed is done. His property joins mine. You would be close to Melina. And when Thessa returns from sea with Ben, you will be near to her as well. If you go away now to Scotland, it will be assumed there is a child. If you stay here and wed the duke—perhaps you can geld him.' He shrugged and gave a pointed look to Rhys's hand. 'Just a thought. I'm sure she'd eventually think of it on her own.'

'His Grace and I would not get on well.' She reached up, pushing an errant lock behind her ear. 'He doesn't even like the way I dress my hair.' She shrugged. 'He does not know how to live for himself, only for others. I do not know how to live that life. I have seen what happens to a woman who falls in love and marries a man when he does not love her back—or think her above his tracks in the dirt.'

'I would not treat you ill.' The duke's words bit into the air.

'But in your heart you would. Now you can promise—anything. Everything. That is easily done.' She looked across at him and slipped a pin from her hair, and tossed it to the table beside her. 'My father promised to return to my mother. He would hurry, he said.' She stared at Rhys. 'He promised most sincere *agape*, love, when he meant it the least. And do you know what my mother's last words were?'

Rhys blinked, forceful. Jaw firm. Solid, unmoving.

'She asked if my father was on the ship in the harbour. But he was not. He was never returning. I knew it.'

'You cannot judge other men by your father.'

'You judge other men by yours.'

He shook his head, causing a strand of hair to fall across his eyes. He put his hand to his temple and thrust the lock back into place. 'I know he was a stickler for convention. But that does not mean—' He used his flat palm to indicate himself. 'He *was* a good man and I can follow his example. All men make mistakes. Even him.'

'You made a mistake and now you must correct it?' She tilted her head.

'We must be married. You cannot hide away in Scotland.'

'I find it nobler to be a spinster than to throw myself under your feet. I do not care who you wed, Your Grace. As long as it isn't me.'

'You should tell him everything, Bellona. Rhys isn't worth much, but he can keep his counsel,' Warrington advised.

Bellona stared forward. Rhys thought she'd looked much gentler when she'd held the arrow to his stomach.

Warrington left the room, his grumbles mixed with curses at her father.

Rhys stood, his face with so little expression she could not read it. Behind his eyes he was secured alone with his thoughts and she suspected they were not charitable ones.

She refused to discuss any more of her life with him. Warrington said Rhys could keep silent, but the earl didn't realise Rhys was the one person she most did not wish to tell.

'We are finished here,' she said. 'You've done as much as you can to help me. You've tried to correct what you see as an error. You should go about your duties and remove this from your thoughts.'

'Remove it from my *thoughts*? And how might I do that?' He moved to stand in front of the painting and pointed to the smallest girl. 'If I wave my hand over the canvas, will it make the scene disappear? Will it make the memories I have go away?'

'Memories are the past. Thoughts are what are in a

person's head at the moment. I do not care what you do with your memories. You may polish them until they outshine the sun. But do not keep me in your thoughts.'

He whirled from the painting to look at her. 'You think I am so uncaring a person that I can bed you in my home and just toss that aside.'

'Did you not do that to a woman once before—a servant?'

'Even that was not as simple as the way you speak of it. It was not.'

'My mother loved my father so much. And she thought she could not live without him. But he was not to stay and she died. Perhaps she spoke the truth of her love. Which showed me so much. The warmth faded from her body while my father painted. I was not with him, but I know—at the very moment my mother died, my father had a brush in his hand, a canvas in front of him and more concern about the light than my mother. She never meant more than being a subject for a painting to him.'

'He will pay for that.'

'He cannot. It cannot be done.'

'You do not have to worry about your father, Bellona. I can ensure he has a set-down. It will be his word against mine. You and I can face this together and it will never be more than a rumour. A tale we laugh away.'

'No.'

'He cannot spread such tales if we are wed. It will be ridiculous for him to do so. I will take care of him for you, Bellona. He cannot cross a duke and get away with it,' Rhys said.

'No. Do not add more coal to the fire.' Bellona shut

her eyes. She should have left England earlier. Now her father would feel he had successfully chased her away if she left, but she did not know how she could stay and watch Rhys wed someone else.

'It is not about increasing the gossip. I will see that he ceases it altogether. We all have our weaknesses, Bellona. All of us. And I can find his.'

'Searching them out will not be hard. They flutter about him like birds over grain. I do not want you to be pulled into his mire. He relishes such things.'

'I will relish this.'

'Do not meddle. I am his daughter.' If she confronted her father, he could tell more truths. More truths she did not want known. She could not lie away the truth. 'His actions do not truly surprise me. I do not wish to be near him and he feels the same about me.' She ignored the way the air seemed to have the scent of her home again and she could hear the waves. 'I am so much his daughter that we cannot bear each other.' Rhys could not get involved in her past.

'You are not like Hawkins.'

'Oh, I am.' She put her hand over her heart and patted. 'I do not use mine to guide my actions. It is to beat and keep me alive, nothing else.' She shut her eyes. 'The letters my father sent my *mana*… My sister read them aloud to her so many times we could recite them. Such words of love. Tears in Mana's eyes. Hope in Melina's voice. Thessa and I would later go to the sea, fall on to the sand in front of the waters, and repeat the words, each of us speaking with all the sincerity we could bring to the speech. None of the fish ever changed the direction of their swimming. The waters continued on as before. Gold did not fall from the heavens. The words were worth nothing. They were not love to Mana. They were words for himself. A painting he created on paper instead of canvas.'

'Words may disappear into the air, but a special licence is binding.'

'My father married twice. Two too many times, but he married for a reason each time. His first wife's funds and my mother's beauty. I will not marry you for your title. Or for your protection of my name.'

'You cannot tell me you do not care for me.'

'No. I cannot. I would say I care for you more than anyone in London does. But no matter what feelings I have, one person's love in a marriage is not enough.'

Chapter Nineteen

She held out a hand to brace herself against the thoughts buffeting her, but nothing fell into her grasp. Rhys stood there, not speaking.

But his past gripped him as strongly as hers held her tight. She'd been marked on the outside and the inside.

Her mother might have called the spot on her body a longing mark, but it wasn't. The mark was her strength. A reminder not to repeat her mother's broken heart. All her father's children had the blemishes—her father's London wife had told her how each of her children had been born with similar marks. They were a legacy, just as a title was. But where her sisters had brown marks, hers had red in it—like a scrape, as if the blood had risen to the surface on her hip and never healed. A heart that was broken.

Now she truly believed that her mother had wished for a torn heart for her daughter.

Better to have a broken heart than a broken soul from loving someone who could not love her in return.

If she didn't turn her back on him in that instant, she

would not have the strength to do it at all. She turned. She could not look at his face.

She left him behind.

Rushing up the stairs, she went to her sister's chamber, not knocking but running inside. Melina sat in there, her son's toy soldiers arranged on the table, and Willa stood at the side, moving the toy men into rows. A governess sat in a corner chair.

When Melina looked up, Willa ran to her aunt and wedged herself against Bellona. For a second, the hug erased the pain deep inside her, but then when she looked at the little girl's tousled curls and cherub cheeks, she realised she had given up her chance to have a child by the one man she loved. Sharp spasms of pain hit her body and she forced herself immobile to let the hurt pass.

Melina looked at her sister's face. 'Take Willa to play in the nursery,' she said to the governess.

'Warrington told me about Rhys.' Melina stood as the governess and Willa left. 'When you moved to Harling House to be a companion to the duchess, I knew you were taking a risk, but how could I warn you?'

'You could not have. I already knew. When I met Rhys in the forest, I knew. No one had ever unsettled me the same way he did.' She'd pointed the arrow tip at him to keep herself safe, but not in the way he'd thought at the time.

She couldn't stay at her sister's house. Rhys had even taken that from her. To see the children grow and watch her sister's family flourish while she stood on the outside looking in would wither her spirit. She had to leave.

'You will survive,' Melina said, walking to put an arm around her sister's shoulder.

'How would you know?'

'You have no other choice.' Melina reached out as if to pat Bellona, but instead pinched her sister's arm.

'Stop it.' Bellona pulled away.

Melina reached out, fingers poised to nip Bellona again.

Bellona took a step away. 'You had better not.'

'It is only because I care for you.'

'Do not let us get in a competition to see who loves the other the most. Your children do not need to see such behaviour.'

'If you do not want me to hurt you, then you must remember that you would not want a husband who does the same.'

'I know. My mind knows that.' She put her hands to her head, pushing back the hair that had fallen at her brow. 'But my head cannot find a way to tell my heart. I do not understand why it will not listen.'

The man of affairs still sat in front of him, patiently awaiting the return to his duties. Rhys didn't know how a man could smell of roses and be content in life, but Simpson seemed to have mastered that. Rhys felt he could kick the chair legs from under the man and he would receive only an apology from Simpson for having placed his chair in the wrong path.

Rhys's jaw hurt from keeping his words careful and precise and all emotion banked.

He began looking over the ledgers again. He spotted an error. One he'd made. He crossed it out, irritated.

He couldn't have been paying attention to have made such an obvious mistake.

Voice ever so solicitous, the man of affairs said, 'I wish to speak with you about a private matter, concerning a bit of rubbish currently being batted about.'

Rhys nodded. Apparently the man of affairs had heard the *on dits*. Rhys could sense a change in the man—an awareness of unsaid things.

'So—' Rhys relaxed his body in the chair, interlaced his fingers behind his head, and fixed his eyes on Simpson '—what is the talk?' Might as well get the words on the table, so to speak, and then get on with things.

'Talk?' The voice was just a tiny amount too shrill. 'I would not call it that. Only small minds repeating things heard. Embellished, I'm sure.'

Rhys didn't speak, but let his eyes pull out the words. He waited. And in the same manner of a gust of air blowing over his body, he viewed his physical self. He'd never sat in a chair in such an informal way. Rhys put his feet flat on the floor, hands on the desk, straightened his back and leaned forward.

'It's said the dark-eyed foreign woman had wild ways, and you, well—' his head swiveled sideways '—did as a normal man would and partook of her favours.'

'That's all?'

'It's said she's even claimed to be that Lord Hawkins's daughter—the one who paints. Trying to disgrace him—though you know how he's viewed by the *ton* as full of himself and rather like a belch that's gone on too long.'

Rhys let his palms feel the smooth wood.

'And we all know,' he continued, 'that the sisters come from Grecian high-born people on an island where the French have been claiming treasures abound from the past. But people are supposing the youngest one is unsettled.'

Rhys's lips firmed and he glared at the man.

'You asked.'

'Yes, I did.' Five heartbeats of silence followed and Rhys reminded himself he had offered to wed Bellona. She had refused.

'One other thing.'

Rhys waited again, wanting to throw an inkpot at the man to hurry him and strangely upset at the thought that the man would not pick up the tossed inkpot and hurl it back.

'Lord Hawkins, he doesn't seem to be taking things well and is blaming the girl. He's said she's hurt his children with her tales.' The man put his fist loosely to his upper lip, as if to blunt what was said next, concentrating on his words. 'Of late, it's said he can't even get along with himself.'

Rhys only response was his usual flick of the brows.

Lord Hawkins wasn't cracked. He knew him. The man didn't have an *un*selfish bone in his body. He could lecture for hours on a bird's beak, as if no one but he could see it. As if everything he saw, he saw in brighter colours and with more meaning than mere humans could digest.

'He's not doing…' The man's words trailed away.

Rhys met his eyes and forced him to continue.

'He's not doing her any good at all, Your Grace.

He's talking about her in a way no lord should talk about a girl who has been a guest at a duke's home.'

Rhys placed his right hand on the desk, above the drawer, and knew that underneath lay a newspaper, with the words neatly printed, not only the reference to *a certain duke*, and most of the things his man of affairs had just said, but repeated several times, as if once wasn't enough.

Bellona was referred to as the Untamed Grecian Temptress from a land of Saturnalian delights, ready to leave a trail of women in tears as she danced about for their husbands.

The simple-lined caricature did not look like her, but a Gillray sketch, hair flowing as a brief covering swirling around her, while she held a tambourine, dancing. The goddess of beguilement. He hoped to be able to return a copy of the newspaper to the artist, personally.

'We're through for today,' Rhys said.

Simpson shuffled the papers together. 'You'll do fine, Your Grace.' He coughed. 'Not a life about doesn't have some struggle from time to time. You've just had more loss than most of recent. Time for a spell of good luck.'

Rhys waited until Simpson left and returned to his examination of the man's meticulous records. Truly, he wondered if Simpson hadn't managed better alone.

Rhys wanted to return his life to normal. To erase the impact of tales that might be told, before the whispers grew louder. To gauge the look in the faces of others and listen, and steer the conversation if they mentioned anything of the improprieties he had caused. But most of all he wanted to forget.

Folding his arms flat over his desk, he rested his head on them, closing his eyes and trying to trick himself into sleeping. In the night, whenever he'd lain in bed, his mind had darted alert, thinking of all the mistakes of the past few days, and the woman whose image he could not erase.

The sound of a rap on the door caused Rhys to raise his head. He brushed his hand over his eyes, uncertain of how long he'd slept. A servant stood there, holding a salver with a calling card.

Rhys straightened, and reached out. The tray was moved to him and he pulled the pasteboard card into view. Lord Hawkins. Bellona's father. He'd sent for him the day before. He tossed the card back on its resting place.

Rhys brushed a hand across his cheek, feeling the bristles.

The grimness of Jefferson's face alerted Rhys. Jefferson had been trained well. With just the briefest narrowing of his eyes, and the extra-precise steps he took as he moved backwards to the door, he told Rhys this was not a congenial guest.

'Show him to the sitting room,' Rhys said, 'and serve him cold tea. Collect me when he has reached a proper temperature to boil the water.' Rhys put his head back on the desk.

He felt he'd just shut his eyes when the sound of Jefferson clearing his throat woke Rhys.

He pushed himself up from the desk, stood, pulled his waistcoat smooth and reached for the coat he'd tossed on a chair, donning it.

'Would you care for a comb, Your Grace?' Jefferson asked.

Rhys shook his head and walked out through the door, running a hand to smooth his hair, but not really caring.

When Rhys walked into his sitting room, the scent of a painting just completed lingered around the man, perhaps linseed oil or painting pigments.

Bellona's father sat, holding a cane, gnarled fingers grasping it, a birdlike flutter to his movements. It felt as if someone had left a raptor in the room and it had flown from place to place, leaving feathers and droppings about. A chair had been moved a bit. A tea cup sat half-empty with crumbs scattered. Rhys examined Hawkins's face, looking for a resemblance to Bellona. He saw none, except perhaps a bit of the chin. And they both tilted their head to the side when showing displeasure.

Hawkins stood. 'Rolleston.' His bow was more the semblance of movement than anything else. 'I have wasted near a day waiting on you.'

'Greetings to you as well, Lord Hawkins. I am going to make you pay for what you did to Bellona. It is nothing personal, you understand. It is justice. You left your daughters to fend alone. You left a family without funds to live in little more than a shack on an island while you lolled about here.'

'I did no such thing.' His lips twisted. 'My only family has always been in England.'

He thumped his walking stick on the floor. 'I hate Warrington for giving refuge to those women when he should have packed them back on the ships they arrived on.'

'They're your daughters, no matter how much you deny it. You know it and I know it.'

'I know no such thing.' He chuckled. 'It's possible I spent some time with their mother while I was away from home. So I can understand how they might be under the impression I am their father. Ridiculous as it is.'

'You make this easier for me.'

'You let her gull you. You couldn't keep your hands off her.' He frowned and looked to the ceiling. His voice softened. 'Not that I don't understand. I had the same problem with her mother. Couldn't leave the woman alone. I'd sail from Melos thinking I'd never see her again and then I'd go back. I couldn't stay away.'

'You were a married man.'

He chuckled, shrugging. 'Only slightly.'

'You are going to *only slightly* pay for deserting your daughters.'

Hawkins raised a pointed finger and softly shook it in the air. 'Oh, no, no, no. You cannot do a thing to me or I will remind everyone how you soiled her. I am no different from other men. I even kept my number of visits to the island to a reasonable amount.'

A flush of intensity blasted Rhys's body.

'You would do well to follow my example.' The voice hit Rhys's ears with a clatter that rang on and on.

Rhys's stomach churned cold.

Hawkins strode past Rhys. The walking stick brushed Rhys's leg. Hawkins looked back over his shoulder. 'She's been nothing but trouble since she arrived. Calling on my wife. Not settling into suitable English society as her sister did. She's nothing to me.

My children—she let my *real* children see her. My daughter cried. Un…for…giv…able.' He dragged out the syllables as if he spoke four words.

Hawkins stopped in the doorway. 'And you…' He pointed the cane at the painting over the mantel. A work by Lawrence. 'Wouldn't know a good painting if you fell over it.'

Rhys didn't speak. He didn't want to give the man even the smallest response, afraid of what his voice might reveal.

Hawkins's walking stick crashed against the door frame. 'You lie to yourself, Rolleston. You think you're better than me, but you're not. Your brother was born to be duke—not you. If he'd been wise enough to wed and sire a son before he died, you'd be living off your nephew's whims. Now you toss crumbs about instead of scrabbling for them. Your dead brother's crumbs. I bet every morning you say a prayer of thanks that he died.'

Hawkins left, pulling the walking stick up and putting it under his arm.

Rhys didn't move.

The foundation of his life cracked, turning into rubble.

Chapter Twenty

Rhys went to a soirée. Louisa was there. She turned her shoulder to him when he walked near and relief surged along with guilt. The relief won when she danced twice with someone else and her eyes shone on her partner. Watching her, it was as if he'd never *seen* her before. This woman he'd hoped to marry, but had never really seen for who she was—because, he now realised, he'd never truly loved her.

He forced his attention to the man who was speaking to him, Lord Andrews.

Lord Andrews leaned closer, winking and smiling. 'So what of the bit of muslin you—?'

'Stop.' Thoughts pummelled Rhys from the inside, causing him to need a moment to sort through even half of them. 'I asked her to marry me. She refused.'

Lord Andrews stared. Rhys didn't think he'd ever looked at Lord Andrews properly either. The man was commanding, of fair face and quick-witted. Yet, Rhys would have compared him to a toad, waiting, watching for insects. They'd shared brandies more times than Rhys could count.

'I am pleased we spoke,' Rhys said. 'But I must be away.'

On his way to the door, he dropped the brandy glass he held on to a footman's tray.

He had to wait for his carriage outside, the unseasonably cool air brushing his face and waking him up to feel even more.

How many times had he truly looked at himself through his own eyes? Possibly never. He'd always used the eyes of others to gauge himself. His father. His older brother. His mother. The things he did privately were deemed to deserve no judgement. No censure. No introspection. After all, he was the second son. It did not matter. Nothing mattered until after Geoff died and then everything tilted in a different direction.

The town-coach door was opened. Rhys stepped inside and made himself comfortable. Even in darkness, he knew exactly what the crest on the door looked like. He'd had the colours corrected as they faded. But he didn't know the face of the man who'd held the door. Didn't know his name.

Rhys touched his cheek with his marred hand.

He had thought, when he'd first discovered that Bellona was not the offspring of someone in the Greek upper classes, that she was scarred by her birth. Perhaps in a way like the statue without arms the sisters had found on Melos. The one that Warrington had told him about and said the sisters thought an ancestor of theirs had posed for. Supposedly, the statue favoured their mother.

But blemishes and perfection did not always appear in the expected forms. The white line at the top of Bellona's nose made him want to kiss it. Her hair tumbling about called to him in a way perfection never would.

He was marred. Bellona had risen from a world of struggle and became someone of strength. He had been handed the world and only had to continue on the path already cleared for him, yet he'd been unable to choose the right steps. She'd made her own path and tossed her head back and fought with all her strength to survive, becoming stronger.

He'd become weaker. Softened by the world giving him his wishes as he indicated them. He supposed— but he would not wish to repeat it—if he had true strength, it had been gained when he'd watched Bellona follow the rules she created for herself.

The feeling of a funeral surrounded him, and now he felt he knew what it would be like to attend his own last service, and see the crypt surround him on all sides, with the grim knowledge that he had done this to himself.

Bellona sat in her room, the needle slowly going into the fabric and moving out on the other side. Her eyes not rising once. Holding the embroidery high into the light, she examined the stitches. She would be better letting the maid sew while she attended the washing. Cleaning she could do well, which no one wanted her to do. Embroidery, which everyone expected of her, was a tangle of threads.

If not for the war with the Turks, she would be wishing for a return to Greece. She couldn't safely sail to Melos now. Or ever. If she did, she'd not be able to see her nieces and nephews grow. She'd not see her sisters again.

Warrington's voice didn't carry through the walls any more. She wondered if her sister had finally quieted him or if his throat had simply given out from the exertion. This was the one time he seemed to have forgotten his rule about servants not hearing family matters.

She looked into the grate. Only ashes left. No more of the vile newsprint.

She wished for more words to burn. Burning the papers somehow seemed to ease the ache in her heart. She could not even look at the mark on her body any more. Once, it had made her feel stronger, the memory of her mother—a trace of the past. Now, even the blemish ached.

Just like her heart and all the rest of her that mattered.

Ruined. That word had carried through the walls a few times.

'She could not be more ruined.' That had spewed into the air and cloaked her with a feeling of being unwashed.

The needle jabbed her finger and she didn't spare her grumbles. She could be more ruined. Warrington was wrong to think otherwise. If not for her sister and niece and nephews, she would be finding out where the scandal sheets originated and marching there with the largest hammer she could beg from the stable master. The printer would be having a holiday from his work long enough for repairs. Then he could write about the angry woman who'd smashed his press and stopped him from being able to put his cruel words on paper.

Rhys could not be sailing easily through this either. He could not.

'A visitor for you.' Her sister spoke from the hall.

Bellona's heart pounded. Rhys. She thrust her sewing to the side.

The quick sideways shudder of her sister's head paused Bellona's movements.

'The duchess.' Melina frowned. 'She's…'

'She's in quite high dudgeon,' the duchess said, walking in behind Melina. Melina rolled her eyes and left.

The older woman's skin hardly covered the bones of her face.

'Embroidery again?' She walked closer, the black crepe of her skirt reminding Bellona of a raven's wings fluttering about. Her reticule matched the clothing and her bonnet completed the effect.

She peered at the sewing while opening her reticule. 'You should conquer reading first. Then dancing. Perhaps leave the sewing to someone else.'

She held up the folded paper and tossed it on to Bellona's sewing. 'I received this unsigned note, but I believe it is from Rhys's man of affairs.' She knotted the ties of her reticule. 'I believe the words are simple enough for you to make out. I brought it for your own good.'

'Your *kali thelisi*, good will to me, is kind.' Bellona forced her lips into a smile and refused to touch the paper, uncertain if she could read it. Refusing to let the duchess see her stumble. 'But I was going to send my sister to tell you I am not at home.'

'Oh, my,' the woman said. 'Neither am I. The stairs weakened my knees. I'll be in bed the rest of the week.'

'You shouldn't overtire yourself.'

'You'd like that, wouldn't you—if I left?'

'Yes. I don't wish to be near you.'

'The house is quiet without you. The servants seem to miss having you about. One of their own has left them.'

'Your maid was very kind to me.' Bellona glanced at the messy fabric beside her. If she'd known what was to happen, she would have stolen a piece of Melina's perfect embroidery and worked on it, pretending to complete it.

'I'm sure the staff here is also kind to you.' The duchess looked around the room. 'The maid does know where her loyalty lies, though.'

'As you know yours.'

'True. I do.' She held her head up, again reminding Bellona of a bird. 'I'm a duchess. I'm well suited to it. But I am a mother first and I only have one offspring left.' She sighed. 'Are you with child?'

'It is a little soon to know.' She shrugged. 'And when I do know, I will not inform you.'

'I will raise the child for you.' The duchess picked a bit of fluff from her gown.

'I will bear that in mind.'

'I'm excellent at selecting nursemaids. I have a gift for it.' She lowered her lids. 'I made sure my children had the best of governesses. Ones that suited them.'

'Perhaps you should have cared for the babies.'

The duchess frowned. 'Child. Think about it. If you were a babe, would you want me or a governess comforting your tears? I am not suited for that duty.' She raised a brow.

Definitely, Bellona would have chosen a servant. 'I see.'

'Even now, I know to put the needs of my son first

and let someone else handle the task of giving him direction.' The duchess's chin bobbed. The lines at her eyes deepened. 'You must go to London and speak with Rhys. He's causing a disgrace to our name by lowering himself to squabble in public. He is not maintaining his dignity at all. You caused this by your presence and you can correct it.'

'But it would not be—'

'Proper?' the duchess inserted. 'Child. You two lost that chance already. I would hope that you could be a bit discreet. Perhaps leave your bow and arrows behind and travel in darkness.' She examined Bellona. 'I'll send a quiet servant with you and you can wear my veil and dark clothing. If anyone sees you, they'll assume I'm visiting him.'

Bellona didn't speak. She shook her head.

'It's not that I particularly like you,' the duchess continued. 'But I think I could—even though I cannot imagine you would ever be a true duchess. But I must have grandchildren and I want them now. There is only one way I know to get them and I will have to accept someone, so it may as well be you.' She shrugged. 'No one's good enough for him, but then no one was good enough for my daughter or Geoff either. You see where that has left me.'

She shook her head. 'I could accept someone as unschooled as you because of the grandchildren.' She leaned towards Bellona. 'I have decided I want the babies strong most of all. I want them to survive. You would have a spirited child.' She sniffed. 'You're tolerable for short lengths of time. And you sing well.'

'I doubt I would let my child meet you. Rhys is not going to be in my life again so you must pick out someone else to breed the next heir.'

The duchess chuckled. She examined Bellona toe to head.

Fingers splayed, the duchess put her palms together and then she interlaced her fingers. 'The butler did the unthinkable. He started a betting book with the staff concerning Rhys and you. Even taking in the possibility of an heir. I am not supposed to know of it, but my maid understands the importance of her duties.' She extended her forefingers towards Bellona. 'All sorts of wagers are being bandied about. I plan for my maid to do quite well. The maid has been informed that she is to wager on you marrying Rhys inside the month and that the first child will be a daughter, because I know you will do that just to spite me.'

'I liked you better when you were crying,' Bellona said.

'Well, child, you should have thought of that earlier. You should have thought about the consequences when you…bathed with my son. The butler has not yet recovered his senses or he would not have started the betting book.'

'You have no say in this.'

'Fine. But you need to alert Rhys that you mean nothing to him.' Unclasping her hands, she stood.

'I have.'

'You have not convinced him.'

'He's a grown man. He can do as he pleases.'

'Oh, he is,' the duchess said. She smiled. 'I have it on good authority—since the staff in London knows I must be informed of events—that an interesting tale could be bandied about at any day.'

'What about?' Bellona couldn't help herself.

The older woman's lips turned up. Bellona thought of Gigia.

'I shall win that wager,' the duchess said.

She didn't walk to the door like a woman with a sore knee. She looked back. 'My son has to have some tenderness for you or he would not be so bound on destroying your father.'

Bellona paused two steps from the room's entrance, listening as she brushed the black veil from her face. A murmuring voice, a male, answered Rhys's bursts of command.

She took a deep breath, moved to the doorway and saw Rhys and a smaller fellow. The diminutive man, face wan, needed a razor, although he had been near one much more recently than Rhys.

'Your Grace,' Bellona spoke, pulling Rhys's eyes to her.

His eyes showed no reaction to her presence. He stood. 'I beg forgiveness that I cannot entertain you. But as you can see we have much to finish.' Papers mounded his desk and a small stack rested on the rug.

She tossed her reticule into the empty chair. 'So no shop owner may dare exhibit any of my father's paintings or they will have the Duke of Rolleston's wrath visited upon them. Even the tradesmen are afraid to sell any artist's supplies to him, for fear of reprisal. His every step outside his house is noted, and should anyone extend any favourable notice to his art they are warned away.'

This time, his face turned directly towards her and his eyes sparked an inferno. Then he switched his attention to Simpson and the man jumped back in his chair. Even Bellona could see the guilt in the face of the man of affairs.

'Rolleston.' She snapped the word out, pulling his gaze. Even though she did not fear him, she didn't like the look he gave her—the calmness a bit too scorching.

'My dear. I am impressed.' Then he pointed a pen to his man of affairs. 'Simpson. For your tale-bearing you are let go without a reference.'

The man's jaw dropped and he gathered his papers as he stood.

She stepped back into the doorway, feet firm. 'Stop,' she commanded Simpson.

'Oh, I could not, miss.' He caught a paper that had slid from his fingers, grasping it before it hit the floor.

She put a hand out, palm against the wood. No one could move through the doorway without pushing her aside.

Simpson stood, looking at her, eyes wavering but feet immobile. 'Pardon, miss?' His eyes begged.

'Tell him,' she commanded the duke. 'Tell him there will be no repercussions for his actions.'

Words knifed the air. 'There will be.'

'Then he may wed me for my *proika, my* dowry.'

Rhys coughed. 'His wife will object.'

She shook her head in frustration. 'You cannot blame this man for his concern—if he did write to Harling House to mention your behaviour towards my father. You have a houseful of servants here and I have noticed that your staff at Harling House cares for you. Or perhaps they just fear the duchess and only pretend affection for you.'

'I am quite well, thank you.'

Her eyes raked over him, and she pressed her palm tightly against the door frame.

Well groomed, he looked like a duke and commanded a woman's attention in a discreet way. Un-kempt, his appearance made a woman's hands beg to straighten his clothing. Or loosen it some more. His eyes looked into the depths of her being.

Rhys need never question whether a woman would only want him for his title and his wealth. But he should always question whether she wanted him only to pleasure her senses. The days Bellona had not seen him had taken her strength and weakened her for his touch.

Simpson needed to stay in the room. She needed to keep him there, for her own well-being. The granite in the duke's eyes told her he would not back down and she could not lose her strength.

'It's said you have been about town, seeing that no man near you has a parched throat, and you've been more affable than people are used to seeing.'

'I see no reason to hide from anyone. My life is my own. To live as I—' Then his breath swooshed on the last word, echoing it in her ears. 'As I wish.'

'Your cravat is a sight,' she said.

'Well, dash my wig,' he said, words light. 'And I have been wearing it in public all day.'

Silence dragged.

'Miss…' Simpson said tentatively. 'Might I pass by you?'

'Not until the matter of your employment is settled.'

'Simpson.' The duke's voice was a commanding boom. 'You will return in the morning to take up where we left off.'

The man took a tentative step towards Bellona.

She left her hand at the door.

'Bellona—' Rhys spoke low, voice curling about her '—must I toss him out of the window?'

Predatory eyes snared her, but she wasn't afraid. Well, not in the mortal sense, anyway.

Rhys made sure he truly looked at her. He needed to see past the hair, the memory of her body and the opinions of other people.

Her fingers slid from the wall and Simpson snaked out through the door before she had fully stepped aside.

'So you are here to tell me all that I have done wrong. You do not have to. I am well aware. More so than you, I suspect.' Rhys put the chair against the desk, but did not release the wood.

'You have enraged my father.'

On that he had not been blinded by any foolishness of his heart. On that one thing he knew he was absolutely right. 'Surely you cannot have concern for that man who did not even give you his true last name, but one he simply pulled from the air.'

'I have no care for him,' she said. 'But his wife has been as kind to me as any *mana* would. I care for her. She suffers with him. It is the way of the world.'

'She's strong. She will survive.' He gave the chair an extra shove.

'If he shoots you, as it is said he has threatened, you might not.'

One side of his lips went up, a smirk. 'It is not in his best interest to be near me. If I die merely from choking on a bone, he will hang. If he does try to do me in and I live, he will be hanged. I have seen to that already.'

'You have convinced people to speak ill of his paintings.'

'I have viewed a considerable amount of them in the past few days as I visited most homes in London where I knew the owners had his drivel displayed. I could not help but notice the subtle flaws in his work, which of course, I asked about before I viewed them. I only spoke the truth. Had he not had the funds of his wife as his patron, he would not have been able to survive on what his paintings earn and he is certainly not worth notice as an artist. Not only my opinion, but the men I talked with.'

'It is in the scandal sheets that the Duke of R. mused about whether this artist painted with his toe or his elbow and suggested he be shown what a brush looks like.'

His lashes flicked down and then up. 'That is actually a compliment compared to what I truly think. They would not even improve the look of a dust bin.' He looked at her.

'Not all of them are that bad.'

'Enough are. Most are. Someone should have taken pity on him and broken his paintbrushes long ago.'

'You are trying to do so now.'

'Yes. The man had left you alone for years. He should have continued to do so.'

'You brought even more attention to the situation.'

'If I did not stand against him, I could not have lived with myself.'

His gaze locked on her so hard she might have become afraid, except something deeper behind his eyes showed a private agony. 'I would not have injured you for the world and yet I live with, every day, how I caused your name to be sullied.' He looked at the ring on his finger. The one passed from duke to duke.

He changed the direction of his gaze. 'What does the crest on my carriage look like?'

She shrugged.

'Tell me about the servants?'

Her eyes tightened. 'Why do you change what we are talking of?'

'Just tell me about the servants.'

'Fenton, I do not like at all. He broke the scullery maid's heart. Thompson makes sure to keep him in hand, though. He thinks of all the women on the staff as his daughters.'

'And the maids. What are their names?'

'Julia. Honour. Susan. Eliza, although she prefers to be called—'

'Enough.' He raised his hand.

'Yes. I know their names. I saw them daily at your house. How could I not?'

'That is just it. How could you not? I dare say you have no thought of the art in the house which could fund a small country.'

'I do have some notion of the paintings on your walls,' she admitted. 'I have never imagined paintings could be so beautiful. Before I left the duchess, I walked through the house to view the art and that took her grief from my mind.' She lowered her chin for a moment before looking back at him. 'Days after I refused you, I realised I had turned away a chance to live with those works.' She shook her head as if she could not believe it.

His response was half-chuckle, half-snort. 'The art tempted you to say yes more than I did.'

She didn't answer.

To speak took more strength than he could immediately garner. Words choked inside him in a way they'd never constricted before. Then everything vanished from his mind except for what mattered most. 'I love you.'

Chapter Twenty-One

He'd not expected the deep intake of breath and the way her lids dropped causing her narrowed eyes to spear him.

He wondered if perhaps he'd been right to let his thoughts be directed by the opinions of others. He could not see what Bellona thought or meant or wanted.

'You say that. But you have not shown it. You have made things so much worse.' Quiet words from soft lips, but with fervour attached.

The words. He had to roll them around in his head to make certain he heard what she was saying.

He struggled to sort things in his mind and then he spoke again. 'I believe that my art collection is one of the best in a private residence anywhere in the world.' He watched her face. 'In case you are wondering.'

'Stubble it, Your Grace.'

'Yes, sweetness.'

She moved within arm's grasp and he could not help it. He moved enough to brush back the hair that had fallen to her temple.

The puff from her lips censured him, but she didn't retreat.

'You are trying to destroy my father and his family,' she said. 'You have no right.'

'I have every right.' She'd taken all his resistance to her and reduced him to the rank of a schoolboy. But then, she'd truly done that days ago. 'The man—he may not have meant to, but he could have caused your death. He left you on that island to fend for yourself.'

'You had no cause to interfere. I told you not to hurt him.'

'His arms and legs are all attached, as well as his head. I would say he is unhurt.'

'How my father treats me is my concern. I will deal with him, but how can I do that now when you have struck out at him and reduced him?'

'And just what were you going to do—thank him for nearly causing your death by deserting you on Melos with no food? Forcing you to use whatever means you might find to survive.'

Rhys was taken aback that she was not more grateful to him, but he didn't care. He cared that she was standing in his house and thought enough of her father's wife to be concerned.

'You are not my protector. You have no right to my life because we kissed.'

'We did more than just kiss, Bellona.'

'And the women before me—did you jump to their aid in this way, too?'

'They did not have such problems as you, but I did not abandon them without a thought. Perhaps the first I did not stand by when I was very young and that cured me of the inability to do so again. I cannot hold a woman near my heart and then forget she exists the next day.'

'That is a poor excuse.'

'Really, sweet? I feel you owe me a bit of understanding. We shared something together I have never shared with anyone else.'

She raised her brows.

He lifted his palm, the cut towards her. 'A very painful bloodletting. I should think you'd have some tolerance for me for that reason alone.'

'You know that was not intended.'

'Just as my actions towards your father are not intended to bear you any ill will.'

She shook her head. 'You have meddled.'

'Meddle? I did not meddle. The man, he needed to be punished. Any man who can cause such harm to a woman should suffer.' He stared at her. 'And you are here now—why? To what purpose? I cannot undo anything that has already happened.' He held his palm where he could see it. He gave a dry chuckle. 'This memento. It will never go away.' He raised his eyes. 'I suspect the true mark you have left on me is not on my palm.'

'That does not give you the right to denigrate my father.'

'I let him off lightly.'

'You destroyed him.'

'He still can sit at a fine table and drink fine wine. I feel no pity for him.'

'You do not even tell yourself the truth.'

He turned from her, shaking his head, and then faced her again. 'If someone strikes at me, Bellona, they can expect me to strike back. It is the nature of the world. It is how one survives.'

'Revenge. That is what you did.'

Her words rasped against the inside of his skin. 'I make the heritage I will pass on to my children. With that in mind you can understand why it is so important I uphold the beliefs I hold close to me.'

He had upheld them. Most of them. Until his world had become fodder for the tongues of the *ton*. But he could trace his madness back one step further than that. When a woman had put an arrow tip to his stomach. 'I had thought to make amends to you by holding your father responsible for his actions,' he said.

She merely shook her head. 'You took away his belief in what he loves most.'

He whispered, 'What he loves most should be— *you*.' He walked forward. He grasped her arms. 'We have both abandoned you, Bellona. He and I.'

'No. I only thought I needed him. I did not. My life is better without him. I did not need his love. I did not. I did not need his presence in my childhood. I only needed food. The funds he did give us came from coin his wife had given him, though I did not know it at the time. When I had nothing, she agreed to give me a dowry, which I now have. She has been my friend even though she could view me with distaste. I do not want her hurt. And you have added to her disgrace. The woman who gave me all she could and asked for nothing. She has treated me with the same kindness as my own *mana*.'

Just like the chimes of the clock sounded too loud in his ears, Rhys heard the pounding of regret in his body.

He loved the woman who had taken away every part of him he believed in and put a mirror in front of his soul.

'I did not tell you all the truth either. My father

could hurt me even more and I did not want him to decide to tell you everything.' She stood in front of him and when she moved, the shoulder of her dress drooped. She pulled it back into place. 'My father came to Melos to paint my mother,' she said. 'He had heard tales of her beauty and of the island's. My mother had no funds and had been forced to sell her body so when my father decided to keep her she insisted he marry her. He did not mind the fact that he was already married. As far as he was concerned it was just words.'

Unthinkable.

The old duke would not even have welcomed Bellona as a guest in the house once he discovered her origins were so tainted. Her mother, selling her body, and her father a bigamist.

The tousled goddess stood in front of him and, like the shattered statue recovered from her homeland by the French, she was indeed more marred than only a dent on the bridge of her nose. But also perfect in a way he'd never seen.

'I don't care about your mother, your father or your grandmother.' Rhys reached out, his forefinger looped under a lock of her hair which barely remained constrained. He slipped the brown strands free. They fell to her shoulders. 'I wish I could be perfect for you. I'm not. Who your father married, or what your mother did to survive, does not matter to me.'

'Rhys, your mother told me how angry you were when a servant did not wear the proper livery once.'

'I was very young when that happened. I was trying to… I don't know what I was trying to do, but I was not acting as I should. That was not the correct way to handle it. I was in error. As I have been many times.'

He held out his left hand. 'Forgive me?'

She didn't step forward right away, but when her body swayed in his direction he moved to her.

'It is not idle words,' he said. 'I do not do that. It is not who I am. It is not what I believe in.'

He rested his forehead against hers. 'I am sorting out who am I to be. What I am to think. All I believed about myself has been a lie. I thought I could forgive myself anything. I was the second son. A second son did not have the responsibility of the first. I am still the second son by birth. I will always be, and yet I am the duke. The thing I wanted most of all, but knew I could not have. Knew I was not worthy of. If I married the perfect duchess, she would hide my flaws. Instead I found the woman who would show me my weakness. You hold it to my face, Bellona.'

'I do not. I would not do such a thing.'

He moved back. His eyebrows rose.

'I could be wrong on that,' she muttered. 'Before you met me, you imagined yourself too grand.'

'Yes. I did want to be grand. Every day I thought of my father and how he would act, or Geoff, and what he would do, and then I did as if they directed me. Mostly. Until you. I could not keep you from my thoughts.'

'What of the woman you courted?'

'She has not even missed me this past year nor I her. But, if I married a woman such as her, without my heart involved, it would be the same as your father did when he wed Lady Hawkins. He married the woman who could give him funds and increase his status, but he could not forget the island woman. I am like the man on the other island. The one in Defoe's book.'

'Crusoe.'

He shook his head. 'No. The one who lived to serve him. I can't be rescued without you, Bellona. I need you every moment of my day.'

'You do not think me good enough for society.'

'Bellona, it is not you that is not good enough. It is me. It was fine for me to be in a woman's bed if the doors remained closed. I felt no guilt at all. But the minute the door opened and others could see me for who I was—then it was different. I didn't ask for marriage to protect you. You were closer than I to that truth. *"Ah, the duke is caught with a woman, but of course His Grace married her. Noble man."'* His words were a sneer. *'"Sacrificed himself to protect a woman."'*

'It is no surprise to me. I told you near the same.'

'You may have told me, but I didn't listen.'

She curled into his chest. 'Put that as another flaw of yours. Along with not listening. But you are very appealing to the eyes…'

'You could not say, *Oh, Rhys, you are perfect just as you are.*' He couldn't help pushing her.

'I do not lie.'

He circled his arms around her, putting a soft kiss on her cool lips before moving back. 'You are here. Why not stay? As my wife?'

Eyes, darker than the darkest stone flickering in the bottom of a pool, looked up at him.

'How do I know you are different now than you were only a fortnight ago?'

He shook his head, letting her slip from his arms, but taking her hands in his. 'Perhaps I am not. Perhaps I cannot truly change. But now instead of using the eyes of my father and brother and mother to look at the world, I wish to use your eyes. I wish to see people the way you see them. Even how you see me.'

'I will think about it.'

'Take the time you need,' he said. 'I am not going anywhere.'

Quite without asking, she moved into his house with the same amount of fuss a mouse made when taking up residence. She found her own room and changed it as she wished. A chamber with the best light which now smelled of linseed oil and paints. She said she wanted a painting of her homeland and wanted to create it herself. He'd instantly sent for a tutor and she'd not said one word against the man.

No one could see evidence of her anywhere else about the house and he did not think she went out often, but contented herself in the room.

She did not come to him in the night. Not once. So finally he went to her. He could not help himself.

Rhys looked in her chamber. All her paints were scattered about and the canvas was there, but he could not find her and the hour was late.

He puffed a breath out through his nose, knowing it could not be a good thing for her to be gone. His jaw tightened.

Rhys returned to his bedchamber and summoned his valet.

'Your Grace?' the servant asked when he walked in through the doorway.

Rhys realised he'd been standing with his hand still on the pull. 'Miss Cherroll, is she about?' He released the rope.

The valet's long face became even longer. His words were spoken as he breathed out. 'I believe you are the only resident of the house, Your Grace. Miss Cherroll received a message and had to rush away.'

'Where did she go?'

'I believe Lord Hawkins has taken ill and she was called to his bedside. It is not certain if he will recover. If you are to request a carriage, I am to instruct you that her father's wife does not want attention called to the matter and it has been suggested that you not follow.'

Bellona stared at the face of her father, noting the bluish tone around his lips. Her oldest sister had already visited him—a quick discreet visit in the night. Their middle sister, Thessa, might never see him alive again because she was at sea. But the ship could dock any moment, or a year hence.

His condition was uncertain. She had asked his wife if she might stay a bit longer and her father's wife had agreed. They had sat, side by side, watching him breathe.

Lady Hawkins wore a dressing gown and no rings or jewellery of any kind. Her face had little more colour than her husband's. Her shoulders stooped. 'This is the end of our years together, I suppose. He is falling more and more away each day.' She took the cover and tucked it closer at his side. 'I don't think he is here any more.'

Bellona tried to think of questions she would ask her father if he roused, but none mattered. The answers would not change anything.

If he hadn't acted so badly, she wouldn't have been given life.

But it had seemed uncaring of her to leave him. Much like he had left them on the island. She stayed at his bedside, if only to prove to herself that she would not do as he had done.

She'd met her half-sisters and brother, and knew they'd only spoken to her begrudgingly after their mother had insisted. She'd felt no kinship for them at all, and yet, for his wife, she did.

'There are no secrets between him and me any more,' his wife said to Bellona, looking at the wan face of her husband. 'They were his secrets, yet he was the one who could not accept them being displayed.' She shook her head. 'The truth of his skill, though, that is what concerned him the most. When he discovered he had no true gift for painting.'

'I am sorry for my part in that.'

'Nonsense.' She waved the words away. 'It's not as if he'd not had it pointed out to him a thousand times before. He just finally accepted it now.' She leaned forward and let her hand rest on the bed. 'His paintings have rarely sold for more than the price of the canvas and frame. The best ones, oddly enough, were the ones of his children and your mother. If he has any talent, it is for capturing people, and of course, he thoroughly detests creating anything but landscapes. Endless landscapes. He doesn't like people. To paint them would mean he might have to look at them. Spend time with them.'

She put her hand on the counterpane covering his arm. 'He lied as much to himself as he did to everyone else. He sneered at the knowledge of others—only believing himself capable of thinking correctly. If he had gleaned from others and used his dedication in the right way, then perhaps he could have had what he wanted most. No one worked as hard to destroy his talent as he did.' She shut her eyes. 'I am only sorry for the pain of my children. For all his children.'

'I cannot begrudge him the past,' Bellona said. 'If I did, then I would be saying he changed me and he does not have that honour. I am who I am because of my *mana* and my sisters and myself. I thank you for what you have done for me.'

'I hated the thought of you children living with nothing. I am sorry he told such lies of you and destroyed your chance of marriage to Rolleston.'

'He did not. Rolleston asked me to wed him. I told him I could not. I was not sure.'

'Bellona.' Her eyes opened wide and she leaned forward to look in Bellona's face. 'After... When you were discovered together, the duke proposed?'

Bellona nodded. 'Yes, but I did not wish...'

'Oh, you may be a bit more your father's daughter than I realised,' she said. 'He turned down his chance to create art because he did not wish to follow his talent of painting portraits. And you turned down a chance to become a duchess—because?'

'I thought he felt he was doing me a boon just asking for my hand.'

The woman took her hand from her chest and clucked her tongue. 'Well, you have the attitude of a duchess already.'

'I will not be married because of pity, or duty or any reason I do not like.'

'Something—perhaps my knowledge of this world—

tells me that Rolleston could have tumbled his choice of women into bed and yet he chose you, and then he had the brazenness to ask you to wed him. The cad.'

'He told me we should be married.'

'Perhaps he's a bit fonder of you than you think?'

'He could be. He thinks he is.'

'I've known his family my whole life. Rolleston is, or was, rather a stick. Much more the saint than most. Pleasant to look at, I thought, but as interesting to talk to as a land steward—'

'He is actually very interesting to talk to,' Bellona snapped.

Her father's wife paused before continuing. '...And quite the duke, until the last fortnight when your father began to denounce you as an extortionist. Then tales about Rolleston's fury began to blossom like weeds in a garden left untended. He became terribly unsettled for a man who'd never caused any kind of stir before.' She raised her brows and looked at Bellona. 'Terribly unsettled.'

'But he was included in the tales. It was said I was using him for gain as well.' Bellona could not keep the pique from her voice.

'He could have easily shrugged it off. Perhaps you should go to him and ask him what madness has grown in him that he had to be restrained in White's because a man dared speak slightingly of you.'

'I had not heard of that.'

'My sister has tried to schedule as many soirées, nights at the theatre and morning calls into her world as she can the past few days to keep me abreast of all the *on dits* because she considers it her duty to know ~hat is being said about her family. Particularly when it concerns my husband. The duke, whether he means to or not, is not letting the talk wither away. His anger over you causes people to note you even more.'

'Rolleston can do as he wishes. I don't know that he cares enough for me even though he says he loves me. I don't know that I can love him enough for both of us if he does not.'

Lord Hawkins's wife looked again at the bed. 'Whomever you marry is a risk. If you don't marry, it is a risk, too. You might look back later and have missed so much.' She took her eyes from her husband and looked at Bellona. 'At least the duke doesn't like to paint.' She smiled.

Bellona didn't nod, or acknowledge the words with anything more than her eyes, but the next morning, as she walked to the carriage, she longed for Rhys more than she'd ever longed for anything in her life.

After directing the servants away, Bellona stepped into the duke's library and saw him at the desk with his man of affairs. He looked up and twisted a pen between his fingers, his eyes fixing on the movement. 'Leave us, Simpson.'

The man stood and hurried by Bellona, but his eyes flashed concern as he passed her.

'I don't think you need worry yourself about my father saying anything bad again,' she said.

'Are you well?' he asked.

She nodded. 'I left before the end came. His children did not want me there. I knew his wife understood. I do not need to be present. As I sat with him, I realised that when he sailed from Melos the last time, he died in my heart. It is as if he is someone I hardly know.'

The duke placed his pen atop his papers. He shifted in his chair and his knee hit the desk leg, but he caught the ink bottle before it tumbled over. 'Blast it,' he muttered. 'I can't keep these things upright any more.'

Still he held the liquid in his hand. He looked at her. 'That never used to happen before.'

She walked to him and took the bottle, their fingers brushing, shaking her in a way she would not let him see.

He put his elbow on the desk, his jaw on his fist, and his eyes flicked her direction. 'What day of the week is it?'

'I'm not certain,' she answered.

'Simpson would know,' he said.

'You can always ring for one of the servants.'

'And let them know I am unaware of even the date? If they have not surmised it already, I will not enlighten them that I am completely distracted.'

'Rhys, why did you ask me to marry you?'

'If you had said yes, we could have discussed it in detail. For years perhaps. But as you said no, I decline to even think about the moment, much less speak of it.' He stared at her, then he took the ink bottle back off her and set it aside.

She put fingertips under his chin and guided it in her direction. 'I have tried to sketch you, but I don't have the skill. I'll learn, then I will always have a likeness of you.'

Eyes, weary with sleeplessness, watched her until his face turned into her hand and he pressed a kiss to her skin. 'You will always have me in person, Bellona, if you wish it, wedding or no. I have committed my heart to you and you will always hold it. You are truly my first love. My only love. If you do not plan to marry me, I understand. That does not change my heart.'

'You think you can continue in your life without a wife?'

'I have not been married in the first decades of my life and have managed very well, and when I look at you and know that it leaves me free for you, I'm very thankful.'

He pushed the chair back as he stood, his body brushing against hers. His hands rested on her hips. 'I will only ask you once more, today, but the question will remain open every day for the rest of your life, if you do not say yes now. Will you marry me?'

She nodded.

Epilogue

Bellona could hardly believe the change in her sister. Thessa had returned from her sea voyage with a young son and enough tales to keep them all laughing for hours, but somehow the talk had changed from the voyage to the husbands, and had become something of a verbal competition to see who had married the most delightful man.

'He talks in his sleep,' Thessa said of her husband, Captain Ben. 'And I find it most entertaining.'

'Rolleston… Well, I do not know if he talks in his sleep or not,' Bellona admitted, covering a yawn, and then aimed a smug smile at Thessa. 'He does not sleep.'

Melina grimaced. 'You are not learning how to be a proper duchess and he is acting more like you every day. You both disrupt all around you.'

A young female shriek of laughter sounded from outside the room.

'See what I mean.' Melina shook her head. 'Willa,' she called out, standing to move to the door. 'Do not—'

Warrington walked in, carrying his daughter under